DEFIANCE

THE BELLATOR CHRONICLES: BOOK THREE

CLARE LITTLEMORE

BRIT ALERT!

If you are reading this book and not from the UK, a brief warning that I am a British author and use British spellings throughout. In Bellator, the pavements have 'kerbs' rather than 'curbs', the students of the Danforth Academy may be disciplined for their bad behaviour (not behavior) and one or two of the characters might, on occasion, have to apologise (rather than apologize).

Happy reading!

Contents

CHAPTER ONE: FAITH

"Wait for my signal."

The order was hissed from the shadows. Faith nodded a response, knowing it wouldn't be seen. The wall they crouched behind was low, and her legs ached. It felt like they'd been here for hours, yet in reality, it could only have been minutes. Still, the mission was important. She had to be patient.

The building ahead was mostly dark, yet a single light still burned stubbornly in a ground floor window. Her team should have been inside by now, but their target was working late and had derailed their plans. For now, all they could do was wait.

Faith glanced to her left, at the other three members of her team. *What were they thinking?*

For three weeks, she'd been a member of the Bellator Resistance, yet many of the women did not fully trust her. Madeleine, the Resistance leader, had insisted Faith go along on tonight's mission. She was not a woman who liked to take chances, and always had a contingency plan. As an ex-student, Faith's familiarity with the location could prove invaluable.

The other women did not seem to agree. Though they had been pleasant enough, there was a cool atmosphere which told her she wasn't quite accepted. Tonight was her chance to prove herself. It had to be.

"Al*right*." Beside Faith, the group's leader allowed herself a muted celebration as the light was extinguished. Robyn was an experienced mission leader, calm in a crisis. Faith wanted to impress her tonight. Tucking a stray lock of her jet-black hair into her cap, Robyn pointed at the building. "Let's give her a couple of minutes to vacate, then get on with this."

Faith shifted the weight to her other leg, hoping to alleviate the pins and needles which were beginning to tingle through the limb. She was rewarded by a sharp elbow in the side from Blake, a short, grumpy woman who had come along as their tech support. Faith stilled, sending her team a look of apology in the near-darkness. Clearly, she needed to learn to be stealthier if she wanted to be asked to join a second mission.

A gentle hand on her arm made her turn. Laura, the final member of the group, shot her a sympathetic grin. Faith returned it, grateful for the bubbly redhead's support. Blake was intimidating, but Laura's gesture proved that not all Resistance members were as unforgiving.

Faith looked back at the darkened building: the Danforth Academy. Being back was strange. The buildings were so familiar, yet it felt like years since she'd been a student. It shouldn't have been a surprise. So much had happened to her in the six weeks since then. She'd learned things. Things which had made her blood boil. Things which had led her here, to the Resistance, where she very much wanted to make a difference.

And tonight was her first real chance. Tonight, she was the one with the inside knowledge, and she had to come through for her team. Inhaling deeply, she focused on the target.

A second light had replaced the first, but she wasn't worried. This one, she knew, illuminated the stairwell in the building's central atrium. It meant Principal Anderson was heading to bed, leaving her office—their target for the evening—empty and unguarded.

The lights in the school were automatic, triggered by motion sensors throughout the building. Once Anderson was in bed, the first job was to deactivate them so their presence in the building would go undetected.

They waited twenty more minutes, making sure the building was completely dark before taking action. Blake spent a few moments at the external fuse box, deactivating the cameras, lights, and alarms.

"It's only a temporary fix," she reminded them. "We *have* to be out of there before the systems start to come back online."

"We know." Robyn was eager to get inside. "You went through it with us a hundred times."

Blake grunted. "People forget when they're under pressure. And I don't even want to think about what will happen if someone accidentally triggers the system reset. I mean-"

"Enough." Robyn eyed Faith. "Let's get on with this. The sooner we're in, the sooner we're out again."

Blake fell silent as they crept across the academy's back lawn together. Though the school was guarded, Resistance members had been tracking the guard patterns over the past week. As long as nothing had changed, they knew when their access point would be unprotected.

Since Jacob's people had set off the explosion in the forest, the city's forces were severely depleted. The number of guards assigned to various important locations around Bellator had been reduced as a result, and Faith's group was fairly certain this would help them to evade capture. All they had to do was make their move between the circular patrols the remaining guards made around the building every half hour or so.

Bending low, Faith tracked Robyn's footsteps, thankful that the grass wasn't damp with dew. No one wanted to leave telltale footprints inside the academy. When the leader reached the pavement on the far side, she made sure she hugged the side of the building, creeping along until she reached the fifth window from the end.

Stopping to make sure that the team was together, Robyn pressed her palms against the glass. Faith felt, rather than heard, her leader's sigh of relief as the pane started to slide upwards. The Resistance often had to rely on insiders to help them, and one such individual had been tasked with making sure the window was unlocked tonight.

Faith didn't know who. The Resistance consisted of a far greater number of people than she'd first anticipated, but many of their identities were hidden from the core group for their protection. Faith found herself wondering if she knew the informant, if they were a member of the school community.

But she respected the importance of secrecy. *Anyone* found to be working for the Resistance would be silenced by the government. They simply knew too much. A mole inside the school would be in terrible danger if they were suspected to be working against Danforth. And, if they were being watched, they wouldn't be able to assist the Resistance.

Thankfully, tonight the insider had played their part. With the window unlocked, it was a simple job for Robyn to ease the sash upwards until there was enough space to crawl through.

"Ready?" she whispered, raising a finger to her lips. "Quiet from here. No unnecessary chatter, got it?"

Without waiting for their agreement, she pulled herself up and over the sill. Faith had to admire the grace with which she managed the manoeuvre. Another elbow from Blake told her it was her turn. Taking a deep breath, she placed both hands on the sill and pulled up, sliding through and easing herself into the space beyond.

Moments later, the four of them were standing in a darkened office. Not Anderson's, but one close by. Their contact didn't have access to the principal's base but had been able to leave the window of another professor's office open for them. It was good enough.

As Laura slid the window back in place Faith was sure her companions could hear her heart pounding. Now the team turned to Faith, waiting for her direction. Creeping to the door, Faith eased it open a crack. The space beyond was shadowy and silent.

Beckoning to the others, Faith stepped out into the hallway. She stayed close to the wall, aware at every step how loudly their footsteps sounded in the empty wing. Grateful that Anderson's office wasn't far, she heaved a sigh of relief when she reached it. The silver nameplate on the door brought back unpleasant memories. She'd been disciplined in this office more than once.

Shaking herself, Faith pointed at the nameplate. The team was ready. Blake stepped forward, placing a small grey device at the side of the door handle. Pressing a couple of buttons on the keypad, she kept her eyes on the small display which was illuminated. A series of numbers scrolled past, rapidly at first, but eventually beginning to slow, until they came to rest on a specific number.

Placing one hand on the door itself, Blake bent close, as though it might whisper its secrets to her. Tapping her fingers against the keypad one last time, she keyed in another couple of commands. The door emitted a quiet click. As Robyn pushed it open, Blake removed the device and slipped it back into her pocket.

Once inside, they slipped off their boots. Laura stood guard at the door while Blake and Robyn turned on slender flashlights and got to work. In the eerie half-light, Faith followed Robyn around the room. They were searching for places to conceal a listening device, though Faith suspected Robyn would be far better at the task than her. Madeleine was hoping to listen in on Anderson's conversations and see what the Resistance could learn.

Blake had gone straight to the state-of-the-art datadev embedded in the principal's desk. Dropping her pack onto the expensive leather chair, she unzipped the front compartment and slipped out a silver disc the size of a penny. It was, she had informed Faith in the meeting they'd held prior to the mission, a tiny chip capable of copying huge amounts of information.

Leaning over Anderson's datadev, Blake used the smallest screw-driver Faith had ever seen to remove its casing. Once she'd exposed all its working components, she brought out an equally tiny pair of tweezers. She used them to pick up the disc and insert it into the heart of the machine. Faith had to admire her steady hand. Her own hands had been shaking since the moment she'd entered the school building.

Once the disc was in place, Blake put down the tweezers, took out a second device and held it close to the datadev. Pressing a finger to activate it, she checked a reading on the display panel before placing it on the desk next to the datadev. That done, she waved a hand to attract Robyn's attention and held up eight fingers—the number of minutes they needed to remain in the room undisturbed so she could copy all the data on Anderson's datadev.

Giving her a thumbs up, Robyn bent close to Faith. "What's through there?" She gestured to a door at the rear of the principal's office.

"Anderson's inner office. Where she holds her private meetings."

"That's where the bug has to be placed, then."

Robyn turned to Blake, indicating that she should switch places with Laura at the door. Once the new guard was in place, Laura joined Robyn and Faith, using the same device to unlock the inner door. Once it was open, the three of them crept into Anderson's inner sanctum. Faith had never been into this part of the office before. Luxuriously furnished, it smelled strongly of lavender. The carpet was a chocolate-brown colour and not very thick. Faith was glad. Though they had already removed their boots, a denser floor covering might still have revealed their footprints.

The office was dominated by a throne-like chair which sat behind a large matching desk. Two slightly less ornate chairs faced it. The walls were mostly hidden by large display boards covered with many complex-looking charts.

"She likes her numbers, doesn't she?" Laura muttered.

"Looks like it." Robyn gestured to Faith. "Start taking photos of those, as well as any files you can access. Laura, we need a place to put this. And let's be quick about it. Clock is ticking."

As Robyn began unpacking the listening device, Laura stalked the perimeter, her eyes searching for the best place to hide it. After scanning the walls with a frown, her eyes moved upwards and her face lit up.

"There!" she hissed at Robyn, jabbing a finger at the extravagant light fixture.

"Perfect."

Both women set to work placing the bug. Catlike, Laura had already hopped onto the desk. Once she was steady, she removed one of the bulbs and dismantled the socket which held it. Accomplishing her task in no time, she held a hand out to Robyn, who passed her the bug. Faith marvelled at their skill. If the bug was well hidden, Anderson would have no idea that the Resistance was listening to her every conversation.

Noticing Faith's stare, Robyn jabbed a finger at her, and then at the charts on display. "Photos!"

"Sorry! Yes." Feeling more than a little chastised, Faith moved towards them.

She didn't know any student who'd ever been inside this office, and a quick glance at the boards was all it took for her to understand why. The amount of data they revealed on each student was alarming. Turning her attention to the new wristclip Madeleine had provided her, Faith activated the camera mode and started snapping pictures.

Once she had a clear image of every chart, Faith turned her attention to the filing cabinets around the room. They were all locked. Frustrated, she glanced at the papers on the desk, but there was nothing more interesting than a couple of bills and a quotation for the resurfacing of the basketball courts.

Leaning against the desk, Faith peered closely at the images from the boards. The numerous columns and numbers were difficult to comprehend. She noted the name femgazipane with a shudder, then traced her finger down the page, noticing the different doses which each Danforth student was being given. Another column contained unexplained percentages. And at the far end of each chart, there were columns labelled Test A and Test B. These simply had the words *Pass* or *Fail* next to them.

Faith shuddered, turning her attention back to the names. Some she didn't recognise. Others, she was familiar with. For now though, there was only one name Faith was interested in seeing. She hurried from chart to chart, running her eye down each one faster than the last, to no avail. When she reached the final one, she couldn't stop her shoulders from sagging.

Sophia's name was nowhere to be found.

If they hadn't brought her back to the school, where was she?

A noise at the door startled her. Blake stood there, her face pale. Laura was just stepping down from the desk, Robyn holding up a hand to help her. As one, they turned to face their teammate.

"Download speed is slower than it should be. And I just heard someone in the hallway." Blake disappeared into the outer office again.

"That's normal." Faith's voice was low. "The guards patrol regularly."

"Will they come inside?" Laura's face was white.

"I don't think so." Faith considered the idea. "Not unless they heard us moving around."

"Let's hope not." Robyn glanced at the time on her wristclip and frowned. Checking that all signs of their presence were erased, she motioned for them to follow her out. "How much longer do you need?" Robyn asked Blake, jerking her head at the datadev.

"Another three minutes still." Blake was staring at the device on the desk, her face grim. "And it's only ten minutes until the security system reboots."

"Alright." Their leader ran her eyes across the room. "The *second* the download is completed, we need to get out of here. We cannot still be here when the alarms and cameras come back on." She motioned to the boots they had abandoned at the door. "Pass me mine. We'll put them back on, so we're ready to go."

It was a long three minutes. The four of them waited tensely. Robyn and Laura stood to either side of the desk, weapons clutched in their hands and trained on the exit. Blake was poised, tweezers in hand, ready to remove the disc the second the information transfer was done. Faith leaned her head close to the door, listening intently.

Blake had been certain there was someone out there. But whoever it was seemed to have gone. For now, Faith could hear nothing. The skin on the back of her neck prickled as she stared across the room at the datadev, as though her thoughts might speed up the process.

She was flooded with relief when Blake set to work with the tweezers once again. Faith had to admire her precision: even under stress, her hands were steady. Within twenty seconds she had removed the disc and replaced the datadev cover. She slid both devices into her pack before glancing at her wristclip.

"Six minutes. Better get going." She turned to Faith. "All clear?"

Startled, Faith refocused her attention on the hallway outside. After a second or so of silence, she eased the door open a crack and peered out. Heaving a sigh of relief when she saw nothing, she beckoned to the others and headed into the gloom. A soft click was all she heard as the door to Anderson's lair closed behind Laura, and the four of them retraced their steps to the office they had entered the building through.

Faith got there first. Grateful their mission was almost complete, she hurried across the room. But when she tugged on the base of the window, it didn't budge. She braced herself and tried again. Was it really so heavy? Knowing she was blushing, she gave it one last try, putting all her efforts into heaving the window upwards.

Behind her, she heard Robyn tutting.

"Perhaps it's locked?" Faith whispered, casting an apologetic glance over her shoulder.

"Let me try."

Robyn stepped forward. But before she could haul on the sash, Blake grabbed hold of her arm. Her grip must have been vice-like, because Robyn's face flashed with pain, then fury.

"What are you–?"

But she stopped speaking. Blake's finger pointed upwards. Above the window, a light was blinking. The light from an armed intruder alarm.

Relinquishing her hold on the window, Robyn took a step back. The truth was up there, staring them in the face. The window had been locked. The alarms reactivated.

They were trapped.

Chapter Two: Noah

It was after midnight, and he was exhausted, but Noah hurried on. Now that they'd made the decision, he wanted to get there as soon as possible. He rounded the final bend and sped up, eager to keep his promise. Reaching the wooden barrier, he bent to unfasten it, trying to loosen the bolt as quietly as possible.

His fingers were stiff and unwieldy, and it took him quite a while, but eventually he loosened them and pulled the wooden barrier out of the way.

"Hey," he called, "it's only me."

He peered inside. A figure was slumped in the far corner of the cave, her head down and her knees hugged to her chest. She didn't move. His heart stopped.

"Ella?"

She raised her head slowly. "Noah? Is that you?"

"It's me." He took a tentative step inside. "How are you?"

She shrugged. "How do you think?"

"Honestly, it doesn't look like you're doing so great."

"I'm not." She let her head drop on to her knees again. "I'm really not."

Noah remained where he was, shifting from one foot to the other as he considered what to say. "Um... we thought you might like to go to the bathing cave..."

"What time is it?" She looked up again, her face creased with confusion. "Sorry... I lose track."

"It's twenty to one."

"In the morning?" Her voice was brittle. "I see. Jacob doesn't know about this, does he?"

"He doesn't."

"That figures."

Noah was hit by a wave of sympathy for the older girl. He thought back to the events which had led to Ella's imprisonment. Immediately following Faith and Diane's escape, the community's first priority had been Carl. Alongside Ella, he'd been guarding the Danforth girls at the cottage during the guard attack on the tunnels. He'd received a severe blow to the head with a heavy branch, presumably delivered by one of the girls.

In contrast, Ella had simply been knocked out with a dose of the sleeping solution. She had woken up with a slight dizziness and contacted the base immediately to ask for help. Despite this, Jacob had doubted her story, claiming that she had helped the escapees.

It didn't help that Carl had told the Eremus leader that Ella had been extremely friendly towards the girls. His head injury had thankfully not caused permanent damage, but it hadn't stopped him using it to gain sympathy from anyone who'd listen. Clearly, he was afraid Jacob might think he was somehow to blame for the Eremus girls' escape, and as a result, he'd been quick to accuse Ella of sympathising with their situation.

He'd also made public Ella's relationship with Helen, one of the Danforth students. Noah knew the relationship had been borne out of Ella's great compassion. She had been the only one able to help Helen when she'd suffered from crippling anxiety after being dragged into the forest at night and used as bait by Jacob himself. Noah also knew that Ella, despite showing real kindness towards the girls and caring for them better than most of the Eremus citizens, would not have simply let two of them leave without raising the alarm.

He'd told Jacob as much. So had Ruth and Anna. But their defence hadn't done Ella any good. Jacob had questioned her repeatedly, but her responses had never satisfied him. No matter how many times she had denied knowledge of the girls' plans, described the way they'd waited until she was sleeping and dosed her thoroughly with the Sleepsol, Jacob remained convinced that she'd played some part in their escape.

Flynn said Jacob needed someone to blame. That he would ease up on Ella in time. But after three days of attacking her with questions, the Eremus leader had flung her into a cave in one of the deepest tunnels in the system and had Harden barricade the door. Since her imprisonment, Ella had only been permitted food, a bathroom bucket, a lantern, and a bucket of clean water in which to bathe.

Worse treatment, Ruth argued, than the Danforth girls. It was the reason for their subterfuge tonight.

Ella rubbed the heels of her hands into her eyes. "You think Jacob's planning to punish me forever?"

"I don't know." Crossing the cave, Noah crouched by her side. "Look, we've been working on him… but it doesn't sound like he's going to come around." At her pained glance, he qualified, "Not any time soon, anyway. For now, sneaking you out is the best we can do."

"We?" She raised an eyebrow.

"Me and Ruth." The older girl brightened at the mention of her sister. "She went to get you some fresh clothes. She's waiting at the bathing pool for you." He glanced over his shoulder at the open door. "We know Jacob's busy checking the outer guard posts, so we figured now was as safe a time as any."

"I'll admit that being properly clean sounds good." Ella hesitated. "But what if you get caught?"

Noah shrugged. "We talked it over. We're prepared to take the rap. Hopefully, it won't come to that."

"Alright, if you're sure." She smiled faintly. "It's the best offer I'm likely to get right now."

She pushed herself into a standing position. Rolling her neck, she groaned. "I haven't moved properly for hours... *days* even. There isn't exactly a lot of space in here."

Noah glanced around the cave. She was right. And Jacob hadn't given her much in the way of provisions. He noted the tray in the corner, the plate untouched.

"You didn't eat your dinner."

Stalking past him into the tunnel, Ella shrugged. "Wasn't hungry."

Concerned, Noah hurried after her. "You need to keep your strength up."

Ignoring him, she kept going. Though her head was high and her step sure, he thought she looked pale. She might have lost weight too, though he couldn't say he'd ever spent much time examining her figure.

He tried a different tack. "Ruth's been pretty worried about you. That's part of," he gestured between them, then at the tunnels, "this. She needed to know that you were alright."

The sisters hadn't seen each other since Ella had been put down there. It was as much a punishment for Ruth as it was for Ella, which seemed horribly unfair to Noah, and was one of the reasons he'd agreed to help.

The older girl strode ahead. "I'm fine."

Noah kept pace with her. "You sure about that?"

"I'm sure," she said, dully.

They walked on in silence. The bathing area was quite a distance from the cave where Ella was being kept. So far, things were going well. They had passed no one. Most citizens would be in bed, or else out in the forest on a night shift. It was one of the reasons they'd chosen the middle of the night for the illicit outing: the likelihood of them meeting anyone was slim.

"How's Helen?" Ella's voice was low, as though she was worried to hear the answer.

"She's alright." He tried to reassure her. "As far as I know, anyway. I'm sorry – they haven't assigned me to the Danforth girls lately. As you can imagine, Jacob's being very cagey about who he trusts."

She jerked her head to meet his gaze. "So they're stuck with Harden... and Sil... and *Carl* looking after them?"

"I think so." He shrugged. "To be honest, I don't know for sure."

Ella heaved a huge sigh and looked at the ground. "I hope she's alright."

"You miss her?"

"Don't you miss Faith?" she countered.

Embarrassed, Noah dropped his gaze. "I guess."

In truth, and no matter how hard he tried not to care, he'd been devastated to lose Faith. He'd told himself over and over that she'd gone back to save her friend, but it still felt like she'd abandoned him. When he thought about her leaving, it was like a dagger to the heart. But behind all the anger, he found himself missing her desperately.

"You're mad at her too though, right?" Ella paused for a second, and when he didn't respond, she pressed on. "I wouldn't blame you." He glanced at her, and her tone grew defensive. "*I'm* mad. I mean... I helped them. I tried to make their lives easier, but they–" She turned away. "And now look at me."

Against his will, Noah found himself leaping to Faith's defence. "She didn't mean to involve you. I'm sure, if she knew that–"

Ella laughed, without humour. "Should've thought about that before she knocked me and Carl out and raced back to Bellator."

"Faith's not like that, though. There's no way she or Diane would've wanted you to get the blame." Noah sighed. "She went because of Sophia."

"And you're okay with her leaving, are you?"

"Don't get me wrong. I'm angry." He shrugged. "But I understand why she went. I mean, if it was Ruth who'd been taken by an enemy, I'd do anything to–"

"Alright." Ella waved away his argument. "You made your point." Abruptly, she changed the subject. "How's everything else?" She swept her arm at the tunnels around them. "What's going on... out here?"

"Things are..." He wondered how much he should tell her. "Difficult."

Since Faith and Diane's escape and Ella's subsequent incarceration, Jacob had been stomping around the settlement like a wounded bear. Extensive searches the night the girls had disappeared had turned up nothing. When they were still empty-handed after several days of scouring the woods, the leader had had to admit the girls were gone.

Where Jacob had once had eight Danforth captives, he now had four. One of the original prisoners was dead, and three had returned to the city. Faith, his prized attribute, was the biggest loss. His big plan to even the score with the Bellator chancellor had taken a substantial hit.

Jacob's fury made him more volatile than ever. Since he had masterminded— without consulting anyone—the explosion which had killed so many Bellator guards, many of the Eremus citizens distrusted him. The council was extremely concerned about what he might do next. There had been a particularly tense meeting where Jacob had suggested various outrageous schemes, all aiming to have a devastating impact on Bellator.

So far, he hadn't been able to muster any support. But Noah suspected he'd go behind everyone's backs if it suited him. He'd done it before.

There was an additional hostage now, of course. A single Bellator guard, the only one who had surrendered after the confrontation in the tunnels, was currently residing in the Danforth girls' original cell. And Professor Kemp, Faith's teacher from Danforth, remained in the other prison cave with the girls.

A member of the Bellator Resistance, she was another asset who might provide them with helpful insight into the workings of the city. But Jacob knew her loyalties lay with Noah's ma, who she'd grown up with, and with the academy students. He couldn't manipulate her, nor could he rely on her silence.

After the infamous meeting where, according to Noah's ma, Jacob had seemed almost manic, there had been an even bigger shift in the Eremus citizens' feelings.

There had been a steady stream of visitors to Noah's cave over the past week, each expressing doubt at Jacob's actions and asking for Flynn or Anna's advice. People were even less sure about Jacob's treatment of Ella, who was a popular member of the community. Their leader had announced that she was being separated from the community for a set period of time as a sanction for assisting the academy students in their escape.

Whilst people had accepted the reason for her punishment, there had been murmurs about the length of time the sanction might last. So far, Jacob had given no indication of when Ella might be released. And Noah was *certain* most people didn't know quite how poor the conditions she was being kept in were. If that became public knowledge, he knew there would be an outcry.

Jacob wasn't a stupid man. He knew of the growing doubt, and hadn't reacted well to it. Instead of retaining his ever-calm exterior, placating people with smooth reassurances, he had taken to snapping at anyone who asked questions and insisting that he had everything in hand. Didn't he always have Eremus' best interests at heart? People just had to trust him, he preached.

But many were no longer certain that they could. And Jacob knew it. At the moment, the lack of faith people had in their leader seemed to be the only thing holding Jacob back from taking drastic action. But Flynn didn't think it would stop him for long.

Noah met Ella's gaze, knowing he'd been silent too long. "Let's just say no one seems to know what Jacob's planning to do next. People seem a little less willing to trust him recently."

"For good reason." Ella snorted. "He's no better than Danforth."

Though the suggestion was shocking, Noah found himself nodding. Lately, Jacob's efforts to make things better for the Eremus citizens seemed to do the opposite.

"He's been in a foul mood. There are rumours that he's planning another attack on the city, *despite* the support he's lost."

"Rumours?"

"Yeah. He's keeping pretty quiet. I think he's frightened how every-one would react right now, things being the way they are." Noah stared down at the ground. "Ma and Flynn are pretty concerned."

"Sounds like they have cause to be."

As they came to the final bend in the tunnel before the bathing cave, they heard footsteps coming from the other direction. Beside Noah, Ella froze. Panicked, he glanced both ways, looking for a place to hide.

But there was nowhere to go.

Stepping in front of Ella, Noah did his best to shield her as the citizen approached. Whoever it was, their stride was confident, pur-poseful. Noah found himself hoping it wasn't anyone who would report back to Jacob. He took a deep breath as they rounded the corner and came to an abrupt stop, almost colliding with them.

"Paulo!"

"Noah?" His brother looked puzzled. "What are you–?" His gaze travelled to Ella. "Oh! I see."

"Hello, Paulo." She stepped out from behind Noah.

Noah watched as Paulo ran his gaze over the other girl. His face clouded with concern and he took a step towards her. "Are you... alright?"

She stiffened. "I'll be better when I've had a bath."

Paulo's gaze flicked back over his shoulder. "So..." his eyes lit up with understanding, "*that's* why..."

"Yes," Noah said hastily, "that's why." He waved his hand at the bathing cave ahead. "Ruth's waiting... would you mind not–"

Slowly, Paulo met his gaze. There was a long pause before he spoke again. "Keep it down. And don't be long, okay? I don't know *what* he'll do if..."

Noah nodded gratefully. With a brief nod at Ella, Paulo continued on down the tunnel. When he was gone, Ella sagged against the tunnel wall. Turning to her, Noah felt a wave of sympathy wash over him.

"He won't tell. Even my brother has less faith in Jacob these days."

"I know. But it could've been anyone." Ella's voice was so sad it broke his heart. "How long do I have to live like this? I mean... I'm having to sneak around like a criminal just to escape my cell for half an hour."

"I know and I'm sorry." Noah met her gaze. "Lots of people are asking about you. Questioning Jacob's actions. I hope things won't be like this for long."

"Me too." With a grimace, Ella moved past him. "Part of me contemplated following Faith and Diane back to Bellator. Bet they wouldn't keep me locked up like an animal."

Concerned, Noah hurried after her. "Really?"

Ahead of them, Ruth appeared at the entrance to the bathing cave. Her face lit up as she saw them, and Ella hurried forward. Noah hung back as they embraced, holding on to one another for a long time.

"So good to see you," Ruth whispered, as they parted.

"You too." Ella managed a small smile.

"Come in then. We don't have long. I have soap and towels for you." Ruth turned to Noah, her eyes shining with tears. *Thank you,* she mouthed.

Before Ella followed her sister inside, she stopped and turned back. Her eyes were serious.

"I don't *want* to run away to the city." She gestured to the caves around them. "I've lived in Eremus all my life. But I can't stand being caged like this. Not for much longer. I miss my freedom. My family." She blushed. "And I know I've only known her for a little while, but I miss Helen."

Her face hardened. "None of us knows what's going to happen. But if there's one thing I'm certain of, it's that Jacob isn't thinking rationally any more. He'll do *anything* to get back at Danforth. And, as far as I'm concerned, if he's in charge, Eremus is doomed. I'd *rather* take my chances in Bellator."

Chapter Three: Faith

The four of them stared at one another. The plan had been to exit the same way they'd entered, bolt across the grass, and get back to headquarters before the sun came up. Now that the window was locked and alarmed, that wasn't an option.

"The cameras!" Robyn's eyes widened in alarm and she pulled the hood of her sweatshirt lower. "Are they back on too?"

Blake was ahead of her and was already slipping the device from her pocket. She frowned as she tapped a button to activate it. "Not according to this. Alarms are back on. But cameras are still offline... for now. Looks like the system's rebooting. We probably have a few more minutes before they start up again."

"What do we do?" Laura hissed.

Robyn turned to Faith. "This is your turf. Where else can we get out?"

"Maybe somewhere that won't be alarmed?" Laura added.

Faith's mind had gone into overdrive. For a few seconds, she turned this way and that, running through the options in a panic. "Not alarmed..." she muttered, her mind going blank, "...surely *everywhere's* alarmed!"

"Gah!" Blake sounded disgusted. "I told Madeleine she'd be a liability."

"Give her a chance." Robyn shot the tech genius a look. She turned to Faith. "Don't panic. Think. Where is there an exit which might not be alarmed?"

"And don't take too long deciding," Blake tapped a finger to her wristclip.

Her heart pounding, Faith racked her brain. Where could they escape the building, through an exit which *wasn't* alarmed, without being seen? She considered the school's layout, picturing it in her head. Here among the staff offices, they'd been pretty safe at night. But there was no way on earth the staff office windows weren't alarmed.

"Um... I g-guess..." Faith was aware of the three pairs of eyes fixed on her. "The bedroom windows aren't alarmed. But that would mean entering a room where there are girls sleeping. Too risky."

But she felt calmer now. In her head, she followed the lines of the map which was displayed on the wall in the academy's entrance. Running her eyes down each hallway, she ticked off each one mentally as she discarded it. Beside her, Blake tutted. Laura shifted from foot to foot. Even Robyn's cool expression had begun to look strained.

Heading for the main building, where the girls and staff alike slept, seemed dangerous. But for now, there seemed to be no other option.

"Come with me."

Beckoning to the others, Faith led them out of the office, hoping she looked like she knew what she was doing. As she walked down the hall, her brain continued to race. There had to be an idea she hadn't considered yet, one exit which might not set off an alarm so loud it guaranteed instant capture.

And then it hit her.

They would have to pass through the central atrium. All the main hallways led away from it. That, in itself, was risky. But if they could get by without detection, there was one door that just might work. Head down, she increased her speed, wondering if it was obvious to the others that the idea had only just come to her.

Her hands were shaking. If this worked, if she managed to get them out safely, surely it would improve her reputation among the Resistance members. She wanted to be seen as someone who was cool in a crisis. It was the only way to secure her position on future missions. To make her part of the positive changes in Bellator, rather than just an onlooker.

She just didn't want to imagine the consequences if it went wrong.

For once, none of the others questioned her as she led them along the hallway towards the centre of the building. As they reached the main atrium, she slowed her steps. It was a large, spacious area, with a high, vaulted ceiling. Between classes, it was thronged with Danforth students hurrying from place to place. Faith could almost hear the happy chatter as the girls called to one another, groaning about homework and making plans to get together after school.

Right now, it was empty. Better lit than the other areas they had passed through, it was also easier to see. And, she thought uneasily, to *be* seen. A grand staircase led upwards to their left, and several hallways ran off it in different directions. Faith knew which one they needed. She was about to dart out into the space when she heard footsteps coming from the corridor leading to the academy's front lobby.

They'd been in the building far longer than anticipated: the security guards must be making their rounds. Motioning to the others to move back, Faith flattened her own body against the wall. If the guard passed this way, they were in trouble. But if she was headed down any one of the other hallways, they might escape without notice.

She closed her eyes as the footsteps came nearer. They paused for a second in what had to be the centre of the atrium, then, one heart-stopping moment later, continued on. Their pace had altered though, it was slower, more measured. Faith knew why. Whoever it was appeared to be going up the stairs to a higher floor. As the sound faded into the distance, she allowed herself to relax.

Peering out into the atrium which was once again empty, Faith moved forward. She took the second hallway on the right and hurried off down it. The passage led to the sports fields. It was on the opposite side of the building to the one where they'd entered, but if the door she had in mind was open and not alarmed, she could make it work.

At night, the door was used by the drudges as they came in and out of the building to complete their outdoor chores. She remembered occasionally thinking how difficult it must have been for them to work in the near-darkness, but somehow, they managed. Every night, the drudges got to work: mowing the extensive lawns, tending to the academy gardens, and removing the rubbish which accumulated in the building.

Her thoughts went to Arden, the kindly drudge that had helped her out once before, when she'd been a student at the school. He, she was sure, would have assisted them tonight. But there was no guarantee she could find him; he was one drudge among many under Anderson's command. Faith would have to act alone, and hope her hunch was a sound one.

Praying they wouldn't bump into anyone, Faith approached the end of the hallway with trepidation. Her hand was trembling as she reached for the handle, hearing the others come to a stop close behind her. When the door yielded to her touch, she heaved a sigh of relief.

Peering outside, she saw no one. With a furtive glance left and right, she hurried through and beckoned for the others to follow. As Robyn eased the door shut behind them, she heard the sound of machinery coming from the other side of the courtyard.

"This way!" she hissed, darting behind one of the storage sheds the school used to keep some of the larger outdoor equipment.

Wordlessly, the others followed her lead. There was only just enough room for the four of them to stand in the space behind it. They waited, breathless, as the noise continued to grow, until the machine was very close. Suddenly, it cut out. The silence that followed was startling. As one, the intruders held their breath.

There was a shuffling of footsteps, followed by a clicking sound, then a faint creak as the door to the storeroom was opened. Whatever machine had been in use was rolled inside. There were additional noises, as though whoever was inside was moving other equipment around.

It seemed to take forever. Faith wondered if the drudge inside might be Arden, but didn't dare risk looking. Finally, the sounds stopped and the door was pulled shut. A lock clicked into place, and the footsteps retreated in the opposite direction.

"Was that a guard?" Laura whispered.

Faith shook her head. "Probably a drudge."

"Perhaps it's–" A frown from Robyn stopped Laura in her tracks. "Sorry," she lowered her voice to whisper-level.

"Come on, we're running out of time." Heaving a sigh, Robyn slipped out from behind their shield. "Which way now?"

They had exited on the opposite side of the building, but Faith knew where they were. Checking for additional drudges or guards on patrol, she broke into a run, leading the rest of her group around the side of the building. Knowing they were less likely to be spotted, she took them into the academy gardens, where she led them through a maze of pathways, marvelling at their familiarity, despite her absence.

They emerged on the same lawn they had crossed to reach the building in the first place. Faith pointed in the direction of the wall where they had entered, but the others had already seen it. They needed no more encouragement. Together, they retraced their steps, scrambling over it before anything else could go wrong.

On the other side, Laura clapped her on the back, panting. "Not bad, for a newbie."

Faith managed to grin, despite her thundering heart.

"Beginner's luck." Blake scowled. "Don't let it go to your head."

"There's no time for this." Robyn pointed at the sky, which was beginning to lighten. "We have to get back."

As they ran back to headquarters, Faith found herself unable to stop grinning.

When she and Diane had first arrived at the library, they had gone straight to the front door. It had been a naïve move, but they hadn't known any different. The Resistance had to protect their base, or risk Danforth's guards discovering it. There was a side door, which was used infrequently, but most of the time the Resistance women accessed headquarters through a tunnel. Leading straight out of the hub, it led them under the main square and came out in a grocery store on the other side. Lucy, the woman who ran the place, was Resistance, and allowed them access whenever they needed it.

At night, they had to be a little more cautious, but the square was deserted and when Lucy let them in, they were pretty sure they hadn't been spotted. The short walk through the tunnel reminded Faith of Eremus and she pushed away thoughts of Noah.

At the door on the other end of the tunnel, Robyn punched in the passcode and they headed inside. The headquarters was quiet, and the group leader spoke in a whisper. "Good job tonight." She shot a glance at Faith. "All of you. Now go to bed and get some rest. We'll update the others in the morning."

When Faith reached the room she shared with several others, she was exhausted. Tiptoeing inside, she crept past her bunkmates until she reached her own bed. Flopping down onto it, she had just closed her eyes when she felt a hand on her arm. Jerking upright, she found herself face-to-face with a pair of inquisitive eyes.

"How'd it go?"

"Diane!" Her heart thundering, she sat up. "You startled me."

The older girl seemed unconcerned. "You didn't think I'd stay awake to find out how your first mission went?"

"Ssh!" Faith held a finger to her lips. "You'll wake them."

Diane cast a doubtful eye over the four other women who shared their room. "Unlikely, but c'mere then." She waited until Faith had slipped into bed beside her. Dropping her voice to a whisper, she went on. "How was the old place?"

"The same." Faith leaned close, keeping her own voice low. "Totally weird to be there."

"Any trouble?"

"Not really. It took longer than planned, because Anderson stayed in her office til way past midnight."

Diane scowled. "Bet she was scheming with Danforth."

"But once she went to bed, we got in okay and planted the bug."

"Did Blake manage to copy what was on the datadev?"

"She did."

"Genius!" Faith frowned. Diane got along with Blake far better than her. Sensing her annoyance, Diane elbowed her gently. "You know she is. Think of what we might find out from that datadev. Information we can really use."

"I s'pose." Faith shifted, uncomfortable in the small space. "There was a bit of an issue on the way out."

Beside her, she felt Diane stiffen. "What happened?"

"It was weird. The window we'd come in through had been unlocked by our contact. But... when we went back, it was locked and the alarm had reactivated."

"No!" Diane gasped. "So how did you–?"

"Had to leave through the door leading to the fields. I figured it'd be open, since–"

"The drudges use it at night!" At an elbow from Faith, Diane lowered her voice again. "*Quick thinking!*"

In the darkness, Faith smiled. Whilst she was tired, she felt proud of her efforts tonight. And Diane was the only person she had left to share it with. Impressing her made Faith feel good, especially considering how tough Diane was.

Her thoughts returned to the person she really wanted to be telling and the smile died.

"What's up?" Diane was more intuitive than Faith sometimes gave her credit for.

She shrugged, not wanting to dampen the mood. "Nothing."

"Nothing my foot!" Diane nudged her sharply. "Spill."

"In the office..." Faith tapped on her wristclip, accessing the photographs she had taken earlier, "there were lists of student names, tests they were undergoing, drug doses they'd been given or whatever."

Diane bent close, peering at the images. "That sounds like useful information."

"Yeah. But..."

"Sophia's name was there?" Diane guessed. Despite her gruff exterior, she understood how much Faith missed her best friend. "They're doing tests on her?" Faith didn't respond. "Wait!" She gripped Faith's hand tightly. "She *failed* them?"

"No. Her name... it wasn't there at all."

"Really?" Faith shook her head. "You must've just missed it." Diane squinted at the tiny writing. "Let's look again."

They looked over the various photographs, scrolling through the lists over and over. There were many familiar names, but no matter how many times they checked, Sophia's was worryingly absent.

Diane was silent for so long that Faith wondered if she'd fallen asleep. Eventually, she sighed. "I'm sorry. I know how much you were hoping..."

Diane had never been great at comforting people. Her best friend, Serene had been the one with the empathy. But she had been the first victim of Danforth's experimentation. Faith reminded herself that Diane understood what she was going through. She just didn't know how to show it.

Giving in to her tiredness, Faith sagged against the older girl, allowing the tears to fall. Sophia would have hugged her, but instead, Diane awkwardly patted her arm.

"Let's try and talk to Madeleine tomorrow. You don't know what Blake got from the datadev. There could be lots of helpful information."

"I know. It's just..."

"You were really hoping to find her tonight." There was another long pause, and Diane shifted away from her. "Why don't you get some rest? I'm sure you must need it."

It was an invitation to leave. Diane liked her space. The conversation was over. Reluctantly, Faith got back into her own bed. As she settled down beneath the covers, she finally allowed her thoughts to go to the boy she had left behind in Eremus. She'd chosen Sophia over him, made her way back to the city to save her friend. Noah was, undoubtedly, angry with her for abandoning him.

And what had it all been for? Three weeks, and no sign of Sophia. Faith punched a fist into her pillow. But as she settled down to sleep, Diane's voice drifted across the distance between the beds.

"I promise we'll find her. Even if we have to go out alone and look."

CHAPTER FOUR: NOAH

"Penny for your thoughts?"

Noah looked up to see his ma standing over him. "Sorry?"

"You were miles away." She peered closely into his face. "Anything you want to talk about?"

He shrugged, trying not to blush. He had been thinking of Faith. Whether he was furious with her or missing her like mad, his thoughts never seemed far from the Bellator girl. He suspected his ma knew it, but knew she wouldn't pry.

"I'm just a bit tired, is all."

"I'm not surprised." She sat down, retrieving a shirt from the table where it lay waiting to be mended. "Don't think I didn't hear you sneak back in last night."

His eyes flew to hers. It had been late when he'd returned Ella to her cell, but he'd thought he'd managed to come in without disturbing anyone else. Clearly, his ma was more alert than he gave her credit for.

He searched for a response which didn't involve him lying. "I was… with Ruth."

"Thought as much." She opened her sewing kit. "It's tough for her right now... what with Ella being..."

"Yeah, she's finding it hard." Noah leaned over, taking a needle and a length of thread from her.

"I think Flynn and I are hoping.... That is, we want to get Ella out. But with Jacob the way he is at the moment, we think it might be safer to keep her out of sight. At least for now."

"I get it." He squinted as he threaded the needle and handed it back to her. "Thanks, Ma."

"What for?"

"I don't know. Just... understanding."

As Anna began to sew, they sat in companionable silence. Noah was tired, it was true. The sisters had spent well over an hour catching up, whilst he had stood guard. He'd been very glad that no one else passed by and found himself daring to hope that Paulo would keep his mouth shut about their nighttime adventure.

Both Ruth and Ella had been extremely grateful for his help, and they'd agreed to try and do it again at some point soon. Ella had asked them if perhaps they could bring her out to see Helen at some point, but Noah didn't think it was a good idea. Attempting to move any of the prisoners around the tunnels in the middle of the night was asking for trouble. Instead, he'd agreed to take a note to Helen for her, though he had no idea how he was going to manage it as yet.

He could understand Ella's frustration. If there was even a chance that he could have seen Faith right now, he knew he'd jump at it. Never mind how angry he was at her. He wondered where she might be. He'd pictured her locked in a room at the academy, strapped to a bed in the med centre, being chastised by Danforth herself. Physical torture for her was mental torture for him, but he didn't seem able to escape it.

"You coming to the meeting?" His ma's voice broke through his thoughts for the second time.

"Of course." He dragged his thoughts back to the moment. "You ready for it?"

The council had met again the previous day. Several members, Flynn and Anna among them, had expressed concerns that there were numerous tensions among the community. People were scared, unsure what was going on, worried about the future.

In response, Jacob had arranged a public meeting where he could update people on what he called "the Danforth situation." Everyone who wasn't on an essential shift this morning had been asked to gather in the canteen. Jacob had told the council he was planning to allay the citizens' fears and bolster morale.

Anna and Flynn didn't believe him. Knowing they had a growing number of citizens on their side, they were preparing to speak out against him if necessary. But they were concerned that the threat of a takeover would send Jacob right over the edge.

"I think so. Gauging his mood will be vital." Anna tied a knot in the thread and snapped it off with her teeth. "We suspect he's going to try and rile everyone up against Danforth and Bellator. He'll have a lot less support than he's used to."

"What do you think he'll do?"

She shrugged. "Honestly, we've no idea." Folding the shirt, she placed it on the table and put away the needle and thread. "I think we managed to persuade him to hold off on taking any action until we have more information from the Resistance."

Noah's heart raced at the thought of getting news from Bellator. "You're going to make contact with them?"

"We're going to suggest ways we might try to." She chewed on her lower lip. "But I've no idea how Jacob will react. He's so unpredictable these days. One awkward question and–"

"You think he'll do something drastic without talking to you?" Noah bent to pick up a sweatshirt, thinking back to the bombs Jacob had detonated in the forest during the recent meeting with Danforth.

"Well, he's done it before." His ma's face was pale. "He definitely keeps a lot from us these days."

"What about Paulo?" Noah's stepbrother was closer to Jacob than most. Perhaps he could shed some light on the subject. "Has Flynn asked him?"

"Yes. He's worried too." She frowned. "You know that Paulo wasn't told about the attack on Danforth's guards in advance. He doesn't feel like Jacob confides in him either."

"You mean..."

"I'm afraid Jacob seems to be talking to Sarah Porter more than anyone these days." Anna grimaced. Noah thought about the woman who'd taken Faith captive on Jacob's instructions and shuddered. "And she just tells him what he wants to hear."

Noah considered what she'd said. "Do you think he'd launch an attack on the city?" His ma's expression confirmed his fears. "I mean... that would put hundreds... *thousands* of innocent Bellator citizens in danger." He felt selfish when he realised he was really only concerned about one.

His ma laid a hand on his arm. "You don't think we know that? Flynn and I have done everything we can to calm him, but I'm not sure we've managed to talk him out of it yet. His actions lately have been on a par with Danforth's." Noah recalled Ella making a similar comment the previous night. "I think..." she paused, "No, I *hope* we persuaded him to wait, at least until we can get in touch with one of our Resistance contacts."

"You mean Madeleine?" Noah frowned. "You think she's alive?"

Part of the Bellator Resistance, Madeleine had helped the Eremus people for years, aiding them with their raids into the city, ensuring they had access to vital supplies which could keep the community going. Since her disappearance a few weeks ago, the council had been extremely concerned for her safety.

It was her home that the Bellator guards had gained access to the tunnels from. Once the raiders had dealt with the threat, they'd been forced to set off explosives at the rear entrance, destroying any evidence that the house had been used as an access point. Madeleine hadn't been seen since. They were hopeful that she had gone into hiding, but no one was sure.

Accessing the city without using her home was difficult, but not impossible. And speaking to her before rushing into action seemed like a sensible move to Noah.

"We hope so. If not, there are others we might contact." His ma glanced at the door. Noah knew she was worried about Flynn. "I actually managed to talk to Charlotte yesterday." Noah knew Jacob had been trying to keep the two women apart. "She thinks they might be prepared to support us. Work things out with a less violent approach. If we can persuade them that we have similar goals, then–"

A noise from outside startled them both. Flynn's head poked through the cave entrance.

"You two ready?" He looked exhausted.

"You only just finish your shift?" Noah's ma hurried to her partner's side. Flynn had been on guard duty in the forest all night. "You sure you don't want to stay here and rest?"

"I want to hear what he says. *First hand*. See that he keeps his word."

"But–"

He held up a hand to stop her. "But nothing. We both have to be there, you know that. I don't plan to interject unless I have to. I'm hoping he was genuine about seeing the sense in our plan, but just in case..." Leaning forward, he pressed a kiss to her cheek. "Don't worry. I can grab a couple of hours afterwards."

Ten minutes later, they entered an extremely crowded canteen. Tensions were high in the community, and everyone wanted to hear what Jacob had to say. Noah followed his ma and Flynn to the front where they stood stiffly, their eyes darting around the room as they waited for the meeting to begin.

Unsurprisingly, Sarah and her son Harden were right beside the podium where Jacob stood. Noah nodded at Harden and was surprised to have the gesture reciprocated. Sarah merely glared at them and leaned over to hiss something in her son's ear. Harden immediately dropped his gaze.

Paulo stood a few feet behind them. He smiled as they approached, but Noah thought he looked tense.

Once Jacob was certain that most of the Eremus citizens were present, he held up a hand for silence.

"Thank you for attending this morning. I know the council has been huddling in corners for several weeks now, without much clarification." He shrugged. "I'll be totally honest with you. We've been struggling to agree on a suitable plan of action."

He glanced down at Flynn as he spoke, and his trademark smile faded slightly. At public meetings, he usually managed to maintain a positive outlook, no matter how he felt. But his fury at the girls' escape had yet to abate. Clearly, he considered Anna and Flynn to be leading the fight against his own plans for Bellator and resented them for it.

"Much has happened in Eremus over the past few weeks, but I want to reassure you that the safety and wellbeing of our community is, as always, of paramount importance to us. Since two of our female prisoners escaped, we have been concerned that they might cause problems for Eremus. We believe the pair have returned to Bellator. How much they would be able to tell those in the city about our community, we're not sure. What we *do* know is, they know enough to put us at serious risk."

Around the room, Noah could hear murmured reactions to their leader's words. Instead of reassuring people, Jacob seemed intent on planting seeds of doubt in their minds. Noah could see why. Making out that Faith and Diane had gone back to the city with the express purpose of revealing Eremus secrets to those in charge was a surefire way of frightening his citizens.

That way, when Jacob presented the people with his solution, no matter how extreme, they would be less likely to question it. Noah hated that aspect of Jacob's leadership. It was too close to what he'd heard about Danforth's methods for his liking. He knew that, given the chance, Flynn and his ma would go about running the community in a more positive way.

And Jacob was dead wrong about Faith. Bellator had done her no favours. He could no more see her feeding information about Eremus back to the Bellator government than he could imagine Jacob sending a map of the tunnel locations to Danforth. But having the majority of his people believing the girls hated Eremus served Jacob's purpose.

"As you all now know, I was born in the city. One of those created solely for the purpose of reproduction. A machine, if you like. Those women treated me, and those in the same situation, like animals," he sneered. "I have no love for them. I'm only sorry that I hid my origins from you for so long. In truth, I was afraid of how you might react."

He lowered his head, as if in shame. As he paused, Noah wondered how many of the Eremus citizens were buying his act.

"I shouldn't have been," he continued. "Breaking out was the best thing I ever did, because it led me here, to Eremus. A place which welcomed me." Raising his head, he swept an arm across the cave as he continued. "I've worked hard ever since to build a community which is free of the male prejudice that infects the city."

Noah ran his eyes over the crowd. There was a sense of mistrust whispering in the air. He tuned into the people closest to him.

"…honestly think we're going to swallow this?" "How can he ask us to…" "…he lied to us…"

The comments were hushed, but the sentiment was clear. The citizens had heard Jacob's act before. Had witnessed what he did behind the scenes and been horrified by it. Did Jacob realise how many of his followers were doubting him now?

"Because of the circumstances of my birth, I *know* Danforth. I *know* the city." Jacob leaned forward, as though confiding in the group. "I believe this gives us an advantage in the coming fight."

Ruth slid into the bench beside Noah, her head down. "Did I miss much?"

Noah shook his head. "He's explaining how his origins can help us." His friend rolled her eyes and tuned into what Jacob was saying.

"Over the years, I have grown tired of the limitations forced upon us by Danforth and her government. And I know I'm not the only one." He swept his hand across the crowd in front of him. "Because of her, we are forced to live in secrecy, to steal to feed our children. We regularly lose friends and family members to her guards."

"We cannot forget Jan, Dane, and Dan, our most recent casualties."

He bowed his head for a second, allowing the names of the deceased to sink in. Noah wondered what Jan would have thought of Jacob's reverent mention of her. She had rarely agreed with him on anything.

Once the murmured reaction had died down, he raised his head again and stared out at the crowd. "But they were *not* the first to die at Danforth's hand. We have lost *so many* people to this tyrant. Over and over, we are forced to witness, first-hand, her capability for bloodshed."

Noah wondered if Jacob considered the bloodshed he himself had caused in the recent bombing. Beside him, Ruth tensed, and he knew she was thinking the same thing.

But the juggernaut at the podium ploughed on regardless. "And why? Because of *false, outdated* claims about the male gender. I won't lie to you. I don't want Eremus to hide anymore."

Flynn took a step forward, as though to protest. Noah knew he was concerned that Jacob was going back on his agreement of the previous night. If he ignored their advice to wait, to gather information before charging in to attack Bellator, would Flynn be forced to publicly oppose him?

Anna's hand shot out. Grabbing his arm, she held on, restraining him.

As the pair exchanged glances, Jacob pressed on. "I want *more* for us. I want us to be able to live without fear, to prosper, to have a choice in the way that we live. That's the reason I have taken action against the city and its rulers in recent weeks. And we must remember that."

At the front of the room, one of the older citizens had raised a hand. "What about the consequences of these actions?" He glanced at the people sitting around him. "I mean... we've seen a lot of change over the last few weeks, as you said. Frightening change."

Jacob held up a hand. "I understand that. And you may be right. Believe me, the council wants you to be able to live *without* that fear. But let me say that I am extremely proud to be your leader. I believe we can change the way things are, if we're prepared to fight. Our goal is to *make* Bellator recognise us as equals, to permit us to live safely either here in the cave settlement or, if we wish, alongside the women of Bellator."

"That's just it, though." Beside the man who had spoken, a woman stood up. Noah recognised Cora, the woman who managed the Eremus food supply in the canteen. "A lot of us...we don't *want* to live in Bellator. And we're worried that we've..." she cast a glance at Jacob, "that *you've* invited trouble from the city... made us even more of a target."

"If I have, then it's all part of the plan. Change comes at a price, Cora." Jacob's tone was brittle. "Of course, we'll have to tolerate some rocky times over the coming days, but isn't that worth it? If it means we can secure the kind of life we want?" Cora opened her mouth to argue, but Jacob pressed on. "Even if you don't want to live amongst the women of the city, you can't deny you'd enjoy a more reliable supply of food, can you?"

Defeated, Cora fell silent. Jacob let the thought settle in before continuing. "As you say, some of the recent attempts to achieve our goals have not gone as planned. But we must focus on what we *have* achieved. Our explosives completely destroyed Danforth's fertility unit. At the moment, she has no seed with which to maintain their current system of procreation. Bellator has used this for many years, and I can't see her easily finding an alternative. At the moment, as males who are capable of procreating, we are her only chance of sustaining life for the community."

"Doesn't that put us in even more danger?" Mick, a raider who had been injured in the very attack where the guard had been captured, burst out. "She might focus her efforts on coming to the forest and capturing some of us."

"That's all the more reason we should take action against her, don't you think?" Sarah's voice was strident. "Protect our men. Stop her from enslaving them."

Nodding at his staunch ally, Jacob continued. "In addition, we still have four Danforth student prisoners." He gestured to Paulo. Taking the girls prisoner had been Noah's brother's idea, but from the expression on his face, Noah wasn't sure he still believed it had been the right thing to do. "We know these girls are *extremely* valuable to the Bellator government. And we have an additional hostage now: the Bellator guard who we captured as part of the recent attack on our community."

"What do you plan to *do* with these hostages, though?" Beth, a friend of Noah's ma spoke from the back of the canteen. "I mean… how much value do they hold for Danforth? Do we know?"

There were louder murmurs from others around the space. Flynn leaned across and whispered something in Anna's ear. Noah wondered if his ma or Flynn might take over the meeting. Seeming to note this, Sarah took a step forward.

"I'm sure they're *very* valuable." She smiled. "Or if they're not, letting the people of Bellator know Danforth doesn't care about them would certainly have an impact on the women of the city." She turned to Jacob. "And speaking of making an impact, let's not forget our recent elimination of a large proportion of Danforth's guard."

"Trust her to dismiss a significant loss of life as *elimination*," Ruth hissed.

"We believe the city's forces are *severely* weakened," Sarah continued. "That means any attempt to infiltrate the city will be far easier."

"Because we killed off a hundred and fifty of their guards in cold blood." Cora had found her voice again.

"Because we killed them before they killed us," Sarah argued. Noah was watching Harden, whose face had flushed a dark red at his ma's words. "How can you say–"

"It was a *necessary* act, I assure you," Jacob butted in. He hurried on, as though afraid other citizens might begin to object. "Listen, I can see that some of our recent actions have been... looked on as extreme by some of you. I wish there was any other way to get through to Danforth, but... honestly, I doubt it." He seemed to grit his teeth as he continued. "I also understand there's a need for caution at the moment, at least until things become clearer.

"The council does not want to further risk the lives of our community. And while we must face the fact that additional battles may have to be fought before we bring Danforth down," he narrowed his eyes at Flynn, "we have *decided* to call upon the assistance of others before taking any further action."

An audible sigh of relief ran around the room. Noah watched Jacob. He wasn't a stupid man. He could see that pushing ahead with his violent agenda wasn't going to work. Not right now. Taking the sensible option, the leader stood aside, gesturing to Flynn.

"Flynn, would you like to explain our intentions?"

"Clever move," Ruth whispered. "He knows Flynn is regarded as less volatile. Plus, if it goes wrong, he can shift the blame away from himself."

Flynn got to his feet, clasping his hands together tightly. Noah wondered if they were shaking from anger or nerves.

"Jacob's right." Flynn began, diplomatically. "Danforth has been weakened. But she is far from defeated." He glanced at Anna, who gave an imperceptible nod of encouragement. "We have decided the safest course of action is to call upon the women of the Bellator Resistance for aid. They have helped us gain access to the city in the past, supported us with gathering food and medicines and so on... and we're wondering if they might be prepared to join forces with us in a more definitive way."

"What does that *mean*, exactly?" A woman's voice came from the back of the room. Noah couldn't see who it was.

"Well, we don't know yet." Flynn was honest as ever. "We plan to send an envoy into the city over the next few days. Undercover. It will need to be a woman, and she will have to blend in with the ordinary Bellator citizens. Her objective will be to get a sense of what's been happening in the city in the past few weeks." He held up a hand to quell the whispers in the crowd. "*Not* to attract unnecessary attention or cause any kind of trouble.

"While she's there, our envoy will try and make contact with Madeleine, or other members of the Resistance. We have an idea of where she might be from Charlotte Kemp, the girls' professor." Warming to his theme, Flynn's voice grew more confident. "If our envoy can locate them, she'll talk to them, gather intel on what's been happening in the city over the last few weeks... and to see how they're feeling about us now. If their goals in any way align with ours, then..." He glanced down at Anna for support.

Noah's ma stood up. "Like Jacob, I came from Bellator. When I left, there were women who felt unhappy with the way things were being run. I've spoken to Charlotte... a little." She glanced sideways at Jacob, who pointedly ignored her. "She has assured me that the Resistance movement has grown in the years I have been away."

She smiled at Flynn, encouraging him to continue. He cleared his throat before he went on. "We want to capitalise on this. Speak to the Resistance. See if their objectives are similar to our own. If so, we're hoping we might... join forces. Work together to ensure that things improve," Flynn cast an eye around the cave, "for all of us."

Noah could feel the tension dissipate. People were far happier with Flynn and Anna's suggested plan than they had been with Jacob's. A sense of pride swelled within him.

But then his eyes moved to Jacob. The leader's face was dark. Beside him Sarah sent an elbow into his side, jolting him forwards. A momentary flash of anger crossed his face, but he quashed it as he held up a hand to speak, ensuring he had the final word.

"*All we want* is to see things improve for Eremus. And I'm sure you'll agree, this plan will allow us to discover more information without risking the lives of any more citizens. We feel the Resistance could be a valuable ally, and we're hopeful we can work alongside them." Jacob cast a glance at Sarah over his shoulder. "But we must be prepared to act alone, *if we have to.*"

The meeting broke up with promises of keeping the citizens informed and not acting without their knowledge. Noah watched, as Jacob pointedly turned his back on Flynn. He took Sarah's arm and began to hurry her out of the canteen, his face thunderous. A few citizens tried to accost him, but he ignored them, waving them away with a hand as he headed for the exit.

"He's not happy," Ruth remarked, as they prepared to head off for their shifts.

"At least he agreed to wait." Noah glanced across at his ma and Flynn, who had stayed to field questions from various worried citizens. The stark difference between them and Jacob struck him again. "Should give us more time to consider what to do next, surely?"

"Maybe." His friend followed him out into the tunnel. "But I don't trust him. Not at all."

Chapter Five: Faith

The next morning, Faith joined the rest of her team to give feed-back to Madeleine. She had not slept well. Images of Sophia hooked up to an IV which sent a never-ending stream of femgazipane into her bloodstream haunted her whenever she closed her eyes. As she took a seat at one of the tables in what the women of the Resistance affectionately called the hub, both Diane and Laura shot concerned glances at her.

Around forty women lived in the headquarters. Hidden in the basement of the Bellator library, they were cramped and not very luxurious, but the space served them well. Central to the city, its old-fashioned purpose rendered it little more than a curiosity, and most people paid it little attention.

There had been plans in the past to bulldoze the building to make way for a more modern structure. The majority of citizens read using digital methods now, the government had argued, but there was strong support for preservation of the city's history, and the library had been allowed to remain.

Still, visitors were limited, and the head librarian had managed to assemble a team of Resistance sympathisers to run it. Providing there were no complaints about the building or its staff, the government paid it very little attention. It worked well as a front. The tunnel beneath it gave them an extra layer of security, protecting them from awkward questions about the number of women who came and went.

Since their arrival, Diane and Faith had been housed here, but there was talk of moving them to one of the safehouses the Resistance had situated around the city. The organisation was far larger than the number of women who lived at the headquarters. Many of its members lived ordinary lives in the city, working in roles which allowed them to spy or obtain important resources for the movement.

Those who lived in the library headquarters were mostly undercover. A lot of their work was done from the library itself, using datadevs to work remotely. They liaised regularly with the Resistance members who lived in the various Bellator districts. These women, in turn, completed tasks which took place in a more public setting.

Faith had been impressed at how organised the network was. As Resistance leader, Madeleine ran a tight ship. Each woman was a cog in a well-oiled machine which worked hard to undermine Danforth's government.

Madeleine was a formidable woman who was used to taking action. Until recently, she had lived in her own house in the city and provided the main link between Bellator and Eremus. A recent brush with Danforth's guards had put her at risk though, and since then, she'd had to go underground herself.

Madeleine was not enjoying life in hiding. The lack of freedom frustrated her, making her sharp-tongued and gruff. Faith had always found her intimidating, and this morning she was no less so.

"The mission was a success?" she barked.

"It was." Robyn wasn't fazed by her abruptness. "As you know, Laura and I managed to place the bug in an appropriate location. And Blake was able to copy information from Anderson's datadev." She pointed to the techie, whose head was bent close to one of the Resistance's own devices.

Blake didn't even look up. "Going through the new info right now."

"Share it with a couple of the others, please. Best to have as many eyes on it as possible, I think. And be sure you let me know immediately if there's anything you think is significant, alright?" Madeleine gestured for Robyn to continue.

"Lastly, I had Faith take photographs of a number of charts which were displayed in the inner office."

"Anything interesting?"

As the leader's gaze snapped to Faith, she jumped. Recovering, she took a breath and willed her voice to be steady. "I-it might just be copies of whatever Blake gets from the datadev..." she cringed at the leader's glare, "...but at first glance–"

"Yes?" Madeleine snapped.

"They appear to be lists of names. Student names." She forced herself to breathe in slowly. "Tests they've undergone, meds they're being given." She ran out of ideas and lowered her gaze. "I didn't have time to read it all properly, but they're definitely being used as part of Danforth's experiment."

Madeleine rolled her eyes. "And Bellator is supposed to be a place where women thrive."

"Hardly." Robyn stiffened. "Danforth's treatment of these girls is no better than her treatment of the Eremus men."

"Spend today going through that information with a fine tooth-comb. Make a note of anything you think might be relevant." Madeleine's tone was severe. "And look over anything Blake finds too, see if you can shed some light on it. As a member of the school community, you might spot something the rest of us miss."

"Of c-course." Faith nodded, not relishing the idea of spending the day working with the tech nerd who disliked her.

Seeming to sense her reluctance, the leader narrowed laser-eyes at her. "I mean… the school *is* your field of expertise. You were the one who spent hours persuading me to let you go along on this mission, right?"

"Right. Yes. I was." Faith gave a nod she hoped looked confident. "Of course, I will."

She glanced at Blake, whose fingers were tapping away at the keyboard. The woman seemed oblivious to anything when she was engaging with technology.

"We were glad to have Faith with us in the end." Laura spoke up. Faith found herself extremely grateful for the woman's support. "She came in pretty useful, to be honest."

Madeleine's gaze sharpened. "How so?"

"We got trapped in the building," Robyn said. Faith watched Madeleine's eyes flash with something like fear. "We went to leave the way we'd come in, but someone had locked the window and the alarm had come back online."

"How did that happen?"

"Not sure. Perhaps a guard locked them while we were in the office." She scratched her head. "Anyway, Faith managed to find an alternative exit."

"We'd've gotten out without her," Blake sniffed, "if we had to." Clearly, she was paying more attention to the conversation than Faith had realised.

"Not without setting off an alarm and alerting everyone in the building to our presence," Laura shot back. "How do you think that would've gone down?"

"Not very well." Robyn attempted to smooth the situation. "We should give Faith some credit for–"

"Sounds like you all did what you had to." Madeleine cleared her throat. "Well done for managing to remain undetected. We don't want Danforth to know any more about our work than is absolutely necessary, for now. Until we have enough citizens on our side... ready to act... we have to lie low."

"Well, there you go." Robyn raised an eyebrow at Blake. "Faith was extremely useful."

Giving her trademark scowl, Blake went back to work.

"On to other business, then." Madeleine turned to another Resistance citizen. "Anything new from you yesterday, Evelyn?"

An older woman sat at the rear of the room. Slender and petite, she looked like a strong wind would blow her over. That was what made her useful, Diane said. She blended in well, escaped notice wherever she went. For that reason, she was regularly sent on solo missions, to gather intel.

When Faith and Diane had first arrived at the library, they had relayed the story of the attack which had led to them being moved out of the Eremus cave system and given them the chance to escape. Guessing that the guards had accessed the tunnels from her old home, Madeleine had been concerned. Ever since, she'd had Evelyn make undercover visits to her old district, to see if the guards had found anything suspicious.

"Far as I can tell, there's nothing much to worry about. Your old place is still boarded up, but the fire investigators seem to have stopped sniffing around."

"Really?" Laura leaned forward. "That's good news."

"Yeah." Evelyn shifted in her seat. "Seems everyone thinks the fire at your place was caused by a gas leak."

Madeleine chewed her lip. "I only hope Danforth believes it. If they dig any deeper, we risk the entire Bellator guard discovering that tunnel. And if that happens, Eremus is in real trouble."

Evelyn frowned. "Well as far as I could tell, no one's looking into it too closely."

"So they think I'm dead?"

"They do." Evelyn nodded. "I spoke to a few of your neighbours. They all believe you were home at the time of the explosion. Planting the charred animal bones there seems to have convinced everyone you perished in the blast. I think the heat's off for now. They won't be looking for you."

"But I'll have to stay hidden." Madeleine scowled.

"Well, yes." Evelyn shot her a sympathetic look. "Sorry. On another note, there *are* whispers that an entire team of guards has gone missing."

Robyn whistled softly. "They'll be the ones in the tunnels that you told us about." She turned to Faith. "The citizens know about that?"

"Only rumours." Evelyn shrugged. "But yes, people are talking."

Madeleine frowned. "What are they saying?"

"Your neighbours seem to believe the women were out on patrol as normal and just... vanished."

Laura looked shocked. "Wait, *none* of them came back?"

"Not according to my sources, no."

"Looks like Eremus got away with it, then." Robyn sounded relieved. "I mean, if they killed every guard that went down there, and the team hadn't reported their location to anyone here before they left, then they're in the clear."

Faith's hand went to her mouth. "You think Eremus *killed* them all?"

"What else do you think happened?" Blake rolled her eyes.

"Whatever happened, citizens are worried." Evelyn shifted in her chair. "About Danforth's ability to protect them. I even heard one woman say she thought the guards might have run away. As though simply being one of Danforth's protectors puts them in a dangerous position."

Madeleine raised an eyebrow. "That would go in our favour, if enough people believe it. We need more people on our side, doubting her."

"Anything of interest in the news today?" Robyn asked Madeleine.

One thing the leader could do while hiding was comb through the news in case there was anything of interest to the Resistance. The media was controlled by Danforth, but the articles sometimes revealed vital tidbits of information if you read between the lines, which Madeleine was good at.

"Not much." The older woman shook her head. "Some more rubbish about the *wonderful* advances being made in technology at BellaLab Corp." Madeleine grimaced at this, and Faith remembered her being fired from the company which had also been the starting point for Chancellor Danforth. "Oh, and something about the repair work on the hospital fertility unit nearing completion."

"Not that it'll do them much good, with all the seed being destroyed." Blake smirked. "Danforth hasn't let that little nugget of information hit the news yet, has she?"

Since the disastrous encounter in the woods with Jacob, Danforth had been busy filling the papers and airways with reports of small skirmishes in the woods with *a few rebel forces*, but the whole thing had been spun as a victory for the guards, rather than a threat to Bellator security.

There had been articles about undercover scouts, who patrolled the woods regularly and had rooted out and executed a few rogue males, plus several guards who had been praised for *bringing down the enemy*. Never anything specific. The dead males had always been *executed on sight* in the forest, and not brought back to the city for questioning. And the news sites always downplayed the number of dead guards. Only a few were mentioned, with the sole purpose of celebrating their bravery and further demonising the masculine villains who threatened the city.

Nowhere had it been mentioned that the people in the woods were part of a large community. And none of the articles had mentioned the female citizens living there. Danforth continued to feed her people a litany of lies about how the city prospered with her in charge. She had informed her citizens that, despite the explosion in the fertility unit causing "slight issues" with their seed supply, the government had "bulletproof backup plans" which they were currently putting in place.

So far, people seemed to be swallowing her lies. How they'd react when they discovered the truth was a very different matter. Madeleine wanted the Bellator citizens to know what was really going on. Her current goal was to gather as much information as possible about what Danforth was up to before making it public. The weight of the combined knowledge would have a greater impact than any smaller nuggets of information which Danforth could easily brush aside.

When Faith had asked Robyn how they intended to do this, she'd been told Madeleine *had her ways*. But the Resistance leader was waiting until she had more information before taking action. The waiting was killing many of the Resistance members who were eager for change, but Madeleine was resolute. She had worked with Danforth, and insisted they couldn't afford to underestimate her power and cunning.

"We're making good progress. But we need to gather more information before we go public with any of this." Madeleine stood up. "Good work, everyone. Let's get on with our tasks for the day. I'll be listening to the conversations in Anderson's office. Those of you going through the information from the academy, report anything you think might be of importance to myself or Robyn *immediately*."

With that, she marched back to her office, which in reality was a small storage closet at the rear of the basement. Once she was gone, Faith attached her wristclip to a datadev and hit transfer, uploading the images so they could be read more easily on the larger screen. One glance at Blake told her not to interrupt now. She decided to ask for the information from the school's datadev later. Better still, perhaps she could delegate that task to Diane or ask Laura about it. Anything to avoid the prickly Blake.

Before she sat down to study the charts, she grabbed a glass of juice, marvelling at the basement's small kitchen and well-stocked fridge. After the days she had spent in Eremus, she would never again take such things for granted. Whilst the food here was not quite of the standard she'd been used to at the academy, it was plentiful and tasty.

She considered the way the Eremus citizens struggled to feed everyone. It seemed a crime for them to have so little when the majority of the women in the city had so much. And it made her angry that the people in Bellator believed all men to be wicked, when in Faith's experience, they were just as capable of being good or evil as women.

Faith took a seat at the datadev and tapped on the first image, enlarging it so the names were readable. She took a sip from her juice and scanned the columns at the top of the page. It looked like the girls were all being given femgazipane, in varying doses. Remembering the devastating effect of the drug on her own body, she shuddered.

Was the academy now filled with girls in various states of ill health as a result of the drug? Or had the scientists made further adjustments to improve it? And to go from the drug being given to Serene and herself, with poor results, to every single student seemed to be an extreme measure. The measures demonstrated Danforth's desperation now that the stores of male seed were gone.

She stared at the column with the pass and fail figures in it. Making comparisons between the levels of femgazipane, she could see that the higher the level of the drug in the girl's system, the more likely the girl was to have failed the test. But the chart gave no information as to the reason the test had been completed in the first place.

She was just zooming in on the column with the girls' year group, aiming to consider what impact their age had on the test results, when Diane shrieked.

The entire room turned to look. Without even being asked, Diane had joined Blake, and they appeared to have been looking over the files from Anderson's datadev together. Right now, the other Danforth student was pointing at something on the screen, but her gaze was fixed on Faith.

"What is it?" Faith pushed herself to her feet. "What have you found?"

"We were looking at the girls' records." Diane spoke quickly. "They're so detailed... diet, vitamin supplements, exercise regime... it's all here... visits to the med centre... individual status of every student... their lives are *entirely* controlled by the academy staff."

"*And?*" Faith closed the gap between them. "What did you find that made you *scream?*"

"It's Sophia." Diane's eyes were triumphant. "I know where she is."

Chapter Six: Noah

The medcave was finally quiet. Noah had worked alongside his ma all morning, cataloguing supplies, laundering all the sheets and towels, and putting it back in good order after the last few weeks of chaos. It was dull work, but satisfying, and it allowed him to think.

The meeting in the woods with Danforth, followed by the arrival of the guards in the tunnel leading to Bellator had kept Anna busy. There had been a large number of patients being taken care of in the cave as they recovered, or didn't recover, from their injuries. The disruption had taken its toll on both the chief medic and her small base.

But Anna had discharged her last patient a few days ago and now only needed to see those with more lasting injuries for brief visits. Noah knew she was hoping the medcave would stay empty for the next few days, to allow her some recovery time, but with Jacob's unpredictable mood, no one could make that assumption.

One thing they did need was more drugs. There hadn't been a supply run to the city in weeks. It had been considered too risky, with Danforth on high alert. But his ma's sigh, as she counted the remaining boxes in the cabinet, suggested they'd have a different kind of crisis on their hands if they didn't restock soon.

"Y'alright, ma?"

She looked over, managing a small smile. "Bit worried, that's all."

"We're running out, right?"

She nodded. "Of batteries and some food products too. I was talking to Cora... she says we're very low on some of the staples we usually get from the city. She's having to ration it." He appreciated her honesty. There had been a time when she might have tried to hide the problem from him. "But I can't see us sending raiders into Bellator right now." She twisted a thread from her sleeve round her finger. "It would be so dangerous."

"We might have to." He held up a hand as she protested. "Maybe a small raid might work for now, just to the buildings on the outskirts. If we let the situation get worse, we'll be facing sickness and starvation, as well everything else."

She grimaced. "You're right. I'm just hoping we can make contact with the Resistance quickly. That way, at least we'll have a sense of what we're walking into if we send raiders in. Without that, we can't–"

A noise outside in the tunnel drew their attention. They both turned to look, as Paulo appeared at the cave entrance.

"Got time to look at another patient, Anna?"

By his side stood the sole surviving guard from the attack on the tunnels. Noah's eyes were drawn to a large scarlet stain on her cheek, the blood creeping out from under a rag she held to her forehead. In contrast, the rest of her face was deathly pale.

Paulo walked the woman through the door, his hand gripping her upper arm. She did not come willingly, and refused to meet their gaze, defiant in spite of her pain.

"What happened?" Anna rushed over.

She reached up to remove the rag, but the woman recoiled as though she'd been shot. Backing away, Anna gestured to Paulo to bring her over to one of the cots they had just changed.

Noah knew the routine. Collecting a bowl, he took it into the smaller cave at the back. He poured some clean water into it, listening to his ma as she murmured to the woman in soothing tones.

"Harden was taking her food." In the outer cave, Paulo began to explain. "Seems she pushed past him. Tried to run."

"Really?" Noah understood his ma's surprise. Up until now, the woman had been a submissive, if silent, prisoner.

"Yeah, really."

Noah couldn't imagine that had gone down well with Harden: the older boy was a bully. Noah knew from firsthand experience that he didn't react well when people tried to stand up to him.

He reentered the main cave with the bowl of water. The woman was perched on the edge of the cot closest to the door, as though she might take flight at any moment.

Paulo turned his gaze to her again, his tone stern. "Not sure where you thought you were going."

For the first time, she lifted her eyes to glare at him. It was, Noah thought, at least some form of reaction. Surprised by the young woman's defiance, Paulo raised an eyebrow.

Taking advantage of the eye contact, Anna stepped forward. "Are you still determined not to speak to us?"

The woman dropped her head again, her lips stubbornly sealed. Paulo clenched his jaw in frustration.

Initially, Jacob had thought the guard might be a good source of information for Eremus. But she had bitterly disappointed him by refusing to speak. She looked to be fairly young, and most of the people who had attempted to speak to her assumed she was a recent recruit. She had been the only one of the guards to surrender, but despite almost daily questioning, had refused to say a word.

Noah had been the one to disarm her, but he hadn't seen her since. As he moved across the space, he wondered whether she'd recognise him. And if so, how she might react.

Placing the bowl on the small table next to the cot, he went to fetch some clean cloths. Once he'd delivered them, he stepped back to let his ma work. Yet again, the woman's eyes remained downcast, as though the brief eye contact she had made with Paulo had been a grave error. He wondered if she was frightened.

"My name is Anna." His ma soaked a cloth in water and squeezed it out. "I'm a medic here." She kept her voice calm and gentle, as she did with all her patients. "I need to attend to the cut on your head. Can you uncover it for me?" The woman didn't react. "If I don't look at it, it could become infected. That's dangerous at the best of times, but down here it could be life threatening." She paused. "Do you understand? Will you let me help you?"

For a moment, Noah thought the woman would refuse. But good sense prevailed, and she eased the rag away from the cut, wincing as it clung to the drying blood.

"Thank you." His ma leaned closer, examining the wound. "How did you get this?"

"I told you, it was–" Paulo began, but closed his mouth at a sharp look from Anna.

"You don't need to worry. It doesn't look too deep," Anna continued, her voice reassuring. "Can you tell me what happened?"

Again, the woman made no response. Noah looked down at her hands. Though she clutched them tightly in her lap, they were shaking. Once again, he suspected it was fear preventing her from speaking.

His ma persisted. "Can you tell me your name?" She ran the wet cloth over the wound and the woman winced. "It's alright. It'll only hurt for a minute. I'm just cleaning it out so it doesn't get infected. You understand?"

The woman gave a tiny nod. Noah and Paulo exchanged glances. It made sense that his ma would be the one to connect with this woman.

Anna continued to bathe the wound with water, her hands gentle. "I'm going to ask you some questions. You can nod or shake your head in response, alright?"

The woman remained silent, but Noah thought her breathing was a little easier now.

"Did you fall?"

A small pause. The woman shook her head.

"Did you do this to yourself?"

A more vehement shake. The woman's head came up a fraction.

"Did someone strike you?"

This time, the woman looked up and right into Anna's eye. She nodded, very deliberately.

"Alright." Noah could hear the slight tone of triumph in his ma's voice. "Was it Harden that hit you?" The woman's brow furrowed. His ma thought again before continuing. "A tall, broad young man. He brought you your food today?"

Another definite nod.

Paulo went to speak, but Noah caught his eye and gave a little shake of his head. This was the closest they'd gotten to speech from the woman. Something told him she would clam up again at the sound of a male voice.

"I'm sorry this happened to you. Harden shouldn't have done that. Were you trying to escape?"

The woman dropped her gaze.

"I can understand you wanting to do that." Anna finished washing out the wound and put the cloth back into the now-pink water. "But you're a prisoner here. You must understand that we would want to stop you from leaving." She peered at the wound. "Alright. Looks clean. Will you allow me to cover it? To protect you?"

The woman inclined her head.

"Hand me a piece of dressing, please, Noah?"

Collecting the scissors from the table at the back, Noah cut a piece of dressing big enough to cover the wound. When he stepped closer to hand it over, the woman's eyes met his. Panic flared in them, and she began to struggle.

"Hold still!" Anna grasped the woman's shoulders and held her down. "Whatever's the matter?"

Noah took a step back. "It's me, Ma." Confusion flashed across her face. "I was down there. In the tunnel, when she... when the rest of her team..."

"Goodness." His ma eased the woman back against the cot. She took the dressing and placed it over the wound, using some tape to fix it into position. She leaned closer to the woman. "There. All done." She hesitated, before continuing. "This is my son. He helps me. Understand?" The woman shuddered.

His ma tried again. "He isn't violent." Still, the woman's eyes were filled with fear. "Look, did he hit you? Like Harden?"

The woman turned her eyes on him. Noah felt a stab of guilt.

"I didn't hit her." He stayed back, hating how scared she was of him. "But I did grab hold of her. Just to disarm her." Noah turned to her. "I'm sorry. But if I hadn't, you'd have..."

The guard lowered her eyes again.

"Can I take her back now?" Paulo tapped his foot, the repetitive sound echoing through the cave. "I've things to do."

"Might you leave her here for a little while?" his ma asked. "I'd like to check her over properly. I'll make sure Noah and I bring her back later."

"I shouldn't."

"There are two of us. She's unarmed." His ma turned to Paulo. "What can she do?"

"Alright." Paulo shrugged. "I guess it's okay. And I really have to go. Make sure you *both* go back with her. She's already tried to escape once."

"We will."

Nodding, Paulo turned and left the cave. Once he was gone, Noah's ma turned to him.

"Go and get some hot water, would you?" He stared at her, unsure of her motives, but she shooed him away.

Thrusting his hands into his pockets, he backed away. As he headed for the canteen, his fingers closed around a piece of paper. Ella's note. He had yet to find an opportunity to get it to Helen. Though Jacob had expanded the number of people permitted to take supplies to the girls' cave, he certainly wasn't ready to permit Noah to do the job. But a promise was a promise. He'd have to find a way to pass it on soon.

As he entered the canteen, he put the thought from his mind. Requesting a flask of water from Cora, he settled down to wait as she prepared it. His ma wouldn't want him to return just yet. She had a knack of getting people to open up, and from what he'd heard, no one else had been able to get anything from the woman. Without him there, she stood a far better chance.

He thought back to the attack. Every guard in the tunnels that day had died, aside from her. She must have felt very alone, since they'd thrown her into a cave with no one for company. Even the Danforth girls, their first prisoners, had been part of a group and able to comfort one another. It was no wonder she didn't trust them.

As he collected the flask and made his way back, he wondered if Danforth would consider their hostage worth negotiating over. Unlike the students from the school, who were part of her mysterious experiment, this woman was simply a guard, and, if they were correct, not a very experienced one. If she wasn't worth much to Bellator, Noah didn't know what would happen to her. He felt an unexpected stab of sympathy.

He approached the medcave entrance with caution. "I'm back."

"Come in." His ma nodded at the flask. "Thanks. Would you pass me some clean clothes, please?" She gestured to the woman's uniform, which was dirty and looked uncomfortable. "Then make her a strong cup of tea. She needs it."

Noah obeyed, moving to the rear of the medcave where they kept a chest of spare clothing. Finding a clean t-shirt and jeans he thought would fit, he took them to his ma and handed them over.

"Thanks." She smiled. "Stay out of here while she changes. I'll guard the door."

Nodding, Noah returned to the back and made the tea as requested, wishing he had a spoonful of sugar to stir into it. The woman looked like she needed some energy. When his ma called his name again, he took in the tea. The guard looked different, younger still, in the new outfit. She was sitting further back on the cot, her knees curled up to her chin. Tentatively, he approached.

"Hot tea?" He proffered the cup. "Make you feel better, maybe?" She met his gaze, but didn't move. "I'll leave it here." He placed the cup on the table to her left and moved back.

His ma was standing on the other side of the cave, putting equipment away in one of the store cupboards. She turned, as he entered, and smiled at him.

"Thanks." She pointed at the tea.

"You want one?" Noah began to move to make it before she'd responded.

"I'm okay thanks." Moving across to the cot, she sat down again. "That's better, isn't it?"

The woman's gaze flicked between the medic and Noah, suspicion in her eyes.

"Listen, I wish you'd talk to us." Anna took a seat beside her. "We're not out to hurt you. We know you've had a rough time since you arrived. I won't promise that you're totally safe here. There are people who don't value you. But *I* don't want anything bad to happen to you." She pointed at Noah. "And neither does my son."

She looked over at Noah, jerking her head towards the woman. Moving round so he stood behind his ma, he took a breath and met her gaze.

"She's right. You have to understand... what happened that night... when your team entered that tunnel, our whole community was at risk. You and your fellow guards would've killed us..." he paused, thinking of Jan and the others, "you *did* kill some of us. We were defending ourselves."

The woman's expression remained unreadable, but she held his gaze.

"We were desperate to find a way to stop you from getting back to Bellator. At the moment, the only thing which keeps Eremus safe is secrecy. If you'd've gone back... told Danforth about the tunnel access..." he shrugged, "...our community would've been in grave danger." He waited for her response for a moment before ploughing on. "I turned out the light and moved into position behind you. I took your gun, because I thought you were going to kill the rest of my group. Understand? But then, you surrendered."

His ma stepped closer. "You did. And it saved you. And I can't promise I know what will happen to you down here. But not everyone wants to hurt you. If you talk to us, we might be able to help you." She paused, smiling in encouragement. "Could you start by telling us your name?"

For a long time, the woman stared at them. Eventually, she averted her gaze, glancing to one side. Noah's heart sank. Perhaps she'd never speak to them.

But then, she moved. Leaning to her left, she reached for the mug of tea. Cradling it between her hands, she brought it to her lips, taking a tiny sip. When she lowered the cup, she kept it hugged to her chest.

Only then, did she look back at them. Staring right at Anna, she took a breath and opened her mouth.

"My name's Charlie."

Noah shivered as she spoke. The woman's voice was familiar. And not only the voice. The name. He racked his brain, trying to think of how he might know her. And then he remembered.

A guard shift, up in a tree, the night after the original kidnapping of the Danforth students. The guard prowling below, stopping beneath him, calling base on her radio. Her name had been Charlie. Instinctively, he knew it was the same woman. He remembered the doubt in her tone, the fear. He remembered thinking that she had sounded as frightened as he was on his first raid.

Charlie. A woman just as human as the Eremus raiders. Not the formidable guards they had come to expect. But a vulnerable woman, wondering whether or not their mission was ethical.

Perhaps she might be the most useful guard they could have captured.

Later that night, as Noah prepared for bed, he felt happier than he had in a while. The conversation with Charlie had been brief, but it had been a start.

They'd been right, she had only recently qualified as a guard, and was so far not at all sure about the role. While Charlie had completed her training, recent events had led to more and more guards being promoted to active status before they were ready. It put them all in danger, she'd told them, when they were sent out on duty with an inexperienced partner.

Noah and his ma had exchanged glances. Clearly, the explosions at the seed bank and in the forest had done more damage to the Bellator forces than they'd previously thought.

Charlie hadn't seen any real action until her team had come face-to-face with the Eremus citizens that night in the tunnel. What she'd witnessed there had terrified her and been the catalyst for her surrender. What she'd found most difficult to deal with was not the treatment she'd received since being imprisoned, but the way she'd been deceived during her training.

Far from the few scattered rebels she'd been taught to expect, Eremus was a force to be reckoned with. Large, well organised, and capable of defending itself. The truth had floored her. Noah understood her confusion, remembering Faith's reaction when she had first uncovered the lies that Bellator told its citizens.

After Charlie had spoken to them, it seemed like a weight had been lifted from her shoulders. She had allowed them to take her back to her cell without a problem. They had left her with the promise that they would try and speak to Jacob about improving conditions for her. Noah promised himself he would do what he could to make sure she wasn't left alone for so long from now on.

He shrugged out of his jeans and pulled on a pair of sweats. Realising he was thirsty, he headed back into the living area of the cave. He crept to the water jug to fill his cup. His ma and Flynn were already in bed, and he didn't want to disturb them.

As he turned to go back to bed, there was a noise at the door. He was startled when a shadowy figure stepped inside. It was Ruth, but she looked odd, somehow.

"I'm glad you're awake." She took a step towards him, her voice a hushed whisper. "Anna and Flynn already asleep?"

He nodded, reaching across to light one of the lanterns. Hurrying to her side, he held it up, then stopped dead. His best friend was dressed in a freshly washed Bellator guard uniform, its buttons gleaming in the light.

He cocked his head, puzzled. "Is this a joke?"

But her face was serious. "No joke. I wanted to say goodbye."

"Good*bye*?"

"I'm heading into Bellator. Undercover." She fidgeted with a button on the front of the jacket. "Looks strange, right?"

"Too right." His brow furrowed. "But what are you–?"

"*I'm* the envoy." Her voice rang with pride. "I'm supposed to blend in with Danforth's guards, see what I can find out. Jacob thinks..."

Noah took a step closer to his friend. "You're working for Jacob?"

"No!" Her eyes flew to his. "Flynn and Anna want me to go too. But they're trying to keep Jacob happy, stop him from doing something stupid. It was his idea to use the uniform to gain the trust of Danforth's protectors."

"But–" Noah found himself struggling for words.

"I'm not going to do anything rash. I've only agreed to wear this," she gestured at her clothing, "and try and start a conversation with some of the guards. See what I can find out. If I don't get any intel, Jacob'll have to live with the disappointment." She smiled. "But if it keeps him from going off the deep end for now, then Flynn..."

"...thinks it's a good idea." Noah finally understood, though he didn't like the idea of Ruth putting herself at risk. "I assume he and my ma have a different objective."

"Yeah. They want me to go looking for Madeleine... see if I can find out what happened to her. Hopefully..." Ruth hesitated, chewing on her lip, "... make contact with the Resistance."

"Really? But–"

"Don't worry. I have a change of clothes for that part." She gestured to the pack on her back. Noting his concerned expression, she smiled. "I'll be careful. I promise."

"And you're going... right now?"

"I am." Lunging forward, she flung her arms around him. "Wish me luck?"

"G-good luck."

The enormity of what she was about to do hit him like a freight train. Alone, in the city which hated Eremus people, disguised as one of the guards paid to kill them. If his friend was discovered... well, it didn't bear thinking about.

"Thanks." She shot him a nervous smile. "Guess I'll see you in a few days." She turned, heading for the door.

"Ruth!" At his call, she turned, a question in her eyes. For a moment, his breath caught in his throat. And then, stepping forward, he took her hand and gripped it tightly. "Please, be careful."

"I will." She returned the squeeze before letting go. "You know me."

A second later, she was gone.

Chapter Seven: Faith

"Absolutely not."

Faith counted to ten, trying not to lose her composure. For two days, she had been trying to persuade Robyn to sign off on a mission. But she wouldn't budge.

"I'll go in disguise." She followed Robyn round the tiny kitchen as she made a sandwich. "I'll go alone."

Ignoring her, Robyn finished buttering the bread and threw on a slice of ham.

"I'll go with Diane."

"No." The older woman finished building the sandwich. Grasping a large knife, she sawed it in half.

"That would only be two of us." Collecting the remaining ingredients from the counter, Faith walked to the fridge and cleared them away. "You can spare that, for one night."

Robyn turned to face Faith, one eyebrow raised. "Send two inexperienced young girls out into the city in the middle of the night on a mission doomed to failure?" She pointed the knife at Faith. "Again, no."

Discarding it in the sink, she picked up her plate, stalked to a table and sat down. Faith watched as she took an enormous bite out of the sandwich, bending her head to read something on her wristclip. A surge of desperation flooded Faith. She couldn't just abandon Sophia. Her friend had been her main reason for returning to Bellator. Ever since Diane had discovered that she was being kept in Bellator Hospital rather than the academy, Faith hadn't been able to stop thinking about it. Now she knew where her friend was, she couldn't just ignore it.

Doggedly, she walked across and plonked herself down opposite the other woman. When Robyn looked up from her first bite, she sighed.

"Look, I'm sorry about your friend. Really." Her face softened. "And we will try to look at how we might help her. But it's too dangerous right now." She took another bite and chewed thoughtfully. "We just can't go charging after every single person Danforth hurts. The Resistance is bigger than that."

"But–"

Robyn's face darkened. "I'm tired of this discussion. Let me make it very clear. Madeleine would go nuts if she found out I'd sanctioned *anyone* to gallivant around the city without her permission, let alone the two of you." She shook her head in disbelief. "The hospital, of all places! It has to be among the most well-guarded locations in the city."

"I've been there before though," Faith protested. "I got in and out without being spotted. I could do it again."

"No. It's too dangerous. The fact that you're asking me and not Madeleine tells me you know how risky it is. Don't think I'm a soft touch." Standing up, Robyn took the plate, sandwich and all, to the door. "I've said no and I mean it."

Once she was gone, Faith slumped down in her chair. She had thought the hard part was over once they'd learned where Sophia was. And after the success of the nighttime visit to the academy, she'd assumed that a similar mission to the hospital would be possible. But she hadn't counted on the Resistance leaders' stubbornness.

They agreed that the information Blake and the others were in the process of gathering from Anderson's datadev was extremely useful. Many of the files were password protected, and though she'd been working day and night, the techie had yet to hack into the more sensitive ones. But the basic information from the student records was more accessible.

Sophia's file was flagged because she was not currently living in the academy itself. The same could be said for the seven other girls who had been kidnapped by the Eremus citizens. But while Faith's file stated her current location as *Eremus*, Sophia's read *Bellator Hospital: Ward FEX2*.

Other than that, they knew nothing. A search of the ward number had revealed nothing. Where other areas of the hospital had webpages about their specialty, the two wards labelled FEX were a mystery. Even more worrying was the fact that the dates on the front of her file suggested she had been in the hospital since the day Danforth's forces had brought her back to Bellator.

There had been no attempt to take her back to the academy, which made Faith wonder if her friend had been injured in the attack. She had imagined everything, from a serious wound, to sickness, to torture. Nothing was more frightening than the complete unknown. But the Resistance refused to risk everything for a single citizen.

Faith slumped down over the table, her head on her arms. She hadn't come all this way to be a mere mile away from her friend and not help her. But going alone, without permission or support, wasn't the most appealing option either. Sneaking out of the academy in the past had always led to trouble on her return. The Resistance was organised. Its members thought things through. Faith would be a fool to ignore Robyn's words of caution.

She was fighting tears when she heard a noise behind her.

"Let me guess." Faith turned to see Diane, rolling her eyes. "She said no again."

Faith wasn't able to voice a reply.

"Thought she might." Diane slid into the seat next to her. "I'm sorry."

Faith swallowed hard. "Not your fault."

"No. But it still sucks." She leaned closer, dropping her voice. "Want to sneak out there tonight? We could go by ourselves. I know where we can get hold of a couple of weapons."

For a moment, Faith considered it. But an image of Diane smacking Carl over the head as they fled from the cottage in the woods flashed into her mind.

"No. Robyn's right." Faith inhaled deeply. "We don't have the experience. Alone, we'd probably make things worse."

Diane raised an eyebrow. "When did you get so sensible?"

Faith rolled her eyes. "I'm not sure."

"Just wish there was some way of finding out *why* she's there." Diane drummed her fingernails against the table. "I wonder if..." She broke off.

Faith frowned. "What?"

Abruptly, Diane stood up. "Come with me."

She pulled Faith to her feet and headed for the door. Hauling it open, she hurried through, towing Faith behind her. Before Faith could protest, her headstrong friend was rapping on a door further up the hallway.

"Blake, you in there?" For a moment, there was no response. "Blake!"

Faith braced herself for the grumpy woman's response to the interruption. Seconds later, there was a grunt from the other side of the door.

Grinning, Diane shoved the door open. "Mind if we ask you something?"

Following her friend inside, Faith found herself in a small room, packed with technical equipment she couldn't begin to name. Aside from several datadevs, there were various screens and consoles installed around the room, and numerous devices both large and small scattered across every surface. Warm and smelling vaguely of sweat, the room nevertheless hummed with energy.

In the centre of it all was an ancient office chair, its wheels allowing the user to roll between the various pieces of equipment. Seated on it, hunched over one of the datadevs, was Blake. She didn't look up as they entered.

"Shut the door."

The command was thrown over her shoulder as she tapped several buttons in sequence and squinted at the screen. Her rudeness didn't deter Diane, who strode across and stood next to her. "You could hack into any security system in the city, right?"

Blake snorted. "Yes."

"Soooo... if we wanted to gain access to, say, the cameras in the academy, you could do that?"

Blake sniffed. "I've done it before."

"What about other important locations?"

"Yeah. Given enough time, I can gain access to most systems." Blake shot her a sideways glance. "We often try to keep an eye on major government targets, places we think things are happening that we need to know about. The issue is there aren't enough of us to keep a handle on all those places at once."

"How about the hospital?"

"Sure." Blake shrugged, turning her attention back to the datadev. "We've kept a close eye on the med centres and hospitals in the past. Especially since Eremus decimated the Fertility Unit."

"Could you take a look now?"

Faith suddenly understood what Diane was getting at. Access to the cameras inside the hospital might well allow them to see Sophia without setting foot in the hospital. That way, they could learn more about her situation. Work out if she needed immediate rescue.

Blake had stopped typing. Narrowing her eyes, she leaned across Diane and looped her fingers through the handle of her coffee mug. Leaning back in her chair, she took a long swig. "Tell me why, and maybe I'll think about it."

Diane looked at Faith, nodding her head towards Blake. Shuffling closer, Faith took a breath.

"As you know, your... investigation into the information kept on Anderson's datadev showed us that my friend Sophia is... well, is currently being kept in the Bellator Hospital. We d-don't know why." Faith found her hands were shaking, but forced herself to continue. "Robyn won't allow us to go to the hospital and rescue her–"

"Too right." Blake interrupted. "Suicide mission, with so little information."

"Yes... I suppose so." Faith stood taller. "But... I care very much about Sophia. She's the reason I came back here. And I need to know... I have to know what's happening to her."

"You want me to hack into their system so you can look at the feed from their cameras?" Blake's eyes widened. "No chance."

"Wait," Diane butted in. "You said yourself that we don't know enough about the situation to risk going down there. Surely your *purpose* is to look into suspicious situations like this... make sure the Resistance is armed with information."

Sensing Blake was tiring of them, Faith pressed the point. "What if you took a break from this and tried to locate Sophia? What if you could find her... *watch* her... see what's happening to her." She shrugged, hoping her words were having some effect. "Might shed some light on what they're doing to the rest of the girls as well.

"Watch her?" Blake drained her cup and set it down on the table with a thump. "I think I just said how we don't have enough people to do things like that. I've enough to do without sitting at a screen staring at a hospital patient all night."

"What if *we* did it?" Diane leaned forward. "We could take turns..."

"...make notes," Faith added, "*detail* what we see."

"Madeleine and Robyn would like that, wouldn't they?" Diane finished.

Blake's gaze went between the two of them. "You're not going to let this go, are you?"

"We're not." Ignoring Blake's scowl, Diane perched on the edge of the desk beside her. Her gaze turned serious. "Haven't you ever had someone you'd do anything for? Someone who you'd defend, no matter what?"

Faith knew she was thinking of her friend Serene, the first victim of femgazipane. Diane had been unable to save her, and had made it her business to stop the same thing from happening to Sophia. Faith looked back at Blake, whose eyes had narrowed. For a moment, she stared at Diane in silence.

And then, without a word, she turned back to her datadev. Exiting her current screen, she opened a different app, her fingers flying over the keys. A form appeared. Without a pause, Blake tabbed through the different boxes, typing in multiple commands, her eyes glued to the screen. Faith found she couldn't read more than the first couple of words on each page before Blake had flashed on to the next.

Eventually, they were staring at what appeared to be the view from a camera.

"Wait, that's..." Faith breathed.

On the screen was a clear view of the reception desk of the Emergency Department of the Bellator Hospital. A woman in a medtech uniform sat behind it, speaking into a microphone attached to a set of headphones. Blake stretched across Diane again, pushing a button on a screen to her left. Seconds later, the same camera feed was displayed on it.

"Grab that." She jerked her head at a stool in the corner. Faith obeyed, placing it in front of the second screen and sitting down. "Watch."

Blake tapped a key on the datadev below the screen. The view changed, now displaying a hospital corridor. A second tap revealed an empty waiting room.

"Every camera the hospital has in operation." Blake changed the view again. "See? You'll have to toggle through them all. I don't have time."

Abruptly, she turned back to her original screen. Diane moved across to stand behind Faith, nodding to the datadev. "Come on. What are you waiting for?"

Her hands shaking, Faith pressed the key Blake had indicated, her eyes fixed on the screen. A medic station popped up next. Numerous technicians and medics stood talking, drinking coffee, typing information into datadevs of their own. Another tap shifted the view to a corridor, then a storage room, not unlike the one in which she had met Noah.

How naïve she had been, simply walking into the hospital that night. If the images on her phone hadn't given her away, the cameras in the hospital would have. Faith wondered how closely they were monitored. Did the hospital have enough security staff to be constantly watching every room? She hoped not.

She found herself with a new appreciation for Blake, someone technical who could deactivate cameras and sensors when necessary. It was the very reason that going solo hadn't worked out well for her in the past. Having a team behind you was, she admitted, very useful.

Faith tapped again, faster this time, revealing a ward with several beds containing patients. She paused to take a closer look. Most of them were sleeping; none of them were Sophia. More images flashed by: a room with a scanner, several offices, a consultation room where all that could be seen was a curtain pulled around a bed. Again, Faith stopped, trying to work out whether it was occupied. When she couldn't, she made a mental note to come back and look at the room again later. Continuing to look, she scanned past a staffroom, the main hospital entrance, and multiple reception desks in different departments.

On and on Faith went, her eyes checking for any sign of a face she recognised before hitting the button again.

"Incredible," Diane muttered, beside her. "Think of what we could learn from this."

Faith ignored her, keeping her eyes glued to the screen. Was she going to have to go through every room in the hospital to find her friend?

And then, she stopped. Tabbing back once, she stared.

On the screen was a narrow view of a very small ward. It contained four single beds with rails around the sides and little else. Dominating the room were a number of large machines, grouped in various positions around one of the beds. Numerous wires snaked between them, interconnecting the different pieces of equipment. Faith shuddered, imagining the sounds emitting from the monstrous devices.

Her eyes travelled to the figure in the bed. It was the only one which was occupied. Pale and tiny, Sophia lay on her back. She was either asleep or unconscious. Faith didn't want to think about which. The tubes twisting out of the machinery were inserted into her body at various points: the crook of her elbow, her neck, her wrist.

As Faith stared, the screen grew brighter, as though someone unseen had flicked on a light. A second figure moved into view. A medic in overalls walked to the bed and leaned in close. Her heart in her mouth, Faith could only watch as the petite woman observed Sophia, tapping information into a datadev she held in her hand.

When she straightened up, the medic moved to each machine in turn. Some, she only glanced at. At others, she pressed buttons and turned dials, making various adjustments. After each one, she studied Sophia closely. Circling the bed like a predator, she continued making alterations until, finally, she seemed satisfied.

And then, with one final cursory glance at her patient, the medic turned away. Faith cried out as she disappeared from view. Seconds later, the screen grew dimmer once again, leaving Sophia in near-darkness.

CHAPTER EIGHT: NOAH

Noah lingered in the canteen after he'd finished his breakfast that morning. On the opposite side of the cave, Paulo sat with Jacob and Sarah. Their heads were bent together, their discussion intense. Paulo leaned forward, gesturing with both hands while the other two looked on, their faces impassive. He wished he could hear what they were saying. He'd considered just walking over and joining in, but knew neither of the council leaders would take him seriously. He could only hope that his brother still had enough sway with Jacob to make a difference.

After his recent encounters with Ella and Charlie, Noah hadn't been able to stop thinking about them. He had sensed their loneliness; seen how much they were suffering from lack of human contact. While he understood Jacob's caution since Faith and Diane's escape, the way he was treating them was downright cruel.

He'd spoken to Flynn and his ma about it, hoping they might intervene. And while they were sympathetic, they were extremely wary of Jacob's behaviour and didn't want to go over his head unless it was absolutely necessary. They'd asked Paulo if he would talk to Jacob first, see if he still had some influence. If he could change their leader's mind without them having to get involved, they were hoping things might remain peaceful.

As Flynn had pointed out, Eremus had seven prisoners, currently housed in three different locations. It required more time and effort to look after them separately. Jacob was a practical man. They were hoping Paulo might persuade him to move all the women into a single cell to save on manpower. Appealing to the leader's common sense might be the way to go, and if he agreed to the move, it would definitely make the women feel less alone. There was safety in numbers, even in a prison cell.

No matter what the future plan was, Eremus owed its prisoners humane treatment. Any future relations with the women of Bellator would be coloured by how the people they had previously dealt with had been treated. He knew Flynn, his ma, and lately, even Paulo, agreed. Jacob was a different matter.

Eventually, Noah made his way to the front of the cave, unable to contain his curiosity. He took his time washing out his bowl, glancing sideways at the table where his brother sat. They had the same shift today, so he could easily have waited for his brother at the tunnel exit, but part of him had wanted to gauge Jacob's reaction to his brother's plea.

He was just placing his bowl back on the rack when Harden approached. Noah was pleased to see he was alone. Without an audience, he was far less likely to give Noah a hard time.

"Harden." Noah lifted his chin.

"Madden." The older boy cocked an eyebrow. "What duty you got today?"

"Fishing." Surprised at Harden's attempt to make small talk, Noah wasn't sure what else to say. "With Paulo."

"Let's hope you snag a decent catch." Harden gestured to his bowl as he plunged it into the soapy water. "I hear we need it."

"Yeah."

"Things get worse, we'll have to start rationing." The older boy grimaced. "We need another raid."

"We do." Noah agreed. "Flynn said we're waiting 'til Ruth gets back, though... see how the land lies in the city."

Grunting agreement, Harden finished washing his dish. He pulled the towel from the rack, giving it a cursory dry before leaning past Noah to stack it away.

"She's brave."

"What?"

"Ruth." Harden turned and met Noah's eye. "Going in alone. The way things are with Danforth. I mean, if she's caught..." he winced. "You have to hand it to her."

"I guess so."

Harden shot a glance at the table where his ma sat with Jacob and Paulo. He stiffened, and Noah remembered his discomfort at the meeting the previous day. "What's that all about?"

Noah figured it was safest to play dumb. "Not sure."

Harden took a step forward, looking like he might join the group. Without thinking, Noah put a hand out to stop him.

"What the–" Harden's eyes flew to Noah's. "What do you think you're *doing*?"

Noah tensed, but before he could respond, there were raised voices from the table where Paulo and Jacob sat.

"Don't question me." Jacob's face had darkened.

Beside Noah, Harden stiffened.

"I'm not–" Paulo tried, but Jacob didn't let him finish.

"Look what happened the last time we permitted those girls some freedom!" The leader jumped to his feet. "We *lost* two of them. And now you want me to–"

"I just thought if we–" Paulo stood up, echoing Jacob's movement.

"No." Jacob flung his hands wide. "I'm past being *understanding*."

Paulo tried again. "But Ella's one of us. She's–"

"One of us?" Sarah exclaimed. "She gave *that* right up the day she helped those girls escape."

She didn't help them! Noah wanted to shake her. *She doesn't deserve this.*

"I won't tolerate betrayal." Jacob jabbed a finger at Paulo, cutting off his interruption before he could make it. "Ella's punishment stands."

"But–"

"I don't want to hear any more about it." With a final glare, Jacob strode from the canteen with Sarah at his heels.

For a moment, there was silence. Noah cringed, waiting for Harden to turn on him. But when he turned to face his old nemesis, his eyes were fixed on the exit.

"Noah?"

At the sound of Paulo's voice, Harden jerked to life again.

"Don't touch me." He turned to Noah. "*Ever.*"

He headed for the exit, not giving Noah time to respond.

"Well, that was a disaster." Paulo joined Noah. "Dammit! Let's get out of here."

After the near-miss with Harden, Noah was glad to escape the caves. Fishing was a job he enjoyed, and he had been looking forward to spending the day with his brother. They collected the tackle and made their way outside.

Sucking in a deep breath as they emerged into the fresh air, Noah shot his brother a sideways glance. "I take it Jacob wasn't very keen on moving the prisoners in together."

Paulo scowled. "You heard him."

"Yeah." Noah ducked under a low-hanging branch. "Not exactly the soul of compassion, is he?"

Paulo grunted a humourless laugh.

"I was really hoping you could get him to change his mind."

"Nope." Paulo strode ahead. "And I think I've pretty much destroyed any influence I had with him now."

"I'm sorry."

Paulo fell silent, his face stormy. Noah let him be, knowing from experience he shouldn't push him. He hurried to keep up with his brother's punishing pace as they headed for Swallow Lake, remembering the last time he'd been there. He'd been with Faith. They'd been fleeing from the battle in the woods, trying to stop the Bellator guards from taking her hostage.

It had been one of the most terrifying hours of his life. And, somehow, one of the most wonderful. Just the two of them against the world. She had kissed him in the rain, offered to sacrifice her freedom to save him. They had hidden in the freezing water together whilst the guards passed within inches of them. He had known that she cared.

He closed his eyes, shutting out the memory. Now that she'd gone, it was painful.

"It's not just today." Paulo's voice cut through Noah's thoughts. "I've been finding it more and more difficult to talk to Jacob lately. He's been distant. Secretive." His pace increased. "He didn't involve me in planning the bombing, mainly because–"

"He knew you'd be against it."

"Yeah." Realising Noah had fallen behind, Paulo slowed his pace. "I suspect, after this, he won't confide in me at all." He turned and met Noah's gaze. "Since the guard attack in the tunnels, he seems really... agitated."

"Don't we all?"

"It's different with him." Paulo stared ahead again. "He seems almost... *possessed*. Like... he knows things could turn against him, and... it's like he's prepared to do *anything* to stop that from happening."

The thought was a sobering one. Noah shifted his pack into a more comfortable position, grateful when Paulo changed the subject.

"Harden still giving you trouble?"

"Not so much these days." Noah's breathing was heavy with effort. "That was the first time in a while, and I think maybe..."

"What?"

"Maybe I asked for it." Noah held a hand up at Paulo's objection. "I was trying to stop him from interrupting you. Physically." He rolled his eyes. "It wasn't the best idea I've ever had."

"No. But still..." Paulo frowned. "It looked like he was threatening you. Want me to have a word?"

"No. Like I said, I got in his way." Noah was happy to see the lake coming into view ahead. "Harden doesn't seek me out to pick on me anymore. Not the way he used to. Lately, he seems more... withdrawn. Angrier. But not with me, particularly."

"That makes sense."

"What do you mean?"

"His ma pushes him pretty hard. She's the one who got him into doing Jacob's dirty work. Like planting the explosives in the forest." Paulo winced. "All those dead guards. It has to weigh heavy on him."

"I suppose." Noah turned to his brother. "I'm not sure I have a lot of sympathy for him. I'm grateful he has bigger things to worry about these days, though. Unless I put myself in his way, he pretty much leaves me alone."

As they arrived at the lakeside, Paulo elbowed him. "I'll bet Harden wouldn't get such a positive reaction from picking on you at the moment. What with you being a hero and all."

"I'm hardly a hero." Thinking back to the incident with the guards in the tunnels, Noah blushed. "I just finished what you'd started."

"Don't put yourself down. If you hadn't had the idea of turning out that light, I wouldn't be here right now. Neither of us would."

"Maybe."

"Heroes aren't always the ones at the front, shouting and waving their weapons." Paulo laid the rods on the ground. "Sometimes they're the quiet ones, the ones we don't notice. And sometimes, their weapons aren't so obvious."

"You'd consider a flashlight a weapon?" Noah scoffed as he set his pack down beside a stout log.

"In the sense that using it protected us, *yes*." Paulo raised an eyebrow. "Yes, I would."

"Maybe." Noah bit his lip to stop himself from smiling. "Harden mentioned Ruth, too. Said she was really brave, going into the city like that..." Noah faltered. "I mean... by herself and all."

Paulo shot him a sideways glance. "You worried?"

"What do you think?" Unzipping his pack, Noah took out a small box and handed it to his brother. "Not much I can do at the moment though, is there?"

"She'll be okay. She has her head screwed on right." Paulo began to bait the first hook. "She's been to Bellator in disguise in the past. She knows how to blend in."

"I hope so."

"Wearing the guard's clothing was a touch of genius." He passed Noah the baited rod. "Bet people don't even notice her face. They'll see the uniform and move past her without even blinking."

Noah considered his brother's words as he cast his line out into the lake. Paulo was probably right. And Ruth wasn't one to draw unnecessary attention to herself. Hopefully, his friend would be able to move around the city safely. She would complete the mission and be home soon.

"What did you make of Charlie?" Paulo kept his head bent over the second rod as he asked the question.

Noah shrugged. "Once she got over her fear, she seemed... decent. Angry... with Danforth, though. For all the lies."

"Guess we all believe what we're told. Until we see proof of something different." Paulo's face screwed up in concentration. When his own rod was ready, he glanced out at the water. "She's not what I expected."

"You mean her age?" Charlie had to be in her early twenties, but most of the Bellator guards who patrolled outside the city were more experienced.

"No."

"She doesn't seem like the loyal soldier we've come to expect from Danforth's guard, I suppose." Noah stared at his brother. "Was that it? That she doesn't seem like the violent type?"

"Maybe. I don't know. There was just something I couldn't put my finger on." He grimaced. "Not that she spoke to me."

"You *like* her." Noah laughed at his brother's discomfort. "Never mind. Maybe you'll have more luck next time. Now that she's spoken to us, she might consider talking to others." He dodged a sharp elbow, struggling to keep his rod still. "Even a grumpy old man like *you*!"

"Whatever." Paulo scowled. "Anyway, it doesn't look like Jacob's prepared to change his mind. Seems like Charlie and Ella are stuck, unless Anna and Flynn are prepared to act against him."

"It's not fair." Noah's hands were gripping the rod too tightly. "Ella doesn't *deserve*–"

Paulo held up a hand. "You don't have to tell me that. I'm well aware that she had nothing to do with the girls' escape." He cursed under his breath. "Her only error was trusting those stupid girls too much. If they hadn't..."

"They're not stupid."

"Don't defend her." Stretching a muscled arm way back behind him, Paulo cast his fishing line way out into the lake.

Noah was patently aware that his brother's line had travelled much farther than his own. "Why not?"

"Because," Paulo sat down on the log, "she doesn't deserve your loyalty. Ella's where she is right now because of your little girlfriend."

Stiffening, Noah considered his response. This was the most positive conversation he'd had with his brother in a long time. He didn't want to spoil it. But, despite his own anger with Faith, he understood her motives.

"Faith's not my girlfriend." He kept his tone even as he could. "And she left because she felt she had to. When Sophia was taken, she–"

Paulo held up a hand to stop him. "You can't have it both ways. Arguing for better treatment of the prisoners is all very well... if they deserve it."

"Why wouldn't Faith deserve it? She's loyal, that's all." Noah flexed his fingers. "Can't you understand her wanting to find Sophia? Her best friend, who's been dragged back to Bellator? *Anything* might be happening to her."

"You're *still* sticking up for her." Paulo leaned closer. "Do you really believe she *cares* about you?"

Noah looked across the lake. That day, when they'd been running from the guards together, he'd been certain that she did. Now, he wasn't so sure.

"You're so sensitive. It makes you a soft touch. I mean, did she tell you she was leaving?" Noah knew he couldn't deny it. Paulo pushed on, shaking his head. "She saw you as someone she could manipulate. A few soft words, a kiss or two..." Noting the hurt on Noah's face, his brother's voice softened. "Sorry little brother, but the evidence speaks for itself."

Noah gave up. It was useless to argue, and he didn't want to alienate Paulo again. Not when he had been so cooperative in speaking to Jacob. Tormented, he lapsed into silence, his eyes on the water. Paulo also seemed happy to let the subject go.

But as Noah reeled in a catch, his brother's words rang in his ears. Paulo wasn't the only one to accuse him of being naïve. Had he just been fooling himself, where Faith was concerned?

The only way to find out would be to go to Bellator and ask her. And in a city where men were not welcome, that was a death sentence.

Chapter Nine: Faith

After a night of poor sleep, Faith arrived at the Resistance leader's office feeling slightly nauseous. Robyn and Madeleine were waiting inside, their expressions serious. Faith took a seat, not sure why she'd been summoned.

"Morning." Robyn smiled.

"As you know," Madeleine began briskly, with no attempt at a greeting, "we have made a thorough study of the photographed documents from the academy. It has confirmed our suspicions that the majority of the senior students are already being given this untested drug."

Robyn leaned forward. "We want to find out more about it before we decide what action to take."

"This..." Madeleine squinted at the report in her hand, "...femgazipane. It's what they gave you at the academy... right?"

"That's right."

"Can you tell us more about the *effect* it had?"

"You can *see* the effect it has." Faith fought to keep the bitterness out of her voice. "You only have to look at Sophia, *in the hospital.*"

"A visual inspection of Sophia's condition is useful, yes." Madeleine gestured to the images on the desk in front of her. "And the information from the photographs you took tells us a little about the dosage each student is receiving." Her gaze pierced Faith's. "But, as you've been given the drug in the past, we're hopeful that you could give us more specific detail."

Faith stared at the Resistance leader, wondering how she could remain so detached.

Robyn seemed to notice her discomfort. "We've been trying to work out the *purpose* of the drug, but we really don't have enough information. We thought..." she glanced at Madeleine, an unreadable expression on her face, "your perspective might help us to help them... in the long run, at least."

Madeleine drummed her fingers against the desk. "Basically, until Blake has more success hacking into the student information on the school system, you're our best source of intel. And we feel your... personal account of your experience with femgazipane would be... a powerful one."

Faith shifted in her chair. Her memories of the drug were uncomfortable. The tiny room she'd been locked in, her loneliness, the terror of the unknown impact of the drug they'd administered so soon after Serene's death. But she had to do what she could. Only by helping the Resistance could she hope to save Sophia.

She sucked in a deep breath. "I was given the femgazipane via injection. I don't know how much they gave me. Then they left me alone, to see if I'd live or die." Faith grimaced. "A lot of it's a blur, really. It made me vomit. I passed out several times... felt extremely dizzy."

Madeleine's fingers tapped away at the keyboard, taking copious notes. "And were these the same symptoms that Serene suffered when she was given the same drug?"

Faith shrugged. "We never saw her afterwards. They kept her away from us." She felt the weight of the two women's eyes on her and searched for more specific details. "I suppose... the effect must have been incredibly rapid with Serene, because whatever went wrong... it happened immediately."

"Really?" Madeleine's fingers stilled.

"Yes. They sent us straight back to the academy." She bit her lip. "None of us ever saw Serene again."

Robyn's hand flew to her face. "That's awful!"

"It was. For Diane especially." Faith recalled the desolation her friend had felt at the loss. Screwing her eyes shut against the memory, she forced herself to continue. "But by the time they gave it to me, the formula must have been altered. Or perhaps the dosage was weakened." She waved a hand in the air as she clarified. "I mean... not that I didn't feel terrible, but... I obviously didn't *die*."

Robyn glanced over at Madeleine. "You think we need to get them out of there?"

"The seniors?" Madeleine looked surprised. "How would we do that without attracting attention?"

"Well, it wouldn't be easy." Robyn sat up straighter. "But don't you think they're at risk?"

"No." Madeleine gestured to Faith. "You heard her. They changed the formula." She leaned back in her chair. "We have to assume the girls are safe for the time being."

"But–"

"If we rescue them now, we risk Danforth discovering our operation. Shutting us down entirely. It's too risky." She turned back to her notes, peering at the datadev screen. "We've discussed this. It's about taking the long view. We need to bide our time. Gather more information before acting."

Whilst both women had an air of authority, Madeleine was definitely the one in charge. Robyn disagreed; Faith could see it in her face. But for now, she fell silent.

Tiredness threatened to overwhelm Faith. Her worries about Sophia had caused a disturbed night. She'd been planning on asking Madeleine to reconsider her decision about rescuing Sophia. But her refusal to consider a similar mission to help the academy seniors did not bode well.

She shifted in her chair. "May I go? That is, if you don't have any more questions for me?"

Madeleine's eyes rose from the datadev screen. "We do have one more question." She glanced at Robyn. "A mission we'd like you to consider."

Faith sat up straighter. Completing a second mission was her chance to impress the Resistance leaders. If she proved herself valuable, she might be able to leverage her elevated status. Get them to consider rescuing Sophia. She forced her weary mind to pay attention as Madeleine continued.

"We've been gathering information on Danforth for a long while now, with the eventual intention of sharing it with the Bellator citizens." The leader's face darkened. "Making them aware of what's *really* happening in their city."

"These recent findings are so shocking." Robyn was back on Madeleine's side now, her tone urgent. "The women of the city *have* to be made aware. And soon."

Faith's mind was racing. *Where did she fit into their plans?*

"We've tried to leak this kind of information before." Madeleine closed her eyes briefly. "It hasn't gone well. Danforth blocks it or casts doubt on its origins. We need to overwhelm the citizens with so much evidence they *have* to stand up and take notice. Last time, Danforth had her guards execute the person responsible."

Robyn shot Madeleine a look of alarm. When she spoke, her tone was much softer. "Faith, we're trying our hardest to turn the tide of opinion against Danforth. But it's not easy. She has the women of Bellator believing every word she says." She met Faith's gaze, her eyes serious. "We *have* to find a new way to get through to them."

Madeleine leaned forward suddenly. "We think you're the answer."

Faith blinked. "But what can I do?"

"We want you to become... a kind of spokesperson for the Resistance." Robyn held out a hand at Faith's look of alarm. "Hear us out. You have *first-hand knowledge* of the academy and the experiments. You spent several weeks living among the Eremus community. You're young, educated, and you speak well. We believe the Bellator women will trust your word, sympathise with you."

"Didn't you just say the last person who did this was executed?"

Robyn dropped her gaze. "We'd do everything we could to keep you safe."

A chill ran over Faith's body. She wanted to help them, to help Sophia. Shame flooded her as she tried to contemplate doing what they asked of her.

"How would you protect me?"

"You'd stay here, inside the library." Madeleine jumped in. "No one knows this is the Resistance headquarters. You'd be safe."

"*Stay* here?" Faith frowned. "Then how would you have me speak to the women of Bellator?"

"To begin with, we thought we'd have a journalist friend of mine interview you. Take your picture. Plaster it on information leaflets which we'd deliver across the city."

"So my face would be known." The reality hit Faith all at once. "I'd never be able to leave the library or I'd be recognised."

Robyn nodded her head. "It would be too risky. Danforth would have her guards out looking for you."

Faith swallowed hard. It wasn't what she'd imagined herself doing when she joined the Resistance. She'd pictured undercover missions where she broke into vital city buildings. Battling Danforth's guards. Finding a way to bring Sophia home safely.

She narrowed her eyes. Perhaps there was a way she could make this work. "If I do it, will you rescue Sophia?"

"No." Madeleine stiffened. "Not necessarily. I won't be blackmailed like that. We will consider rescuing your friend when it is the best thing to do for the women of this city *as a whole*. Not on a whim. Or because you try to bargain with us." She resumed her typing, glancing down at the datadev keyboard. "We could, of course, ask Diane to undertake this mission instead."

It was an empty threat. Though Diane had knowledge of Eremus, she hadn't experienced the femgazipane. And she was far too spiky to come across as sympathetic. But Faith held her tongue for now. She had to stay on Madeleine's good side if she ever wanted support getting Sophia out of the hospital.

"I'm not sure. I mean, it wasn't what I imagined myself doing here."

Madeleine frowned. "But it's a role we think you'd be perfect for."

Faith stood up, wanting to look as though she meant business. "I'll think about it. And, in the meantime, will you allow me to participate in other missions, *outside* of the library?"

Madeleine glanced at Robyn, who gave an imperceptible nod.

"Very well." She turned back to Faith. "We need more time to gather additional information anyway."

"Thank you." Faith turned to leave, but Madeleine's voice stopped her in her tracks.

"Faith?" Madeleine's tone was distinctly cool. "Don't take too long, will you? We'll need an answer soon."

Nodding, Faith left the office. She forced herself to close the door quietly, though every part of her wanted to slam it.

Two hours later Faith was a little less agitated. After leaving Madeleine's office, she had headed upstairs to the library, glad to see the amiable Laura on duty. She had permitted Faith to stay, as long as she remained out of sight. Since the library was huge, and mostly empty, it had not been a problem.

Strolling the length and breadth of the shelving at the rear of the space, she had browsed all the books available to her. Faith was fascinated to find they were mostly classics, written hundreds of years ago. The front section of the library, she presumed, contained more modern works by Bellator writers who were still living.

She sighed. All of the older books had been modified, a movement propelled by the Women's Independence Party when the city had begun to rid itself of males. Texts which included instances of male violence had been given forewords warning of their shocking content, proof of innate male tendencies the city was trying to get rid of. Large sections had been removed from many books, and others had been rewritten, at least in part, to contain only female characters. Many books from the old days, Sophia had once told her, had been lost altogether. Faith remembered her friend's anger, so uncharacteristic, over the words of writers long dead which were gone forever... at least to the citizens of Bellator.

She drew in a shaky breath. Sophia was never far from her thoughts, but memories of her from the time before Eremus were especially painful. Curling her nails into her palms, Faith stalked towards the only section of the library she had yet to explore. A side room off the main chamber, its sign declared it the *Records Room*, and she suspected it contained dusty documents which pertained to the city and its inhabitants.

Slipping inside, she gazed around the space. It was no less beautiful than the rest of the building, but had more of a functional tone to it. In addition to the sofas which were arranged around the fiction section, this room contained several tables surrounded by wooden chairs, presumably so that the user could sit and peruse documents which interested them. Around the edges, instead of shelves, there were several filing cabinets, each carefully labelled.

Faith wandered to the first, which read *Laws and Policies 2090 – 2110*. The next three were similar, with different dates. But the fourth was titled *Genealogy*. Curious, Faith stopped in front of it and pulled the top drawer open. Inside, separated by scrupulously labelled dividers, were a number of slender record books. Faith's heart jolted. Would there be a record of her mother's pregnancy in here? Of Sophia's? Of Noah's, even?

She ran her finger along the tops of the dividers, stopping at the one marked 2100-2110. Her hand shaking, she slid the book out and closed the drawer. Moving to the large oak table, she slid into a chair and opened the cover to the first page. The book was organised into sections, each one pertaining to a different year of births. Faith flipped eagerly to her own, and found the name Grace Hanlon, her mother, in the middle of a table of names.

The entry gave dates and times of impregnation, a complex code labelled as Seed Origin and the number of attempts with successes or failures. After that, there was a record of maternity appointments, the various tests the pregnant Bellator citizen underwent, and, finally, a date of birth and given name at the end. Faith located Sophia's entry easily, but it took her a little longer to find the one for Noah, as she had no idea when his birthday was.

Eventually, she stopped at an entry a few pages before her own. It stood out because many of the columns were empty, and one of those was filled out with a large black letter M, for male foetus. Anna had fled from the city when she'd discovered she was expecting a boy, and none of the subsequent tests had been done. The final column was simply marked with a black X, presumably noting Anna's disappearance and the lack of information about Noah's birth.

Fascinated, Faith flipped back several more pages, searching for Diane's entry. She found it, and felt a pang of sadness when she spotted the name Serene Joseph two rows above. Another victim of Danforth's experimentation, she had not deserved to die. Faith knew how much Diane missed her old friend. And thinking of what had happened to Serene only made Faith more frightened that the same fate might easily befall her own best friend.

Desperate to distract herself from her depressing train of thought, Faith ran her finger down the rest of the page, searching for more familiar names. She found Farrah, and noted that she was older than Diane, which surprised her. Was Avery older or younger, she wondered? She had to go forward another page to find the blonde girl's name and chuckled to herself. Avery was actually younger than Diane and Farrah, despite her superior attitude.

She ran her eyes idly back along Avery's entry, wondering who had given birth to the arrogant young woman. When she reached the name, her heart stopped.

Avery's mother was Abigail Danforth. A fact the chancellor had obviously wanted to hide. Despite the lack of connection between daughters and their mothers in Bellator, girls did retain their mother's surnames. But Avery's last name, at least the one she'd gone by at the academy, was Lassiter.

Faith's mind was swirling with questions. If Danforth was Avery's mother, why didn't anyone know? Did Avery even know?

It made sense that Avery would act superior to everyone else if her mother was the chancellor of the city, but Faith doubted the older girl would have been able to keep that nugget of information to herself. And why would Danforth put her own daughter in the academy, knowing its true purpose?

She had to tell someone. Someone she trusted.

Faith stood up. After replacing the book, she exited the anteroom and hurried along past the towering shelves to the front of the library. Behind the main desk, Laura frowned at her.

"You alright? You look like you've seen a ghost."

"I'm fine." She forced herself to slow down. "Just realised how hungry I am!"

Patting her stomach, she bypassed Laura and headed for the door. Her heart pounded as she took the stairs two at a time, almost stumbling as she reached the bottom. Regaining control, she raced along the hallway towards the hub.

She found Diane at their usual table, drinking coffee as she pored over some documents on a datadev. Throwing herself down onto the bench beside her friend, Faith filled her in. When she had finished, Diane's eyes were wide.

"This is *huge*."

"I know."

"Do you think *Avery* knows?" Diane rolled her eyes. "I can't imagine her keeping something like that to herself."

"Me neither." Faith kept her voice low. "And I don't get it. Why would Danforth put her in the academy. I mean, now that we know its purpose? She surely didn't want her own child to be subjected to..." Faith shuddered.

"Maybe she was there to spy." Diane's eyes lit up. "Yes! I bet that's it. She had to report back to *mother dearest*."

"But that would mean she knew about their relationship." As a couple of Resistance members entered the hub, Faith leaned closer. "And I *really* don't think she does."

"Hmm." Diane shrugged. "Maybe not."

Faith voiced the question which had been running through her head. "You think I should tell Madeleine?"

"Of course, you should. Why wouldn't–" A look of understanding dawned on her face. "You want to use it as a bargaining tool."

Faith could feel herself blushing. "Well, she's still refusing to help Sophia. I thought–"

"You thought this might persuade her?" Diane took a sip of her coffee as she considered the idea. "Perhaps. Though she doesn't seem like she's the sort of person who responds well to blackmail."

"No." Faith recalled the leader's earlier words. "I'm sure she doesn't. But if I could... choose the time when I reveal this information, maybe... maybe it could help my case?"

"Maybe." Diane drained the remnants of her mug. "But if she finds out some other way and then discovers that you knew, it won't go well. I wouldn't wait too long to tell her. Or the whole thing might backfire."

Chapter Ten: Noah

Things were tense the next morning at breakfast. Jacob point-blank refused to speak to Paulo when he approached him. Instead, he took his meal to a table in the corner where he sat, his head bent closely with Sarah, Carl and Denton. The group's body language was hostile, their faces dark. Not a single citizen approached them during the meal, and, when they had finished eating, they left without a word to anyone.

Despite Noah and Paulo bringing back a decent catch the previous day, things were still difficult. The fish had proved a welcome addition to their dwindling supplies, but Cora had salted and saved most of it, serving up a thin, watery stew for dinner, which had satisfied few. But at times like this, rationing was key. They couldn't blame the cook for the situation.

Ella's note was still burning a hole in Noah's pocket. Today was the day, he decided, that he had to deliver it. After finishing his tiny portion of oatmeal, his eyes scanned the canteen for Mick. He'd checked the schedule. The older man was supposed to take the Danforth students their breakfast.

Unlike Jacob's close supporters, he was a man who Noah had always gotten along with. And since the recent attack on the tunnels, Mick was struggling to cope with a shoulder injury. This, Noah was sure, was the way to approach the situation.

"Hey, Mick." Noah sidled over to the man's table with a smile. "How're things?"

"Not bad, considering." The older man shrugged, gesturing to his arm. "Bit of ongoing pain, but…"

"You been to see my ma?"

"Sure. But you know how things are at the moment. No painkillers to spare." Mick shrugged. "Can't be helped."

"Can I do anything?" Noah cocked his head to one side. "To help you, I mean. Did I see you on the schedule to take supplies to the prisoners this morning?" Mick nodded. "I could do that for you. Let you have a bit of extra rest."

Mick shooed him away. "Don't be daft, lad. I'll be fine."

"Honestly," Noah pressed him, "I'm happy to do it." He bent closer to the man's ear. "You'd be doing me a favour, to be honest. I'd like a word with one of the girls."

Mick eyed him closely. "'Bout that girl who ran away?"

Noah hesitated for a moment, before deciding to tell at least part of the truth. "Yes, if you must know. I want to ask the others some questions. That's all."

Mick stared at him, considering. "Alright. If that's all you're after. I suppose I would appreciate the extra down time."

"Thanks!" Noah grinned, already on his way out. "Enjoy the rest."

The cave was quiet when Noah pulled away the barrier. So quiet, he thought there might have been no one inside at all. But when he poked his head in through the entrance, the prisoners were sitting or lying in various positions around the space.

"Morning," he called, reaching down to grasp the tray that held the girls' meals.

He stepped inside and placed it on the ground. For a moment, nobody moved.

"Everything okay?" he asked, concerned.

"Noah?" The voice came from the opposite side of the cave. "That you?" Helen pushed herself to her feet and came forward.

Surprised that the usually quiet girl was the first to come forward, Noah managed a smile. "It's me."

Helen crept closer. "Is... everything alright out there?"

He knew she was asking about Ella. As he considered how to respond, Avery stood up and crossed the cave towards him.

"About time." Bending down, she took a large slice of bread from the plate. "We're starving in here."

Noah rolled his eyes at the exaggeration. "Sorry to keep you waiting." He wondered how she'd feel if she knew that starving was a realistic prospect.

Catching the sarcasm in his tone, she flushed. "Thanks." She bent to help herself to some of the oatmeal. "This looks..." she paused, as though searching for a word to describe the meagre portion, "good."

"Avery, make sure you–"

"I know, I know, Professor. Take a fair portion." Avery stood up and thrust the bowl in her teacher's face. "Happy?"

"Yes. Thank you for being considerate."

Tight-lipped, Avery retreated to the other side of the cave.

Noah turned back to answer Helen's question as the other girls gathered around the food. "Things are okay, I guess."

Helen stepped closer to him, dropping her voice low. "It's just that I haven't seen Ella for a while now. Is she–?"

"She's fine." Noah met her gaze. "Well, not exactly fine, but…" He fished in his pocket for the note and pressed it into Helen's hand. "Here. This should explain." He glanced around at the other girls, thankful that they were paying too much attention to the food to notice. "Maybe read it later."

"Thank you." Helen pushed the folded piece of paper into her pocket, but her worried eyes stayed on Noah's face.

Noticing Helen's expression, Professor Kemp abandoned her bowl of oatmeal and crossed the cave to join them. "Something wrong?"

Noah beckoned them to move a few steps closer to the door. Aware of Avery's ever-watchful eyes on them, he kept his voice low.

"Jacob's blaming Ella for Faith and Diane's escape." He heard Helen's sharp intake of breath. "Can I ask… I mean… did any of you know about it in advance?" He glanced between Helen and Kemp. "*I* don't believe that Ella helped them. Did any of you?"

Kemp glanced at the girls. Though most of them were tucking into their oatmeal, Avery and Farrah had shuffled a little closer. They were definitely listening.

Gesturing to the entrance, Kemp raised her eyebrows. "Could we…?"

"Sure."

Ignoring Avery's tut of annoyance, Noah ushered them into the tunnel. Once out of earshot, Kemp continued.

"We've talked about this a lot over the past few days. No one here knew anything about their plans. As you know, I didn't want Faith to go back. I'm devastated that she has." The usually calm woman twisted her hands together. "They would *never* have told me. And, honestly, if they'd told any of the others, I'd know."

"How?"

The professor turned her shrewd eyes to him. "As you've just seen, this is a small space. Very difficult to keep secrets. If the others had known, they'd have battled to stop them or rallied to join them. There was none of that. They kept it very quiet."

Noah could see the truth in her words. From what Faith had said about Avery, he was pretty sure she'd have wanted to return to Bellator. Farrah, too. But while Helen was frightened of Jacob, he didn't think she'd want to leave Ella. And Mary was so young. She had recently lost her friend and seemed pretty lost. He couldn't imagine the others would have burdened or trusted her with the important details of an escape plan.

He turned back to Helen, whose face was white in the gloom. "Ella's alright. Jacob has her locked up," he gestured back at the cave, "just like you. But not everyone agrees with his actions. We've been talking to him, pleading her case. So far, he... he seems pretty set on punishing her." He reached out and took Helen's hand, pleased when she didn't pull away from him. "We'll keep trying, I promise. Go back inside – eat. Before it's all gone."

Helen returned the squeeze, leaning close to him. "Thank you for..."

"No problem." Before Noah could respond, Helen had released his hand and slipped away.

Once she was out of earshot, Kemp leaned close to him. "Any more news on Faith and Diane?"

Noah shook his head. "We searched the woods for several days after they left. There was no sign of them. And we've heard nothing from the city since we destroyed the entrance to Madeleine's house."

"I'm certain they've gone to look for Sophia. But I don't think they'd march right back to the academy." Kemp looked thoughtful. "They might be reckless, but they're not stupid."

"Where do you think they'd go, then?"

She frowned. "I've been thinking about this. They'd want to stay under the radar. Hide during the day, and move around the city at night, unseen. Try to gain access to the academy, see if they can locate Sophia."

"Would they be able to manage that without being spotted?"

"Perhaps." The professor shrugged. "The school is guarded, but they know it well. I told them a little about the Bellator Resistance. I'm wondering if–"

Noah's heart pounded. "You think they'd try to find them?"

"Well, it would be a safer option than trying to go it alone." Kemp sighed. "But I've no idea how they'd know where to start looking."

Noah recalled his final conversation with Faith. "What if I told her?"

Kemp frowned. "*You* told her?"

"In the medcave a couple of weeks ago, you were talking about where Madeleine might have gone..."

"You mean the library?"

"Yeah. The last time I spoke to Faith, she was asking me questions about the Resistance." He shifted from one foot to the other. "I didn't see it at the time, but she was obviously fishing for information." Paulo's words came back to him and he felt foolish. "I'm pretty sure I mentioned the library."

Noah braced himself for the professor's criticism. It never came. Instead, Kemp's face was flooded with relief.

"Perhaps it's a good thing. They were obviously determined to go." The teacher shrugged. "If Faith and Diane can locate the Resistance, they'll be in a much better position." Noah thought of the few times he had met Madeleine on raids, and knew Kemp was right. The older woman was extremely experienced and had helped them many times.

"They might be able to use their contacts to access key locations, like the academy. Find Sophia."

"You mean there are people who would help them get inside without being caught?" Noah felt hope swell in his throat. "But who?"

"The Resistance has people undercover in many walks of life. People who Danforth has no knowledge of. I was one of them, within the academy. But there was another."

"Another professor?" Noah's eyes snapped to Kemp's as he waited for her response.

"No. The school has several drudges." Noting his puzzled look, the professor paused. "Bellator's serving class? They're bred to serve the women of the city." Noah recalled Paulo telling him about them before their first raid, but he didn't recall ever seeing one. "They work in the larger institutions mostly... aiding the women with menial chores. They wear face coverings, they don't speak... and they're mostly ignored, which makes them excellent spies. There is one in the school in particular that has helped me out in the past. If Faith and Diane can get his help, they might well have a way in."

Noah sagged against the wall of the tunnel. "So that would mean..."

"That they haven't walked straight back into the lion's den?" Kemp raised an eyebrow. "I don't think so."

Relief flooded over him. "That's the best news I've had in a long time. I can't tell you how worried I've–"

He stopped abruptly as the sound of footsteps echoed from further down the tunnel. Heart pounding, he gestured for the professor to return to the cave. But it was too late. Jacob strode towards them.

"You shouldn't be here." He glared at Noah, before turning to Kemp. "And *she* shouldn't be outside the cave without my permission."

"I'm sorry." Noah searched for an explanation. "Mick was scheduled to bring the breakfast but..." he opted for the truth, hoping it wouldn't get the other man into trouble, "his shoulder's been giving him trouble. I said I'd take the job off his hands... let him have a bit of rest."

Jacob glared at him. "You have no business being in this area. Or talking to our prisoners alone."

Taking the professor by the arm, he escorted her back into the cell. Once she was inside, he stared into the cave, as though checking Noah hadn't brought the girls anything illegal. Seeming almost disappointed when all he could see was a tray of food, he stalked back to his prey. Grasping Noah's shoulder, he spun him around and propelled him back the way he had come. Noah winced as Jacob's fingers dug into his skin.

When they reached the place where the tunnel forked, Jacob stopped. He bent his ear close to Noah's.

"I'm *sick* of your family disobeying my orders." Noah could feel hot, sour breath on his cheek. "*I'm* the Eremus leader. No one questions me."

His grip on Noah's arm intensified. Noah had to fight not to cry out from the pain.

"If I find you down here again, you won't like what happens. I don't care who your parents are." He gave Noah a shove. "Got it?"

The expression in Jacob's eyes was fierce, burning, almost manic. Noah took a step back, suddenly very frightened. He nodded, afraid that any words he spoke would betray his fear.

"Good." Seeming satisfied, Jacob jabbed a finger at the main tunnel. "Now get out of here."

CHAPTER ELEVEN: FAITH

As she walked beside Evelyn, Faith tried to breathe evenly. Though she'd asked to be included in more of the Resistance's missions, she hadn't anticipated one happening so soon. Nor that it would be a two-person job, in broad daylight.

She hadn't been told what the mission entailed. Ever since she'd been reluctant to accept the role of Resistance spokesperson, Madeleine had been brusque with her. All she had told Faith was that she would be working with Evelyn and that the job would take most of the day.

She didn't know her partner well. The older woman moved through the city with a quiet confidence Faith wished she could emulate. She was also one of Madeleine's closest confidantes, and Faith couldn't help but think she'd been sent out with her so Evelyn could judge her performance.

Faith hadn't found the right moment to tell Madeleine her discovery about Avery. Concerned that Madeleine might look on it as Faith having kept the information from her, she was praying the mission went well. At least then the Resistance leader would be in a better frame of mind to receive the information.

After emerging from the library tunnel on the opposite side of the square, Faith followed Evelyn in a southerly direction, heading towards an area of the city which was unfamiliar to her. Eventually, they began to pass offices and businesses, rather than the museums and shops and cafes in the centre.

They'd been walking for more than a mile when a uniformed guard appeared in the street ahead. The woman was heading straight for them. Instinctively, Faith stiffened.

"Act normal." Evelyn cautioned. "There's no reason for her to suspect anything of us. We're just a couple of Bellator citizens going about their daily business."

Trying to appear relaxed, Faith dropped her gaze to the pavement.

"That's odd." Evelyn's voice was hushed. "Her weapon doesn't look..." Faith looked up as the figure got closer. "It's not standard issue."

Marvelling at Evelyn's knowledge of Bellator weaponry, Faith squinted her eyes at the approaching figure. The guard walked rigidly, as though marching in a parade. Her eyes darted left and right, vigilant, searching for danger. But Faith had to agree with Evelyn: there was something odd about her.

"Stop staring!"

A sharp elbow from her companion had Faith sucking in a breath. She jerked her gaze away, hoping the guard hadn't noticed. She was much closer to them now.

"...and would you believe it, the machine had broken down!" Beside her, Evelyn chuckled loudly.

For a moment, Faith didn't understand. But as the other woman laughed again, she realised the sudden outburst was for the benefit of the guard. Evelyn was striking up what Faith assumed would sound like a natural conversation for two Bellator citizens to be having on the street.

"Really?" she managed to reply, hoping she wouldn't be required to contribute anything more detailed.

"Yes! We couldn't believe it, but–"

Tuning Evelyn out, Faith glanced up at the guard's face as she was about to pass them.

She stopped dead.

Evelyn had travelled several paces ahead before she realised Faith was no longer with her. Spinning around, she hurried back to Faith and the guard, who stood completely still, staring at one another.

"What are you *doing*?" Evelyn took hold of Faith's arm. "I'm so sorry." This was directed at the guard. "I'm sure she didn't mean to stop you."

But Faith resisted Evelyn's effort to pull her away. "Ruth?" She stared at the face of the guard. "What are you–?"

"You *know* this guard?" Evelyn hissed.

"She's not..." Faith closed her mouth. Glancing both ways, she made sure that there was no one close by. "She's from Eremus."

Evelyn's face paled. She took a slight step backwards, then recovered herself. "We were just out for a walk around the city, officer."

Ruth seemed to find her voice. "It's a beautiful day for it." Faith had to admire her courage. "My patrol takes me through the city centre today. A lovely route through the main square and past the *library*."

Faith jumped at the emphasis on the final word. Ruth was heading for the Resistance. Her heart was pounding. She opened her mouth to speak, but nothing came out.

Luckily, Evelyn did not have the same problem. "Such a beautiful building. Have you ever been inside?"

Ruth gave a small shake of the head. On the opposite side of the street, a small group of Bellator citizens emerged from an office building. Evelyn continued, waving an arm enthusiastically.

"It's gorgeous. And of real historic *importance*, wouldn't you agree." She shot a deliberate look at Faith.

"Oh yes." Faith echoed Evelyn's enthusiasm, wanting to show Ruth she was on the right track. "The library's a place *everyone* should visit at least once."

The group of women moved off, paying them little attention. Faith found herself heaving a sigh of relief as they disappeared down the street. Beside them, Ruth remained silent, but her eyes lit up and Faith knew she understood.

"Anyway officer, we'll be on our way." Evelyn took Faith by the arm and began to steer her away. "Nice to talk to you."

As they walked away, Faith couldn't help but glance back over her shoulder at Ruth. Noah's best friend, in the city, in broad daylight. And in a guard uniform. The other girl was still standing gazing after them. She caught Faith's eye and nodded, very slowly. And then, making an abrupt about turn, she marched off in the opposite direction.

They said nothing for several minutes. Eventually, Evelyn slowed her pace. "Well, that was unexpected."

"Yes." Faith felt strangely close to laughter.

"But not, I suppose, a total surprise." Sensing Faith's questioning glance, she explained. "Now that we've lost Madeleine's house it's more of a challenge for Eremus people to access the city." Evelyn motioned to Faith to keep up with her. "From now on, they'll have to find new ways to enter the city. Travel a lot further above ground."

Unbidden, Faith imagined Noah entering Bellator. Twin feelings of excitement and fear surged through her at the prospect. Shaking her head, she tried to rid it of the idea, forcing herself to focus on what Evelyn was saying.

"It'll increase the risk for them, though. A disguise is probably very sensible."

Faith considered Ruth's guard uniform. She had managed to fool them for a few minutes. But could she keep it up?

"They must be starting to run out of supplies." Evelyn mused. "They can manage a fair amount of food without Bellator's help. They forage, and fish, and hunt. There are other things they *like* to have though... when they can get them. But when it comes to things like batteries and medicines, they need us."

Faith thought about the supply shed at the cottage. It had been filled with boxes clearly taken from the city, but most of them had been empty. How long would it be before Eremus had to risk a raid?

She wondered how many of the citizens had been killed or injured in the skirmish with the Bellator guards. How would Anna manage to treat them without medical supplies? If she didn't have the resources to help them, how many more would die? Taking a deep breath, she pushed away the unwelcome thoughts. Worrying about the citizens she had left behind wouldn't do any good. She couldn't help them.

Beside her, Evelyn shrugged as they turned the corner into the next street. "Anyway, let's put that from our minds. We have work to do. See that building ahead?" She kept her voice low. "The one with all the glass?"

Faith's eyes followed Evelyn's. The building she indicated was one of the tallest on the street. She gave a small nod.

"That's BellaLab Corp. Danforth worked there, before she got into government. Madeleine, too." She glanced both ways, checking the street for other citizens. "She was fired from the place after asking too many questions about their research." Her lips pursed primly. "The Resistance is *very* interested about what goes on inside those walls."

"Why?"

Ignoring her question, Evelyn ducked her head. "We're just going to walk past, for now. Act natural."

Faith kept pace with her guide as they continued on down the street. On the other side of the laboratory, Evelyn directed Faith into a side street. She stopped in a doorway which bore the words *BellaLab Corp: Private*.

"Our mission involves trying to find out more about what's going on in there." She gestured back towards the building. "But security is extremely tight. Madeleine and Blake have been working on a project to allow us to gain access, but they haven't perfected it yet. We're going to need to use old-fashioned tactics."

Faith waited for her to continue.

"Last night, Blake managed to open one of the files from Anderson's datadev. She looked at Anderson's search history and found a report about this drug Danforth appears to be testing."

"Femgazipane?"

"That's the one. According to the scientist in charge of the trial, it's been in trial mode for more than three years now, but up until a couple of months ago, they were only using it with animals."

"Really?"

"Really. Mice, at first, and then a smaller species of monkey."

Faith's mind was reeling. If Evelyn was suggesting what she thought she was suggesting... A wave of anger rolled over her.

Evelyn grimaced. "I can see from your expression you've already worked it out. The report states quite clearly that femgazipane is not to be administered to human subjects until certain alterations have been made. The chemist in charge requested an additional *six months* to test the drug before the project went ahead."

"The project involving the academy students?" Faith felt sick. "And when was the report dated?"

"You're a smart girl, aren't you?" Evelyn gave a wry smile. "The report was only two months old."

Faith felt like she'd been punched in the stomach. Serene had been dosed with femgazipane a month ago. Faith herself had been given it not long after that. Now, it was being administered to the Danforth Academy students en masse. All before it was considered safe to use.

"Those bastards..." she whispered. "How could they give it to us when they knew it wasn't safe?"

Evelyn glanced up and down the street, ever-alert. "Danforth doesn't care."

"The report mentioned her by name?" Faith asked.

"Oh yes." Evelyn's eyes flashed. "Our dear chancellor set this project up... she's *very* interested in what femgazipane can do. Especially when used in conjunction with another drug... I think Blake called it... melatidine."

"Never heard of it."

"I don't think it's in use. Not *yet*, anyway." A hot sweat invaded Faith's body as Evelyn continued. "Unfortunately, Blake wasn't able to discover the new drug's purpose. We know it's linked to fertility, but that's all." Her eyes flicked to the building behind them. "Femgazipane ensured a more successful rate of conception in the animal tests... perhaps gave them more control over the breeding process, but we don't know any more than that."

Faith felt a sudden wave of dizziness sweep over her. Putting out her hand, she steadied herself against the wall.

Evelyn peered at her. "You alright?"

Faith swallowed. "Yeah. Just..."

"Angry? Join the club." Evelyn gestured at the BellaLab Corp headquarters. "It's exactly why we're here today."

Without warning, she turned and headed further down the street. Faith followed, curious to discover the specifics of their mission. Evelyn stopped beside a large metal gate. Once Faith had joined her, she continued.

"Madeleine wants us to find out more about the testing. We know the animal experiments were done here." Evelyn jabbed a finger at the gate. "This is the loading bay. We're here to observe the comings and goings. Track deliveries going in and out. Later, we can use the information for other missions. Have our people trail the delivery trucks, work out where they're taking things. But we have to stay under the radar."

As she finished speaking, a door banged on the other side of the gate. Footsteps sounded from the space beyond, followed by a voice.

"No. That's not big enough." The tone of the speaker was sharp, as though they were used to giving orders. "It needs to be a similar size to the first." There was a pause while the speaker listened, and Faith realised the woman was on the phone. "And, as usual, the utmost discretion will be needed once the deliveries start to arrive."

Evelyn and Faith exchanged glances. The information was fascinating. But their position was a delicate one. If they stayed to listen further, they might easily be spotted.

"Yes." On the other side of the gate, the conversation continued, sounding closer this time. "The first warehouse is almost at capacity." Another pause. "We have a final order going out in a few minutes. We'll look to be diverting resources to the new location over the next few days."

There was a creaking sound, like that of a lever being pulled. Faith and Evelyn leapt backwards as the gates whirred to life. Evelyn gestured to the opposite side of the street, where there was a door on the side of the next building. As they hurried across, Evelyn fumbled in her pack. By the time they had reached their goal, she was holding a couple of cigarettes and a lighter.

She lit one, then the other, offering it to Faith. "If anyone asks, we're..." she squinted at the signage on the door they stood outside, "employees of MedTech on a smoke break."

She inhaled deeply, motioning for Faith to do the same. At the academy, the girls had been warned against the dangers of smoking so often that Faith was frightened to start now. Gingerly, she brought the cigarette closer to her face. The smoke burned her eyes. She held it between her fingers, hoping the act would be convincing enough without her having to breathe it in.

The gate was completely open now, revealing the yard behind. A delivery truck was waiting on the other side. As Faith watched, the engine roared to life.

"*Look at me*, Faith!" Evelyn's voice hissed in her ear. "You have to act the part."

Faith jerked her gaze to her companion, attempting to smile as though they were two colleagues having a casual conversation.

"That's it." Evelyn angled herself so she could look over Faith's shoulder. She broke out into laughter and took another drag from the cigarette. "I'll watch. You just stay still."

Faith heard indistinct voices calling out over the sound of the engine.

"They just loaded the truck with a few extra boxes." Evelyn narrated. "Now they're closing it up ready to leave." She nodded, as though she was agreeing with something Faith had said. "The boxes had wording on them, but it was difficult to make out from here. There was a symbol on each one, though. I'm pretty sure they're medical supplies of some kind. If only we had some way of finding out where they're going."

Faith longed to turn, but willed herself to stay where she was. "Can you see the woman who was on the phone?"

"Yep. She's giving instructions to the driver."

The truck's engine revved again. The engine noise increased as the driver moved the vehicle out onto the street behind them. Eventually, it faded as the truck drove off into the distance. Evelyn watched it go before looking back towards the loading bay.

"Okay. The woman who was on the phone is about to close the gates, I think. Then we can–" Evelyn dropped her gaze suddenly.

"What?"

Evelyn raised her eyes to meet Faith's. "She sees us."

Faith felt her heart start to beat faster. "Is that an issue?"

"I hope not." Evelyn paused to shoot a rapid glance across at BellaLab Corp. "Just act as though we're having a normal conversation. I'm sure it will be fine."

"Okay." Faith's mind had gone blank. "How has your day been so far?"

"Okay, thanks. I'm glad of the break though." Evelyn put the cigarette to her lips. "She's staring at us." Tension had begun to leak into the older woman's body. "Now she's on her phone."

Desperate to appear as normal as possible, Faith took a deep drag of the cigarette. The second she did, she knew she had made a mistake. As the smoke hit the back of her throat, she knew she was going to cough. Though she struggled to contain it, moments later a huge coughing fit enveloped her entire body.

Evelyn stared, panic flaring in her eyes. Instead of reassuring the BellaLab employee that they were an ordinary pair of workers, Faith had just attracted more attention to them. But she couldn't stop coughing. She bent over, fighting to control her breathing. Evelyn thumped her on the back. When Faith had regained control, the two of them glanced back at the space between the gates.

They were empty. But they weren't closed.

"Did you see where she went?" Faith managed to croak.

Evelyn shook her head. "I'm not happy with this. We should go. And *now*." She pointed at Faith. "Put your hood up." Faith obeyed the command without question. "Now let's go."

They had barely taken a step into the street when an armed security guard came out of the BellaLab building. Spotting them, she headed for the gate immediately.

Evelyn picked up the pace, glancing across at Faith. "Run!"

The older woman set off at a sprint down the street. Faith attempted to follow, but the guards were faster. Stronger. Evelyn was at the end of the street as the hand closed on Faith's arm. She was brought to a sudden halt, her arm jerking out of its socket, as her partner disappeared around the corner.

She turned to face her assailant with dismay. This was it. She had wanted the chance to be a part of active missions, and now one was staring her in the face. But the guard looked fierce.

"Who are you?" The woman had several inches on Faith. She loomed over her, her voice gravelly. "What are you doing here?"

Faith glanced back at the end of the street. There was no sign of Evelyn. She was on her own. The mission was an undercover one, and she hadn't been given any weapons as such. She would have to improvise. All she needed to do was incapacitate the guard so she could run away.

The cigarette! In her haste, she had yet to dispose of it. And it was in her free hand.

Without hesitating, she pressed the glowing end into the arm which held her. Yelping, the guard let go. The millisecond that followed was all Faith needed. She took off down the street, running as fast as she could.

It wasn't long before she heard pounding footsteps behind her. *Damn, the guard was fast.* Keeping her eyes on the end of the street, Faith kept going. Looking back would only make her lose time. The main road was just a few steps ahead.

But it was too far. And she wasn't fast enough. This time, the guard didn't go easy. Leaping forward, she tackled Faith, sending her crashing to the street.

She didn't have time to put her hands out to break her fall. Cringing as the road came up to meet her, she turned her face at the last second. Her cheek slammed into the ground. As the guard landed on her, a pain so intense she had no comparison for it shot through her body.

When the guard's weight lifted off her, she curled into a ball. But it wasn't over.

"You're coming with me." The woman loomed over her. "Get up."

Faith contemplated running again. But as she rolled on to her back, she saw the gun. Forcing herself into a sitting position, she raised a hand to her cheek. It came away stained red. Fighting the dizziness, she tried to focus on what Madeleine had told her before the mission.

Don't get caught. And if you do, don't give them anything.

But the agony of her swollen cheek was enough already. She wasn't sure she could stand much more. The guard's eyes were narrowed. She reached a hand down, closing once more on Faith's and jerking her upright.

But just as Faith was attempting to regain her balance, the guard lost her grip. Faith tumbled to the ground again, her knee twisting awkwardly as she landed. The guard pitched forward and Faith had to roll sideways to avoid the woman falling on her again.

She glanced around, puzzled. *What was going on?* And then she knew. Evelyn stood on the other side of the fallen guard, wielding a sturdy chunk of wood. Her eyes were blazing.

"Come *on*!" she hissed. "They'll notice this one's missing any minute. We have to *go*!"

Faith took a deep breath and hauled herself to her feet. Leaving the guard lying on the ground, she limped after Evelyn, pain from the wound on her cheek radiating through her entire body.

Chapter Twelve: Noah

The raiders had been called together for the first time in weeks. As Noah hurried into the training cave, he was shaking. He hadn't seen anything of Jacob since their encounter outside the prisoners' cave, and he had no idea how the man would react when he came face-to-face with him again for the first time. Keeping his head down, he hurried to Flynn's side.

As he settled in next to Flynn, he cast his eyes around the room, very aware of those who were missing. Jan had been one of the most experienced leaders in the group. She would be missed the most, but Dane and Dan had also been a reassuring presence on raids. Now, along with several others lost in the clash with Danforth's guards, they were gone.

He wondered if Jacob would suggest the need to recruit more raiders. No one seemed to know why the leader had called them together. Ruth had yet to return, though his ma had assured him that they expected her to be away for several days, so Noah had tried not to worry. Since his conversation with Professor Kemp, he had even entertained the hope that Ruth might find Faith among the Resistance.

The thought was a selfish one, he knew. But he was desperate to know that Faith had managed to return safely to the city. And if she was with the Resistance, she wasn't lying in a bed somewhere being injected with a dangerous drug. If she was with the Resistance, maybe they were fighting on the same side for once.

Once the majority of the raiders had arrived, Jacob stepped forward. Noah was grateful that the size of the group made it difficult for the leader to pick him out.

"I'm sure you're wondering why I called you down here today," he began. "I wanted to make sure we were keeping up with our training. Making sure our weapons were ready. We mustn't be caught unprepared."

"Unprepared for what?" The interruption came from one of Harden's buddies, but he wasn't standing with him. Noah searched the cave for the older boy, finally spotting him skulking close to the back, almost as though he wanted to remain out of sight.

"For *anything*." Jacob frowned. "Don't be fooled. We're at war with Danforth now. Just because we haven't seen anything of her since the last confrontation, doesn't mean she's not still plotting against us. We have to be ready for her."

He swept an arm across the group. "To that end, I want all our remaining weapons categorised, checked over, and cleaned this morning. Our explosives, counted and readied for use. Then, we can run some training drills."

Beside Noah, Flynn stiffened. "Sounds like you're planning an attack. Did you forget we agreed to wait until Ruth got back before we took any action?"

Jacob cocked his head to one side. As his eyes turned in their direction, Noah cringed. But the leader didn't even spare him a glance, focusing his glare on Flynn.

"I didn't forget, no." He paused for a second, seeming to consider the mood. "But, sooner or later, we're going to have to act. Before Danforth gets the chance to." His voice grew in volume and intensity. "She needs to know we're not done yet, that we still have the power to get to her. To damage her beloved city."

Noticing Jacob's fists clenching at his sides, Noah again thought of madness. Paulo had mentioned it, and Noah had seen the same, slightly crazed expression in Jacob's eyes the day he'd met him in the prisoners' cave. There was no more talk of Eremus gaining equal rights, of the need to preserve life, not to harm the innocent. He seemed bent on revenge, and little else.

Perhaps aware of the way he was coming across, their leader calmed his tone. "As Flynn says, a few days ago Ruth was sent into the city as an envoy, to connect with the Resistance and do a little investigation of her own." Noah thought about his friend's mission to infiltrate the Bellator guard with a shudder. "We fully expect her to return with key intel, which I assure you will be shared with the council. But we will need to act on it. And quickly."

He glanced around the room, noting his raiders' concern. Holding up a hand, he quelled the growing murmurs of discontent.

"I'm aware that we have other worries. Our resources are severely depleted. Anna informs me that we have almost no meds left." He began to tick off items on his fingers. "We are low on batteries to supply our flashlights and walkie talkies, and, whilst we have some sources of food, we need to stock up on items which will see us through the next few months. Be reassured. We will make this a priority."

Beside Noah, Flynn tensed. "You mean alongside preparing to launch an attack on Bellator."

Jacob's gaze hardened. "Yes. As I said, we can't afford to sit back and do nothing."

On the opposite side of the space, Paulo stood up. "Which mission takes priority for you?"

"What?" Jacob looked stunned at the doubt in Paulo's tone.

"What I think he means is," Flynn looked thrilled by his nephew's support, "do you still have the best interests of your community at heart? Is it more important that you crush Danforth? Or make sure your people are fed and cared for?"

For a moment, Jacob was silent, his eyes wide. When he did speak, his gaze was steely. "How dare you accuse me of–"

"It's a valid question." Flynn turned to the rest of the raiders. "And one which I think we deserve an answer to." A murmur of agreement ran around the room. Flynn seemed to take courage from the support. "I mean, you seem more focused on the problems in the city than those we're experiencing right here within these caves."

"I can assure you that's not the case," Jacob spluttered. "The well-being of my people is of the utmost importance to me. You know that."

"All your people?" Flynn raised an eyebrow. "What about Ella?"

"*This* again?" Jacob spat out a laugh. "She's being fed, she hasn't been harmed. She is enduring a punishment for acting against the Eremus people."

"But you don't have any real proof that she did act against us." Paulo turned to the other raiders. "We all know Ella. It would be hugely out of character for her to go against her community. She loves Eremus." He looked back at Jacob, his voice calm and even. "Could you consider releasing her? I think it would go a long way towards..." He gestured around the room.

"I thought I made myself clear that I won't be releasing her," Jacob huffed. "Not until I'm certain she can be trusted."

"I truly hope you decide she can be trusted soon." Flynn's voice had an undertone of steel which Noah hadn't heard before. "Because–"

"You're naïve if you think Danforth can be ignored." Jacob cut across Flynn, steering the conversation in another direction.

"I wasn't suggesting we ignore her," Flynn pushed on. "I just think there are better, more constructive things we could be doing to tackle our issues with Bellator. And I firmly believe that *caution* is the way forward."

"I agreed we would wait, didn't I?" Jacob's voice rose in volume. "I won't take action until Ruth has returned."

"And you'll make sure the council meets with Ruth altogether?" Flynn insisted.

"Of course." Jacob's smile did not reach his eyes. "But once we hear from her, we will need to act quickly." Jacob gestured at the boxes of weapons which were stacked at the side of the cave. "Hence our task today. Now if we could just–"

"Sorry." Flynn's eyes flashed. "But I'd like to know more about your plan of action. The one you've put on hold until Ruth returns. Don't tell me you don't have one, because I know that's a lie."

"Of course, I have a plan." Jacob's eyes flashed with annoyance as he spoke. "The first part of it involves getting our weapons ready for use. Beyond that, I will brief the relevant citizens about their role when it becomes necessary. For security reasons, it's better not everyone knows the plan."

"You mean you don't trust some of us," Flynn wagered.

"Not at all." Jacob smoothed his words with a smile, but it looked strained. "Secrecy is vital in any plans we have against the city. If Danforth gets her hands on any of us, who knows what she'll do? The fewer people who know the details, the better."

"I disagree." The voice came from the other side of Flynn, where Mick was sitting. "You keep claiming you have our best interests at heart, but your previous actions... reckless actions, I might add, have thrown Eremus right in Danforth's path. What have you done to further the Eremus cause lately?"

Jacob met Mick's gaze head on. "Firstly, you all know that my plan to destroy their fertility unit was a success. Bellator now has no male seed and will therefore struggle to reproduce. Tell me that hasn't furthered the Eremus cause." His eyes flashed with triumph as he ploughed on. "The effects of this will only be seen in the *long term*, though. For now, we must continue to take action which makes Danforth and her government uncomfortable. To that end, we recently disposed of a large number of the city's guard force."

Noah thought about the explosion in the forest, and the number of guards it had wounded or killed. The word *dispose* made him shudder. The dead guards might be their enemy, but they were also still people... women who lived in the city Eremus claimed it wanted to unite with. To hold this as a point of triumph seemed wrong, somehow.

"You say *we*," Mick continued, "but it was a very small minority who participated in that little plan. And we weren't given the chance to object to the enormous loss of life it involved."

Noah glanced towards the back of the room, where Harden was seated. The older boy's head was down, his shoulders slumped, as though the mention of the bombing was painful for him. Paulo was right, he realised. All around him, there were growing murmurs of disagreement.

"That loss of life," Jacob spat out, "was a necessary move. With so many guards out of action, Danforth is weakened. Severely. It gives us a chance we've never had before. You *must* see that."

Flynn held out a hand to calm the growing discontent in the cave. "And you *must see* why we'd like to be included in your future plans."

"Alright!" Jacob's jaw was rigid with tension. "My plan is to disrupt the city in other, more immediate ways." He gestured to the boxes of weapons. "We still have a good number of explosives. I'd like to use them to target various important city buildings over the coming days and weeks. A series of continuous attacks will show we're a force to be reckoned with... Danforth won't be able to ignore us. And each attack will take us a step closer to being on an equal footing with the city."

"These targets," Flynn asked. "Will destroying them mean endangering *more* Bellator citizens? And innocent ones, at that." He looked around, meeting the eyes of the other raiders. "Doesn't that make us as bad as them?"

Jacob was quick to react. "Of course, every effort will be made to ensure that the buildings are empty when we attack."

But Flynn wasn't ready to give up. "Isn't our goal to share their resources, in the end?" He pressed their leader. "To have them accept us as their *equals*? Destroying their facilities will severely impact their way of life. How can we ever expect them to accept us, to look on us favourably if we devastate their city?"

"And," Paulo chimed in, "from a selfish perspective, if we raze half of Bellator, what resources will be left for us to utilise if and when we gain an equal footing with the women of the city?"

Jacob regarded Paulo coldly for a moment. Then, slowly, he smiled. "Of course, I want to minimise damage to the city's resources. The targets I intend to destroy will be considered very carefully."

"In discussion with the rest of the community, of course." Flynn added.

"Of course." Jacob said tightly. Turning, he jabbed a finger at the group in front of him. "Make no mistake, though. We've seen what

Danforth is prepared to do. We can't underestimate her. In the end, we *must* be prepared to fight."

Ignoring the storm of muttering which filled the room at his final comment, Jacob stalked out of the cave. After a few moments of stunned silence, Flynn stepped into the place Jacob had vacated.

"I think that's probably enough discussion for now." Noah marvelled at how calm he sounded after the unpleasant confrontation. "Let's get on with the task at hand."

He gestured to Paulo, who began giving out instructions to the individual raiders. "Alright, grab a partner, take a box. You know the drill."

Waving his hand, he moved around the cave, assigning a range of maintenance tasks to the different raiders. Noah was happy to find Flynn wanted to partner with him. Together, they dragged out a trunkful of guns to clean and check over.

Whilst the task wasn't a familiar one for Noah, Flynn demonstrated how to unload and disassemble a few different guns. Soon they were working quietly side-by-side. The job involved using various rods and slender pieces of rope soaked in oil to clear the residue from the gun barrels. At first, Noah found himself handling each item gingerly, as though it might go off at any moment. When he imagined the lives the weapons might have taken, it made him shiver.

But each gun was different. Eventually, he found himself enjoying the challenge. Eremus' weapons had been picked up in different places over the years. It took care and focus to break each one apart and clean it well, and the satisfaction of conquering a new one was rewarding.

Flynn was preoccupied. Noah suspected he was brooding over the spat with Jacob. Unusually quiet, he worked with ferocity, snapping each gun apart, clearing out the barrels far faster than Noah could, then polishing the weapons until they shone. Methodical and precise, Flynn took pride in everything he did.

Not for the first time, Noah wondered how different the raiders' plans might be if his ma's partner were the one in charge.

"When do you think Ruth might be back?" he asked, tiring of the silence.

Flynn looked up, blinking, as though he had forgotten Noah was there. "I'm not sure..." he said eventually. "When did she leave?"

"Sunday evening."

Flynn frowned. "At the earliest, later today or tomorrow. And that's if things went well. If she gets stuck... delayed at all... it could be much longer."

"You think Jacob will wait for her to get back before he does anything? I mean..." he hesitated, "after everything that just happened?"

Flynn's face darkened. "I don't know. It depends." He placed the gun he'd been working on in the trunk and picked up another. "He's feeling threatened. That makes him unpredictable. And Anna and I are just as concerned about our resources." He turned the oil can upside down, shaking the last remaining drops onto the rope, as if to demonstrate the shortage.

"But I think he'd be stupid to act before we have more intel." Wrenching the empty gun barrel open, Flynn set about cleaning it with verve. "We need more information. If Ruth has managed to speak to Madeleine... if the Resistance is prepared to work with us. It changes everything."

"What do you mean?" Noah frowned.

Flynn stopped what he was doing and looked Noah in the eye. "Charlotte told your ma the Resistance wants to make real changes to the way the city is run. So do we." He shrugged and went back to the gun he was working on. "If we can settle on doing it *together*," he dropped his voice, "in a less destructive way than Jacob is currently suggesting, we might reduce the damage to vital city locations in the process. That would be better for everyone."

"Agreed." Noah swapped his own gun for another, dropping his gaze as he continued. "But... um, what if they won't help us?"

Flynn shrugged. "I don't know. Without the Resistance, Eremus doesn't have enough knowledge of the inner workings of the city. From what Charlotte told your ma, they have many members stationed in key locations around the city. People who watch what's going on, feed information back to them, help them out."

"Like spies?"

"I suppose." Flynn smiled at the word. "Having access to that kind of information would be amazing. Can you imagine? We could minimise damage to vital buildings, reduce the threat to life." Flynn's tone was earnest. "Your ma and I feel the Resistance would really show the Bellator citizens we're on their side... that we're not monsters who plan to just charge in and mount a vicious attack."

"As Jacob plans to."

"Exactly."

Noah cocked his head to one side, his mind working overtime. "So... having people on the inside is useful?"

"It most definitely is."

"What about sending Eremus people into the city undercover? In disguise, to blend in with the people and gain a better sense of what's going on." Noah lowered his voice. "Wouldn't it be useful to have some of our own people there too?"

Flynn drew the rod out of the gun he was working on and stopped. "You mean like Ruth?" He stared at Noah, puzzled. "I'm not sure she'd get away with living among the people dressed as a guard. She wouldn't know enough to be convincing... not if she were side-by-side with the other guards every day."

The older man looked thoughtful. "I mean, I suppose as an ordinary citizen she might have more success. Perhaps the Resistance *might* allow us to place a few female citizens in Bellator. Find them housing, supply them with clothing and so on. They'd all have to be female, of course."

"Would they?" Noah raised an eyebrow.

Flynn stared at him, uncomprehending. "How could we get away with sending men into an all-female city?"

Noah hesitated before speaking. "Listen, I had an idea... after I talked to Professor Kemp..." Noah tried to gauge his stepfather's reaction. "There is *one* way we could send a man into the city without attracting attention."

"Go on." Flynn narrowed his eyes. "I'm listening."

"Someone could go in as a drudge." Noah hurried on, watching Flynn's face carefully. "They're the ones who–"

"I know what they are."

"Kemp tells me there are lots of them in the city, often placed in locations of importance. They're male, but they go mostly unnoticed..." He held up a hand to stop Flynn's protest. "And I know what you're going to say. It's dangerous. But it's definitely possible." He rushed on, not wanting to give Flynn the chance to protest. "They even wear face coverings as part of their uniform. The women barely acknowledge them, as long as the jobs they're assigned get done."

Flynn looked thoughtful. "I suppose you're right. *In theory*, a man from Eremus could get away with posing as a drudge. But they're bred a certain way, aren't they? Engineered to be... smaller?"

"It's true, they're usually quite slender. A muscular man wouldn't get away with it. But they're wiry... strong. They have to be, to do their job. I think... I feel like, if he were properly prepared, a slim, fit Eremus man could get away with posing as a drudge." He leaned closer as he warmed to his subject. "Think about it. The *intel* he might gather, in addition to the existing Resistance members. We could use it to *connect* with the citizens, persuade them we're on their side, avoid blindly destroying half the city's resources."

Flynn's eyes narrowed. "Think of the danger they'd be putting themselves in." He eyed Noah closely, his expression changing from uncertainty, to doubt, to horror. "Wait. You're not thinking...?"

"I am." Noah took a deep breath. "Think about it. I'm slight. I'm subtle. I know how to go unnoticed." He watched for Flynn's reaction. "I think I'd be the perfect choice."

Chapter Thirteen: Faith

Faith was miserable. Whilst she and Evelyn had made it back to headquarters safely the previous night, things were bad.

Thankfully, the pain from the twisted ankle had eased. But the wound on her cheek was painful. Evelyn had brought Lily, a Resistance member who acted as their unofficial medic, to look at it.

"Sheesh!" the willowy woman had exclaimed when she saw Faith. "That looks painful."

It had taken her half an hour to clean Faith up. When she showed Faith her reflection in the mirror, it had been all she could do not to cry. Her face was swollen and bruised, and the bleeding had come from several cuts which she had sustained as her face collided with the concrete. The deepest of these was more than an inch long and had taken several stitches to seal. She knew it was going to scar.

But there had been worse to come.

Upon hearing Evelyn's mission report, Madeleine had summoned Faith to the office. Dragging her feet all the way, Faith had gritted her teeth through a ten-minute lecture on how she had proved she wasn't ready for undercover ops. At the end of the speech, Madeleine had gestured to her face.

"I thought you were considering acting as a spokesperson for us. How do you think you'll come across now?" She had grasped Faith's chin, making her wince. "With a face that looks like you've gone ten rounds with a prizefighter? Danforth will be very quick to use your injuries as further proof of the Eremus' men's brutality. You know how she twists things."

Faith left the office with her head down. Far from impressing the leader, her inability to act naturally and to flee when the necessity had arisen had ruined the mission. It would now be impossible for Evelyn or Faith to go anywhere near BellaLab Corp.

The hands-on mission had not been what Faith had expected, and the job of spokesperson had started to sound like a far more suitable option. But she'd ruined her chance to play the role. The way Madeleine had glared at her, she'd be lucky to be assigned anything above cleaning duty from now on.

Avoiding company, Faith had headed for bed. She had a killer headache, and Lily had urged her to rest properly after her ordeal. She hadn't thought she would be able to sleep, but the minute her head had hit the pillow, she'd passed out.

When she woke up, Diane was sitting on the bottom of her bed. "Mission didn't go as planned, I take it?" She gestured at Faith's face. "What *happened*?"

"We had to run." Faith put a hand to her cheek. It hurt to talk. "It appears I wasn't fast enough."

"Ouch." Diane peered closer. "Are those *stitches*?"

"They are, yes." Desperate to change the subject, Faith sat up. Her head spun, but she forced herself to speak. "Any news on Sophia?"

"Nothing new. She's still unconscious." Diane sat back a little, her eyes narrowing. "You tell Madeleine about Avery yet?"

"I forgot." Noting Diane's sceptical look, Faith turned defensive. "I *did*!" She gestured to her cheek again. "I've kind of had other things on my mind." She slumped down again. "In case you hadn't noticed, I'm not really her favourite person right now."

Diane smirked. "That's an understatement."

"Alright. Alright." Faith held out a hand. "I'll tell her today. Right now, if you want me to."

"Now might not be the best time." Diane pushed herself off the bed. "I think you'll want to come with me."

Faith stared at her suspiciously. "Why?"

"Because," Diane rummaged under the bed and pulled out a sweatshirt. "There are other things going on."

"Like what?"

"Like *Ruth* just arrived."

Faith sat bolt upright. Noah's best friend had not appeared by the time she and Evelyn had gotten back the previous night, and she hadn't had the energy to wonder why. But if she was here now...

"I want to speak to her." Grabbing the sweatshirt from Diane's hand, she pulled it on. "Why didn't you *tell* me!"

"I just did." Diane rolled her eyes. "And the Resistance leaders took her straight into the office to grill her, so you won't be speaking to her just yet. But if you wanted to grab a shower and come with me to the hub, we can catch her as she comes out."

Faith headed for the door with renewed energy. "See you downstairs in ten minutes."

The Resistance leaders did not finish talking to Ruth for several hours. By the time they emerged from the office, the majority of the library's inhabitants had gathered in the hub, curious to learn more about the visitor. Madeleine emerged from the office with Ruth, now dressed in jeans and a sweatshirt. The room fell silent.

"Ah," she began. "I was going to call everyone together, but I see it's not necessary. We wanted to update you on a few... new developments." She gestured to Ruth. "I'm sure you're all well aware that this young woman arrived here earlier today."

As Madeleine continued, the attention in the room shifted, every eye zeroing in on the newcomer.

"Ruth was sent by the Eremus council. As you know, we lost touch with them a little while ago. A lack of batteries has meant they've been unable to use their walkie talkies of late, so Ruth came here to update us on their status and to ask us if we might provide them with some much-needed resources." Madeleine glanced at Ruth with an unreadable expression. "She also came to present us with... an offer, of sorts."

Once again, every eye in the room travelled to Ruth, who dropped her gaze and shifted from one foot to the other. For a moment, Faith thought Madeleine was going to have the Eremus raider address them, but after a few seconds, she continued to speak.

"Eremus is as tired of Danforth's treatment as we are. For very different reasons, obviously. There are hundreds of people, decent people, living in those woods. Hiding from the Bellator guards. Terrified for their lives, should they be discovered. I'm sure our other recent arrivals can attest to that." Her eyes searched the room. "Faith? Diane?"

Startled, Faith sat up straighter. Beside her, Diane had tensed. A look of pure panic flashed over her face as she glanced at all the people in the room.

Feeling Madeleine's eyes on them, Faith searched for the right words. "It's true." As everyone turned to look at her, there were several gasps at the state of her face. Ignoring them, Faith ploughed on. "There are more citizens in Eremus than we could count. And their network of underground tunnels is impressive." Her eyes met Ruth's and she felt a surge of loyalty towards Noah's people. "Danforth wants us to think they're all monsters, but they're not. These people's lives are basic, but they survive. Not only survive... they *live*. There are women and children down there, *families*... They've... adapted well to their underground home." She shrugged. "And I can't say they were *all* kind, but some of them went out of their way to help us."

It was more words than she'd spoken all day. Her cheek ached from the movement, but the fascination on the surrounding faces made her push on. "The Eremus people are forced to hide because if they don't, Danforth has her guards hunt them down and execute them. Most Bellator citizens believe they'd be in mortal danger if they came across an Eremus citizen, but it's simply not true. The people of Eremus have acted with violence in the past, but only as a reaction to the violence they have experienced *all their lives* at the hands of our city's so-called defenders. Fear is all they know." She stared around at the Resistance members. "It's Bellator's fault. And it's not fair."

As Faith sank back in her seat, she felt faintly embarrassed. She hadn't meant the speech to become so impassioned. To her surprise though, most of the women in the room were nodding, their expressions sympathetic. Watching Madeleine hide a smile as she moved forward to speak again, Faith realised why the leader had requested she speak up. She'd wanted to prove that Faith's words could have an impact. The reactions of the other Resistance members showed that they could. That *she* could.

Madeleine was right. The role of spokesperson was important. And it was something she could do well.

"Everything Faith says is true. The people in Eremus are mostly decent. It's why we've helped them in the past. Any aggression they have shown is a result of their frustration. Or self defence." Madeleine gestured to the Eremus citizen who stood by her side. "But Ruth tells me the citizens feel things are coming to a head. Recent events have frightened them. If that patrol had radioed back their location, Danforth would have sent her guards in to destroy the entire community. This has strengthened their resolve to fight back. To be accepted. Which they cannot do with Danforth still in power."

Robyn stepped forward. "And so, it seems that we have a common goal. Ruth came here to offer Eremus' support to the Resistance. To see whether we can work together. The people of Eremus want to change the way men are perceived in the city. *Prove* they're not monsters... and that they belong here just as much as women do."

Her final comment provoked a flurry of conversation.

"What?" "They want to *live* here?" "You mean–" "In the city? With *us*?"

"Perhaps," Madeleine held up a hand for silence, "we could ask Ruth herself."

Ruth stepped forward, her hands clenched in front of her. "Some of us would like to have the option to live here, yes. To work here, forge relationships with the women of the city." There were murmurs from the Resistance members, but she forged ahead bravely. "Others would be happy to stay where they are, in the community we've worked so hard to build... but mostly we're tired of hiding. We want Danforth to acknowledge our existence... and if she won't, then we want someone in power who will."

"In short," Madeleine spread her hands wide, "Eremus is prepared to take the next steps against Danforth. They sent Ruth to ask if we'd be prepared to work *together*, to align ourselves, to fight for a fair and independent society which is accepting of all genders.

"Of course, it's too soon to assume an alliance between the two communities would work." She smiled. "For now, Robyn and I have agreed to listen to what the Eremus council has to say in return for Eremus giving us certain assurances. Ruth will be heading back there later today with our message."

Robyn stepped forward. "We want to reassure you that we won't dive into this without ensuring both groups have similar objectives. No one from Eremus will be permitted to walk in here and start making demands. To secure our trust, the community will have to prove their loyalty. Ruth understands, and will convey this to the Eremus leaders when she returns."

"That's pretty much it for now," Robyn finished. "We promise to keep you informed."

As the Resistance members began to disperse, Faith and Diane stayed where they were.

"Thanks." Diane muttered. "I'm a terrible public speaker. Always have been."

"It's fine." Faith kept her gaze on Ruth, who was still deep in conversation with Robyn. "Anyone could have done it."

"Not anyone. And definitely not *me*." Diane cringed. Then her tone became one of admiration. "Where did that speech come from? It was pretty powerful."

Faith flushed. "I only told the truth."

"Well, you did better than I could have." Diane punched Faith's arm gently. "You're very believable."

"I am?" Faith turned to face her friend.

"Didn't you *see* people's faces? You had them hanging on your every word." She grinned. "Even Madeleine."

Faith's eyes searched the room for the Resistance leader. It took a while to find her. Instead of being in the thick of things, she was standing to one side. And her eyes were fixed on Faith's. Slowly, she raised an eyebrow. Faith knew what she was asking.

Despite her beat-up face, Faith's words had been powerful, convincing. The women had believed her, been willing to trust her words. Madeleine and Robyn had seen something in Faith that she hadn't seen in herself. She thought back to the failed mission the previous day. If she was honest with herself, the front-line fighting had terrified her.

But telling her story, honestly, eloquently, had been easier than she'd thought. It was a powerful way to contribute. And Madeleine had known it all along.

She held the leader's gaze for a second. Inclined her head twice. *Yes.* She would accept the role Madeleine had in mind for her. A welcome smile broke out over the older woman's face. Returning the nod, she turned and strode back to her office.

The room was almost empty now. Ruth finished speaking to Robyn and headed to Faith and Diane's table. There was an awkward silence.

Eventually, Ruth raised an eyebrow. "Well, it's good to see that the two of you are safe." Her voice was cool. "And that you found your way to Madeleine rather than the academy."

"You really thought that's where we'd go?" Diane burst out.

"We weren't sure *where* you'd go." Ruth said pointedly, her expression accusing. "Since you disappeared in the middle of the night without a word."

Diane rolled her eyes. "It's not like you'd have let us leave if we'd asked nicely."

Ruth's eyes flashed with a sudden anger. "Jacob's blaming Ella for what you did."

"What? No!" Faith's hand flew to her mouth. "But we... we made sure that we knocked her out."

"With Sleepsol. Which is *harmless*." Ruth emphasised the word. "Not like Carl, who you clobbered over the head with a pretty sturdy branch."

"Is he alright?" Faith asked tentatively.

"I didn't–" Diane looked horror-struck. "He's not dead, is he?"

Ruth's eyes came to rest on her. "No, thankfully. But his injury was pretty severe. And once he told Jacob how Ella was nice to you all..."

"We're sorry." Diane leaned forward. "*Really* we are. We only wanted..." she glanced at Faith.

"We came back to help Sophia," Faith finished for her. "We never meant for–"

"I know." Ruth sat down with a heavy sigh. "I told them. I knew that was why you'd gone." She shrugged helplessly. "But it didn't help. Jacob has her locked up like your academy friends."

Faith felt a stab of guilt. "Can I ask how the rest of the Danforth girls are?"

"He didn't blame them too, did he?" Diane scowled.

Ruth shook her head. "He presumed they'd have gone with you if they'd known." She shifted position on the bench. "I haven't seen all that much of them to be honest. Jacob's being very picky who he allows to see them. But they're not being mistreated. He values them more, since…"

"…since he lost us," Faith finished.

There was an awkward silence. Diane drummed a finger against the table. Eventually, she jumped to her feet.

"Are you hungry?" She glanced at Ruth, her expression eager. "I could make you something. Toast and coffee, maybe?"

"Yes, please." Ruth's instant acceptance made Faith wonder when she'd last eaten.

"How come you didn't make it here til this morning?" Faith asked as Diane moved away.

"As well as making contact with the Resistance, I was supposed to infiltrate the Bellator guard." She shuddered. "Hence the uniform you saw me wearing. After I saw you yesterday, I spent the day trying to talk to some of Danforth's protectors."

Faith suppressed a shudder. "Weren't you afraid you'd be discovered?"

"I was terrified." Ruth admitted. "But since the explosion in the forest, Danforth's been doing a lot of recruiting. I guess there've been a lot of new faces."

"You discover anything useful?"

"The new guards are incredibly inexperienced." Diane returned with a cup of coffee, which Ruth accepted with a grateful smile.

"Toast's on its way." Diane wandered back towards the kitchen.

"The older guards don't feel safe fighting alongside the newbies. They haven't had more than a couple of month's training. And," Ruth took a sip of her coffee, "there are a lot of rumours going round about guards disappearing."

"Understandably so." Faith thought about the missing patrol. "Are the guards who stumbled on the tunnel dead?"

Ruth grimaced. "Most of them. One surrendered. She's now a prisoner with the others." Ruth grimaced. "Not that we can spare the extra food. Jacob insists they're all important, though I can't think a single guard with minimal experience will be valued as highly as Helen, Mary, Farrah, or Avery."

At the mention of her old enemy's name, Faith's heart lurched. Speaking of Avery, there's something you should know."

Ruth raised an eyebrow but waited for Faith to continue.

"I was in the library a couple of days ago, looking at old documents. I found some birth records going back years. There was a lot of info there, but one which I feel the Eremus council should know about specifically."

"About Avery?"

Faith nodded. "She's... well, she's Danforth's daughter."

Ruth's eyes widened. "You're kidding."

"No." Faith watched the steam rise from Ruth's coffee. "It makes sense, though. She's always been a stalwart believer in Danforth's philosophy about the male of the species. *Unswerving*. Even when the evidence in Eremus was to the contrary."

Ruth glanced at the door to the office. "How did Madeleine react?"

"Haven't had the chance to tell her yet." Nerves shot through Faith as she considered how the leader might react. "I'm going to do it today."

"And you're okay with me letting people in Eremus know?"

"I think the council should be aware of all the information. If Avery comes back to the city, knowing what she does about Eremus, she'd pose an extremely dangerous threat." Faith shuddered.

Diane reappeared with a plate of toast. "Here you are." She peered into Ruth's face. "You look exhausted. Faith can show you to the dorm once you're done eating. Grab a couple of hours sleep before you head back, okay?"

"Thanks." Ruth spoke through a mouthful of toast. "I will."

"Make sure you say goodbye before you leave." She turned to Faith. "I have to go and help Blake with something."

The Eremus girl's eyes followed her. "Who's Blake?"

Faith watched her devour the food, wondering again how hungry she had been when she'd arrived. "Blake's our resident tech genius. Has a whole room crammed with devices that do who-knows-what. Diane finds them fascinating." She rolled her eyes and was grateful when Ruth smiled.

"It's odd that you said *our*," Ruth said, without malice. "You really feel like you belong here?"

Faith considered her words. "I didn't. Not at first. But maybe I'm adjusting." She shrugged. "Seriously though, Blake's brilliant. Scary," Faith mock-shivered, "but brilliant. She can access cameras in key locations all over the city. It's how we found Sophia."

Ruth's eyes widened above the steaming cup of coffee. "I've been meaning to ask. You got her to safety, then?" She cast a gaze around the room. "Where is she?"

"We didn't rescue her. Not yet." Faith took a breath to quell the tears that pricked her eyes at the thought of her friend. "She's in the hospital, hooked up to a ton of machines. Security's pretty tough. But we're working on it." *I hope*, she added silently.

"At least you know where she is. That's the first step." Finishing the last bite of toast, she yawned. "Could you find me that bed now, please? I'm shattered, but I should set off back to Eremus as soon as it gets dark."

"Of course." Faith stood up and motioned to the door. "It's this way."

As they walked along the hallway towards the dorm, Ruth nudged Faith. "I *told* him she was the reason you left."

Faith's heart beat a little faster. "What do you mean?"

"Noah. I told him you came back here because of Sophia." She glanced sideways at Faith. "Was kind of hoping you'd rescued her already. He might feel less..."

Faith's eyes filled with tears. "He's angry, isn't he?"

"He misses you."

They reached the dorm and Faith gestured for Ruth to follow her inside. "This is my bed. You're welcome to use it for as long as you like." She turned to face the other girl. "He really misses me?"

"Of course, he does." She sat down on the bed and began pulling off her boots. "He's just... angry... because it felt like you abandoned him. I tried to tell him you hadn't left *him*, you'd gone *to* your best friend."

Faith choked back tears at the other girls' understanding. "Did he get it?"

"Not at first. Not until I put it in terms he couldn't argue with."

"How did you manage that?"

She grinned wickedly. "I just asked what he'd do if I'd been kidnapped."

"And it worked?"

"Oh yes."

"Thanks... for convincing him." Faith swallowed hard. "I couldn't bear the thought of him hating me."

Ruth laughed. "I don't think he could ever hate you. See, as I said, he cares about me. A lot." She lay back on the bed, giving Faith an appraising look. "But the way he feels about you? That's something totally different."

Chapter Fourteen: Noah

"Where do you think you're going?"

Noah stopped short. Ahead of him, leaning against the side of the tunnel which led to the raider training cave, was Harden.

"I heard..." Noah paused, puzzled at the expression on Harden's face. He looked almost... guilty. "Someone mentioned they'd seen Ruth coming in. Said she was heading for the canteen, but she isn't there, so..."

"What makes y'think she's here?"

Noah leaned to one side, peering at the darkened tunnel ahead. ""The weird way you're acting, for a start. Something's not right."

Harden took a step towards him. "Everything's fine, Madden. Go back the way you came."

Noah took a breath. He had no wish to tangle with Harden again. Not after their previous altercation. But something was going on.

Ever since his conversation with Flynn the previous day, he'd been anxiously awaiting his friend's return. The more he thought about his drudge idea, the more excited he was to see if it could work. Ruth's news from the Resistance headquarters would give him a better idea of how he might pull it off.

He'd been on his way home from a foraging shift when he'd heard she was back. He'd set off right away to find her.

Several people had directed him to the canteen, but there had been no sign of her when he'd arrived. Cora had shooed him out, shaking her head and muttering about the ridiculous number of people expecting food early today.

When he'd pressed her on the subject, Cora had rolled her eyes and told him Sarah had already been in to collect enough food for four or five people. *Before* dinner was actually ready, she'd complained. *And* when rations were so tight. Curious, Noah had headed for the council meeting cave. On the way, he'd run into Mick, who mentioned seeing Jacob heading for the training caves. Following his instincts, he'd done an abrupt about turn.

Harden's caginess was the last straw. Ruth was here, and, if he was right, Jacob had hurried her away so he could grill her about her time in the city before anyone else. Frustrated, he went to step past Harden, but was stopped as a hand squarely hit the middle of his chest.

"Are you seriously on *guard*?" Noah gestured up the tunnel behind him. "Stopping anyone from getting through until Jacob's finished torturing her?"

"He's not torturing her, he just wanted to question her without–" Harden snapped his mouth shut.

"So she *is* down there." Noah should have been triumphant, but all he felt was a growing sense of concern. "She was supposed to talk to the entire council when she got back. That was the agreement. Not just Jacob and your ma. That is who's down there with her, right?"

Harden raised an eyebrow but refused to be drawn in any further.

Don't touch me. Ever. Harden's words rang in Noah's ears. But Ruth was in trouble.

Taking a deep breath, Noah tried to push past, but this time he found himself crashing into Harden's very solid chest. He was as strong as ever. A fierce shove and Noah found himself staggering backwards.

Fire flared within him. Recovering his balance, he tried to dodge around him the other way, but only made it a few steps before Harden was on his heels.

"You are *not* getting past me," the older boy hissed, grasping Noah by the hood of his sweatshirt. It choked him as he was hauled backwards.

There was a ferocity in Harden's manner which put Noah on edge. He sounded desperate, as though he were spoiling for a fight. Noah struggled for a moment longer, but the grip was vice-like. Noah remembered the time he'd made the mistake of punching Paulo. He'd lived to regret that. And Harden wasn't his brother. Harden would never go easy on him.

Eventually, he stilled, allowing his body to relax. "Alright, alright."

Harden let go of him abruptly and he staggered backwards again. "Didn't think so."

Noah felt a small surge of satisfaction as his enemy recovered himself. His struggle had forced Harden to get out of breath, at least. And as the other boy folded his arms across his chest, he seemed a little rattled.

Noah was about to turn and leave, but something stopped him. Instead, he wandered to the side of the tunnel and leaned against the wall, keeping his gaze on Harden.

The other boy frowned. "You planning on staying there?"

"Maybe. I mean, you won't let me pass, and I know my best friend's down there with people I don't trust, so…"

Harden shifted, clearly uncomfortable. "You'll be there a long time, Madden."

Noah shrugged. "That's fine." The other boy looked away and fell silent. "I thought you said you admired her."

Harden's gaze jumped to Noah's. "What?"

"The other day when we spoke. You said Ruth was brave."

"She is. So?"

"So you admire her, but you're prepared to do this?"

"Just following orders." Harden shrugged.

"Do you always follow orders without question?" Noah thought back to the last job Harden had done for Jacob. "Even if you think they're dangerous?"

"She's not in any danger." But there was a flash of guilt in Harden's eyes.

"Do you know that for sure? I mean… did you see her?" Harden gave a terse nod, and Noah couldn't resist continuing. "Was she okay?"

He glared but answered. "Looked fine to me."

Noah hesitated, wondering how many more questions Harden would tolerate before turning violent again. "You get the impression things went well in the city?"

"No idea."

"Did she mention Madeleine?" Harden remained silent, but his expression told Noah she had. "She found the Resistance, then?"

"Like I said, I *don't know.*" Harden's face darkened "Shut up. Unless you want a punch in the face?"

Knowing he'd pushed his luck, Noah fell silent. He was debating what to do next when he heard the sound of raised voices coming from the direction of the training cave. Pushing off the tunnel side, he took a few steps forward, straining to hear what was being said. Harden had also tensed, one hand going automatically to the knife in his belt. Noah wondered who he was anticipating using it on.

Frustratingly, though the voices were loud, none of the words themselves could be made out. But there was definitely one male and one female voice. Noah's heart lurched in his chest.

"*Still* think she's not in any danger?" He snarled at Harden.

"She's fine." But the glances his enemy kept shooting back over his shoulder told a different story.

Noah drew in a deep breath. Ruth was alone, with Jacob and Sarah. There was an argument going on. He owed it to his friend to at least attempt a rescue. But Harden had just proved he wouldn't be an easy target. He was racking his brain for the best way to outwit him when he heard footsteps behind him.

Harden's face fell. Noah turned to see Flynn and Paulo approaching, with several other council members in tow. Relieved, he stepped towards them.

Flynn's face was filled with concern. "Is Ruth–?" He jerked a hand down the tunnel.

"Yes. She's been here around an hour, I think. Jacob and Sarah are–"

Flynn waved him away impatiently. "Suspected as much." He turned to Harden, who looked far less sure of himself now that he was facing a larger opposition. "What's going on back there?"

For a moment, Noah was sure that Harden was going to attempt to argue with the older man, but after a second's pause, he scowled.

"Jacob and my ma are speaking to Ruth, that's all."

"That's all?" Paulo stepped closer to Harden, his voice icy. "Why does he have her alone? How does *that* show his trust in the council as a collective?"

"This isn't what was agreed." Flynn gestured behind Harden. "It doesn't encourage trust. It's just Jacob going behind our backs. *Again.*"

Harden flushed. "He's only talking to her. Asking her how things went in the city."

"Why didn't he wait for us though?" Flynn fumed. Shooting another look down the tunnel behind Harden, he glanced at Paulo. "We have to get down there."

Nodding, Paulo grasped hold of Harden's shoulder, pressing him back against the tunnel wall. Harden yelped as his back hit the rock.

"What's Jacob's aim?" Paulo's gaze was piercing. He leaned closer, pushing Harden further into the wall. "What's he trying to achieve?"

Harden's face was purple as he twisted uselessly. He was no match for Paulo.

"He only wants to know what Ruth found out about Danforth's guard." He was breathing hard. "He... he has plans for the city if... if the guard is as depleted as he thinks they are."

"Plans?" Paulo's voice was cold. "Then we'd better get down there and discuss them with him, hadn't we? I'm sure he doesn't want the council to *miss out* on his plans. Especially when we specifically agreed he wouldn't keep things from us anymore."

With a final shove, he released Harden. Sweeping him out of the way with his arm, Paulo and Flynn charged down the tunnel. Harden recovered quickly and trailed after the two men, closely followed by the other council members. Left alone, Noah glanced in both directions. On the one hand, this was private council business. But no one had told him he couldn't be there. Flynn and Paulo might need his support.

Pushing any concerns aside, he hurried along the tunnel to the training cave. Inside, Flynn and Paulo faced Jacob, whose face was a mask of fury. Ruth stood to one side, a grim smile on her face now that she was no longer alone. And in the far corner, Harden had moved to stand beside his ma, whose body was rigid with tension.

Noah slipped inside without notice. The only eyes which were drawn to him were Ruth's. Her smile widened for a second, and then her focus snapped back to the men in the centre of the space. Noah's gaze followed hers, attempting to gauge the mood.

"We agreed." Flynn's face was stone. "You said we would make the next decisions together, openly, without any of this subterfuge."

Jacob had regained some semblance of control. "Of course. I merely spotted Ruth returning and was curious to discover what she had learned in the city."

"Nice try." Paulo was almost spitting. "But that's not what this looks like."

"You just keep on disappointing us." Flynn glared at Jacob. "We only heard by accident that Ruth was back."

"I assure you," Jacob's voice was tight, "we were about to send for–"

Noah had taken a step forward before he knew what was happening. "That's not true." Every eye in the room jumped to him, and he took a breath to prevent his voice from trembling. "When I got here, Harden was on guard. He wouldn't let me past. He'd been put on guard to keep people away."

"Interesting." Flynn's tone was cold. "Sounds like you're trying to feed us lies again." His eyes flicked from Jacob, to Sarah. "*How* can we trust you, if you keep doing this?"

Jacob stepped forward, his eyes flashing. "How can *you* be so naïve?" There was venom in his voice. "You continue to believe we can beat Danforth without playing dirty. It's almost amusing how dense you are. At least it would be, if it didn't make Eremus so *weak*."

"What?" Flynn recoiled from the verbal attack. "I don't think–"

"You think too much, that's your problem. And you don't *act*." Flynn began to protest, but Jacob pressed on, counting off the issues on his fingers. "You refuse to consider my ideas to defeat the chancellor. You insist on waiting, taking our time, making sure we limit the loss of life when we attack." He sneered. "It's ridiculous. I take out a *huge* proportion of Danforth's guard and you don't want to take immediate action? You want to delay, when we have our best chance in years to get at her? Seems to me you're scared." He took a step back, gesturing to the other council members in the cave. "*All* of you."

"We have *always* attempted to limit the loss of life." Flynn was tightlipped, and Noah knew he was fighting to keep control. "Of both Eremus citizens and those in Bellator. They are not all responsible for our situation. Most of them know nothing about who we really are."

"You're right they're not responsible. But who is?" As he jabbed a finger in Flynn's face, it crossed Noah's mind that he might be crazy. "Danforth. And it's Danforth we have to stop. Now. While her defences are down. We need to get in there, *now*, all guns blazing, destroy vital buildings, show the city we're–"

"Show the city we're *what*?" Paulo burst out, so loudly that Noah jumped. "I can't *believe* I used to think so much of you. If we do what you're suggesting, we cement the Bellator citizens's belief that we're violent, murdering bastards. It plays right into Danforth's hands! How would we go about living alongside them after *that*?"

Jacob gave a twisted smile. "And to think I had such high hopes for you as my lieutenant. Danforth controls the city. Danforth tells her citizens the lies about us. Danforth has treated men like dirt for years. We destroy Danforth, we have control. We can change the narrative. Danforth's the key."

"Danforth's who you're obsessed with, more like." Flynn spoke, his voice quiet and menacing. "And what you're suggesting is *not* what's in the best interests of Eremus. Not at all." He turned to the council members around him. "Are we agreed?"

Noah watched as the others in the cave nodded slowly. Jacob's gaze narrowed, and he took an uncertain step back. Whatever was being agreed on, he wasn't privy to it.

Flynn turned back to him, his face calm and determined. "We'd like you to leave while we speak to Ruth."

"What?" Jacob laughed. "Not likely."

"Yes." Flynn continued, his voice even. "We gave you the chance to show us that we could trust you. You failed. Spectacularly. You do not deserve to hear what she has to say. We fear you'll use any information about Bellator to your advantage and we will no longer allow you to have that power. You are hereby dismissed from the council."

"I don't think so." Jacob spluttered. "Do you really think, after *all* my hard work, I'll just walk away from this position?"

"We're hoping that you will, yes." Flynn took a step towards the leader. "And that we don't have to take any further, harsher action against you."

Several things happened at once. Jacob leapt forward, his fist flying towards Flynn's face. Paulo knocked Flynn sideways, out of harm's way. And Sarah was suddenly at Jacob's side, her face twisted. She hauled him backwards and hissed something in his ear.

Whatever she said, it had some impact. Jacob dropped his hands, but his body remained tense. Breathing heavily, he placed his hands on his knees. Noah glanced at Flynn, whose face was impassive. He waited, calmly, for Jacob's next action, anticipating anything, saying nothing.

Eventually, Jacob stood up. "If that's how you feel, I'll go." He sucked in a long breath. "For now. We'll talk again later, when things are calmer."

"We'll see." Flynn gave a tight nod. "If you demonstrate calm and sensible behaviour over the coming days."

Jacob glowered but returned the nod. "Fine."

Jerking his head at the door, he swept past the remaining council members. Sarah stalked after him, her head high. At the door, she paused and glanced back at her son. Harden was frozen in place.

"Harden?" she hissed.

As though emerging from a trance, his gaze snapped to hers. "Coming." He ducked his head and trailed after her.

Silence fell. For a few moments, the remaining citizens in the cave listened to the retreating footsteps. When the sound had gone, Flynn turned to the group.

"Well, we suspected that might happen." He rolled his shoulders tiredly. "I guess it could have been worse."

Ruth crossed the cave to him, her face earnest. "Thank you."

"No problem."

"When I got back it was almost like he'd been waiting for me." She chewed on her lip. "Carl was scouting in the forest, on Jacob's orders, I guess. Must've seen me coming. The minute I stepped inside the tunnels, Harden was there. Said the council was waiting. Hurried me here like we were running from an enemy."

Noah stepped forward. "They didn't want people to see you."

Ruth shuddered. "I can see that now. Once I got here and it was just Jacob and Sarah, I knew something was up. I tried to leave, but he assured me you were all on your way. Started to ask me what happened. I told him a little about my journey, but then I got suspicious and said I'd rather wait." She winced. "That's when he started threatening me."

Paulo's face turned red. "Threatening you?"

"Yeah. Told me Ella would suffer if I didn't tell him exactly what I'd learned, and before the rest of you arrived."

"Really?" Flynn turned to the others. "He's out of control, if he's threatening members of our own community. Do we agree this was the right thing to do?"

"You had a plan in place for this?" Noah asked.

Flynn glanced at the door of the cave. "We did. We've been working on the assumption that he isn't trustworthy for a while now. Decided we'd give him the chance to prove himself. But he's done quite the opposite."

"It's vital that we keep information from him now." Paulo said. "The more he knows, the more dangerous he is."

"I agree." Flynn's face was creased with concern. "But being shut out isn't going to go down well either. We need to watch him. And carefully." He turned to Ruth. "I'm sorry he put you through that. But I don't want him roaming the caves unchecked for long. Think you can give us a brief rundown of what you discovered in the city?"

Nodding, Ruth went to her backpack. "Of course." She opened the top and pulled out some items. "I was able to make contact with Madeleine. She gave me some basic resources to tide us over. And she said the Resistance was happy to help us with a supply raid in the near future." She turned to Flynn. "You should contact her to arrange it soon. I'm sure they want to make sure we're not going hungry."

There was a sigh of relief as she held up packs of batteries and some medicines. When she had displayed her wares, she sat back on her heels. "They're open to talking about us working together to change the situation with Danforth. She wants you to use the walkie talkies to contact her for more information now that we have batteries. She was a little cagey about it – said we'd have to prove our allegiance before they were willing to share confidential information. I'm not sure what she was after. But I guess you can discuss that with her yourself."

"Did you manage to infiltrate the guards at all?" Paulo cocked his head to one side. "I mean... it was Jacob's request, but if you did get some information, it might be useful."

"I did speak to a few of the guards, yes." She flushed. "Wasn't too hard to convince them I was just another newbie, since there are so many at the moment."

"Danforth's trying to fill the gap left by the guards we killed in the forest?" Flynn asked.

"Yes. But the older guards aren't happy. The new ones aren't properly trained, and the rest believe their lack of experience puts them all in more danger than if they weren't there at all."

A noise at the cave entrance made them all jump. But when Noah turned to see who was there, he was relieved to see his ma.

"Sorry – took me a while to find you all." She walked to the centre of the room. "I have the rest of the council waiting in the canteen." She cocked an eyebrow at Flynn. "How'd it go with Jacob?"

Flynn grimaced. "As expected."

"I'm sorry." Anna frowned. "Where is he now?"

"Unsure. He left of his own accord in the end, but he wasn't happy."

"Better keep a close eye on him, don't you think?"

"Of course." Flynn turned back to Ruth, who had started to pack the supplies away. "Was there anything else we needed to know?"

"One thing." Ruth zipped up her pack. "When I was at the Resistance headquarters, I saw Faith and Diane."

Noah's heart leapt. "Was she–" he caught Paulo's stern gaze and modified his tone. "I mean, were they...?"

"Both safe. They reached the library around a day and a half after leaving here." Ruth paused. "There's a lot more to fill you in on, but the main information Faith wanted me to pass on was something she herself discovered quite recently."

"Go on," Anna encouraged.

The cave was silent now, every person in the room hanging on her every word.

"She was in the library searching through some old papers when she found a record of births which showed the parentage of each Bellator citizen." She turned to Noah. "Bet you were in there, with a huge question mark over your whereabouts." She grinned, but catching Flynn's frustrated look, refocused quickly. "Anyway, she found an entry which indicated that *Danforth* has a child."

"What?" Noah's ma's face had gone white. "She's never made that public."

"Apparently not." Ruth chewed on her lip. "But it's not the fact that she has a daughter that's the most shocking. It's who the daughter is."

"Faith knew her?"

"We all know her." Ruth dropped her voice low. "In fact, she's here in Eremus. It's Avery."

A ripple of shock ran round the room. Flynn was the first to recover. "So you're saying we have Danforth's daughter here, with us. Our prisoner?"

"I am." Ruth turned to face him. "Faith and Diane didn't seem to think Avery knows... unless she's very good at hiding things. And since Danforth has never claimed Avery publicly, it seems likely she isn't that important to her, but... it's a revelation."

"It certainly is." Flynn scratched his head. "Alright. That information *definitely* doesn't leave this space, okay?"

There was a round of nods.

"Let's get out of here, then." Flynn waved a hand. "Speak to the rest of the council, start making plans. I'll contact Madeleine and see what assurances she wants, and we can start setting up a raid as soon as possible." He turned to Ruth. "Thank you."

She shrugged awkwardly. "It's fine."

Anna moved forward, pulling her into a hug. "You don't know how much you've done for us. Well done." Letting her go, she stood back. "Guess you deserve a break." She turned to a tray of untouched food which lay on the ground nearby. Noah remembered Cora's complaint about Sarah's earlier visit to the canteen. "We can't let that go to waste. How about you two eat it and take a break... I'm sure you'd like to catch up. Bring the leftovers to Cora when you're done."

The council members who had accompanied Flynn to confront Jacob had already begun to leave. Anna hurried after them. As their footsteps retreated down the tunnel, Noah settled down next to Ruth against the wall on the opposite side of the space. Leaning their heads back against the wall, they sat in companionable silence for several minutes. Noah had questions, so many questions. But they could wait.

Reaching a hand out, he squeezed Ruth's and smiled. "I'm glad you're–" he began in a whisper, but her grip tightened on his.

They both froze. From the cave behind the one they sat in, there was a sound. A shuffling, followed by a single set of footsteps moving across the space. Noah met Ruth's gaze with a look of alarm. The cave next door contained weapons supplies stored in boxes stacked on top of one another. It provided an excellent place to hide. And also, they knew from experience, was a good place from which to hear the conversations which were going on in the raiders' cave.

Holding a finger to his lips, Noah slipped off his trainers and pushed silently to his feet. Tiptoeing across the cave, he halted at the entrance and peered out. Further along, a figure darted out into the tunnel and hurried in the direction the rest of the council had just gone. It was dark, the space shadowy, but the figure's bulk was unmistakable.

Noah's heart sank. When Jacob had been sent away, he had left behind a spy to listen to Ruth's information. A spy who would no doubt now report straight back to him. A spy who had sneaked into the adjoining cave while Jacob and Sarah had retreated.

Harden.

Chapter Fifteen: Faith

Faith quaked as the journalist's eyes bored into her. On the surface, she was a mousy-looking woman, but as soon as she'd started asking questions, Faith's opinion of her had changed. The timid exterior she'd perfected made a good front, but Stella Thane was sharp as a tack.

A Resistance sympathiser, she worked undercover at the *Bellator Blade*. As soon as Faith had agreed to act as Resistance spokesperson, Madeleine had brought Stella in for an interview. The city's media was government-controlled, and the news channel wasn't able to print or broadcast anything which wasn't approved by the chancellor.

Stella's position was delicate, and she had to be extremely careful what she wrote in the *Blade*. But she conveyed her real thoughts through an anonymous broadcast where she could comment on political issues freely. Madeleine had been feeding her pieces of information for *Bellator Exposed* for months, but Faith's input would be the start of a more targeted campaign, aimed at waking up the citizens to the constant lies they were fed by their chancellor.

In addition to the online newspaper, the *Blade* also printed a number of old-fashioned physical copies, popular with some of the city's older residents. This gave Stella access to a printing press, which Madeleine wanted to commandeer. A leaflet containing information about the existence of Eremus or the suspicious medical experiments going on in the city was the leader's initial aim. She was hoping it would help them to spread the word more widely and get the message across to those citizens who weren't aware of Stella's underground broadcast.

Madeleine was convinced that Faith's information would be vital in opening the citizens' eyes to the corruption. Faith wasn't so sure. Despite having made the decision to help the Resistance in this way, she was nervous. And Stella's gruelling questions hadn't put her any more at ease.

They had been talking for what seemed like hours now. Faith had recounted her experience with the femgazipane in as much detail as she could. The dizziness, the vomiting, the exhaustion. How she had struggled to even walk across a small room to use the bathroom. The reason she'd been alone, locked in the small room. The food she'd been permitted to eat. The amount of exercise she'd managed to complete whilst imprisoned.

So much had happened since the experience that Faith struggled to remember the details. Those she did recall, she had trouble recounting as they only reminded her of what Sophia was going through at the moment, alone in her hospital room. But as the interview rolled on, she had done her best to answer honestly.

How long the drug affected her? Which symptoms had stayed with her the longest? What follow up tests had she been given? When she'd gone to Eremus, what kind of diet had she experienced? Had her symptoms worsened or improved as a result of the food or the limited exercise she'd been permitted whilst staying at the cave settlement?

The questions went on and on, many of them seeming irrelevant. The journalist was thorough, Faith had to give her that. And Faith really wanted to be useful. She couldn't shake the feeling that Sophia's fate was directly related to the depth of her responses.

But after two hours of grilling, she was exhausted. "I really don't think there's any more I can tell you. I'm sorry."

Blinking, Stella looked up from her datadev. "That's alright. I just want to make sure I have everything I need." The journalist glanced at Madeleine. When her eyes returned to Faith, they were serious. "You said when you first arrived in Eremus you weren't conscious."

"That's right."

"When you regained consciousness, where were you?"

Faith frowned. "In the large cave which acts as their canteen."

"And you were dressed the same way you had been when you were kidnapped outside the hospital?"

"Yes."

"You're certain?" Stella pressed. "They hadn't stripped you off... couldn't have—"

Realising what she was suggesting, Faith's cheeks flushed. "No!"

Stella gestured to Faith's jeans and sweatshirt. "Can you describe what you were wearing when you left the academy?"

"My uniform." Faith forced her tone to remain polite, resenting the implication that she might not be remembering the experience accurately. "We all were."

"And that includes...?" the journalist prompted. Noting Faith's mutinous expression, she clarified. "I just want you to be *certain* you were still dressed the same way when you woke up in the caves."

"I *am* certain." But Faith could see Stella wasn't going to be happy until she answered. "Black tailored trousers, a shirt... a white shirt..." She ticked off the items on her fingers, "a jacket with the school badge on the lapel."

Stella raised an eyebrow. "*Every* item, please."

"Black shoes, socks, underwear, bra, academy pendant..." Faith blushed as she thought of the necklace she'd left with Noah. "Wait... no. I didn't have the pendant on."

Stella sat forward. "They took it from you?"

"No! I didn't have it on when I left the academy. I hadn't..." She hesitated, unsure of how much to tell the stranger. A glance at Madeleine's face told her to tell the truth, or at least as close to the truth as possible. "I'd, um... lost it. A couple of days before Anderson locked me up."

"Alright. And the uniform... you were *definitely* dressed the same way once you got to Eremus?" Faith nodded. "Alright. Thank you."

Relieved that Stella finally seemed satisfied, Faith sneaked a look at Madeleine. Was she satisfied with her responses? She was still hopeful that the leader's stance on rescuing Sophia might change if Faith helped her in this way. But Madeleine wasn't even looking at Faith. Instead, her gaze was fixed on Stella, the intensity of her gaze quite frightening.

Finally, the journalist looked up. "Alright. I think I have what I need." She turned to Madeleine. "I'll write this up tonight and try to broadcast it tomorrow. You know how it is... I might not get all the information out the first time. Depends how long it is before they shut me down."

"Shut you down?" Faith was puzzled.

"Danforth always has her tech staff on alert. They try to get me off the air as fast as they can, once they know I'm broadcasting." Stella shrugged. "Madeleine even sent Blake to look at my set-up, but even with her help they usually find my frequency sooner or later. Once they have, that's it."

"That's it?"

"Until the next broadcast, when I set up on a different channel and try again."

Madeleine gave a sly grin. "They never manage to shut you down completely though."

"Nope." Stella chuckled. "Not so far, anyway." She turned back to the Resistance leader. "The physical leaflets will take a little longer. I can only access the presses on certain nights."

"Alright. When you have them ready, let me know. I'll arrange for them to be collected. We're aiming to distribute them throughout the city but doing that without being detected will be a real challenge."

Stella turned to Faith. "Thanks for being so honest with me. There's just the picture left now." She frowned at the cuts and bruises, which were still inflamed. "Though we might want to take it at an angle."

Faith's heart sank. "Do you *have* to have a photograph?"

"We do." Madeleine was firm.

Stella leaned forward. "There's *nothing* more powerful than an innocent victim endangered by those in power. But we need them to *see* you. To know how young you are, how innocent."

"Okay." Faith glanced around the room. "Where do you want me?"

Stella was already glancing around the room looking for potential places to take the picture. "Stand against that wall, please." She turned to Madeleine as she hustled Faith into place. "I'll crop out anything that would give away her location, of course."

"Sure." Madeleine had returned to her usual position behind her datadev.

"Can you turn your head towards the door?" Stella gestured with her hand. "A little more... that's it. Now we can't see your injuries at all."

Faith allowed herself to be posed and positioned as Stella wished. As the Resistance's representative, she needed to look professional, to present the group as serious and organised. Not like its spokesperson was a bareknuckle fighter who'd been dragged off the streets. Or someone who had been beaten by the Eremus men, if Danforth spun the story the way Madeleine suggested she would.

When the journalist was finished, she patted Faith on the shoulder. "All done."

As Stella began to pack her camera equipment away, Madeleine looked up from her work.

"Thank you, Faith. I know this wasn't an easy thing for you to do, but I'm certain it will make a difference." Madeleine shrugged. "I hope you can see now that this is where your strengths lie. You've more than made up for the issues you caused on the BellaLab mission. I mean, between this and your discovery about Danforth having a *child*..."

Faith felt herself blushing at the mention of the failed mission. She hurried to cover her embarrassment. "What will you do with the information about Avery?"

Madeleine pursed her lips. "Not sure, as yet. I'm waiting for Eremus to get in touch. For now, the best thing to do is to keep her there, out of sight. I do have a few of our spies trying to discover more about the relationship, but a secret that's been buried this long, well... I suspect very few people know about it."

"You won't... do anything to put her at risk though?" Faith disliked the older girl but didn't want her to be hurt. Being so closely linked to Danforth would make her a pawn in a very dangerous game, should the wrong people decide to use the information to their advantage. "Or let Eremus hurt her."

"No!" The reply was rapid and definite. "She's a Bellator citizen, same as you or me. We would never wish her harm." Madeleine stood up and moved towards the door. "Would you excuse Stella and me? We've much to discuss, and we're finished with you for the time being."

Dismissed, Faith followed the Resistance leader to the door. As she pulled it open, Madeleine's voice stopped her. "I meant what I said. Thanks for agreeing to do this. I know it's going to make a real difference."

Faith heard the door close behind her. Outside in the common area, she found that her hands were shaking. It was over, for now. But what was she getting herself into?

She headed through the hub towards Blake's room, wanting to check on Sophia. In all the chaos of the last few days, she'd had little time to dwell on her friend's situation. Easing the door open, she peered in. It took a few moments for her eyes to adjust to the low light, but when she made out a single figure, her heart sank.

Hoping that Blake might be so involved in her work that she hadn't heard her enter, Faith began tiptoeing backwards. The other woman was leaning close to one of the monitors, engrossed, as usual. But she wasn't seated in her usual position. Instead, she was staring at the monitor which displayed Sophia's hospital bed.

Faith froze. It wasn't like the tech genius to involve herself in the drama going on at the hospital. She had actively gone out of her way to state how she had no time to sit staring at a girl who did nothing but sleep when she had so many other tasks to complete. Yet here she was, transfixed.

Reversing her retreat, Faith took a step into the room, craning her neck to see what had the other woman glued to the screen. Her movement alerted the other woman to her presence. But instead of shooing her away or glaring, Blake turned and beckoned her over.

"Something's happening." She frowned, tapping a finger on the screen. "Not sure what as yet. But something."

Keeping her eyes on Sophia, Faith hauled a second stool over from the corner and sat down. Blake was right. There were two people in the room, when Faith had only ever seen one. The first was small and wore the ordinary scrubs of a medic. The other was tall and thin. She wore a lab coat, denoting her status as a doctor. Faith squinted at the screen, her hackles rising. It was Dr. Sanders, who had visited Faith in her prison cell at the academy and injected her with femgazipane. Sanders had first arrived at the academy dressed in a technician's uniform, presumably hoping no one would recognise her. The next time Faith had seen her, she had realised Sanders was actually the doctor in charge of Danforth's entire experiment.

Breathlessly, Faith counted the machines which surrounded her friend. There were still four, and they didn't look to be set up any differently. Not for the first time, she wished that she was able to zoom in on the dials and readouts on each one. Lily had used her limited medical knowledge to try and explain their purpose, but she hadn't been able to identify what procedure Sophia was undergoing.

The atmosphere in the hospital room seemed to change, somehow. Faith could tell, even without sound. She and Blake strained closer to the screen.

"What are they...?" Blake whispered.

Dr. Sanders had moved to one side of the bed. She was bending over Sophia, partly obscuring her body from view. But as the petite medic moved towards one of the machines, she straightened up. The two exchanged glances, nodding at one another. Slowly, the woman twisted a dial on the front of the large metal machine, her eyes were glued to the numbers on the readout.

"Looks like they're altering her dosage," Blake muttered.

"Increasing it, do you think?" Faith felt sick.

But Blake was consulting a set of notes on a different screen. "I don't think so. Lily said that machine is probably administering a sedative." She looked back at Faith. "It's making sure she stays unconscious."

"But too much of that would be harmful, surely." Faith's stomach flipped over, and she found she was digging her nails into her palms. "If they're increasing the amount of that, they could kill her."

"I don't think they're *increasing* it." Blake tapped a finger on the screen.

Dr. Sanders was leaning over Sophia again, obscuring their view. The other medic returned to the bedside, lifting Sophia's head so she could slide another pillow underneath it. When the pair backed away, their eyes were glued to their patient.

"She's *reducing* it." Blake hissed. "Look!"

Faith leaned closer to the screen again. Now that Sanders and the medic had moved, she could see her friend clearly. Sophia lay, propped up on the extra pillows. And her eyelids were flickering.

"She's awake." Blake slapped her hand on Faith's back, almost choking her. "She's actually awake."

CHAPTER SIXTEEN: NOAH

Noah closed his eyes and willed himself to stay calm. They were going round in circles, and had been for the past half hour. So far, his ma refused to budge.

"How many times do I have to say it?" Her fingers twisted in the wool of her cardigan. "Flynn and I think it's too dangerous." Her voice softened. "What you did in the tunnels was brave. We acknowledge that. And I know you *think* you'd be prepared for this, but–"

"I might *not* be prepared, Ma," he leaned forward, "but I have to do *something*."

The moment Noah had mentioned the idea of posing as a drudge, he'd known he was going to struggle to bring his parents round to the idea. His ma hadn't quite forbidden him to go yet. But no matter how many times he explained his plan, she was resolutely against it.

"I'm trying to do the mature thing, Ma. Talk to you about it. Get your blessing." Her lips tightened, but he tried again. "I can't just sit here while other people fight for my freedom. I'm not a child anymore."

"I know you're not." She sighed. "And I understand that you want to play your part, believe me."

"Then why can't you–"

"You don't know Bellator the way I do." Pulling away from him, she wrapped the cardigan around her tightly. "You weren't brought up in a world that contained drudges." Her eyes flickered to his, pleading with him to understand. "The way they act, move, *serve*... it's so different from what you're used to."

"But surely I can *learn*. I know I'm not like them now, but–"

"You're *nothing* like them." Fierce pride shone in her eyes. "You've grown up with freedom, independence, the ability to speak your mind. You're rational. Educated, at least as well as I could manage." She gave a faint smile. "I'd even call you confident, these days."

"You admit I've grown up, then." Noah seized on the praise. "So why can't you trust that I'd be–"

"I trust *you*, Noah." She shuddered. "It's the people in Bellator I don't trust. As a drudge, one tiny slip is all it would take for–"

"Look at what Ruth just did for Eremus." Leaning forward, Noah grasped his ma's hand. "Her visit to Bellator, *undercover*, has been the start of something new. She's opened up the possibility of Eremus working much more closely with the Resistance. Helping them, the way they've helped us in the past. Acting *together*, because, in the end, we want the same thing." He paused, making sure she met his gaze. "That's huge. It brings us a step closer to gaining equality for our community. It's what we've always wanted."

Since Ruth's return the previous day, a lot had happened. Furious with the council for demoting him, Jacob had retreated to his own quarters. Nothing had been seen of him since the confrontation. Sarah was keeping him supplied with food and he had so far refused the council's offers to talk. Some claimed he was sulking, nursing his wounds. But others were concerned that he might have more sinister plans in mind.

With everything he knew about Eremus, Jacob was certainly capable of causing trouble. The complete loss of power would not sit well with the man who had spent so long building up the community. The council was keeping a close eye on him. But so far, all he had done was to shun the company of everyone but his inner circle.

More worrying was the conversation that Harden had overheard. Flynn had gone to speak to him about it after Noah had returned to the cave the previous night, but Harden had denied all knowledge. He had returned to collect a sweatshirt he'd left in the tunnel, he'd said, and knew nothing of any conversation between Noah and Ruth.

Flynn hadn't believed him, but unless he admitted it, there was little they could do. They had agreed to keep a close eye on the young man, but with so much going on, they could barely spare the manpower.

In Jacob's absence, Flynn and Anna had taken charge. Their first priority had been to contact Madeleine and arrange the supply raid. But they had also begun to discuss their common goals, putting forth the idea of working more closely with the Resistance to achieve them.

Madeleine had been fairly open to the idea. With a few caveats which would demonstrate Eremus' loyalty, she felt the two groups would be stronger together. Her first request had been that they allow Professor Kemp, an important part of their spy network, to return to Bellator. Anna had spent the previous day discussing a possible cover story with her old friend, and Noah knew she was excited about the prospect of positive change.

But she had dropped her gaze from his. "I know all that. And we're so grateful to Ruth for taking on the mission, but–"

"But *what*?" Noah took a breath, aware that his tone was growing dangerously close to anger. "Ruth's the same age as me. She just doesn't have a ma around to stop her anymore."

When his ma pulled her hand away, he knew he had gone too far. Ruth's ma, Dawn, had died a few months ago, leaving Ella and Ruth to fend for themselves. It had brought the sisters closer, in many ways, but meant they didn't have an authority figure to make their decisions for them.

Anna had been close to Dawn, and still missed her. It had been a low blow to mention her now.

"I'm sorry." He hung his head. "That wasn't fair."

For a second, she didn't reply. He raised his eyes to hers, expecting the worst. But instead of looking angry, she was wiping away tears.

"You're right." Her voice was a whisper. "I'm being overprotective. I just can't stand the thought of losing you."

This time, she reached for *his* hand. But before she could say anything more, there were hurried footsteps in the tunnel. As they turned towards the noise, Flynn burst into the cave, his eyes wild.

"He's gone."

Anna's eyes widened. "Who's gone?"

Tugging the privacy curtain across the cave entrance, Flynn moved inside. "Jacob. We've searched the caves. There's no sign of him."

Anna got to her feet. "You're sure?"

Flynn threw himself into a chair. "I checked his cave. A lot of his personal stuff is missing. And not only that. Sarah and Harden's living space has been cleared out. Carl too. And Denton."

"You think they all went together?" But Noah knew they had. The missing people were all Jacob's supporters. "Where would they go?" His mind reeled as he considered the consequences. "What did they take with them?"

Flynn rubbed a tired hand across his forehead. They had known the loss of Jacob's leadership position would infuriate him and suspected they hadn't heard the end of it. But to leave the settlement altogether seemed extreme.

"My guess is they're camping in the woods somewhere." Flynn threw up his hands. "For now, at least. I don't think they have enough provisions to get anywhere else."

"You think he'll come back?" Anna began pacing the cave. "Break in and steal from us?"

"Well, he's not going to come crawling back with his tail between his legs." Flynn stared at her. "Not after the way he was ousted."

"Do you think he might head for Bellator?" Noah asked. "Go for Danforth again?"

"It's definitely a possibility." Flynn had paled. "With what he knows about Avery, he might not be able to resist."

"Let's hope he manages to. He could ruin everything we're trying to build with the Resistance!" Anna continued to pace. "What are his other options?"

"Maybe he'll head away from here altogether." Noah suggested. "Start again somewhere else."

It was rumoured that other communities like Eremus still existed, but nothing had been heard of them for years. Even if they were real, they had to be quite some distance away.

"Maybe." Flynn shrugged. "But he can't do anything unless he has more weapons. Additional food stores."

"So we're back to him threatening Eremus. When we barely have enough supplies to care for the people who *aren't* rebelling." Anna whirled to face them. "Like we don't have enough to worry about with planning the raid."

"We'll have to revise the schedule. Move some of the supplies so he can't find them. Post extra guards on the entrances." Flynn counted off the measures on his fingers. "Let everyone know to keep a look out for Jacob's group."

Noah frowned. "Can we spare people to do all that?"

"Not really." Flynn's tone was terse. "But we can't risk losing any more supplies to him. Damn his stubborn pride! Why wouldn't he listen?"

The council's plan had been to remove Jacob from his leadership role as peacefully as possible. While no one had expected him to take it well, they had hoped to avoid coming to blows over it. The intention had been to ask him to step down to a less central role in the community for a little while, until things calmed down. Or, if he wished to leave, they were prepared to provide him with supplies once the raid to Bellator had gone ahead.

But he hadn't given anyone the chance to explain. And now he was gone.

"Jacob knows the tunnels better than anyone." Anna resumed her pacing. "He knows we're planning a raid. What if he just waits til we're under-defended and barges right in? What's to stop him from taking whatever he wants?"

"We'll have to do the best we can with the manpower we have." Flynn stood up. "We should call a council meeting."

"I'll gather people together." Anna headed for the door. She turned to Noah. "Can you fetch Ella for me, please? She'll be with the prisoners."

"Yeah." He stood up. "You want me to–"

"Send her to the canteen. Thanks. And Noah?" She shot him an apologetic look. "We can discuss the other matter later, okay?"

Grateful that she was still willing to discuss it, he managed a smile. "Okay."

"See you later." And she was gone.

Along with contacting the Resistance, Anna and Flynn had also freed Ella the moment that Jacob was out of the picture. She had been punished enough, they had told the community, for a crime she was innocent of. At the same time, they had moved Charlie, the guard who'd surrendered in the tunnel attack, into the same cave as the other prisoners. Both decisions had been accepted by most citizens without complaint.

It was no surprise that Ella's first request had been to see Helen, but she had also approached Anna the next morning and asked about joining the council. She wanted to help them with their efforts to fight against Danforth's control, she'd said. Her imprisonment had made her angrier, more determined to fight injustice, wherever it occurred. Anna had tentatively given permission for her to attend meetings, with a view to her supporting the upcoming mission. Noah only wished his ma would show the same level of belief in him.

Bidding a hasty goodbye to Flynn, Noah hurried to the cave where the girls were being kept. During the conversation with his ma, he'd had an idea. To bring Flynn and Anna on board with him going to Bellator, he had to have a solid plan. To arm himself with as much information as possible about the drudges.

As someone who was close to his ma, Professor Kemp was the ideal person to help him. If she was also travelling back to the city, he'd have her support on the journey back. Perhaps that would go some way towards persuading his ma that he could do this. Knowing he would find her in the same place as Ella, he picked up the pace.

When he reached the cave, the barricade was already leaning against the tunnel wall. Cautiously, he poked his head inside, relieved to see Ella sitting just inside the doorway talking to Helen.

"Hey, Noah." Helen was beaming. "How are you?"

It struck him how much happier she looked in Ella's presence. He glanced across to find Ella's face similarly content. Ignoring the wave of jealousy which swept over him at their reunion, he forced a smile.

"Okay thanks." He turned to Ella. "My ma asked me to fetch you. Council meeting in the canteen. Right away."

She frowned. "Something wrong?"

He cast a glance over the others, knowing he shouldn't let them know. "She can fill you in when you get there."

"Alright." Giving Helen's hand a squeeze, she stood up. "I'll come back and see you all later, okay? I promise I'll talk to the council about our discussion."

She beckoned to Noah. Curious, he followed her to the exit.

"I was wondering, since..." she bent closer, dropping her voice, "things have changed... whether we might permit them to be let out of here a little? Get some exercise, and so on. I was going to talk to your ma about it."

"Today might not be the right time." He felt bad as her face fell. "But I agree with you. Just... go speak to Ma. You'll understand."

Nodding, she turned to go. "Alright. See you later."

Wondering how he might approach Kemp with his request, Noah ducked back inside. Six pairs of eyes turned to him and he felt instantly embarrassed.

"How are you all?" he tried. "Okay? Aside from being cooped up in here. I know it's not ideal."

There were various nods and murmurs from around the space. All the girls seemed to accept they'd suffered worse treatment. Apart from one.

"We'd certainly be better if you'd allow us out of here for a little exercise every once in a while." Avery's tone was strident, but for once she was making a valid point.

Turning to her, Noah wondered how much to say. "Yes, I'm sorry about that. We've felt it was a necessary step, since–"

"We know," Avery rolled her eyes. "Since our fellow captives managed to escape you."

"Yes." Noah hesitated, not wanting to mention the extra protection she might need now that Jacob knew of her origins. "You can understand why, can't you?"

The older girl opened her mouth to reply, but an elbow from Farrah stopped her. She dropped her gaze. "I guess so. But we're..."

"I know. You must be." Noah watched as Avery's gaze snapped up to meet his, startled by his empathy. "Listen, I'll see what I can do about you being let out soon. Maybe we could manage it, for a little while, at least."

Her eyes wide, Avery seemed to have lost the use of her tongue. Beside her, Farrah leaned across. "That would be wonderful, if you could. Thank you."

A movement on the other side of the cave caught his eye. With agility which demonstrated her guard training, Charlie pushed herself to her feet and crossed the space until she reached him.

"Could we...?" She gestured to the cave mouth.

Ignoring Avery's glare, Noah led her towards the doorway.

"Wanted to say thank you," Charlie said, once they were out of the others' earshot. "For whatever part you played in getting me moved in here."

"Wasn't really me. Not just me, anyway." He shrugged. "We just thought it would be nicer for you if you had a little company. The isolation didn't seem to be doing you any good."

"It wasn't." She grimaced. "This is so much better than being on my own. You've no idea."

"I'm glad." Noah smiled. "How are you…" he gestured inside the cave, "finding the company?"

"Not sure I'm quite fitting in just yet," Charlie glanced over at Kemp, who was sitting just inside the cave door. "But I'm working on it."

Noah wondered if Kemp was nervous around the guard. Charlie's first loyalty, on the surface, at least, was to Danforth. The very woman Kemp was working against as part of the Resistance. But from what Noah had seen, Charlie hadn't been the most devoted of the chancellor's followers, and the discoveries she had made since arriving in Eremus had definitely made her question the Bellator teachings. They were, very possibly, on the same side. But Kemp didn't know that.

"Helen's been quite friendly," Charlie mused. "And Avery."

"Really?"

Noah wondered if Avery's pleasantness had more to do with her belief that Charlie might fight to protect them, rather than being a genuine offer of friendship. Of course, someone so devoted to the Bellator ways would favour those who were in charge of protecting its leader.

Since they'd received the news of Avery's unusual parentage, Noah had seen her through different eyes. Now that he knew she was related to the chancellor, her entitled attitude made sense.

His ma had asked Kemp about the connection between Avery and Danforth. Staff at the school were aware that Avery was treated differently, Kemp said, but not the reason why. Whenever a member of staff had cause to discipline her, Anderson would take over, and more often than not, Avery appeared to be let off lightly. Kemp thought it made sense that Avery was related to Danforth, but the reason for her presence at the school remained a mystery.

They had decided, for the time being, not to speak to Avery about her background. If she already knew and was keeping the information a secret, they might jolt her into action by letting her know that her cover was blown. If she didn't know, then discovering her connection to the chancellor might make her behaviour even more volatile. So for now, with Madeleine's agreement, they had decided they would keep the news to themselves. But her friendliness towards the guard made Noah suspicious.

"Yes." Charlie glanced at him, curious. "That surprises you?"

"Helen, no. Avery, however–" Noah forced himself to shrug carelessly. "A little. Just... be careful what you tell her."

"You don't trust her?"

"Let's just say her past behaviour hasn't given me a lot of confidence."

"Alright. I will." Charlie turned to go back in. "Thanks."

She ducked back inside and he followed her. Conscious of time, he turned to Kemp.

"Professor? I have a message for you," he almost stumbled over the words, "from my ma. Would you step outside for a moment?"

The older woman looked a little surprised but got up and followed him. Behind them, the other girls resumed their conversations without suspicion. Once he and Charlotte stood in the tunnel out of earshot, Noah didn't waste time.

"Sorry – that was an excuse. I just needed to speak to you alone."

The professor's eyes sparked with interest, but she said nothing.

"I wanted to ask you more about the drudges. You mentioned them the last time we spoke?" He paused, trying to gauge her reaction, but her face remained expressionless. "With only having been to the city a couple of times, I've never seen one. You said they wear a specific uniform... with a face covering?"

"They do."

"How many are there in the city?"

"I don't know, maybe four hundred or so?" If Kemp was surprised by his questions, she didn't show it. "They're mostly used in the larger establishments... schools, hospitals, labs, laundries... not many of them work in individual homes. A few of the wealthier citizens in the city have one, I suppose, but on the whole they're used in wider public service." She cocked her head to one side. "Why the sudden interest?"

"You spoke to my ma yesterday, right?"

"I did. I hear I'm to go back into the city soon."

"Yeah." Noah paused, holding the professor's gaze. "How do you feel about that?"

"I'm glad, I suppose." The professor rubbed a hand against her forehead. "It's killing me right now that I can't be part of it. I mean... coming here to find Faith was important, but now she's gone and I'm stuck here, totally out of action. I was in a great position at the academy... it took me years to work my way up... to gain Anderson's trust. I'm useless, stuck here." She blew out a breath. "But I'll admit, I'm nervous about returning. I just hope this cover story we're cooking up holds."

"I hope so too." Noah hesitated. "Ma told you Faith's safe, right? You know she's not back at the academy?"

"That was one piece of good news." Kemp's face darkened. "Sophia, however... that's a different story."

"You're hoping to help her?"

"If I can." Her face fell. "She's not at the academy though."

"Ruth said there are lots of others there, though. And many of them are being dosed with this drug."

"Sadly, yes. If I'm able to get back to my original position at the academy, I'll do what I can for them." She paused, staring at Noah. "Sounds like you have enough of your own issues here in Eremus. Your ma filled me in on what happened with Jacob." The professor grimaced. "I never had much respect for him. I'm sure Flynn and your ma are already doing a better job of liaising with Madeleine."

"They are." Noah seized on the change of topic eagerly. "We have lots of plans. One thing we've offered is to send some Eremus citizens into Bellator—additional eyes on what Danforth is doing. We feel the more eyes we have in the city, the better."

"So Anna said. Sounds sensible."

"And, well, at the moment the only citizens we could realistically send into the city are female. Unless..."

Kemp's eyes lit up. "I think I see where you're going."

"I thought..." Noah hesitated, "I wondered if I talked to you about the drudges... the way they work, where they live, the roles they fulfil... how they move and talk and – oh, anything you think is important..." he paused before voicing the idea, afraid that she might laugh. "I wondered whether I could get away with posing as a one... to enter the city, undercover."

Kemp looked impressed. "It's a daring idea. And not without danger." She leaned back, running an eye over him from head to toe. "Most Eremus men wouldn't manage with it. But with you... it might work. You're slim. With the mask, in uniform... taught how to walk, how to behave... you might get away with it." She paused, a look of amusement crossing her face. "Your ma didn't mention this. She's alright with it?"

Remembering the earlier conversation with his ma, Noah dropped his gaze. "No. Neither's Flynn. But I was hoping if we talked, if you taught me what I needed to know, I could show them how convincing I could be. And maybe they'd come around to the idea."

"Well I can't promise to convince your ma," Kemp shrugged, "but I'd be happy to help you."

"Thanks. I've been wondering... if the first few citizens we send in manage to blend in, whether there might be the possibility of a larger number of our citizens going undercover too..." He hurried on. "I mean... Ruth managed it. If myself and a couple of others pull it off, then perhaps going forward we could..."

"You've thought about this a lot." The professor looked amused.

"I have, I suppose." He could feel himself blushing. "It's important."

"Yes, it is." Kemp turned serious. "Listen, if Eremus can pull this off, it will really help them to align with the Resistance. I mean... offering citizens to go undercover... to actively work against Danforth from the inside... it's clever. It will be useful. And very much appreciated." She paused, leaning closer to him. "I can understand why your ma is reluctant to let you go, though. Have you *really* thought what you'd be getting yourself into?"

Noah gritted his teeth. "I have, yes."

Kemp chewed on her lip. "Drudges who have disobeyed orders in the past have been executed."

"As have innocent Eremus citizens who did nothing but try to live their lives." Noah paused, finding himself breathless. "Honestly? I'd rather die trying to do this than stay here and let others fight for me."

Kemp stared at him for a long time before continuing. "Alright, if you're sure, I'll help you. It's not going to be easy, though. You'll have to be constantly aware. Not let your guard down for a moment."

"I know. But I have to do *something*."

"It's very commendable." Kemp patted his arm. "And I do believe you might do this quite well. Do you want to start right away?"

"I can't." Reluctantly, he turned to go. "I have a shift."

"Alright. But come back as soon as you can." She raised an eyebrow. "I may not be here for much longer."

Chapter Seventeen: Faith

"Any change?"

Diane's voice startled Faith. Realising she'd fallen asleep in the chair in front of Sophia's monitor, she tried to focus. She stretched widely and brushed a hand across her face, wincing when her fingers brushed against the tender skin on her cheek. The wound was healing well, but was still painful to the touch.

"Not the last time I looked, which must have been..." she consulted the time at the bottom of the screen. "Wow. I've been asleep a while."

Diane tutted. "You need to actually go to bed. This isn't doing you any good."

Bending over Faith, she peered at the screen. "Looks like you're right. No change."

Faith rubbed her eyes. Since Sanders had woken up Sophia, Faith had spent as much time as she could watching the monitor, trying to work out what was happening to her friend. The checks on her had become more regular, and more thorough. The same petite medic took blood from her every day, and she was supervised at all times now by a small team. Faith suspected those looking after her were specially selected to keep Sophia's presence at the hospital a secret.

Sophia had also been removed from the room on two occasions. The first time, Faith had curled up in the chair, terrified as to where Sophia had been taken. After several desperate minutes spent jumping from camera to camera, Faith had clicked back to the original room to find that her bed had been wheeled back in again, with no visible alteration to her condition. Blake said they'd probably taken her for a scan. When she disappeared for the second time, Faith had been less anxious, but it had still been a difficult thirty minutes.

Even more disturbing were the bouts of sickness Sophia underwent on a regular basis. Since she'd woken up, she had been vomiting at least three times a day. Faith didn't know how she was keeping any food down, but she hadn't seen her eat any either. Again, Lily had told her that one of the tubes Sophia was hooked up to was providing her with sustenance. But watching her friend retch every few hours was awful.

"You had any breakfast?" Diane said. "A shower?"

Faith shook her head.

"Madeleine wants to see you." Diane took hold of Faith's arm and pulled her upright. "Go and clean up. I'll make an excuse til you're ready."

"But–" Faith gestured towards the screen, where Sophia lay, eyes open, but completely still.

"You're not doing her any good." Diane shooed her away. "You'll make yourself ill. How can you help her, then?"

Faith began to protest again, but found her head was spinning.

"When was the last time you ate?" Diane scolded. "You need to look after yourself." She reached into her pocket and pulled out a slightly crushed cereal bar. Pressing it into Faith's hand, she pushed her towards the door. "Get out of here." She jabbed a finger at the screen. "I'll watch her, I promise."

Knowing her friend wouldn't give up, Faith made her way out of the tiny room. She hurried down the hallway with her head down, grateful to find their shared sleeping space empty. Still feeling light headed, she devoured the cereal bar. Then she grabbed soap, shampoo, and a towel and headed for the bathroom.

Half an hour later she felt a little refreshed. She walked to Madeleine's office, wondering what the older woman wanted. Over the past few days, she and Diane had been given fairly light duties, and Faith had spent the majority of her time in Blake's room. Whenever she had entered the hub to grab some food, the door to the leader's office had been firmly closed.

She'd heard a couple of whispers about the current Resistance priorities, but she'd been so preoccupied with Sophia that she hadn't really paid much attention. Now, she wished she'd had the sense to ask Diane about the reason for the meeting. Still, it was too late now.

She knocked softly on the door. Hearing a sharp "Come," she obeyed, easing the door open and peering inside.

"Faith!" Robyn was the first to greet her. How's the face?"

It was sore, but Faith didn't want to admit weakness. "S'fine." She resisted the urge to bring a hand to her injuries.

Madeleine was less sympathetic. "About time. I sent Diane to fetch you ages ago."

Faith scuttled in with what she hoped was an apologetic expression. Madeleine sat behind the desk, a number of papers spread out in front of her. Without preamble, she waved Faith into a chair.

"We received a report from one of the safehouses on the outskirts of the city last night. Seems Ruth put those batteries we gave her to good use. Eremus has been in touch. I was able to speak with Flynn for a little while."

"Flynn." Faith was puzzled. "Not Jacob?"

"It seems there has been a leadership change in the community." Madeleine frowned. "He didn't give me details, but said Jacob wasn't available to speak to me."

Faith's heart began beating faster. If Jacob was out of the picture, would Madeleine still be happy to work with Eremus? "And that was okay with you?"

The older woman's face was impassive. "I've worked with both men for years. Jacob has always been," she paused for a second, searching for the right word, "somewhat hot-headed." She shrugged. "I suspect the explosions in the forest went a bit too far for some of the Eremus citizens. I trust Flynn though. He's headed up many raids in the past and always done it well. He's a man of his word and he's made some very interesting proposals which I think might well feed into what the Resistance wants to achieve in the long run."

Faith was flooded with relief. "You're still looking to work with them then?"

"I am. Providing Eremus shows they're willing and lives up to our conditions."

"Conditions?"

"We're not prepared to jump in with both feet until I know Eremus isn't just using us to get what it wants. We have to have common goals."

Faith's heart leapt. "What did you ask them for?"

"First, I asked that they return Charlotte Kemp to Bellator." Madeleine fingered one of the papers on the desk absentmindedly. "She's been a faithful Resistance member for a long time, and her cover at the academy took years to set up. There is another person within the academy who helps us, but they don't have the same access to the professors as she does."

"You're hoping Professor Kemp can go *back* to the academy?" Faith burst out. "After all this time? Where will they think she's been?"

Madeleine frowned. "We're working on a cover story which could explain her absence. If it's successful, she may be able to return to her old position and continue to support us from there."

"And if she can't?" A feeling of dread crept over Faith as she asked the question.

Robyn shrugged. "We'll get her out and she'll have to work under-cover from here instead."

"Like me." Madeleine frowned. "Anyway, Flynn has agreed to bring her back here. Eremus is planning a raid in the next couple of days. Mostly for supplies." Madeleine tapped a list on the screen in front of her. "We know what it is they need, and we'll attempt to assist them, as we always have."

"How will you do that?" Faith asked, curious.

"We'll provide access to the city through some of the safehous-es, make sure that the locations they want to raid are unguarded..." Robyn ticked the items off on her fingers. "Give them access to the more complicated targets... that kind of thing."

Faith's heart started to beat a little faster. Might Noah be among the raiders? She pushed the thought away. She hadn't been permitted to leave the library since the first mission to the academy. It was hardly likely that Madeleine would permit her a jaunt out in public simply to meet with a random Eremus boy.

"Flynn suggested they send some of their people here to swell our forces... show they're serious about joining with us. Undercover, of course." The Resistance leader shrugged. "It's an experiment, ob-viously. See whether or not they can blend in, go unnoticed." As

Madeleine went on, Faith found herself shivering at the thought of what would happen if they couldn't blend in. "I think it will go a long way towards proving their dedication to our cause."

Faith swallowed. "You mean they're coming here?"

"They are." Madeleine's tone made it clear she was closing the discussion. Abandoning her datadev, the Resistance leader stood up. With a piercing gaze, she walked around the table until she stood right in front of Faith. "Now, I'm told there have been some changes to Sophia's condition." Madeleine leaned back against the desk. "Blake told us you've been watching that damn monitor permanently since they woke her up."

"Um, yes." Faith wondered if she was about to be disciplined. "I suppose I have."

"We'd like you to give us a thorough update on her condition." Madeleine said. "What with the information Blake dug up on the drug, and your description of its effects, we're curious to find out more."

Faith sat up a little straighter, leaning forward. "Well, as you said, she's now awake," she began. "The medics made some adjustments. It seems they had her sedated, before."

"Interesting." Madeleine exchanged glances with Robyn. "Do we know *why* they've woken her up?"

"Not at the moment." Faith searched for words which would sound logical, rather than emotional. "They seem to be monitoring her more closely. She's awake most of the time... I mean she does sleep, but normally... at night, as you'd expect. The medics have taken her out of the room a couple of times. Not for long, though. Lily said they probably took her for a scan of some sort."

Robyn nodded. "That would make sense."

"What's more worrying," Faith paused, "is the fact that she's being sick. A *lot*."

Madeleine raised her eyebrows. "How often, would you say?"

Faith shrugged. "Two... sometimes three times a day."

"Any other significant symptoms?"

"Well, it's difficult to tell, without being able to hear what's going on in the room." Faith had spent a lot of time thinking about it. "Sophia appears to be able to speak to them, but obviously, we can't hear what they're saying, so that's a dead end. When she gets up to use the bathroom, someone has to help her, so it looks like they're worried she might faint." She glanced between the two women. "You remember me telling you that I experienced extreme dizziness when I was given femgazipane? At times, I could barely make it across the room. If Sophia's being given multiple doses, it's no surprise that she's the same way."

Madeleine leaned closer to Faith. "You might be wondering why we're so interested. As you know, we've been listening to the conversations in Anderson's office regularly since your team planted the bug. So far, most of it's been pretty dull. But yesterday, Robyn heard them talking about Sophia."

Faith bolted upright. "What did you hear?"

"It seems," Robyn frowned, "since Sophia is the only one of the missing students to have been returned to the city, they've decided not to broadcast her return. Instead, her return has been kept quiet so they can... let's just say... *accelerate* the testing on a subject no one knows about."

"You mean–" Faith stammered, "they can cover up what happens to her because no one knows she's here?"

"We think so." Madeleine sighed. "This way, if she dies, they have an easy out." Faith went cold at the thought, but the Resistance leader pressed on without noticing. "My guess is they'd just blame her death on the rogue men who kidnapped her, spin some story, tell the citizens she died in the forest... or they brought her back to the city severely injured, then couldn't save her."

"It's disgusting." Robyn started pacing. "Anyway, I'm pretty sure Anderson was speaking to Danforth herself. The call was audio rather than video, though, and I could only hear Anderson's side of the conversation." She turned to face them. "What she confirmed is that Sophia is on higher doses of femgazipane than any other student so far. Anderson said they've kept her sedated to allow her body to adjust to the drug."

"The fact that they've woken her up implies there has been a breakthrough..." Madeleine mused, "or at least they were hoping that–"

"Surely the vomiting implies her body *hasn't* gotten used to it?" Faith interrupted.

"You'd think so, wouldn't you?" Robyn rolled her eyes. "But Anderson implied that, given the large doses of femgazipane, they were expecting a far more severe reaction. Apparently, they're quite pleased with her progress."

"As we know, they have large numbers of the girls in the academy on lower doses of the drug, but the effects have been pretty severe." Faith gasped, and Madeleine hurried on. "No one has died. You were right. Whatever they did to the formula between giving it to Serene and to you has prevented that from happening."

"Thank goodness." Robyn massaged her temples.

"But the sickness you described, the dizzy spells, the disorientation, they're all experiencing that." Madeleine shook her head. "According to Anderson, many of the senior girls aren't making it to their classes, the effects are so extreme."

"And they keep giving it to them?" Faith was incredulous.

"So it seems." Robyn resumed her pacing. "They have them on rotation. They take the drug for a couple of days, then they're given a week off it, to rest and recover. But then they begin all over again."

Faith thought back to the photographs she had taken of the girls' charts. "The test they're given? That one on the charts Anderson has in her office. Did we work out what that's about?"

Madeleine drummed her fingers against the table. "It seems to be linked to their tolerance. Once the levels of femgazipane in the bloodstream reach a certain point, the side effects are so severe that the girls fail this test and have to be taken off the drug for a few days."

"But they're straight back on it as soon as they're recovered." Robyn bit her lip. "It's barbaric."

"But Anderson's conversation indicated something interesting about Sophia." Faith clenched her teeth as Madeleine picked up the story. "By keeping her sedated, it appears they've managed to get her body to tolerate far higher levels of the femgazipane for a far lengthier period of time."

Faith shifted in her chair, hoping the conversation would at some point lead to a way they might look at rescuing her friend. The expression on Madeleine's face did not give her much hope, though.

"As we know," she continued, "femgazipane is linked to fertility in some way. Now that they've had what they consider to be real success with Sophia, they've made some alterations."

"Obviously, they woke her up." Faith said. "Do we know *why*?"

"Not exactly. And there have been other changes too." Robyn said, her voice gentle. "Not only the scans, and Sophia's alertness, but Anderson mentioned a *second* phase of the process."

Something stirred in Faith's memory. "When I got over the worst of my reactions to the femgazipane..." she cast her mind back, suppressing a shudder as she recalled the barren room she'd been locked in, "Anderson mentioned something to Danforth about a Phase Two."

Madeleine frowned. "And what did that involve?"

"I'm not sure." Registering Madeleine's look of disappointment, Faith tried to explain. "It sounded like they wanted to somehow... take things a step further, based on the fact that I had survived the first dose."

Robyn sat forward. "We think she was referring to a second drug." Robyn paused, glancing at Faith as though monitoring her reaction. "You understand? It looks like Sophia's being given something *in addition to* the femgazipane."

Faith's heart was pounding. "But what will it do to her?"

"We're not exactly sure, but we think it might have already had the desired effect."

"What do you mean? What have they done to her?" Faith glanced between the two women. "Is she dying?"

"I'm sorry, Faith..." Madeleine was unusually hesitant, "but it seems there's been a... a *change* in Sophia's condition."

"A change?" Faith could hear her voice rising in pitch but could do nothing to stop it. "What kind of change?"

"Well, with all the sickness she's experiencing," Robyn's voice was gentle, "we believe she might be pregnant."

Chapter Eighteen: Noah

Ruth stared at him. "You're *certain* you want to do this? That it's a good idea?"

"I'm sure." Noah didn't hesitate.

They were sitting shoulder-to-shoulder in the den. It had been difficult to get a minute alone together since his friend had returned from the city. With the constant threat of Jacob hanging over them, and all the planning for the supply raid, there had been a lot to do. Plus, Noah had been spending every moment he could spare with Kemp, who was putting him through his paces training him to be a drudge. The professor couldn't be sure when she would be sent back to Bellator. Noah needed to make his time with her count.

It was the reason for his friend's question. Like his ma, Ruth was not very enthusiastic about his plan to go undercover in Bellator. It seemed like every conversation he'd had over the past few days had been linked to this decision.

Having had longer to get used to the idea, his ma seemed to have come round to it. She had admitted that, if she put her feelings aside, he was perfect for the role. Noah knew the incident in the tunnel with the Bellator guards had gone a long way towards demonstrating how capable he was and he appreciated the newfound trust she had in him.

Ruth was another matter.

She shifted her position. "And Kemp thinks you'll be convincing enough?"

"You're doubting me?" Noah tried to make light of the situation. "You know she's been drilling me non-stop in the mysterious ways of the drudge."

It was true. Over the past few days, Noah had spent what felt like hours training with Charlotte Kemp. Flynn had permitted them to use one of the smaller training caves, so they had space to practice and were away from Avery's prying eyes. The professor had explained the way the drudge system worked, suggested the kinds of jobs he would be expected to do and the clothing he would wear. She thought the best idea would be for him to start off at Resistance headquarters, until they could work out a plausible placement for him.

Kemp was hoping it might be somewhere vital, where he could really be of some use. A laboratory, a government office, even the academy. Many drudges were required to work in small teams, so they would need to look carefully to make sure he was assigned to a position where there were few drudges, or where the drudges were sympathetic to the Resistance movement. After that, he'd have to find a way to report back to the headquarters without being caught.

It was vital that he fit in. Kemp had made him walk with his head bowed low, not making eye contact, never speaking. It was harder than he'd expected, but that morning she had proclaimed herself happy with his progress.

"Not perfect," she'd said, "but you're getting there."

He had resisted the urge to look up at her and remained silent. Laughing loudly, she'd clapped him on the back and declared their session over, moving across to work with the other citizen who had volunteered for the mission: Ella.

Her suggestion that she enter the city had come as a shock to most. But it made sense when Noah considered her recent experience at Jacob's hands, her relationship with Helen, and her recent interest in joining the council. She was tired of Eremus being forced to live in the shadows.

She'd done a good job of persuading Flynn and the others, stressing how personable she was, how well she knew the Danforth girls, and how her recent imprisonment had given her a newfound desire to move out of her comfort zone. Paulo, who she'd grown up with, had been reluctant, arguing that she wasn't a raider and had never been to the city before. She'd responded by reciting the raider rules to him, which she knew by heart from Dawn's teachings growing up.

In the end, even Paulo had to admit that Ella had a way of getting people to confide in her which would make her the perfect spy. It had been decided: Noah and Ella would travel to the city the following night with Professor Kemp. Together, they would be the first to attempt to infiltrate the city and live amongst its citizens. If they were successful, more might follow.

One or two of the Eremus citizens had expressed concern over Ella's inclusion in the mission. Most had seen the light after Jacob's recent betrayal, but a few still didn't quite trust her. For a while, Ella had been concerned that she might not be able to go. In the end, Flynn and Anna had vouched for her personally. Their opinion carried a lot of weight in the community, and eventually everyone had agreed to give her a chance.

She had embraced the mission wholeheartedly. Her only regret was leaving Helen, but since she saw the mission as something which would eventually allow them to be together, she had come to terms with it. Noah had never seen her so determined. But working towards a Bellator which welcomed Eremus citizens as equals, she'd told Noah, was the best way to secure the kind of future she wanted. She was excited to be a part of it.

Whilst sympathising with Ella's regret at leaving Helen, Noah had to admit he was happy to be moving closer to Faith. When Ruth had told him she was alive and well and living at Resistance headquarters, he'd been so relieved. It had been even better hearing that she'd asked after him and told Ruth she'd regretted the way she'd left.

"Honestly," he sat up, turning to reassure his friend, "I'm ready for this. If I could stand up right now and show you my drudge walk, I would." He winked. "It's *very* convincing."

Ruth scowled at him. "Don't joke about this."

"I'm *not*!" He lowered his voice as she gestured at the cave entrance. It was unlikely they'd be overheard, but the outer tunnel was used on occasion and they always tried to keep it down to ensure their sanctuary remained a secret. "Listen, if there was ever a role Noah Madden was born to play, it's this one. A skinny little runt who's not up to the difficult jobs?" He slapped a hand on his chest. "That's me."

"That's Harden talking." Ruth elbowed him. "Those drudges might be slight, but they do difficult jobs. They're not weaklings. And neither are you." She gazed at him, her face softening. "It's not going to be easy."

"I know that."

"It's not just a raid... in and out and get back here as fast as you can." She jabbed a finger at him. "We're talking about staying there, *living* there, among women who'll report you the second they discover who you are. You'll have to keep up the act all the time. Twenty-four seven."

"I *know*." Noah was beginning to tire of her warnings. "Give me some credit. I mean, *you* did it."

"Did what?"

"Infiltrated the city in disguise."

"That was different," she snapped. "I'm not a man."

"I'll be fine. I'm–"

But his friend cut him off. "I was scared, you know. Wandering through the city, in full view of Bellator citizens. I mean... I've only ever been there at night before. Apart from that time Paulo and I were delayed." She dropped her voice to a whisper. "Every time I passed a citizen, my stomach was churning. I was just *waiting* for one of them to call me out as a fraud."

Noah didn't interrupt. Ruth hadn't told him much about her visit to the city, aside from the details of her conversations with Madeleine and Faith. She didn't like to appear vulnerable, so her admission was quite a shock. He fought the urge to reach out and take her hand.

"When I bumped into Faith, she stopped dead." Ruth twisted her hands in her lap. "*Right* next to me. Honestly, I thought that was it. Thank goodness it was her and not someone else."

"We'll have to hope I'm as lucky as you then," Noah hedged. The talk of getting caught was alarming. He didn't want to lose his nerve before he'd even left Eremus.

"And if wandering around was difficult, when I had to try and *talk* to people, it was downright terrifying." Her entire body tensed. "Blending in with the other guards like I was one of them. I was lucky they just assumed I was a new recruit. Meant most of them just ignored me or sneered. But the ones who did speak to me... well, my hands were shaking the entire time." She turned her head to face him. "It was so stressful. And I only had to do it for a couple of hours."

"Alright, alright, I get it!" Noah threw up his hands. "It won't be a picnic, I'll be petrified the entire time, I won't–"

"Noah." Ruth's tone stopped him dead. "I know you're going to do it, whatever I say. I'm not trying to talk you out of it. But I *need* you to understand how difficult it's going to be. I don't want you going in there trying to be a hero."

"Me? A hero?" Noah went for humour, which fell flat. "Unlikely."

His friend narrowed her eyes. "A lot of this is about Faith. Isn't it?" She didn't wait for a response. "You might not see her at all, you know. It's a big city. Once you're established as a drudge, you won't have regular access to any of the Resistance members. You'll be stuck in whatever role they give you, day after day. You'll be *extremely* vulnerable."

"Don't you think I can do it?" Noah snapped.

"It's not that." She wrapped the drawstring of her hoodie around her finger, pulling it tight. "I have faith that you're prepared. That this isn't just a spur of the moment decision. I'm just... worried for you. And for Ella." She dropped her gaze. "I can't believe I'm losing you both at once."

Noah felt a stab of guilt. Ruth was going to the city but would be returning to Eremus with the raiders involved in the supply mission. Alongside Paulo and several other raiders, she would take much-needed resources from an assigned location and head back to the community with them. Flynn was staying behind with a second party of raiders, still mindful of the threat from Jacob. This meant more pressure on the raiders who were travelling to the city, as there were fewer of them than the council would have liked.

Ruth's was a vital role, and one she was proud to fulfil. At the same time, when she returned to Eremus, she would be leaving behind the two people who meant the most to her.

"You're not losing us." He leaned closer to his friend, nudging her. "And we'll be just fine. Back before you know it."

"You think so?" She shifted away, turning to stare at him again. "Because this feels like the start of something huge. Something that's likely to change things forever."

There was a ring of truth in her words that couldn't be denied. Noah lay back and looked up at the stars which twinkled high above them, visible through the slender gap in the rocks above. The den had always been here for him, a place of comfort to run to when things got too much. Would he have an escape like this in Bellator? He had to admit the prospect was unlikely.

"Noah?" Ruth's voice had taken on a tone of appeal. "Be careful, won't you?"

"I will." He rolled on his side, and this time he did take her hand. Squeezing it, he hoped his words had comforted her at least a little. "You know me. I'm not reckless. I'll make sure I–"

But her grip on his hand had tightened, and her face was pale. Outside in the tunnel, there was the sound of urgent voices, followed by the thunder of footsteps galloping past.

"Disturbance... south side..." "Flynn called..." "...need support..."

The jumble of voices mingled with the hissing of a walkie-talkie.

"What–?" Noah whispered.

"Jacob?" Ruth frowned.

"We'd better go and see."

Once the sound of footsteps had retreated, they shuffled through the gap in the rock and out into the tunnel. For a moment it was eerily silent, the panicked passersby long gone. They peered in the direction of the exit, then back towards the central tunnels.

"Which way should we go?" Noah glanced at his friend.

"No idea." She shrugged. "Pick one."

With a final glance towards home, Noah turned towards the exit and hurried off in the wake of the people who had just raced past. If they were answering a distress call, he and Ruth might be of assistance. His hands shook as he ran, his fingers closing around the knife in his belt. Yet again, it was his only weapon. But he would fight with his hands if need be.

As they neared the end of the tunnel, the problem became clear. Thick smoke was billowing into the tunnel, and the visibility was reducing quickly. Noah slowed down, mindful of the possibility of running headlong into something. An injury was not what he needed right now. Nearing the exit, he hoisted his t-shirt up to cover his mouth and put his head down.

As he reached back to grasp Ruth's hand, he was reminded of a fire in the forest which he'd been trapped by with Faith. That one, they'd been able to avoid by seeking refuge in Swallow Lake. This time, there was no large water source nearby. His heart pounding, he slipped through a narrow crack in the rocks and pushed away the foliage which hid the entrance, pulling Ruth behind him.

They emerged together into a dense fog. The trees around them were barely visible and the cries of the citizens already outside were eerie and muffled.

"Which direction's the fire?" Ruth called, her mouth close to his ear. "We have to protect the bushes around the entrance."

She was right. Noah's gaze circled the space. The foliage which concealed the passage into Eremus was not yet burning, but if they caught fire, the entire community would be vulnerable. They forged ahead until they found a group of Eremus citizens already forming a circle in a clearing between some trees. Noah and Ruth hurried to join them.

The first person they came across was Beth. At the rear of the group, she was handing out blankets which they would use to beat out the fire. Seeing them, she pressed one into each of their hands.

"It's mostly smoke. Fire's not that bad, actually." She jabbed a finger up ahead. "Should be able to contain it without too much difficulty. There are more people on the way."

Grabbing the blanket, Noah sped past, unfolding it as he went. He joined the rest of the citizens, who had already spread out and begun to smother the flames. Remembering his training, he held the section of material aloft, wrapping its edges around his arms and hands to protect them. Moving into place beside Harriet, he bent low and stretched the blanket over as large an area as he could manage. On his other side, Ruth did the same.

They had prepared for this. Fire was a huge threat to their community, and they couldn't afford to let one spread. Not only would it consume sections of valuable foraging land, it could expose the very cave system which protected them. But they were always so careful. Every Eremus child had the dangers of fire drilled into them from birth. It was threaded through many of the stories passed down through the generations, which most of the children were able to recite by the time they were six.

That there had been two fires in as many weeks was shocking. The first had begun when Jacob had set off the explosives in the forest which had killed so many of Danforth's guards. It had been a reckless action on their leader's part, but luckily, they'd had rain soon afterwards which had helped to extinguish the flames and reduce the damage.

To suffer a second fire so soon after the last one was coincidental, to say the least. Noah glanced around at the Eremus citizens who were fighting the flames on all sides. A threat like this brought everyone to help, and the number of people flooding out of the tunnel exits was growing by the second. Under normal circumstances, this would have made Noah proud.

But something nagged at the back of his brain. If every available Eremus citizen was out here, fighting the fire which threatened them, who was guarding the rest of the community?

"Ruth!" he yelled.

Hearing the panic in his tone, his friend looked up, frowning. He gestured to the area around him. Everywhere he looked multiple citizens beat the flames. The fire was almost out, the smoke already beginning to dissipate.

"Think they have this?" He jerked his head back towards the tunnels. "Could we go?" For a moment, she scowled, perhaps assuming he was attempting to dodge the work. He stepped closer, leaning in so only she could hear him. "Trust me?"

She hesitated for a second. "Alright. Let's go."

Leaving the others to finish the job, they raced back to the entrance and hurried inside. As they jogged down the tunnel together, she turned to him.

"I hope you have a good reason for making me abandon my community."

"I do." He huffed. "Or at least, I think I do. Though I hope I'm wrong."

They gave up on speech as they hurried onwards, through the tunnels. Noah had one destination in mind. As they reached the canteen Noah swerved down the right-hand tunnel and barrelled straight into his ma.

"Noah!" She staggered backwards, her hand going to her forehead where there was a gash. "I need– I have to get to Flynn."

"Woah. You're hurt." He steadied her. "Is it Jacob?"

She nodded frantically, fear in her eyes. "The fire. It's a distraction."

Noah's heart sank. He'd guessed at the ex-leader's plot too late. Tearing the edge from his t-shirt, he folded it over and pressed it gently to his ma's wound.

"Did he attack you?" Noah's blood boiled.

"Not really. He shoved me aside, that's all. Hurting us wasn't his aim."

Ruth's eyes widened. "Jacob's here? Inside the tunnels."

"He was. So was Harden and a couple of others." Anna sounded out of breath. "I think they took weapons. Maybe some explosives. Not sure how many. I was rounding up the rest of the raiders to send them out to the fire when I stumbled across them by accident." She tried to move forward. "I need to find Flynn."

Ruth placed an arm around her. "We'll do that. You need to sit down. The fire's almost out. It wasn't all that big, to be honest."

"His aim wasn't to destroy the forest. Just to get enough of us out there that the settlement was vulnerable." Noah fought to keep the bitterness out of his tone. "Let's get you back to the canteen ma, where you can sit down."

They turned to go back along the tunnel when another set of footsteps came pounding towards them. Tensing, they turned to face the new arrival. It was Paulo. His face was taut and he was breathing hard.

"I was down in the cave with Charl-" He checked himself. "I was looking in on the girls." He paused, his entire body shaking with rage. "*Sarah* came charging in."

Anna's hand flew to her mouth. "What did she want?"

"The girls were terrified." Paulo shook his head in bewilderment. "Sarah was swinging a rifle around... shouting at us all. I didn't..." He steeled himself to continue. "I didn't have a weapon with me."

Noah knew how much his brother would regret this lapse. "What happened?"

"I tried to take her down, but..." Paulo looked shamefaced. "The weapon was loaded... I mean, she definitely meant business. I tried to stand in front of the girls... protect them.... but there are so many. Anyway," he paused, resting his hands on his knees while he gasped in a breath, "in the end, she shoved me out of the way, grabbed her and took off."

"Took off with who?" Noah demanded, dreading the response.

"Avery." Paulo's eyes were desperate. "She knew *exactly* who she was after."

"No." Anna stumbled forward and Noah shot out his hand to catch her. "They weren't just here for the weapons then. They've..." her voice cracked, "they've taken Danforth's daughter."

Chapter Nineteen: Faith

Faith stared through the window at the darkened square. It had been raining earlier, but the downpour had finally stopped. Now, the streetlights were glinting off the wet pavement, sending reflections dancing across the metallic surfaces of the surrounding buildings.

Not that Faith could go outside and enjoy the view. Madeleine had forbidden it, for the time being.

"You're our figurehead now." Her tone had been brisk. "We can't afford to lose you."

It wasn't lost on Faith that she was almost as much a prisoner here in Bellator as she had been in the Eremus caves or at the academy. Desperate for escape, she had retreated to the only place she was permitted which wasn't officially within the Resistance headquarters: the library.

She understood the reason for Madeleine's caution, but it didn't ease her frustration.

Stella Thane had attempted to broadcast Faith's story a couple of times since their interview but, so far, she hadn't had much success. Each time she had tried, she'd only gotten through the first few sentences of her report before Danforth's tech team had found her show's channel and shut her down.

She'd had more success printing the physical leaflets, and had brought them to headquarters the previous day. Faith's picture was front and centre on one side, below a headline which read *Danforth Academy Student Speaks Out*. The rest of the page was filled with quotes taken from her interview. The other side of the sheet was dedicated to Stella's online broadcast, *Bellator Exposed*. Under the headline *Citizens of Bellator Unite!* were a number of bullet points. Each one stated a lie Danforth had told the Bellator citizens, followed by the reality.

The Resistance's most pressing job now was to distribute the information around the city, as widely as possible, without being caught. Once the leaflets had been distributed, Faith feared she'd never escape the headquarters again.

The delivery mission was huge, but she knew she couldn't be a part of it. No matter how much she wanted to. She had spent a large portion of the afternoon helping Robyn and Laura to fill bags with the leaflets, but it hadn't felt like enough.

Catching Faith's despondent expression, Laura had taken pity on her. "I know you'd rather be coming with us. But you're the focus of the operation. The Resistance will be in trouble if *any* of us are caught. But if Danforth gets her hands on *you*?" She had whistled under her breath. "We'd lose our biggest advantage."

"She's right." Robyn's tone had been gentle, but firm. "I know it's frustrating, but I'm afraid, for the moment, you're stuck here." She had nudged Faith's elbow. "There are other ways you can be helpful, though."

"How?"

Robyn had gestured to a datadev. "How about you take another look at the reports from the academy?"

"I've gone over them a thousand times." Faith had cringed inwardly at her exaggeration. She knew she sounded childish. "There's nothing else there that I can see."

"Alright." Robyn had given her a sympathetic smile. "I'll ask Madeleine if you can listen in to Anderson's office bug tonight. We've been trying to have someone listen 24/7, but with so many of us out on the leaflet run tonight, we might be shorthanded."

Faith had brightened. "You think she'd let me?"

"We can ask."

Grateful that Robyn understood her need to be useful, Faith had felt a little more positive. But when Madeleine had given her permission to take on the task, Faith had regretted it. Anderson's office was silent for large portions of the day, while the principal worked alone, or went out and about around the school. So far, she'd listened to Anderson placing her lunchtime sandwich order and disciplining a junior citizen who had repeatedly failed to complete homework. Faith's job might have been vitally important, but it was also dull.

And once the majority of the Resistance citizens had disappeared down the tunnel on the leaflet run she had felt lonely. She wanted to be outdoors with the others, actively doing something which made her feel like her escape to the city had been worth it. But she was stuck here while everyone else worked hard for the cause. Even Diane had been permitted to go.

Faith had spent four hours sitting in Madeleine's office with a set of headphones on, staring at a blank datadev screen. Eventually, she'd asked if she could take the equipment up to the library.

"Please?" She'd prayed Madeleine was in a charitable mood. "Just for a change of scene."

"If it will stop you from sighing every five minutes, I'd agree to anything." The leader had said, glancing up from her work. "Take the back stairs, mind. No sneaking out via the street."

The jibe only served to remind Faith how trapped she was. Tearing her eyes away from the square below now, she took a deep breath and tried to draw comfort from her surroundings.

The library was quiet, and she liked the slightly dusty, papery scent of the books. Madeleine had linked the earbuds to her wristclip so she didn't have to carry the datadev around with her. This made her more mobile. And whilst walking laps of the library wasn't quite running around the track at the academy, or walking through the forest close to Eremus, it was better than nothing.

But Faith was tired of wandering in circles while Anderson's office remained silent. She needed to do something to distract herself. Spotting the Records Room at the rear of the space, she headed towards it. Her last visit had revealed some shocking truths. Perhaps the files warranted further study.

Locating the book filled with the genealogy records, she flipped it open. The first time she had looked through it, she'd been too focused on the basic information the document contained, and the shock of discovering Avery's parentage had distracted her.

Now, with a clearer head, she scanned her own entry for a second time. Her mother's name was no surprise. This time, she was more interested in the Seed Origin code. She snapped a picture of it and moved on to Sophia's listing. This time, the code was different. Snapping another picture, she looked for Noah's entry. The code was different again.

Just how many seed donors had there been? It was unlikely that she would ever know her father. All the men kept by Danforth for procreation purposes had been executed, aside from Jacob. But it had struck her, since spending time in Eremus, that she might have sisters out there, or a half-sister, at least. And, with horror, she had wondered if she might even share a genetic bond with Noah. It was a relief to know she didn't.

Her eyes scanned the different entries, beginning to find links between some of the girls in the list who she knew from the academy. There were several girls who had the same seed code listed as she did, but she didn't know any of them well. Sophia, it appeared, had the same father as Mary, but otherwise she couldn't find many connections between the academy girls. There were hundreds of other citizens who had the same Seed Origin code, but they were not girls who attended the academy.

She traced her finger across her best friend's name. The failed mission, her injury, and the leaflet delivery had distracted Faith temporarily, but she was still desperately worried about Sophia. And with the confirmation that Danforth's testing was linked to reproduction, Madeleine had rejected the idea of a rescue. They had a responsibility to observe her a little longer, she had said. Discover once and for all what Danforth was up to.

But watching her friend lying in the hospital bed, pale as milk and vomiting regularly, was too much for Faith. If, as Robyn and Madeleine believed, she was pregnant, did Danforth somehow have a secret store of seed? What part did the two drugs play in the experiment? So far, Sophia appeared to be the only student who'd been given both drugs. Clearly, she was their prime test subject.

Did Sophia know she was pregnant? Was she *aware* of what they were doing to her? Was she too weak to fight? Faith had tortured herself over and over with questions. Robyn had tried to reassure her, telling her that Sophia was important to Danforth, that there was no way they would risk her death when she was the only candidate currently showing a promising response to the experimentation.

But Faith wasn't just worried about Sophia dying. Being confined to a bed for so long, with no company other than the medics who were overseeing her, had to be affecting her mentally. What of the long-lasting effects of the cocktail of thus-far-untested drugs she was being given? Faith shuddered just thinking about it.

Until the leaders permitted a rescue mission though, there was little she could do.

She snapped a few more pictures of the seed codes, making sure she had a record of all the people she knew for future reference. As she was sliding the genealogy book back into the file, there was a crackling in her headphones. A firm click Faith knew was Anderson's office door closing. A slight creak of the chair as the principal sat down. And then, the intermittent buzzing that suggested an incoming call.

Faith moved across to the table where she'd left the datadev. Anderson was probably ordering dinner, but she should pay attention, just in case. Dropping into the nearest chair, she listened.

The buzzing stopped, and she knew the call had been answered. There was silence, as the call recipient spoke first. On Anderson's reply, Faith froze.

"Put me through to the chancellor, please."

Faith held her breath through the pause which followed. Eventually, the academy principal spoke again, her voice low and terse.

"Abigail, we have a problem."

Chapter Twenty: Noah

Walking through the city was a different experience, now that Noah knew his visit was more than a fleeting one. The streets seemed more dangerous, yet at the same time full of promise. Here, perhaps, he could actually make a difference. To the people of Eremus, to the citizens of Bellator, to the students at the academy.

And, of course, to Faith. She was here, somewhere. He might see her soon. He couldn't decide whether he was excited or worried by the prospect. Slipping a hand inside his pocket, he brushed his thumb along the delicate chain of Faith's pendant. The one he had once taken without her knowledge. By the time he had confessed to stealing it, they had grown close. She had told him to keep it as a token of her affection. It had become his good luck talisman.

After Jacob's devastating visit to the caves, Flynn had decided there was little point in delaying the dual mission into Bellator. A thorough examination of their resources had revealed a well-executed raid by the ex-leader which had left them missing numerous guns and explosives, some of the batteries they had just received from Madeleine, and one very important Danforth student.

Jacob had always been a meticulous planner. Even with a limited force behind him, he had managed to manipulate the community into doing exactly what he wanted. Dividing his followers, he had sent them in three different directions while the Eremus citizens were dealing with the fire. Sarah, Harden, Jacob, and a couple of others had gotten in and out with their various prizes before anyone had known what was really happening.

Most citizens had been completely unaware of Jacob's actions until he was long gone. Those who had come face-to-face with them had been threatened with weapons but left unhurt as long as they didn't try to stop him. Flynn didn't think they would return. The only person at risk now was Avery, who Sarah had forced out at gunpoint.

According to Professor Kemp, she'd been truly frightened, and clung to Farrah for several minutes while Sarah had threatened them all. When she had left, she'd been quiet, shaking and quite unlike her usual self. As Danforth's daughter, she was an important hostage to Jacob. Noah's ma seemed certain she wouldn't be hurt. Whether Avery knew that was a different matter entirely.

The council was frustrated by Jacob's actions, but at the same time Noah knew they were grateful that the problems caused by the raid were minimal. No one had been hurt or killed. The cave system had been mostly empty because of the fire, which had been purposefully minor. The damage to their foraging space had not been serious, because Jacob had not intended the blaze to be a destructive one.

He didn't want to reveal the tunnel entrances to Danforth. He didn't want the Eremus people to starve. He just wanted to continue his vendetta against the Bellator chancellor. And to do that, he needed weapons. And a hostage.

Now that he had them, there was no telling what he would do. But Flynn and Paulo had felt it important to continue with the original mission as planned. Noah and Ella had been instructed to fill the Resistance in on recent happenings in Eremus, and hope that they didn't regard Jacob's absence as a stumbling block in the planned alliance.

After leaving the rest of the raiders at the tunnel exits, Noah, Professor Kemp, and Ella had made their way to a safe house on the outskirts of Bellator. They'd been met by Evelyn, a member of the Resistance the community had prior involvement with. Greeting Kemp with a brief hug, she had confirmed their prior instructions: the professor was to remain in the house until later, when Evelyn would return.

They planned to use a cover story about how Kemp had been captured by rogue men while searching for the missing Danforth girls in the forest, but for this to work she would have to act as though she had staged an escape. Evelyn would assist her with this, but right now her job was to guide Noah and Ella safely to the Resistance headquarters at the library.

"Busy night." Evelyn had frowned. "There's a lot going on. Stay quiet and do what I tell you at all times."

The Resistance's presence on the streets, she had told them, was riskier of late. There had been issues with a recent mission and they were keen to avoid more clashes. They would stay out of sight as far as possible, keeping to the less-travelled routes. Noah was not yet acting the part of a drudge, so it was vitally important he acted with caution, as though he was on an ordinary raid.

Noah had tried to keep his expression neutral at Evelyn's words, though Ella stiffened beside him. They needed to stay calm, no matter what. As Evelyn had set off with a gritty determination, he had reached for Ella's hand, hoping his reassuring squeeze would be enough to carry her through the journey.

Since then, they had been following their guide for more than an hour. She knew the city well, leading them along narrow side roads and darkened alleyways with assurance. At every junction, she paused to check that the route ahead was clear. When forced to cross a major street, she did so swiftly, darting from the shadows at one side of the road to the other.

As they headed into the heart of Bellator, the buildings around them grew taller and taller, until they seemed to scrape the sky above. Built with concrete, steel, and glass, the solid structures were symbols of everything Eremus was not. They screamed of wealth, of modernity, of permanence. The lantern-lit tunnels of their own community seemed a world away.

Noah had to force himself to keep his eyes at street-level. He had a responsibility to be aware of his surroundings, to use what raiding experience he had to keep Ella safe. Back in Eremus, he'd made promises to Ruth that he intended to keep. But the glamour of Bellator at night fascinated him. Brief glimpses of partially-lit store windows and office reception areas, the highly-decorated front of what his reading had taught him was a theatre, and a stylish-looking food-provision place the citizens called a restaurant taunted him, fighting to pull his attention away from their goal.

Beside him, Ella shivered. She wasn't a raider, and this was her first visit to the city. She had shown courage in volunteering for the mission, but he could see the reality made her nervous. Unlike him, she kept her gaze lowered, her eyes darting from side to side only when they moved across open areas where they were more vulnerable.

"Look out for her, would you?" Ruth had asked, her face tense. "As best you can. I know she *wants* to go. For the Danforth girls, for Helen, to change things... but she's frightened too." In an uncharacteristic show of emotion, she had grasped his hand tightly. "It won't be easy. Try to help her adapt."

Noah had promised that he would. And now, with the usually vivacious young woman mute beside him, he could see why Ruth had been worried. He took Ella's hand, pulling her closer to him. She glanced up at him, her eyes wide.

"It'll be okay," he murmured, wishing he had more knowledge of their final destination. "Not much longer now, I'm sure."

She opened her mouth to reply but was silenced by a harsh *"Sshh!"* from the woman who strode ahead. Glaring back at them, Evelyn held up a hand as they reached the end of yet another alleyway. Leaning her back against the wall, she motioned for them to do the same.

Noah squeezed Ella's hand as they obeyed. He watched the Resistance member edge forward, until she could peer out into the street ahead. For a moment, she was still. When she turned back to them, her face was white. She mouthed a single word.

"Guards!"

Chapter Twenty-One: Faith

Faith's body ached with tension as she listened.

"*...just back from a meeting at the medcentre.*" Anderson's voice was shaky. "*There's an extremely worrying leaflet tacked up on the wall outside the academy.*"

In the silence which followed, Faith presumed Danforth was responding. She stifled her laughter, wondering which Resistance member had been brave enough to place one of the leaflets so close to the school building. She hoped one of the students would see it. Perhaps it would give them hope.

Not that Anderson let them outside the academy buildings these days.

"*So you're already aware.*" Anderson's tone changed. "*And you've had the printing press shut down?*" A short pause. "*You're **sure** it's the only one?*" Faith could hear Anderson's sigh of relief. "*That's good. Do you think–*"

She fell silent again. It was very clear who had control of the conversation. Faith strained closer, as though it would help her to hear what Danforth was saying. She found herself hovering between elation and terror. Danforth was concerned about the leaflets. And she had acted quickly to close down the printing press at the *Bellator Blade*. She crossed her fingers that Stella had been nowhere near when the chancellor's guards had stormed the place.

It was several minutes before Anderson spoke again.

"Faith Hanlon." Faith jumped at the sound of her name. *"Well, she was always trouble, but…"* Another pause. *"She's obviously back in the city, then. And working with the Resistance."*

There was a repetitive sound, as though Anderson was tapping the desk with a pen. Faith wondered if it was a nervous habit. She certainly hoped so.

"Didn't we think she was still in Eremus?" Anderson asked, waiting for Danforth's response before continuing. *"But if she's back in the city, won't it be easier to get our hands on her now?"*

Not if I can help it, Faith thought. Begrudgingly, she admitted that Madeleine had been sensible to keep her inside. Being featured on the leaflet clearly made her more of a target.

As Anderson waited for the principal to reply, Faith cursed. It was difficult to judge what the chancellor was saying from Anderson's responses. She would have given anything to hear Danforth's side of the conversation.

"Unfortunate, yes… How many do you think there are?" A few murmurs, as though Anderson were agreeing. *"And if I've seen one, other citizens will have too."* A pause. *"What are we going to do?"*

Again, Faith wished she could hear what the chancellor was saying. There was a lengthy gap in the conversation now, so long that Faith thought perhaps Danforth had hung up. Eventually, there was a long sigh.

"I see. Yes, of course. You know I'll back you on that." Anderson cleared her throat, sounding almost uncomfortable. *"I can see how we would explain away the claims about Eremus... but the information about the drugs will be a lot more difficult."*

Faith felt a surge of triumph at the mission's success. She found herself grinning as Anderson continued.

"Yes. Things here are the same. We've made no significant progress, though we've been trying different concentrations as Sanders suggested. I'd appreciate some extra security, if you can spare the–" Anderson stopped abruptly. *"I see. No, of course not. Catching Stella Thane has to be your priority. I'm sure you'll have her in custody in no time."* She hesitated before continuing. *"How's the Thompson girl doing?"*

At the mention of Sophia's name, Faith stiffened. She didn't have to wait very long to hear Anderson's reply.

"And you're certain the Fertility wards are totally restricted? No one could get inside?" Faith imagined Anderson biting her lip. *"Because if anyone managed to verify what we're doing to her,"* her voice shook, *"that could be very difficult for us."*

Faith's hands curled into fists on the table in front of her. The fact that Danforth and Anderson were concerned about their experiment being discovered when her best friend lay pregnant and alone in a hospital bed was horrific.

"I'm sure you have." Anderson's tone turned placatory, and Faith wondered if Danforth was angry. *"No, I'm sure it won't come to that."* A pause. *"I'll let you go. Yes, of course. Goodbye now."*

But as Faith kept listening, the deep sigh which Anderson gave as the call ended told her more than the entire conversation. Anderson was frightened.

The leaflets were doing their job.

Chapter Twenty-Two:
Noah

Tightening his grip on Ella's arm, Noah began to inch backwards. Evelyn followed, mirroring their retreat. The footsteps in the street ahead grew louder.

As they reached a door in the wall of the alleyway, Evelyn held up a hand for them to halt. It had to be the rear entrance to a restaurant. The scruffy-looking door was set back in a slight recess, which would allow them a small amount of cover. Directing Noah and Ella into it, Evelyn positioned herself at the front, blocking them from view.

They had made the move just in time. From his position, the sounds were muffled, but Noah heard the footsteps stop somewhere close by. Tensing, he pushed Ella further into the recess and reached for the knife in his belt.

Evelyn remained stock-still as the guards' conversation floated towards them.

"I'm so tired." There was an exaggerated sigh. "I can't believe that she has this many of us out tonight searching for these damn leaflets. I mean, we're stretched thin enough as it is."

There was a pause before the second guard replied. "Danforth seems pretty concerned about their content, though. I s'pose, if they're being delivered as we speak, we stand a good chance of catching whoever's responsible."

"Guess so." But the first woman did not sound enthusiastic. "But if I have to work *one more* double shift this week, I'm going to scream."

There was a short pause, then a clicking sound echoed down the alley. Beside him, Ella whimpered, clamping a hand over her mouth to stifle the noise. Seconds later, wisps of smoke began to drift past. Noah pointed it out, miming a smoking action. Though Ella remained tense, she calmed enough to remove her hand from her mouth and gave him a tight nod.

Glancing around, Noah wondered what part of the city they were in. The route Evelyn had led them on had been unfamiliar to him. He hoped she was trustworthy, because he had no idea where they were. She could lead them right to Danforth's front door, and he'd be none the wiser until he was standing in front of her.

In an attempt to distract himself from the uncomfortable thoughts, he peered at the restaurant door. *What kind of food did they serve?* His ma had told him about eating out. She had fond memories of delicious meals out she'd shared with friends in the years before she had fled the city. The concept of paying for food to be served to you by a stranger had blown his mind.

He ran his gaze over the doorway. The signage said *Staff Only* in faded lettering. To one side of the door, there was a message board. Several notices were pinned on it: advertisements for comcar firms, the restaurant's menu, and a torn slip of paper with half a phone number scribbled on it. At the top, a newer-looking leaflet took precedence. *Citizens of Bellator Unite!* It proclaimed. *Your government is lying to you. Tune in to Bellator Exposed to find out more.*

Noah reached up and pulled the page down from the board. *Was this what the guards were talking about?* No *wonder* Danforth had half the guards in the city looking for them. Ignoring Ella's look of alarm, he turned it over and froze.

On the back of the leaflet was a photograph of Faith. She was unsmiling, her head angled to one side, but the look in her eyes was one of determination. Underneath, the headline read *Danforth Academy Student Speaks Out.* Noah shuddered. Just *how* involved was Faith with the Resistance? And in such a short time, too. But he didn't have time to read it properly now. Folding the paper in two, he slipped it into his pocket. His questions would have to wait.

As more smoke filled the air around them, Noah felt the urge to cough. Forcing himself to breathe slowly through his nose, he managed to regain control of his lungs. He strained his ears, hoping he might hear more. When they spoke again, it sounded like the pair had moved closer.

"How can we go on like this? I mean, Hammond keeps saying there'll be more recruitment, but it's not even like the new ones are properly trained, is it?"

In front of him, Evelyn shrank backwards ever so slightly. Noah pressed himself and Ella as close as possible to the wall as the guards continued to complain.

"You're right. There's been no time." The second woman spoke more softly. "And after the attack in the forest..."

"Yeah." The first guard barked out a humourless laugh. "Who wants to join her ranks now that we know what Eremus is capable of?"

"I heard rumours there might be another attack..." the woman sounded worried. "Perhaps in the *city* this time..."

The first guard scoffed. "Eremus would *never* attack Bellator."

"I'm not so sure. I mean..." The rest of the woman's words were lost as a delivery truck drove past the end of the alley.

"...struggle to hold them off," the other guard sounded dejected, "the way things are right now, it could be–"

The guard fell silent at a shrill beep. Seconds later, a disembodied voice cut through the night air.

"Suspects spotted on Bramwell Street. Backup requested."

"Must be one of the rebels delivering the leaflets." There was a grinding sound as the woman crushed her cigarette under her boot. "Danforth *will* be pleased."

"Bramwell Street's not far." There was another beep and the guard standing feet from where they crouched spoke again. "Unit 6 responding. Affirmative. We can be there in five."

"Thanks." Even over the intercom, the voice sounded relieved. "I'll hold off on making a move 'til you get here."

"Understood. Over and out."

A clicking sound, followed by a sudden shifting of feet indicated the guards were leaving. As the boots retreated in the opposite direction, Noah's heartrate slowed. But when he turned to face Evelyn, her face was white.

"This suspect. Are they part of the Resistance?"

"Most probably, yes."

"I'm sorry."

Evelyn shook herself. "They haven't caught whoever it is yet. And I can't worry about that now. You're my priority. We're almost there. But let's hurry."

With a smile of encouragement to Ella, Noah joined Evelyn at the end of the alleyway. This time, the route ahead was clear, and she beckoned them to follow her again. When Noah stepped out of the shadows, he found they were in a square, rather than a street. Impressive buildings flanked the open space, which also contained several benches and an ornate fountain.

On the far side of the square was an odd-looking building. Far shorter in height than the others, it was nonetheless attractive, in an old-fashioned sort of way. Solid and welcoming, it was totally out of character with the rest of the area, yet Noah found he liked it better than the skyscrapers which almost engulfed it.

"That's where we're headed." Evelyn waved an arm towards the older building. "The Bellator library."

Noah started towards the building Evelyn had indicated, but felt her grip on his arm.

"We don't access it that way."

She turned around and headed around the square rather than across it. Exchanging nervous glances, he and Ella followed her down yet another alleyway. A moment later, they found themselves being let into the side door of a shop. The woman who opened it acknowledged Evelyn before relocking the door and disappearing into the darkness.

Evelyn led them down a set of steps into a cellar. Moving to the far wall, she pulled aside a curtain, revealing a small door. When she opened it, Noah found himself looking into a tunnel.

"I'll bet we're more at home down there than most people."

But Noah's attempt at lightheartedness fell flat. Ignoring him, Evelyn gestured for him to move ahead. With a sudden burst of nerves, Noah stepped into the darkness.

Chapter Twenty-Three: Faith

E ager to share what she'd overheard with Madeleine, Faith headed to the office. As she approached, she could hear excited voices coming from inside. Knowing better than to enter without knocking, she tapped on the door.

"Come in!" Madeleine sounded far more animated than usual.

Faith pushed the door open, starting to speak before she even crossed the threshold. "Danforth knows about the leaflets. I just heard her talking to Anderson about it."

As she moved inside, she noticed Robyn sitting on the far side of the room.

"How long have you been back?"

"Not long."

"Well, I'm glad you're here." Faith closed the door behind her. "You'll want to hear this too. They sounded worried. I mean, *really* worried."

Robyn and Madeleine exchanged grins.

"Anderson said–"

"That's great." Robyn cut her off. "And it ties in beautifully with what's about to happen."

Faith glanced between the women, puzzled.

"Stella's trying to broadcast again." Madeleine gestured at the datadev.

"She's *safe*?" Faith gaped at the Resistance leader. "But... Anderson implied it was only a matter of time before Danforth–"

"Don't worry." Robyn's tone was soothing. "We anticipated this."

Faith spun to face her. "You did?"

"Of course, we did." Madeleine frowned. "As soon as Stella printed the leaflets, we knew she'd be a target for Danforth. Once she'd delivered the leaflets to headquarters, we moved her into one of the safehouses. It wasn't easy, transporting all her equipment so quickly, but she's well-hidden. Danforth won't find her."

"That's a relief."

"We're hoping the leaflets will give her a larger audience." She waved Faith into a chair. "Sit."

Faith obeyed. "How'd the leaflet distribution go, Robyn?"

"*Well*, I think." Robyn grinned. "I'm the first one back, but the others should be back any minute." Noting Madeleine's frown, she lowered her voice. "I'll fill you in properly later."

"Listen!" Madeleine was tapping buttons, adjusting the volume, her eyes glued to the screen. "Should start any minute."

Robyn leaned forward, whispering now. "Stella's trying a new signal blocker. Something Blake's been working on. We're hoping she'll get more information out before they find her this time."

Faith felt a surge of excitement. *It was all coming together!* Her eyes moved to the screen, where a black logo with the letters *BE* stood out against a white background.

After a few seconds of silence, a disembodied voice rang out from the speaker. *"Good evening citizens of Bellator, and thanks for tuning in."*

Faith turned to Robyn. "Stella disguises her voice?"

"Shh!" Madeleine glowered at them. Hiding a smile, Robyn nodded and raised a finger to her lips.

"A huge welcome to any new listeners out there!" Stella sounded almost gleeful. *"I'm hoping my audience tonight is larger than usual, due to a certain publication which has been... finding its way into the hands of the Bellator citizens tonight. For the benefit of any newbies, let me explain.* Bellator Exposed *likes to bring you the very latest insights into what's happening in our beloved city. Regular listeners will remember me mentioning the rumours about the explosion at the Bellator Hospital in previous broadcasts."*

There was a dramatic pause before the voice continued.

"We were told... officially, anyway... that it was an accident... a gas leak... but as you know, I had my doubts. As always, I kept on digging, and yesterday... guess what? I managed to grab an exclusive interview with a young woman who actually witnessed the event."

Robyn jabbed a finger at Faith in excitement. Trying not to blush, Faith kept her eyes on the datadev.

"My subject tells me she was at the hospital on the night of the explosion for some tests. Tests, I hear you ask? In the middle of the night? Very suspicious, I'm sure you'll agree. And definitely something that our well-respected chancellor doesn't want us to know about."

At the mention of Danforth, Faith turned to Robyn. "*Anyone* can listen to this?"

Robyn leaned closer, whispering to avoid Madeleine's wrath. "Anyone who knows about the broadcast."

At a glare from Madeleine, they turned their attention back to the broadcast, where Stella was talking about Eremus.

"...would have us believe that this place of legend was destroyed by our beloved guards many years ago. Of course, from time to time we hear about a few dangerous men who hide in the forest, waiting to attack the city, but we're always reassured that Danforth's forces eliminate them."

Faith considered how, not long ago, she had believed everything the chancellor told them. Madeleine was right. Most Bellator citizens just blindly accepted whatever they were told. If the Resistance was going to fight to improve things, it had to start by opening people's eyes. She felt proud to be part of it.

"The subject of my interview, Faith Hanlon," at the sound of her name, Faith shuddered, *"told me how she was taken from the hospital that night to a large community hidden deep in the forest. That's right, folks. Contrary to everything we've been told, Eremus still exists. And that's not all–"*

There was a short pause, a clicking sound, and the strange voice was silenced.

Robyn glanced at her wristclip. "Eight minutes. Not bad."

Faith swallowed her disappointment. "Blake's signal blocker worked, then?"

"It did," Robyn confirmed. "Stella got a lot more out than her previous attempts. And she'll set up from a different frequency tomorrow."

"And reveal a bit more?"

Robyn grinned. "That's the plan. Unless Danforth finds out who's responsible for the broadcast, she'll just keep at it."

"But Stella would be..." Faith chewed her lip. "I mean, she has to remain anonymous. Or... she'd be in danger?"

"She would, but she takes multiple precautions." Madeleine raised an eyebrow. "As we have with you."

Faith blushed. "So tonight's mission. If the leaflets reached enough people... if Stella's broadcast is more widely heard... if citizens begin to realise Danforth's been lying to them–"

"They join us. Or at least support us." Madeleine stood up. "And finally, we can start to make significant change."

"And you believe it will happen?"

"I do." Madeleine regarded Faith with a steady gaze. "It's complicated, it's frustrating, and it's dangerous." She folded her arms across her chest. "But with your words, and with Eremus on our side, it's looking more possible every day."

A buzzing sound emanated from Madeleine's datadev. She glanced down at it. "People in the tunnel. Probably some more of the raiders returning."

Robyn leapt up. "I'll let them in."

As she bolted from the room, Madeleine turned to Faith. "Go get Blake. Tell her to come see me with her notes. I don't need a full report, but I want to know how many were listening just now."

Reluctantly, Faith obeyed.

At the door of the hub, she glanced towards the tunnel exit. *Was Diane among the returning raiders?* As Madeleine cleared her throat loudly, she thought better of staying to find out. Head down, she hurried to Blake's office. The sooner she relayed the message, the sooner she could return and check on her friend.

Chapter Twenty-Four: Noah

Once the door was closed behind them, Evelyn turned on a flashlight and led them farther into the tunnel. They walked for several minutes, stopping when they reached a second door. When Evelyn opened it, Noah could hear voices on the other side. He began to understand. Instead of walking across the square itself, in full view, the tunnel had brought them to the library via an underground route. It was a far safer entrance, and made Noah feel a lot more secure about the place they were about to enter.

"Come along." Evelyn beckoned to them, before disappearing through the door.

Noah followed her with caution, towing Ella behind him. Her hand trembled in his. The room on the other side of the door was large and filled with a haphazard mixture of tables and chairs. Most of them were empty, which made sense with the late hour. On the other side, Evelyn stood talking to a dark-haired woman. Their expressions were serious, but the unfamiliar woman's face broke into a smile as she spotted him.

"I see you brought us some new allies." Leaving Evelyn, the woman moved towards him, her hand outstretched. Ella released Noah's hand and took a step back. "I'm Robyn. Welcome to the Bellator Resistance."

"H-hi." Noah hated that his voice faltered. He accepted the hand, shaking it more firmly than was necessary. "Thanks for…" he glanced around the room, "well, for having us. I'm Noah," he added hastily, "and this is Ella."

"Come in." The woman moved immediately to Ella, recognising her reluctance. "We don't bite!"

Ella said nothing, but allowed herself to be ushered into the room.

"I'd better go." Evelyn moved past them to the door again. "There's still Kemp to take care of."

"No rest for the wicked, eh?" Robyn nodded. "Stay safe. Try not to worry about…" Noah knew she was referring to the conversation they had overheard between the guards. "It might come to nothing."

"Let's hope so."

As Evelyn closed the door behind her, Robyn returned her attention to Noah and Ella.

"Come this way," she called over her shoulder, leading them towards another door at the back of the room.

With no other choice, they followed her. Inside, a familiar woman with silver hair was waiting behind the desk. Noah smiled in recognition. Unlike the last time he'd seen her, her hair was pulled back severely, but her eyes glittered with the same intensity.

"Noah!" She peered at him. "It is Noah, isn't it? Paulo's brother?"

"It is, yes. Hi, Madeleine. This is Ella." He noticed Robyn close the door behind them. "It's good to see you again."

"Good to see you too." She stood up and circled the desk. "Just the two of you?"

"Yes," Noah replied. "For now."

"We weren't sure exactly how many to expect."

"Flynn felt we should start small. See how it goes."

"Always was a sensible man." Madeleine stopped right in front of Noah, narrowing her eyes.

Noah opened his mouth to tell her about Jacob, then closed it again. Perhaps it could wait until tomorrow, when they were more rested. The Resistance leader was a formidable woman, more so now that he didn't have Paulo to protect him. Right now, she was staring at him in quite an off-putting manner.

She seemed to size him up, her gaze roving over him from head to toe. Taking hold of one of his arms, she circled it with her fingers, nodding with apparent approval when they almost met on the other side. Finally, she took hold of the sweatshirt he was wearing and pulled it in tightly around his waist.

"What–?" he gasped, taking a step back.

"Yes, I think you'll do nicely." She let go of him, glancing over at Robyn, who had been watching her with amusement. "Oh, stop it. I just wanted to check that they'd sent someone who'd fit the bill. No good sending a great hulking oaf like Jacob or Paulo. They'd make useless drudges."

Turning her attention to Ella, she screwed up her eyes. "And we'll need to place you somewhere too, I suppose. I have a few ideas, but it will depend on where you might best blend in." She paced around his friend, who shrank away from the scrutiny. "Won't be as tricky, what with you being female, and all." She peered into Ella's face. "What are you good at?"

"I do all kinds of jobs in Eremus." Ella stood taller. "I'm experienced in foraging, preparing food, cleaning, I've supervised the children, trained others." Her courage failed. "But perhaps those aren't useful skills here." Madeleine said nothing and Ella sucked in a breath. "I can read and write fairly well. I help Anna in the medcentre occasionally, though Noah has more experience in that department."

"That's all good to know." Madeleine narrowed her eyes. "I was thinking about–"

"Madeleine!" Robyn interrupted. "Our guests have come a long way. They must both be very tired." She cast a sympathetic glance at Ella and Noah. "And, I'm guessing this is a lot for you to take in right now." She leaned closer. "Don't worry, we aren't going to send you straight out into the city to fend for yourselves. Not tonight, anyway." She waved them away as Noah shot her a panicked glance and Ella gasped. "Kidding. I'm just kidding."

"It will need to be soon, though." Madeleine had retaken her seat behind the desk, not seeming to share Robyn's sense of humour. "After tonight, things are really going to ramp up. If you're truly going to join us, and be of use, it needs to be sooner rather than later."

"Just having you here is an excellent start, though," Robyn chimed in, noting Ella had paled. "It shouldn't be too difficult to prepare and place the two of you." She turned to Madeleine. "Evelyn had some new intel which we should discuss. And the others will be back soon. Shall I get our guests settled? Then I'll come back and talk to you?"

Madeleine frowned. "Alright. But don't be long. You'd better put our male visitor in the storeroom." She turned to Noah. "My apologies, but I don't think it would go down too well with the women here if I were to place you in one of the shared bedrooms."

"Of course not," he murmured. "Don't worry, I'll sleep anywhere."

Madeleine was already turning back to the screen in front of her.

"Come on, then." Robyn ushered them out the door.

A moment later, they were standing in the shared area once more.

"We call this the hub." Robyn waved a hand across the room. "It's where we gather to eat, chat, and so on. You hungry?"

"No," Ella said, as Noah was about to say the opposite. Closing his mouth, he decided not to undermine her.

Robyn caught his eye. Changing direction, she moved to open a cupboard in the kitchen area at the front of the room. When she returned, she was holding a chocolate bar. She pressed it into Noah's hand.

"That should keep you going til breakfast."

"Thanks." Noah found himself warming to her. "Appreciate it."

She winked at him. "It's nothing. Now let's get you a place to sleep."

As they crossed the hub, a short woman burst in from the opposite side. She took in the newcomers, a look of suspicion crossing her face.

"Great work tonight, Blake." Robyn smiled.

The woman grunted something as she passed, heading for the office they had just left.

"Don't mind her," Robyn muttered, "She's always like that. It's nothing personal." She glanced at Ella with concern. "You look like you're about to collapse." She led them back to the hallway they'd entered through. "The storage room's this way."

Ella hurried to catch up. "Couldn't..." she faltered.

Robyn stopped. "What is it?"

"Um... I don't want to be any trouble, but is there some way I could stay with Noah, just for now?" Ella chewed on her lower lip. "I'd be fine in the storage room too."

Robyn burst out laughing. "It's *tiny*. We won't fit you both in there." Ella's face fell, and Robyn leaned close. "Listen, don't you worry. Most of us are very friendly. I promise, we'll look after you, and I'll make sure someone brings you right back to Noah here in the morning."

Halfway down the hallway, Robyn stopped. Pulling open another door, she revealed a storage space. Both sides had shelving from floor to ceiling. The only free space was a small rectangular section of floor in between.

"See what I mean?" Robyn rolled her eyes as she turned to Noah. "Would you mind waiting here while I take Ella to the dorm rooms?" She shot him an apologetic smile. "Most of our residents are out right now, but they'll be back soon."

"No problem." He stepped back into the store room. "I'll wait here, out of the way."

"Great. I'll bring down some bedding for you in a few minutes." She turned to Ella. "Ready?"

"Sure." But as Ella was led further down the hall, she turned back to Noah, her eyes filled with concern.

"See you in the morning." He gave her what he hoped was an encouraging smile as she disappeared down the hall, hoping she would manage to get at least some sleep.

Peering around the space he had been allocated, he contemplated his own exhaustion. He wasn't used to much in the way of comfort, so the floor would be fine, but he did wonder how the other women might react to him. Robyn had seemed quite concerned that he stay out of sight until his presence had been explained.

Would it frighten them so much, having a man in their space? He remembered his first encounter with Faith and decided it would. *What if one of them came across him by mistake?* It was a store room. Surely many of them used it.

Leaving it open so he could see, he stooped to study the door, hoping it might have a sturdy bolt. He would definitely feel more secure knowing he couldn't be disturbed while he was sleeping. But though the door did have a lock, it looked like one which required a key. A key Noah was pretty certain Robyn wouldn't allow him to have.

A noise further down the hallway startled him. Expecting Robyn's return, he was alarmed to see another door much closer to him begin to open. He tensed, stepping back inside the store room to avoid startling the newcomer. Easing the door closed, he waited in the darkness, feeling foolish.

For a moment, there was silence. And then, the sound of footsteps, moving towards him. Noah froze, praying they would go right past. But they didn't. He heard them stop right outside the door and his heart sank. His intention had been to stay out of sight to avoid frightening the woman. But if she opened the store room door to find a man hiding in the darkness, it would be so much worse.

There was a clicking sound. Noah imagined the handle turning. Hardly daring to breathe, he wondered what he should do next. Attempt to hide? Call out to the woman, alerting her to his presence?

But it was too late.

The door was opening, the crack of light widening. He blinked at the sudden brightness. The figure on the other side seemed young, a similar age to him. Her head was bent over a handheld device of some kind, a tumble of hair falling over her face.

She reached out absentmindedly, hitting a switch on the wall to his left. As the store room was flooded with light, Noah braced himself. But when she finally looked at him, he was just as shocked as she was.

Chapter Twenty-Five: Faith

"Noah?" She stumbled backwards, a gasp escaping her lips. "What are you...? Where did...?"

The world around her seemed to be spinning faster and faster. She tried to make sense of it, wondering if she was suffering the effects of sleep deprivation. She'd delivered Madeleine's message to Blake. As she'd left, Blake had asked her to fetch some batteries so she could replace those in the datadevs which had been used for the mission that evening. When she opened the store room door, *Noah* was standing there.

Faith wondered if she was hallucinating. But as she blinked and looked again, there he was. He took a step forward, then stopped.

"Faith?" The voice was familiar. "I was hoping to find you here, but I didn't think..."

"Why are you–? How are you?" Faith pressed her hand against the doorframe to steady herself. "I don't understand..."

"Madeleine didn't tell you?" Noah looked unsure of himself. "I-I mean... you didn't know?"

"That you were coming?" Faith frowned.

"Not that *I* was coming... not specifically." Noah shrugged awkwardly. "But that Eremus was sending people into the city."

"Yes." Something stirred in Faith's mind, "I do remember her saying something about that."

Faith stayed where she was, a slow smile creeping over her face. First, Danforth's fear about her appearance on the leaflets. Then, Stella's broadcast, even from her new location at the safehouse, lasting for such a long time. Now, Noah was here. Perhaps things were finally starting to improve.

She blinked again. "You're really here?"

"Yeah, I'm here. Flynn and Madeleine agreed that some Eremus citizens would come into the city. To support the Resistance." He smiled faintly. "Discuss an alliance."

"So..." Faith's mind was racing. "You're... staying here? In the library?"

She took a step forward, closing the gap between them. Stretching out a hand, she touched his arm. He felt solid enough. He was really standing right in front of her. As she brought her other hand up to his face, the air around them seemed devoid of oxygen.

His eyes moved to her hand on his arm. She became aware of how close they were standing. Blushing, she took a step back.

A burst of sound came from the hub.

"That'll be the women from tonight's mission coming home." Beside her, she felt Noah tense. "Don't worry. They've been out all the night. They'll probably head straight to bed."

He didn't relax. Laying a hand against his chest, Faith pushed him backwards until they were both standing inside the store room. She pulled the door closed behind her and turned to face him.

"We'll just wait here until they pass." She sent him a reassuring smile. "It won't be long."

"Alright."

He let out a slow breath. Suddenly, the space seemed tiny. Faith shifted slightly, turning so her body was side-on to his. There were things she wanted to say. And she couldn't do it when he was standing so close.

But before she could open her mouth to start speaking, Noah began fumbling with something in his pocket. Puzzled, she waited. When he brought out a bar of chocolate, she almost laughed.

"Sorry. It was a long journey." With an expression of reverence, he removed the top corner of the wrapper and broke off the first couple of pieces. He held them out on the palm of his hand. "Want one?"

"Thanks."

Feeling shy, she leaned forward and picked up one of the chunks. As she withdrew her hand, he tossed the other one into his mouth. A look of contentment came over his face.

"Been a while since I've tasted anything this good."

"I heard Eremus was struggling."

He finished chewing and swallowed before responding. "We definitely need supplies. But the raid tonight will make a real difference. And the fact that I'm here... about to join the Resistance." He beamed, and she wondered at how easily he seemed to have forgiven her betrayal. "It feels like I'm finally part of something, you know?"

He snapped off another piece of chocolate and offered it to her. When she shook her head, he ate it himself.

"I know *exactly* what you mean." Faith had been thinking the same thing only an hour ago. But she focused on what she wanted to say, not wanting to get distracted. "And I'm glad you're here... because I hated the way I left."

He finished chewing and she saw him swallow, but this time, he didn't take another piece. Instead, he dropped his gaze, waiting for her to continue.

"You have to know that I came back here for Sophia." She stood up straighter. "She's my best friend, and... and I was frightened for her. I couldn't just abandon her to her fate. Not when Danforth–" she stopped, not wanting to break down before she'd had the chance to finish explaining. "You have to believe me. I didn't *want* to leave you... Not after–"

He looked up at her, his eyes glowing with intensity. "Not after what?"

Now it was her turn to turn away. She stared at the shelving, stacked with boxes of supplies. "Um... not after we'd..." Reaching out, she straightened a couple of boxes. "Well, I mean, we had..." she turned to face him. "Hadn't we?"

"*What* had we...?" He laughed softly. "Talked? Started to get to know one another? Enjoyed each another's company?" He leaned closer, his voice dropping to a whisper. "Kissed?"

"Yes. That." She willed herself not to get distracted. "All of that." Reaching for his hand, she clutched it tightly. "I wanted to say I was sorry."

"I know."

"You do?" She glanced up at him, surprised.

"I do." He shrugged. "I mean... It's not like you could've *told* me you were leaving... I couldn't have just let you go, could I?"

His simple acceptance of her apology humbled her. "If it hadn't been for Sophia, I'd never have..." she dropped her gaze. "Well, I'm not saying I'd have wanted to stay Eremus' prisoner forever, but... I didn't leave because of anything you did. I never want you to think that." She took his hand again. "Honestly, nothing could be further from the truth."

"Is that your way of saying you missed me?"

She blushed. "I guess so."

He leaned closer. "I missed you too."

"Are you..." She dropped her gaze, flustered by his closeness. "Will you be staying for a while?"

"Not sure how long we'll be here."

"We?" Her eyes flew back to his. "Someone came with you? Who?"

"Ella."

"Jacob let her out? I mean, Ruth told us she was–"

"It's a long story." Noah was too tired to fill her in on the situation with Jacob. "But my ma managed to release her. And she volunteered to come here."

"Volunteered?" Faith was confused. "What for?" She glanced at the door. "Where is she?"

"She was exhausted." Dodging Faith's first question, Noah jerked his head towards the hallway. "Robyn took her to a dorm of some kind."

"And where was Madeleine planning on putting you?" Faith felt the colour rise in her cheeks. "Not in with us, I'm assuming?"

"Right here, would you believe?" He chuckled at her appalled expression, waving off her concern. "I've slept in worse places."

"I guess they're worried... about the way the other women might react to you."

"They definitely are." He turned to her. "Should *I* be worried?"

As she opened her mouth to reply, the door to the hub banged open. Noah stiffened. Finding his hand, she tucked her own inside it and laid a finger on her lips. The sound of voices grew in volume, accompanied by the thunder of footsteps, but none of the women even paused outside the door.

When the hallway was silent again, she smiled. "We're good." She let go of his hand. "See? They just want their beds."

He relaxed slightly. "You think they'll accept me?"

"Honestly, I don't know. They're not used to being around men here. You can understand that, right?" He nodded. "But I think, as long as Madeleine explains who you are and why you're here, they'll come around."

"I hope so."

"They've been out all over the city tonight. Delivering leaflets." She felt a surge of excitement at the impact they'd already had. "Ones which tell the truth about Danforth. About the experiments at the academy. About Eremus." She grinned. "I listened in on a conversation between Anderson and the chancellor earlier this evening. Sounds like they're really worried about the content of the leaflets."

"Content *you* provided, I suppose." Noah's hand went into his pocket. When it emerged, he was holding a screwed up piece of paper. He straightened it out and Faith gasped. "Found this on my way into Bellator."

"They really did put them everywhere."

"Guess so." Noah's face clouded over. "Isn't this dangerous? I mean... putting your face out there? On such a dangerous document?"

"No more dangerous than you or Ruth or Ella coming into a city which would execute you in a second if it caught you." Faith held her head high. "Or hacking into Bellator's computer systems." She stared up at him. "It's how I'm making a difference. Like you coming here. Can't you understand?"

"I understand. Doesn't stop me from worrying about you, though."

"Don't worry about me." She made a sweeping motion with her hand. "Madeleine won't let me out of the library now that my face is out there. She's been very strict about it. I'm perfectly safe."

"I'm glad to hear it."

"And I'm hoping..." she leaned closer, "that if I keep it up, if Madeleine is pleased with me, that she'll consider rescuing Sophia from the hospital soon." She bit her lip. Things were going well. If they continued to do so, there was no reason why the Resistance couldn't bring Sophia back from the hospital. She *had* to believe it would happen.

"Sounds like you're fitting right in." Noah smiled. "And making such a difference. Sophia will be home in no time at all, I'll bet."

"I hope so."

"In the meantime," Noah stepped closer once more, circling his arms around her. "Did I tell you how much I'd missed you?"

"You did." Faith found her whole body was trembling. She slipped her arms around his waist, pulling him even closer. "But feel free to tell me again, if you like."

"What if I show you instead?"

Noah bent his head closer, his lips hovering over hers. She held her breath in anticipation of the kiss.

And then the door behind her burst open.

"I take it you two know each other?" The voice from behind made them both jump. Faith spun round to see Robyn standing in the doorway, holding a rollaway sleeping mat and a blanket.

Noah let go of Faith so fast she almost fell. By the time she had recovered herself, he was standing at the very back of the store room, his face flaming.

"Don't let Madeleine catch you." Robyn glared at Faith. "A relationship with an Eremus boy won't go down too well around here. You don't want people doubting where your loyalties lie, do you?"

Blushing, Faith struggled to regain her balance. "It's not– I mean... We're not..."

"It's okay." Robyn broke into a smile. "It's nice to see someone with a bit of happiness for a change. Just keep it quiet, okay?"

"Of course." Faith glanced at Noah, who was still staring at the floor. "I think I'll go to bed."

"Good plan." Robyn stood back and waved her through. "As for you, Noah, let's get you settled in this closet." She glanced at Faith as she scuttled past. "I don't need to lock him in, do I?"

Her tone was teasing rather than accusatory, but as Faith hurried away down the hallway, she found her cheeks were on fire. When she reached the dorm where she and Diane slept, she was relieved to see Ella fast asleep on an empty bed in their room. Not wanting to disturb her, she tiptoed past and slipped under her own covers as quietly as possible.

In the morning, Faith woke early to find Ella deep in conversation with Diane at the end of her bed. Scooting over to join them, she found herself smiling for what felt like the first time in weeks.

"Hey!" Ella hugged her. "It's good to see you."

"Wait, you're not...?" Faith pulled back. "I thought you'd be angry."

"We've already been through this." Diane rolled her eyes. "She knows why we came back. She doesn't blame us. It was Jacob who locked her up."

Faith turned back to the older girl. "Is that true?"

Ella nodded. "I mean... I get why you couldn't tell me you were going. I'd've been forced to try and stop you, wouldn't I? And poor Sophia..."

Diane shot a sideways glance at Faith. "What happened to you last night? I thought we were going to catch up when I got back from the mission, but you were nowhere to be found."

Faith knew she was blushing. "I was just talking to Noah. Didn't Ella tell you he was here too?" Ignoring Diane's amused expression, she ploughed on. "I bumped into him last night – in the supply room, of all places... We were talking... then Robyn came down and–"

Diane clapped a hand over her mouth. "Robyn caught the two of you together! What did she *say*?"

Faith slapped Diane's arm. "We weren't *together*. Not like that." Diane closed her mouth, but the smirk remained. "Isn't it time for breakfast?" She turned to Ella. "Come on, we'll take you down."

Ella looked grateful. "Thanks."

When they reached the hub, it was busier than usual. But despite the number of people in the room, the mood was muted. Something was wrong.

Once she had shown Ella where the food was, Faith grabbed a bowl of oatmeal and honey, some juice, and an apple. Taking a seat next to Diane at their usual table, Faith looked around.

"What's up with everyone this morning?" She glanced over at Diane. "I thought everyone would be thrilled that the mission went so well. Blake told me the number of people listening to Stella's broadcast had shot way up."

"I heard that too." Diane frowned. "When I got back people were celebrating."

As she finished speaking, a Resistance member called Olivia leaned across from the next table.

"You didn't hear?" Her face was pale. "Not everyone made it back from last night's mission."

"What?" Faith sat bolt upright. "How many people are missing?"

"Just one." Olivia dropped her voice. Faith braced herself for the name. "Laura."

Chapter Twenty-Six: Noah

He hadn't slept well. Despite Robyn providing him with perfectly adequate blankets, bed roll, and a pillow, a combination of nerves and excitement had proved difficult to ignore, and Noah had tossed and turned all night. When he had managed to sleep, he'd been haunted by dreams filled with faces: Faith's, Ella's, his ma's, the mysterious masked drudges. Eventually, he'd woken up with his heart pounding and a sheen of sweat on his face.

Robyn had returned not long afterwards, taking him to a small private bathroom on the other side of the building. He'd managed to work out the shower, revelling in the constant flow of warm water which was a far cry from the chilly waters of the bathing cave. He had just finished dressing himself when Robyn arrived and took him back to Madeleine's office.

The woman herself was absent, but Robyn directed him to a chair and left the room. A moment later, she returned with the sour-faced woman Blake. Robyn provided him with a hot cup of coffee, a circular bread product she called a bagel, and some fruit, before holding a hissed conversation with the other woman in the doorway. It sounded like they were arguing about something, but before Noah could begin to work it out, Robyn was gone.

Scowling, Blake moved around the desk to the far side. Sitting down in front of the device he'd heard called a datadev, she began jabbing away at the keys as though she had a score to settle with them. Noah assumed she hadn't wanted to be left babysitting, and didn't try to engage her in conversation. Clearly, the Resistance didn't want to leave him in the office alone with potentially sensitive documents. He decided he couldn't blame them.

On the opposite side of the door, he could hear the women gathering for breakfast. Slowly, at first, just a couple of voices, but as the moments ticked on, the clattering of dishes and chattering conversation grew in volume. He ate his bagel, marvelling at the way mealtimes here were at the same time both similar to and different from those he shared with his fellow citizens in Eremus. The element of companionship was much the same, but the food was a world away.

As he finished eating, his thoughts went to Ella. Was she stuck out there alone, as nervous as she had been the previous night? Concerned he couldn't fulfil his promise to protect her when he wasn't with her, he stood up and moved towards the door.

"What are you doing?" Blake's gaze snapped up from the screen.

"I just…" he gestured at the door. "I wondered when I might be able to go…"

"Not yet." Blake continued to tap away at the keys, despite the fact that she wasn't looking at them.

"When, then?" Noah took a step towards her, hoping she might be less hostile if he didn't appear to be disobeying orders. "I mean… I understand that I might be… unnerving… to some of them, but I thought the idea was to tell them about me so they were… prepared."

"Don't think we're *all* frightened of you." Blake looked him up and down. "I mean... don't underestimate us, will you? Us women... we're not all terrified little rabbits, you know."

"I'm sure you're not." Noah held up his hands. "Look, I came here with a friend... Honestly, *she* was a little nervous. I was hoping I could–"

"You'll do what you're told." Blake stood up. "Madeleine requested we wait for *her* to tell the rest of the women who you are and what you're doing here."

"And where is Madeleine?"

Blake frowned. "Taking care of some business. She'll be here soon."

"But until she's back...?"

"You stay here." Blake eyed him for a moment, sighing. "It shouldn't be much longer."

Noah moved back to the chair and sat down again. "Alright."

The other woman relaxed slightly and looked back at the screen. The speed with which her fingers moved over the keys increased.

"What are you doing?" Noah enquired.

Blake glared at the second interruption. "Sorry?"

"What is it you're doing?" Noah cocked his head to one side. "Apart from babysitting me, of course."

She didn't smile. "Research."

"Seems like you're pretty good at what you do there." She frowned, as though she thought he might be mocking her. "I mean, all that time you were looking at me, you never took your fingers off the keys."

She glanced down at her hands, then up again. "I touch type. I know where all the keys are... don't need to look."

"We don't have..." Noah waved a hand, "devices like that in Eremus."

She sat back in her chair, appraising him. "I don't suppose you do."

"Seems like they're very... useful."

She allowed herself a small smile. "I don't know how you can live without them. I know I couldn't."

Noah shrugged. "You could if you'd never known they existed."

Before Blake had a chance to respond, the door burst open and Madeleine strode in.

"Any sightings?" Blake's face clouded with worry.

"'Fraid not." The leader ran a hand through her hair. She seems to have disappeared into thin air."

Blake hissed a curse under her breath. "So Evelyn's fears were grounded."

"It's looking like it." Madeleine grimaced. "Of course, we'll keep searching."

"Do you think the guards caught her, then?" Noah asked, without thinking. He was rewarded by a withering look from Madeleine. "Sorry. It's just... I was with Evelyn when we heard–"

"I'm aware. And yes, we think that Danforth's guards probably have her, which is not good news. Still, we carry on." Madeleine returned her attention to Blake. "He's not here yet. Can you keep an eye out for him while I bring everyone up to date?"

Noah wondered at the male pronoun. But he didn't dare ask who Madeleine was referring to.

"Sure." Blake was already on her feet, anxious to leave. "You'll come up when you're done?"

"We will."

Noah wondered whether the *we* included him. As the door closed behind Blake, a buzz of chatter flooded in from the hub.

Madeleine stood looking at him expectantly. "They're waiting. Shall we introduce you?"

He made sure he met her gaze head on. "Before we do, I need to speak to you. I should've told you last night, really, but…"

A faint annoyance crossed the older woman's face, but she circled the desk and sat down in the seat Blake had just vacated. "Go ahead. We don't have a lot of time."

"Flynn asked me to let you know that," he glanced down at his hands before taking a deep breath, "there have been some changes in Eremus, recently. Ones you're not aware of yet."

Madeleine raised an eyebrow. Noah felt the chatter of the room outside fade as he steeled himself to tell the Resistance leader about Jacob. He had no idea what her reaction would be. His ma had insisted they couldn't lie. Honesty was the only way, she'd said, of securing an alliance between the two sides. But he had no idea whether she would be prepared to work alongside them now that Jacob was no longer part of the equation.

"You're aware, I believe," he began, "that there have been some… disagreements between the various council members."

"I was." Madeleine's gaze was shrewd. "Jacob's recent actions had upset some people, right?"

"That's right." Noah bit his lip. "In fact, Jacob is no longer in Eremus."

Madeleine frowned. "Where is he?"

"We're not sure." Noah hurried on before Madeleine could inter-ject. "When it became clear how many of the Eremus citizens were unhappy with what he'd done, the council tried to speak to him about it. He didn't react well."

"I can imagine." Madeleine raised an eyebrow. "What did he do?"

"He left."

"He *left*?" Madeleine echoed his words. "Where could he possibly go?"

"Well, at first he must have stayed close by. Not in the caves, but..." Noah's hands trembled, but he folded them together and forced himself to continue. "He returned a few days ago without warning. Took things from the community, then disappeared again. Flynn doesn't think we'll see any more of him for a while. Not now that he has what he needs... what he wants..." Noah trailed off.

"And what's that? Food? Batteries? Weapons?"

"Yes. Items which will ensure the survival of the people he took with him."

"How many people?"

"Five. All his allies."

"And you don't know where they've gone?"

Noah steeled himself to tell her the worst. "We suspect they're headed here, into the city." Madeleine narrowed her eyes as he continued. "When he came back to raid the tunnels, Jacob didn't just take supplies. He took Avery."

The Resistance leader scowled. "With full knowledge of who she was, I assume?"

"He knows she's Danforth's daughter."

"We can expect him to take action in the near future, then." Madeleine tapped a finger rapidly against the desktop. "Another threat. That's all we need."

Noah stared down at his lap. *Was this the moment where she called off the alliance?*

After a moment, she inhaled deeply. "Alright. I'll instruct my associates to keep their eyes peeled for Jacob and his associates entering the city. Can you give me a list of the people he's with? Describe them for me?"

"Of course. Whatever you need."

"We'll watch for him. Attempt to stop him if he tries anything." She shrugged. "Who knows – maybe his actions might work for us. If Danforth's distracted by an attack from Jacob, it might take the heat off the Resistance."

"You're okay to go ahead with the alliance, then?" Noah tried to keep his voice neutral.

"It's not what I'd have wanted." Madeleine leaned closer. "But the way things are at the moment... we're close to a breakthrough." Her eyes lit up. "*Really* close. But we're putting our people in danger every day. This alliance with your community gives us new opportunities, a larger force with which to act against Danforth.

"I've known Flynn almost as long as I've known Jacob. I trust him. The fact that he's sent you and Ella and Charlotte back to us is evidence of his commitment. I won't throw this opportunity away because of one rogue agent."

"That's great!" Noah flushed at the eagerness in his voice. Embarrassed, he changed the subject. "Did the professor make it back to the academy safely?"

"I'm waiting to hear." The older woman twisted a stray strand of hair behind her ear. "Evelyn accompanied her most of the way, but she had to do the last part alone. To keep up the backstory," Madeleine explained. "It was vital that she arrive at the academy doors looking as though she'd escaped from an Eremus capture. Evelyn made sure she looked a little dishevelled. Gave her a few bruises."

"What? But–"

Madeleine gave him a stern look. "We had to sell the idea that she'd been mistreated." Abruptly, she stood up. "Now, as I said a while ago now, time is of the essence. Are you ready?"

Noah's heartrate quickened. But Madeleine had been more than fair. He owed her this. It was what he had come here for.

"Sure." He stood up. "I'm ready."

Motioning for him to wait, she disappeared through the door, leaving it ajar. He heard her rap her knuckles on what sounded like a table to get everyone's attention.

"Morning," she began. "I'll start with the matter I am sure is uppermost in your minds. Despite a thorough search of the city, Laura has not been located. We do suspect that Danforth has her." Noah heard a muttering run through the crowd of women. "I'm sorry we don't have better news. For now, though, we carry on as usual. I know there have been rumours of some arrivals last night, so I won't pretend this is news to you all. Two Eremus citizens will be staying with us for a few days as we prepare them to join us, taking on undercover roles in the city."

Noah tensed. It was almost time. *How would these women react to his presence?*

"Most of you will have seen, if not met, Ella over there." Madeleine paused, and Noah imagined his friend's embarrassment as all eyes focused on her. "But her companion has not been placed in the dorms with any of you because he is male." She waited again, as there was a murmur of a different kind. Once it had died away, she continued. "They arrived in the middle of the night, and we did not wish to startle anyone, so we kept him out of sight. However, I'd like to introduce him to you now."

Pushing the office door fully open, she beckoned to him.

"Come on out." Noah obeyed, feeling very much like an exhibit at some strange museum. His eyes roamed the room, where the women's gazes conveyed every emotion, from outright fury to fear to curiosity.

"This is Noah."

As Madeleine named him, he searched the crowd for Faith, spotting her in the far corner. Her eyes were fixed on him, steady and kind.

Beside her sat Diane, and on the bench opposite, to his great relief, was Ella, who looked a lot more comfortable than she had the night before. With a sigh of relief, Noah smiled and tuned back in to what Madeleine was saying.

"…worrying unnecessarily about his presence here. I know we have varied opinions about the male of our species, but Noah will be kept close to a trusted Resistance member at all times and not permitted to roam headquarters at will. Your contact with him should be limited, and he will not have an opportunity to be alone with any of you unless you're happy with it."

Remembering Kemp's drudge training, Noah bowed his head and tried to look as unthreatening as possible.

"You don't have to speak to him at all, if you don't want to. For those of you who are very uncomfortable with the idea of men, bear in mind that he won't be here for long and, so far," something in Madeleine's voice made him look up, "he seems to be a long way from the violent male specimen we've all been told horror stories about."

Noah smiled at the praise. Catching Faith's eye again, he felt a surge of hope. They were together again. They could play their part in making things better. The future could be very different for them both now. He focused on what Madeleine was saying.

"…we're hoping he will be able to masquerade as one of the Bellator drudges, and infiltrate a key location in the city."

As Noah watched, all the colour drained from Faith's face.

Noah understood why. Last night, he had purposely avoided explaining the role he'd be assuming within the city. Faith had seemed exhausted, and he'd been so happy to see her that he hadn't wanted to risk ruining things between them. Because he'd known, the moment Faith knew he was intending to masquerade as a drudge, she'd be frightened for him.

Posing as a citizen of Bellator would be difficult enough for Ella, who was female. But if she were discovered, the city would probably try and help her. But as a man?

If Noah was discovered, he wouldn't stand a chance. He had always known this, but the terror on Faith's face brought home the danger he'd be in. Laura's disappearance was a stark reminder of the risks taken by the Resistance members. And if Danforth discovered the alliance between Eremus and the rebel group within her own city, anyone supporting them would be in grave danger.

As Madeleine finished her speech, he held Faith's gaze, determined not to flinch. He would do this. He *could* do this. He willed her to believe in him.

"For the time being, get on with things as best you can. Until we find out Laura's location, there is little we can do for her. I know it's difficult, but try to put her from your mind and do your work as usual. We all know the risks." She paused, her sombre expression morphing into something more businesslike. "Also, please keep out of the library this morning. Noah will be completing some training in there." She waved a hand at the door to the rear of the room, signalling the meeting was over. "That's all."

As he followed Madeleine through the hub, Noah felt a stab of guilt. He should have told Faith the truth when he had seen her the previous night. He tried to catch her eye when he passed her table, but she dropped her gaze, hiding her face beneath her hair.

Once Noah entered the library itself though, all thoughts of Faith were forgotten. Filled with row upon row of books, all housed in gorgeously-carved wooden shelving which stretched from floor to ceiling, the room was magnificent. Fervently wishing his ma was here to share the moment, he wandered to the first shelf, stroking his hand across the spines reverently.

Behind him, Madeleine cleared her throat. "Come on, no time for delay."

"I'm sorry." He hurried to join her. "I've just never seen so many books. It's... heaven."

Rolling her eyes, she sped ahead, leading him to an area at the rear of the space. Blake stood there, next to a figure Noah didn't recognise. Head bowed low and dressed in the uniform Kemp had described in such detail, he could only be one of the Bellator drudges.

"You're here." Madeleine turned to Noah without giving the man a chance to respond. "Noah, this is Arden."

The man slipped off his mask, revealing a thin face which was knotted with worry. He was older than Noah had anticipated, perhaps thirty.

"He works at the academy," Madeleine continued. "But he also works for us."

She glanced at the drudge and seemed to notice his expression for the first time. "Something wrong?"

Blake stepped forward. "There definitely is."

"What is it?" Madeleine glanced between Blake and Arden then back again.

Arden kept his head lowered, as though he were uncomfortable speaking in front of so many people. With more understanding than she had shown Noah earlier, Blake turned to Madeleine, speaking for the drudge.

"It's Kemp." Her face darkened. "She made it back to the academy alright, but they didn't buy her story. Not fully, anyway."

Noah's heart began to beat faster again. Beside him, Madeleine tensed.

"What happened?"

This time, when Blake paused to judge Arden's reaction, he opened his mouth to speak.

"She returned late last night. I was on garden duty… saw her come in." He paused, raising his eyes for the first time. "Anderson herself came out to meet her. Only she was pretty suspicious."

"Where is Charlotte now?"

"They have her locked up." Arden dropped his head again. "And I heard Anderson speaking to the gate guard. Danforth's heading to the academy this morning. To question her."

Chapter Twenty-Seven:
Faith

Fighting the urge to pound up the stairs to the library and demand to know what Noah thought he was doing, Faith retreated to Blake's room instead. Met with a vision of Sophia vomiting violently into a bowl, her face pale and distorted, she felt a sinking sensation settle over her.

She'd felt so positive the previous night. But everything she had thought was going well had come crashing down around her in a matter of hours. The leaflet run had led to Laura's capture. Noah's appearance was marred by the knowledge that he too would soon be put in grave danger when he posed as a drudge, of all things. And Sophia was no better.

Her only comfort was that the leaflets were out there. Surely, once the women of Bellator realised how many lies they had been fed, things would change?

But for now, she felt totally helpless.

The door banged open and she hid her face, wiping a tear from her eye. When she turned, expecting to see Blake, she was surprised to see Madeleine and Robyn. As Blake moved to her usual station and began twisting dials and tapping buttons, Madeleine took a seat and Robyn closed the door.

Their expressions grim, they settled around Blake's main datadev. Faith wondered whether she should leave, but as she opened her mouth to ask, she heard a familiar crackling. They were listening to the bug in Anderson's office. *But why were all three of them there?*

Faith's interest sharpened. Whoever the meeting was between, it had to be important.

A conversation was already in progress. Unlike the conversation Faith had listened in to, this meeting was taking place in person.

"...you're claiming you managed to escape their clutches?" The first voice was Anderson's. *"How exactly did you do that?"*

There was a pause. A shifting. And then, another familiar voice.

"I told you. I observed their movements the whole time I was held captive."

Faith's heartrate increased at the sound of Kemp's voice. *She had made it back to the academy!* But it didn't sound like her story was going down too well.

"...permitted me to visit a local lake to bathe once a week. I was blindfolded, of course."

Faith marvelled at the story. No one in Bellator knew about the bathing cave. They would swallow a lie about people washing at Swallow Lake because they knew very little about Eremus. And if Kemp had been blindfolded, she wouldn't be able to tell them anything about Eremus' location. It was a clever ruse.

"I knew the lake was my best chance of escape," Kemp continued, *"so when they took me there yesterday, I took my chances and ran."*

"How did you get away from them?"

Faith shivered at the cold voice. *Danforth was there!* No wonder Madeleine and Robyn wanted to hear the outcome.

"I had a knife... concealed it after a meal..." Faith marvelled at how calm Kemp's tone remained. *"I used it to stab the male who was supposed to be guarding me."*

*"You expect us to believe that you overcame an Eremus male with an **eating implement**?"*

"He was only a teen," Kemp continued, offering a plausible response for every question. *"Same age as the academy girls. He didn't expect me to attack him."*

"Is he dead?"

"I very much doubt it." Faith imagined Kemp shaking her head. *"I didn't wait to find out. I just ran."*

Faith almost clapped her hands. The story was perfect. Covering all bases, and performed with just the right amount of plausibility. She glanced at Robyn and Madeleine, whose faces were less pleased.

"Do you think she–" Robyn began.

"Shh!" Madeleine held up a hand, gesturing to the speaker. "I don't think so."

There was a lengthy pause. Inside the principal's office, there was the sound of rustling, as though someone was moving across the room. Faith heard a creak as the door opened. Muffled voices. And the sound of the door being closed.

By the time Danforth spoke again, Faith's body ached with tension.

*"That's a very... **convincing** story, Charlotte."* A chill ran up Faith's spine at Danforth's tone. *"But I'm afraid it does sound like a story. A very carefully constructed story, which permits you to return to us with no useful knowledge of your captors, no route with which you can show*

*us the Eremus location, no evidence **at all** that you were kidnapped and held hostage in the forest."*

"I assure you, Chancellor–" Kemp began.

"I'm afraid," Danforth paused, *"that I will need a little more convincing before I accept this as the truth. You understand my suspicion, of course. The Eremus males have tried to dupe us in the past."* Once again, Kemp started to speak, but was cut off by Danforth. *"You might recognise the commander of my guards, Lieutenant Hammond."*

With a shudder, Faith remembered the woman from the incident in the Eremus woods. The other occupants of the room were similarly disturbed: they knew Danforth's attack dog too. Trembling as one, they waited for Danforth's next words.

"The lieutenant is here to find out if what you are telling us is, in fact, the truth." Danforth sounded like she was enjoying the conversation. *"If it is, you have nothing to worry about. And we will, of course, accept you back in your old position. But if not..."* she let the thought dangle, *"an alternative course of action will be necessary."*

Faith leaned closer to the speaker, waiting for something to happen. For a moment, there was silence.

And then, a sharp crack. For a moment, Faith was confused. And then, as the sound reverberated around the room for a second time, she knew.

Kemp was being beaten. Tortured for information.

Faith's face creased in horror as a succession of ever-more-violent sounds continued. Kemp was strong. She was loyal. But was she strong enough to withstand this?

When Kemp let out a piercing scream, Faith covered her ears and began to pray.

CHAPTER TWENTY-EIGHT: NOAH

Noah tugged at the uncomfortable drudge mask. He was unsure he'd ever get used to wearing it.

After spending the entire morning shut away in the library, Arden felt Noah was ready to test out his new persona in front of others. The prior training with Kemp had paid off, and the drudge was pleased with Noah's progress. His training with Arden had involved completing numerous tasks: simply walking around the library, moving items from one place to another, reorganising books on the shelves, pouring drinks, and serving plates of food. Every task had to be completed maintaining the correct posture and keeping his eyes lowered.

It was harder than it looked.

After the news of Laura's capture and Arden's concern about Professor Kemp's return, it was all too easy to see what a dangerous position he was putting himself in. It was vital that he get everything right. But Arden was a good teacher, and a great model to follow. Noah marvelled at how he managed to convey so much with barely a word: small gestures, his posture, a nod or shake of his head, all sent an important message. He didn't think the other man had said more than a handful of words to him in the entire time they'd been together.

Noah was also questioning the term *man*. He knew the drudges were bred specifically for servitude. His ma had told him they weren't men like Flynn, or Paulo, or himself. But beyond that, he knew little. Arden looked male, however his behaviour was so unlike any man Noah had ever known that he struggled to place it. He didn't act like any of the females Noah knew either.

It was as though the drudges were a totally different species. Trained to be submissive, to go unnoticed, to be ignored. Yet every now and again, Noah caught a look in Arden's eye which suggested there was so much more to him than his obedient exterior. Kindness, empathy, personal opinions, even humour. Certainly, Danforth's servants deserved better treatment than they received.

Kemp had told him the punishment for a drudge who disobeyed was death. Yet, if drudges were bred to be like this, perhaps Danforth believed they'd never rebel. Yet Arden worked for the Resistance. Behind his quiet, submissive exterior, he wanted more. And that told Noah a lot about him. He was brave, intelligent, determined to make things better. Noah found it fascinating.

When he led Noah to the door of the library, Arden resecured his mask before opening it. Beckoning, he motioned for the two of them to move down the stairs together and into the hub. Noah walked by his side the whole way, working hard to mirror his actions and demeanor.

The room was far quieter now, with only Robyn seated at a table on the opposite side, close to the office door. Her head was down, and she seemed subdued, but she stood up as she saw them enter.

"Wow." She ran her eyes over Noah. "You're pretty convincing in the costume, I have to admit."

"I'd like Noah to serve lunch to a few people." Arden murmured from behind his mask. "Good practice for him."

"Sure." Robyn got up and moved towards the door. "I'll just fetch a few of the others. He'll need to convince more than just me."

As Robyn disappeared through the door, Noah followed Arden into the kitchen. His heart was pounding. Once inside, Arden gestured to the cupboards.

"Start by serving some drinks. Just as we practised." He nodded encouragement as Noah began setting up a tray of glasses. He was filling a pitcher with water when a door banged in the hub. Stiffening, his gaze followed the sound.

A cool hand on his arm brought his attention back to the task. He looked at the drudge who stood beside him. Unusually, Arden held his gaze. His eyes were calm and serious.

"Try to stay calm."

"That's easier said than done." Noah shut off the water and placed the pitcher on the tray with shaking hands. "I don't feel ready. I'm not–"

"If you mess up, just stop what you're doing and take a breath." The drudge smiled. "Fake a cough or sneeze, if you have to. You can get away with a lot under the cover of a tickle in the throat."

Arden relinquished his hold on Noah's arm, stepping back so Noah had space to work. Inhaling steadily through his nose, Noah tried to calm himself. *One step at a time.* To begin with, all he had to do was retain the drudge posture while pouring drinks. He had been working at it all morning. If he wanted to play his part in the Resistance, this was his chance.

He carried the pitcher over to the tray, making sure he could access everything he needed without issue. Outside, the sound of voices grew in volume as whoever Robyn had gathered came closer. He caught snippets of the various conversations as several women assembled around a table just outside the kitchen door.

"Still no news of Laura." The sharp tone belonged to Blake.

"Do you think Danforth will torture her?" *Diane,* Noah thought. "For information?"

"After what we heard Kemp go through this morning, I'd say it's fairly likely." The more reasonable voice belonged to Robyn, he was sure. *But who was she talking about?*

"Hammond gave her a real going over," Blake sounded disgusted. "Right there in Anderson's office."

Noah shuddered. Professor Kemp's return to the academy had obviously not gone as well as they'd been hoping.

The next voice he heard was lower in volume than the rest, but he identified it instantly.

"I thought it would never stop." His heart went out to Faith, clearly a witness to Kemp's beating. "It was *awful.*"

"But she didn't give us away?" Diane was more practical. "We don't need to worry that Danforth knows where we are?"

"No." Robyn's voice rang with pride. "Kemp was amazing. Kept her mouth shut, no matter what Hammond dealt her."

"Do you think they'll leave her alone now?" This was Ella. Of course, she was concerned for Kemp's safety. "They believe her?"

"We hope so." Robyn's tone was sober now. "The assault lasted about fifteen minutes, but Kemp said nothing." He imagined her shrugging. "I guess they might try again later, but we're hoping her performance was convincing enough."

A silence settled over the group for a moment. Eventually, there was an impatient shifting and a voice called out.

"Noah?" Robyn sounded impatient. "You going to keep us waiting all day?"

Shaking himself, Noah grasped the tray firmly. With a last nod at Arden, he made for the door. He made sure to keep his head down as he entered the hub. Aware that every eye around the table was on him, he walked quietly to the table. Pausing to prop the tray on one hip, he removed the first glass and placed it on the table without issue.

"How's your training going, Ella?" Robyn piped up, as though she was aware of the pressure he was feeling. He found himself grateful for the distraction as he continued to make his way around the table.

"Okay, I think." As Ella began to speak, he could feel the women's eyes sliding away from him. "We've been studying maps of the city. I think I have a handle on the names of all the districts already. Diane has been testing me on the routes between the key landmarks, and..."

With his eyes downcast, it was difficult to know who he was serving. He recognised the red jumper Robyn had been wearing, and the ring Ella wore on her middle finger which he knew had belonged to Dawn, but others took him longer to identify. The drudge view of the world was a very different one. He was going to have to learn to read cues in other ways, relying on his hearing and peripheral vision.

But he *would* adjust. Relaxing slightly, he circled the table until he had placed a glass in front of every woman. Now for the pitcher. He inhaled slowly as he picked it up from the tray.

Moving back to Robyn, he leaned across to fill her glass. It was a tricky process, as she was deep in conversation with Ella and waving her arms enthusiastically as she spoke. She wasn't about to make this easy for him. But, he supposed, the false situation would become real life very soon, and the ordinary women of Bellator were unlikely to go easy on him.

Still, he was proud when her glass was full and he hadn't spilled a drop. And as she swooped forward to grasp the glass and bring it to her lips, he stepped out of the way without missing a beat.

Soon, Diane, Ella, and Blake had full glasses of water in front of them. He had kept his eyes cast downwards throughout, resisting the temptation to glance up and check the women's expressions to see how they thought he was doing. At last, there was only Faith left.

He lined himself up on her left side, exactly as he had with all the others. Faith sat very still as he leaned in and positioned the pitcher so it was directly above her glass.

But when he bent forward, he could smell her scent. Something slightly floral, reminding him of woodland flowers after a spring rainfall. Memories of their time in the forest came flooding back. He tensed, praying that his hand would stay steady while he was so close to her.

As he began to pour, Diane asked her a question and she turned her head towards her friend. The movement put her eyes on a level with his face. She opened her mouth to reply to the question and he felt her breath whispering across his cheek. The lips he had been about to kiss last night were only millimetres away from his.

Inhaling deeply, he fought to retain control. He would keep a steady hand if it killed him.

"Oh!" Ella exclaimed from the other side of the table.

Noah's eyes leapt to Faith's glass. For the first time in several moments, he focused all his attention on his task. He'd been concentrating on the wrong thing. And, whilst his hand was steady enough, the glass was overflowing.

Noah jerked back instantly, righting the pitcher. His eyes filled with horror. Faith stood up, pushing the bench back and leaping sideways to avoid the flood of water which was headed for her lap. On the opposite side of the table, Diane snickered.

"Way to lose focus," she muttered.

"I'm sorry," Noah looked up, his eyes meeting Faith's, "I didn't mean–"

Her face blanched and he froze, realising what he'd done.

Knowing it was too late to look away, he moved his eyes around the table. Ella's were filled with concern. Diane was stifling a smile. He was certain she'd asked the question in some effort to see how he would react to Faith's proximity.

But the more senior-ranking Resistance members were not laughing. When his gaze met Blake's, her eyes were cold. He looked at Robyn, the last person at the table. She had been nothing but nice to him since his arrival. Surely, she would understand?

But she was shaking her head. "Clean this up."

"Of course." He made for the kitchen door, his face flaming. "And then I'll start again."

"No." He turned back to face her. "Not today."

"But–" he started, closing his mouth and casting his eyes down at the dark look on her face.

"But nothing." Her tone brooked no argument. "Arden said you were ready. This was a simple task. The issue is not with you making the mistake and spilling the water. It's with your reaction to the mistake." She sighed. "Drudges are like another species. Perhaps we were too optimistic with our hopes that you could pull this off."

"Please," he held out a hand. "Give me another chance. This was just–"

"It was a failure." Blake's tone was harsh, but he knew she was right. "If you do that in Bellator, in front of real Bellator women, you'll be dead before the end of your first day."

A gasp ran around the table. Even Diane looked shamefaced.

"Blake's right." Robyn cast a glance at Faith. "If something as simple as proximity to an attractive young woman can put you off your game, how would you react to something going seriously wrong? How can we keep you safe? How can we rely on you to be useful, rather than a liability?"

"I'll do better!" He clenched his jaw, fighting to keep control for the second time in as many minutes. "I didn't come all this way for *nothing*. Just let me try again, and I'll–"

"The very fact that you're debating this with me proves our point." Noah lowered his head in shame at Robyn's disappointed tone. "Drudges don't talk back. They are subservient. They go unnoticed. We don't have the time or the resources for intensive training."

"I'm not sure it's worth the effort," Blake muttered.

"Perhaps not." Robyn gestured to the office. "Shall we get on?"

As Blake joined her and they stalked away, Arden emerged from the kitchen. He began mopping up the spilled water without a word. Noah knew he was simply being helpful, doing his job. But the perfect manner in which he executed the drudge-task made Noah feel ten times worse.

Unable to even look at Faith, he made his way back into the kitchen. He'd known what he needed to do. The task had been simple.

But he'd failed.

Chapter Twenty-Nine:
Faith

F aith was reeling. It had been hard enough to watch Noah playing the part of a drudge. But to see him mess up so badly? She glared at Diane. At least her friend had the grace to look ashamed. The question had been her idea of a joke, a deliberate effort to distract Noah by taking advantage of his relationship with Faith.

But Robyn and Blake's reaction had demonstrated the severity of the error.

"Do you think they'll send him back?" Ella's gaze rested on Faith, her eyes filled with concern.

As the real drudge finished cleaning up the water, she slumped down in her seat again. "I don't know."

The morning had started badly. After the horror of Hammond's attack on Kemp, she had attempted to occupy herself with Ella's training. She and Diane had begun to familiarise the young Eremus woman with the city's layout using a number of maps and photographs, but images of Kemp being beaten had kept swirling through her mind.

When they'd been asked to assist with Noah's training, she'd been glad to have the distraction.

But to have him fall at the first hurdle, in front of Blake and Robyn? Things just kept getting worse.

She glanced at the *real* drudge. Having replaced her glass with a fresh one, he was now pouring her a fresh glass of water. His hand was steady, his motions subtle, just as a drudge's should be. Her eyes wandered to his face.

"Arden!" she stuttered, recognising the large, expressive eyes. "Is that you?"

Behind his mask, he looked as startled as she did. But once he recovered from his shock, she was certain he was smiling behind the face covering.

"I thought you said drudges didn't have names." Ella looked puzzled.

"They don't. Not usually. So who..." As Faith stared at the man, something clicked into place. "Madeleine was the one who named you?" He nodded. "And *you're* the one who's helping Noah train?"

"Yes." Arden bent his head.

"So you work for the Resistance?"

"I do." He straightened his back, looking less like the drudge that he was. "Recruited by Professor Kemp. I keep an eye on what goes on at the–"

"Wait! You're from the academy?" Diane flushed. "But I don't recognise you."

"Why would you?" He met her gaze shyly. "Most Bellator citizens don't give us a second glance."

"I know." Diane looked shamefaced. "I thought–" she lowered her gaze, "I thought I was different. But I don't feel like I've ever seen you before."

"That's normal for me." Arden shrugged. "I'm not offended."

"Do many drudges work for the Resistance?" Ella asked.

He shook his head. "We are bred to be subservient. Many drudges are too afraid. That's why–" He cast a glance at the kitchen door.

Faith followed his gaze. "You want things to work with Noah."

Arden looked back at her. "He would be an effective ally. And he's good. It will just take him... a little time."

"Yeah." Diane jerked a hand at the closed office door. "Time they don't seem to think we have."

Silence fell over the table for a moment. Faith contemplated Noah's failure again. It had been wonderful to see him. Would she feel better if he were sent back to Eremus and its relative safety? Or if he could remain here and manage to become a convincing drudge? Both would mean him leaving her, but perhaps the drudge training would keep him in the library a little longer. She had to admit just being near him soothed her.

And it wasn't like she hadn't put herself in danger for the cause. There had been the mission to BellaLab Corp, and the previous one to the academy itself...

A thought struck her. She turned to Arden. "Were you the one who left the window open for the Resistance? The night we came to the academy?"

Arden hung his head. "I meant to say how sorry I was."

Faith frowned. "Sorry? What for?"

"The window." He looked sheepish. "I opened it as instructed, but when I came back to secure it afterwards it was already locked. I realised later..." He bit his lip. "We had a new guard in that night. Really inexperienced. She had sneaked into that office to smoke, not knowing about the alarm system. I guess..."

Diane groaned. "She opened the window to let the smoke out."

"She must have," Arden agreed. "And it would have automatically locked when she closed it." Faith felt a growing sense of horror. "That's why the alarm system reactivated faster than we expected."

"She obviously didn't expect the window to be alarmed, otherwise, she wouldn't have tried to use the room in the first place." Faith frowned. "Did no one ask questions about why the alarm didn't go off in the first place?"

"Oh, they questioned everyone about it. Had the whole security system reset the next day. And one of the other drudges overheard the guard being severely disciplined a few days later."

"Good job you didn't try to exit while she was smoking." Diane whistled under her breath. "It could've turned out quite differently."

Faith felt sick at her friend's words. They had been so close to getting caught. She thought of Laura, of Sophia, of Noah's mistake. They were *always* so close to getting caught.

She glanced at the kitchen door. There was still no sign of Noah. She stood up, ready to go and check on him. But she hadn't taken more than a step when the door to Madeleine's office burst open, making them all jump.

Robyn stood in the doorway, her eyes wild. "Danforth's about to make an announcement! We're betting she'll give her reaction to the leaflets." She beckoned to Faith and Diane. "Want to listen?"

Leaving Ella and Arden at the table, they hurried towards the leader's office. Inside, their attention was drawn to the ever-present datadev on the desk. Madeleine and Blake were already hunched over it, concern etched on their faces. On the screen, the chancellor stood behind a podium, her face sombre.

"Citizens of Bellator," she began, a serious expression on her face. "It has come to my attention that some very disturbing information may have reached you recently. It may have come in the form of an illegal broadcast which you could have stumbled across. It is more likely, however, that you have received a leaflet making numerous libellous claims about myself and my government."

"Libellous!" Faith hissed. "They were far from–"

Madeleine held up a hand as Danforth continued to speak. "These pamphlets, I can assure you, are filled with vicious lies. We have long been aware of the rogue males living in the forest. Despite my tireless efforts to rid our beloved city of their influence, it seems that some of them might have contacts *within* the city."

Robyn and Madeleine exchanged horrified glances.

"Yes, you heard me correctly." Danforth raised an eyebrow. "A small number of women within Bellator, who know of the vicious horrific influence that men had over females in the past, appear to be supporting these men in their efforts to disrupt and even overthrow our way of life." On the screen, Danforth leaned closer. "Now I don't want you to be concerned. These women are clearly troubled, and in some way being controlled by the male influence. And, as I said, there are not many of them. However, as I'm sure you will agree, they need to be *stopped*, before they can destroy our city and its way of life forever.

"Please know that I have not been idle on this matter. It is of extreme concern to our government that these women might gain the ear of any Bellator citizen–"

"I'll bet it is." Diane's comment was rewarded with a stern stare from Robyn. She fell silent as Danforth continued to speak.

"...to that end, I have begun to identify and hunt down any Bellator citizen who might have found themselves... involved in such treachery. Rest assured, I will treat these women with care and respect." At this, even Robyn spat out a bitter laugh. "They are sick. They have been infected by the male plague and should therefore be supported and helped to see the damage that such thoughts can cause." On the screen,

Danforth gave a little shudder. "But if you suspect that anyone you know might be involved in some way, it is your civic duty to report them."

Everyone jumped as Madeleine banged a hand down on the desk. "She wants us to turn tail on one another! Control us by fear, have us so afraid for our own lives that we're prepared to betray others to save ourselves."

"Will this undo the good the leaflets might have done?" Diane asked.

"Of course, it will." Madeleine snapped. "The more the women of this city fear their lives are at risk if they side with the Resistance, the less likely they'll help us."

"Not only that," Blake spoke for the first time. "She's encouraging them to help her hunt us down."

"That only works if she knows who we are." Robyn attempted comfort. "As long as we remain anonymous, as long as no one knows who we are or where we are, we should be–"

She stopped speaking as a familiar face appeared on the screen. A gasp of horror ran around the room as they all recognised Laura. Her face was pale and her hands were bound. She sat on a bed at what appeared to be a medcentre. The camera crept ever closer to her face. She looked tired, the dark circles under her eyes reflecting exhaustion, as well as terror.

"This is one of the women my guards caught last night. She was delivering the poisonous leaflets I'm sure many of you have seen."

"Women like this," Danforth continued, "are a danger to themselves and to the integrity of the community we've fought so hard to build. This rebel will remain in one of the Bellator medical facilities. She will be given medication and therapy to rehabilitate her."

"Rehabilitate her!" Robyn snapped. "Not likely."

After Kemp's experience earlier that day, they could all imagine what kind of treatment Laura was receiving.

"However," Danforth continued to speak, her tone hardening, "It is not only those *delivering* the leaflets who have been brought to my attention."

The video feed of Laura disappeared, replaced by an image of the leaflet itself. The camera zoomed in slowly as Danforth paused. A sense of dread settled over Faith as the entire screen was filled with her face. She felt the eyes in the room flick to her and back to the screen before the voiceover continued.

"This young woman," Danforth's tone was cold and forbidding, "disappeared from the city after the recent explosion at the Bellator Hospital. I have had guards out searching for her, to no avail." The chancellor's voice filled with fake concern. "We had assumed that she was a victim of some kind of kidnapping. But now, it seems she is being used as a prop for those people who wish to hurt this good city."

Faith bristled at the word *prop*. It implied she hadn't chosen to be part of this. That she was being manipulated by the people around her. That she didn't agree with the words Stella had quoted her saying on the leaflet.

"It is *vital* that Faith Hanlon is found and brought to me," Danforth continued. "We must give her the treatment she needs, take her away from the evil influences which control her. Before it's too late."

The camera returned to Danforth's face and she smiled directly into it, reminding Faith of a predator about to pounce on its prey. As she delivered the final blow, Faith felt sick.

"Good citizens of Bellator, I must ask for your help. Look out for Faith Hanlon. If you see her, it is your civic duty to alert the authorities. Anyone who has information on her whereabouts will receive the enduring gratitude of the city of Bellator." She paused, smiling slightly. "And a *significant* monetary reward."

CHAPTER THIRTY: NOAH

Though Danforth's broadcast had taken the heat off him a little, Noah knew the Resistance leaders hadn't forgotten about his error. No one had broached the subject of sending him back to Eremus. Not yet, anyway. But he suspected that a conversation was coming.

For the past two days, Robyn, Madeleine, and Blake had been locked in the office. Ella had told him the trio was trying to work out a way forward now that the leaflet campaign had failed. Noah noticed Ella was doing a superior job of fitting in at the library. The Resistance members trusted her, and she was included in more conversations than Noah.

Instead of actively working as a drudge, Robyn now had him sitting in the hub working his way through a stack of documents with Ella. Maps of the city, lists of the various workplaces, historical documents, the city's laws. Unlike Ella, who had been by turns fascinated and appalled, he had found it difficult to focus on the information.

After rereading the same section of one research paper three times, he tossed it on the desk in frustration.

Ella cocked her head to one side. "You *still* dwelling on the issue with the water yesterday?"

"Can't help it." He rubbed the back of his neck with his hand. "They really don't trust me now. I feel like this," he gestured to the papers, "is my punishment."

"This sort of stuff is just as important as the practical tasks. It's important that we both know the city well."

"I know." He grimaced. "But I've been at it all day. At least you get to do a mixture of both."

It was true. Ella had been taken out into the city that morning, permitted to go shopping, run errands, speak to actual Bellator citizens, whilst he had been downgraded to reading endlessly dull documents with no end in sight.

He understood the reason why. Whilst they were both spies, Ella's role would be quite different. Other Bellator citizens would expect her to talk to them, exchange ideas, act as though she'd lived in the city her whole life. It was important that she prepare for it.

But he needed to prepare too.

"Sorry," he muttered. "But I'm so sick of just... *sitting* here."

"So I see." Ella pushed back her chair and stood up. "Come on then."

Noah looked up. "Come on where?"

"Let's get you some drudge practice." She gestured to his clothing. "You're still dressed for it."

It was true. He had dressed in the drudge tunic in the hopes that he would be allowed to use it. So far, he had been disappointed.

Ella disappeared inside the kitchen. When she emerged, she was holding two bags of rubbish. "I heard Robyn complaining that no one had taken these out at lunchtime. You do it."

"Without permission?" Noah glanced at the office door. "If they–"

"They'll be in there for hours." Ella waved his concern away. "It's exactly the kind of job a drudge would do." He hesitated. "If you do this well, they'll be pleased with you. They might start to believe in you again."

"But where do I–"

Ella handed the bags to him and beckoned for him to follow her. When she reached the door to the tunnel, he knew where she was heading.

"The tunnel comes out in that shop across the square." She opened the door. "The bins are in the alleyway just beside it. All you'll have to do is walk outside, keep the drudge posture, lift the lid of the bin and throw in the bags, then get back here. Simple!"

He felt a wave of nerves flood over him at the prospect. "Alright." He heard himself agree.

She shot him a nervous smile. "Good luck!"

The bags weren't heavy, but as he walked through the tunnel, Noah felt a trickle of sweat make its way down his spine. Ella was right. It was a small job. One which he felt he should be rehearsing, if they were ever going to use him. But the fact that his actions were unsanctioned by Madeleine made him wonder how sensible he was being.

At the end of the tunnel, he opened the door to the shop's cellar with no issue. Making his way through, he kept his head lowered and prayed he wouldn't meet anyone.

At the top of the stairs, he heard voices coming from his left. The shop was open and presumably filled with customers. Trying not to shudder, he turned right and headed out the door to the alleyway. It was a cold, grey day, the shadows telling him that darkness would soon fall.

The bins were straight ahead. Only a few more steps and he could complete the task and return to the relative safety of the hub. Suppressing the urge to run, he made his way across the space as he knew a drudge would. He lifted the lid of the first bin and heaved the bags inside.

It was already quite full, and he had to compress the existing rubbish to allow his load to fit inside. As he was struggling to close the lid, a wind whipped through the alleyway, lifting some of the bin's lighter contents and scattering them on the ground around him.

His heart racing, Noah bent to pick them up. The alleyway had been spotless when he'd arrived. He had to leave it the same way. But as he collected the papers, he realised they were leaflets. Hundreds of the Resistance leaflets, gathered and dumped. Madeleine was right, Danforth hadn't wasted any time getting rid of them.

He reached for the last one, desperate to get it back inside the bin before he was spotted. Before he could grasp it, the wind whispered through the alley again, whisking the errant paper farther from his grasp. Cursing under his breath, Noah darted after it, but it leapt away for a third time, like a child teasing him. This time, it landed behind the bin.

Wondering how the posture would be affected when a drudge was on all fours, Noah gritted his teeth and dove. At last, his hand closed around the piece of paper. But as he was about to stand up and get rid of the escapees for good, he heard the sound of the shop door opening and closing. Footsteps approached the alleyway.

"Can't be too careful." A strident female voice spoke. "Not with these rebels on the loose."

He tensed. Glancing back down the alleyway, he could see it led nowhere. Surely, the women were just exiting the shop and passing by on their way elsewhere? For now, he would stay where he was.

"Thank goodness the chancellor has acted so quickly." The woman continued, pausing at the end of the alleyway to chat to her companion. "I mean, can you imagine the danger we're in from the *bastard* males behind this?"

Noah reeled from the words. Clearly, the women of the city believed everything Danforth said. It was a slap in the face, after all the Resistance's hard work. He could understand why Madeleine was so downcast: their efforts to change the Bellator citizens' minds had failed. Not only that, the recent mission had risked the lives of several Resistance members.

The women were passing the end of the alleyway now. He crept closer, desperate to catch more of the conversation before they moved out of earshot.

"As for this *Faith Hanlon* girl..." The voice was dripping with disdain. "I hope they catch her soon."

Noah was beginning to despise the speaker. *Did all Bellator females think like this?* Finally, her companion managed to get a word in.

"Poor thing." This voice was softer and lower in pitch. "I wonder what they've done to brainwash her."

"Brainwash?" The first woman scoffed. "I heard a rumour that she went willingly. You know, one of those rebel types..." She let the thought dangle. "I'm not sure she deserves rehabilitation."

"Really?" The softer-voiced woman sounded more sympathetic. "You don't think she could have been manipulated by the men in the forest? She's *sixteen*." There was a pause. When the strident voice did not respond, Noah could feel her disapproval. Eventually, the woman went on. "But yes, of course, it's worrying. I hope they catch her soon."

Noah couldn't help but feel she had changed her attitude as a result of the first woman's criticism. Being different was difficult. And fear was a powerful thing.

"With every eye in the city looking out for her?" Strident-voice laughed, apparently appeased by the other woman's acquiescence.

"Danforth will have her before the week is out. Now I must go. I've a busy day tomorrow."

The women bid their goodbyes and headed off in different directions. It was several minutes before Noah dared to stand up again. Disposing of the leaflets in the bin, he quickly crossed the alleyway and made his way back to the library through the tunnel. Ella was waiting where he had left her.

"Alright?"

He closed the door and headed back to her. "Well, I didn't get caught, if that's what you mean."

"Then what?" she puzzled. "You look like you've seen a ghost."

By the time he had finished telling her about what he'd heard, her face was as serious as his.

"I guess we have to try something else to show the Bellator women."

"But what?"

"I don't know." She shot a glance at the closed office door. "And the length of time they've been in there, well, I'm not sure they do either. But we can't give up now."

As though summoned by their gaze, the door to the office burst open. Robyn strode into the hub, her eyes fixed on Ella.

"Would you come in here please?" She looked more positive than she had all day. "We have news of a possible placement for you.

"Already?" Ella's eyes widened. "How?"

"We have a Resistance member working in the office which assigns government jobs to citizens. Let's just say she's very good at assigning Resistance sympathisers useful roles in places where Madeleine wants them." She turned back to Ella.

"Where will she be working?" Noah asked, then wondered if he should have kept his mouth shut.

But Robyn didn't seem to mind. "The position is in the main government building, Matriarch House. There's been some sickness recently. It's knocked out quite a few of their staff. They need people in their catering section to assist with food preparation, service, and so on." Catching sight of Ella's expression, she softened slightly. "Nothing you can't handle. More importantly, you'll be close enough to Danforth to maybe get your hands on some vital information."

"But where will I sta–" Ella began, but Robyn waved a hand at her.

"That's what Madeleine wants to go through with you. If you'll come and speak to her now, she'll explain everything."

When Ella had disappeared inside the office, Noah turned back to the papers on the table in front of him. But before he could start reading again, there was a noise at the far side of the hub. He glanced up, disappointed to see Diane. When she made a beeline for him, he tensed.

"She's in the library, if you were wondering. *Alone.*"

Noah frowned. "Sorry?"

"Faith." Diane raised her eyebrows.

"Did she say she wanted me to go up there?"

"No." She rolled her eyes. "But she does."

As he entered the library, Noah glanced around, marvelling once again at the magnificent room.

As it had earlier, the scent of the ancient texts washed over him. He could never have imagined so many books in one place. He thought about his ma. *Had she ever been here? In the time before she ran away to the forest, had she visited this place?* She was a huge lover of books, and the lack of them in Eremus had always been hard on her.

He followed the faint glow of a lamp which led him to a room at the rear of the library. Faith was sitting at a desk, her head bent over a record book of some kind. Unsure whether to call her name or simply approach and let his footsteps announce his presence, Noah paused on the threshold, watching her.

A strand of hair had escaped her ponytail and lay against her cheek. Her brow was furrowed in thought as she ran a finger down the page. She shifted her attention to a second book, glancing between the two, making comparisons. Seemingly frustrated, she brought a hand to her mouth and chewed on a nail.

What was she thinking about?

He was just about to call out to her when she sat up and looked right at him.

"Noah?" She stood up suddenly, one of the volumes slipping out of her hand and falling to the floor. "What are you–?"

He was at her side in seconds. Stooping down, he rescued the dropped book. When he came back up, she was staring at him.

"Diane said…"

"She sent you up here?"

"Yeah."

He held the book out to her. As she took it from him, their fingers brushed against one another. He felt a familiar jolt of electricity and held on to the book, their fingers remaining in contact.

"She knew I needed to be with you." Faith blushed. "Better than I did myself." She paused. "I think she's trying to make up for the other day. When she–"

She broke off, but Noah knew what she was talking about. "I know she didn't mean to get me into trouble. And I should've been more prepared for…" Now it was his turn to blush. "You have that effect on me. I know it. I shouldn't have let it throw me off the way it did."

Breaking their contact, Faith replaced the book on the desk. Then she turned back, reaching for his hand again. "You have the same effect on me."

He stepped closer. "I'm glad I'm here, despite the disaster the other day." He knew as he spoke the words, they were true. "I wanted to join the Resistance. To play my part. To change things." Gently, he circled his arms around her, revelling in the closeness of her body. "But I needed to be with you too."

He felt her relax against him. For a moment they stood there, unmoving. The peace of the library enveloped them. It was bliss, he realised, to be alone with her. To have no one questioning their being together. But it wouldn't last.

When he felt her shiver, he pulled away. "What is it?"

"We came here to make a difference. But our problems seem... *insurmountable* right now. Sophia's still in the hospital, and we have no way of getting to her. Kemp has been tortured once already – who knows if they'll go back a second time... Now Danforth has Laura, and *you* might be sent out into the city at any moment..." Jerking away from him, she slammed a fist into her palm. "*Everyone* I care about is putting themselves in harm's way and I don't seem to be able to do a damn thing to protect them. The one thing Madeleine wanted me to do seems to have had no effect at all."

"You mean the leaflet?" Noah glanced down, not wanting her to catch him in a lie. "I'm sure it's had *some* impact."

But she wasn't looking at him.

"I doubt it. And now Danforth's declared me public enemy number one, Madeleine's never going to let me out." Faith slumped back into her seat at the table. "I feel so useless! I came back here to rescue Sophia. Everyone talks about sacrificing the needs of the individual for the good of the cause, but I can't help feeling like I'm failing my friend." She brought her hand to her mouth. "Noah, if you could see her... She's not herself. She's clearly suffering. I have to convince

Madeleine that Sophia's worth rescuing. But I'm no closer to doing that than when I was stuck in a cave in Eremus."

"I guess you'll have to convince Madeleine you can support the cause in another way." Noah's heart went out to her. He gestured to the books. "What's all this?"

She followed his gaze. "I was doing a little research. Ruth told you about Danforth being Avery's mother?" He nodded. "Well, this is where I found that information. I've been looking over the records ever since."

"What for?"

"Firstly, I wanted to work out if there were any biological connections between myself and the people close to me. You know – Sophia or Diane or Helen..." She flushed. "Or you."

"Woah." Noah glanced down at the columns of information. "*I'm* in there?"

"You are. Took a bit of finding, but you're definitely there. Not too much information about you, for obvious reasons."

And I'm not–" Noah's heart started beating a little faster. "I mean, we're not–"

"No. Our seed donors definitely had different codes." Her cheeks flushed. "We don't share a father."

He met her gaze. "Well, that's a relief."

"Yes." She looked away. "See here?" She pointed at a column on one of the charts. "The codes indicate the specimen that the seed sample was taken from. So, the *father*, I suppose, in Eremus terms, at least."

"Is there any indication who these men were?" Noah asked, leaning closer. "Or are they considered so worthless that they don't deserve an identity?"

"I've been looking, but I haven't found anything so far." Faith flipped through the book's pages idly. "They're dead now, though, so I suppose it doesn't really matter."

"I guess not." Noah shrugged, wondering why he cared. "Not to the Bellator women, anyway."

Catching the bitterness in his tone, she turned. "Don't be like that. I didn't mean–"

"I know."

Not wanting to take his anger out on the wrong person, he moved away from the table, striding to the side of the room which had a window overlooking the street. Faith cared who her father was, or she wouldn't have been up here pouring over the books. But how many of the other Bellator citizens would care? How long would it take them to change the minds of women who'd had it drilled into them that men didn't matter, that men were evil, that men were scum? He thought back to the conversation he'd overheard on the street. The women of Bellator truly did hate and fear all men.

A comfortable-looking sofa lay underneath the window, facing outwards. He ran a finger along the arm, revelling in its softness. He'd never known furniture like this. In Eremus, everything was practical, functional. But here, it was comfortable, even beautiful. And most of the women didn't even appreciate it. The idea of having the time, space, and security to sit here and read a book filled him with an overwhelming sense of envy.

He glanced out of the window, trying to regain the calm he'd felt only minutes before. Outside, the street was empty. The thought of it filled with people, both male and female, all with the same rights, the same opportunities, the same fears and hopes and dreams, seemed impossible. Were they totally naïve to imagine it could happen?

A movement to his left startled him, and he turned to see Faith at his side. Shoeless, she had moved stealthily, appearing beside him like a mirage.

"Careful," she murmured. "There are regular patrols. The library's supposed to be empty at night. If anyone saw you–"

She stopped speaking as they both spotted the pair of guards at the same time. Approaching from the opposite side of the square, they walked in silence, their gaze roaming from side to side like a pair of prowling tigers.

Panic seized Noah. Grasping hold of Faith's arm, he pulled her down onto the sofa, out of the guards' line of sight. She landed awkwardly on top of him, the air rushing out of her lungs. Clutching his shoulders, she braced herself as though she thought she would fall. Once again, he pulled her close to prevent her from tumbling onto the floor.

For several seconds, they lay together, panting.

"Think they saw us?" Faith's chest rumbled against his as she whispered the words.

He shook his head. "We're okay."

Faith shifted so she lay more comfortably along the inside of the sofa. Relaxing his arms slightly, Noah became aware of how close their bodies were now that the danger was over. From shoulder to hip they aligned, and he could feel every breath she took.

He thought of Ella's new assignment. His own could happen just as quickly. Or he could be sent back to Eremus. There might not be many more chances to be with Faith like this, alone, again.

Bending close, he pressed his lips to hers.

Chapter Thirty-One: Faith

Her head was spinning. Faith wanted this kiss. Had wanted it ever since Robyn had interrupted them in the store cupboard the night of Noah's arrival. But with everything that had happened since he'd arrived, it didn't feel *right*. How could she lose herself in his embrace when Kemp and Laura were in danger? When Sophia's life hung in the balance? When things were more wrong than they'd ever been?

But in the back of her mind, she had a nagging feeling that this might be their only chance. At any moment, Noah could be sent somewhere else in the city. Or sent home. Once that happened, she had no idea when they might next be together. When he'd appeared in the library, she'd silently thanked Diane for sending him. For understanding how precious their time together was and knowing how much Faith needed him.

And now, as he bent his lips to meet hers, she responded with a fervour she hadn't known she possessed.

As the kiss deepened, she slid her arms higher, her fingers curling through the stray hairs which lay against the nape of his neck. Closing her eyes, she sighed. Noah broke their contact, leaning away from her.

"Is this alright?" Uncertainty clouded his face. "Me kissing you, I mean."

"Yes." She felt her cheeks heating as she opened her eyes. "It's alright."

He brought a hand up to cup her chin. "You want me to?"

Words failed her, but she managed to nod.

"With everything that's been going on, you must feel..." he began, then paused. "And I know this must be confusing for you. The romance side of things, I mean."

Inhaling deeply, she made herself meet his gaze. "It is. I mean, I understand how the... physical side of things *works*, but... we were only taught about it in negative terms. The relationships between men and women were shown to us as violent, forceful, destructive." She dropped her voice to a whisper. "Male-female relationships are what our society fought *against*."

"But I don't–" A look of horror dawned on Noah's face. "I didn't–" He attempted to shift away from her.

Securing her arms around him, Faith kept him close. "You don't understand." Leaning forward, she pressed her lips to his very softly. "I've seen the relationships between the Eremus citizens. Your ma and Flynn, for example. Anyone with half a brain can see how much they care for one another. I *know* the Bellator teachings are wrong. I *know* we only get half a story, one that's spun to the government's advantage."

Relaxing slightly, Noah listened.

"What I'm saying is, yes I want you to kiss me. I'm enjoying kissing you. But," she hesitated and glanced away, "I still find it odd. Unfamiliar. I'm not sure what to *do*, even."

She stopped speaking as he chuckled, the vibrations rumbling through his chest pressed against her. "It's not that difficult. I'm not exactly an expert myself."

She felt herself blushing fiercely. "But I don't want you to think–"

"I'm not thinking anything." His tone was warm, firm. "Except how often I've thought about doing this. How much I want to. How, when I'm not with you, the world doesn't feel quite... right."

A silence fell between them. Faith regarded him steadily, feeling slightly more confident than she had previously. "It's the same way for me."

A broad smile spread across his face. "I'm glad."

"But with things the way they are right now..." She chewed her lip, unsure of his reaction. "I'm not sure that we should–"

"I agree." He smiled. "Why don't we just leave it at kissing for the moment?"

"You wouldn't mind?"

"I wouldn't mind. Well, maybe I would, a little." He pulled her close. "But you're right. There'll be time later to take things further... if we want to." A shadow crossed his face and she knew he was questioning the truth of his words. "At least, I hope there will be."

"Me too." She rested her head against his chest, comforted by the knowledge that they were in agreement. "Noah?"

"Yeah?"

"I'm glad you came up here tonight. I really want this thing between us to work."

"Me too."

"I just feel..." she hesitated, not knowing how to explain it, "unless things change here in Bellator, there isn't all that much hope for us. To be together, I mean."

His arms tightened around her. "I know exactly what you mean."

She pulled away, looking up at him. "You do?"

He nodded. "Until men are at least tolerated in Bellator, I don't see us being together." He smiled sadly. "Unless you're on board with running away to Eremus like my ma did."

She returned the smile. "You think that could work?"

He raised an eyebrow. "You'd consider it?"

"I might." Embarrassed, she pressed her head against his chest again. "Honestly though, with the way things are going..."

"I know." He paused, shifting his body slightly so they were better aligned. "It all feels a bit of a mess at the moment, doesn't it? Like... things are starting to get out of control."

She felt like crying. When she'd arrived back in the city, she'd been filled with hope. Optimistic that she'd be able to change things, play her part in making Bellator a better place. She knew Noah felt the same. But so far, all the Resistance efforts had come to nothing. All that had happened was people close to her had gotten hurt.

"So we're agreed?" She nestled closer to him. "We can't think about being together until things change for the better?"

"We're agreed." He pulled her closer still. His breathing deepened, and the rise and fall of his chest beneath her was reassuring. Closing her eyes, Faith allowed herself to drift.

The next thing she knew, someone was calling her name, their tone sharp and urgent.

"Get up!" It was Diane. "Faith! Noah!"

Faith opened her eyes, wincing as the sunlight from the window above pierced her retinas. "What are we–?"

Beside her, Noah stirred. Faith shifted her body slightly, her muscles cramping in the small space.

"Come *on*!" Diane stamped a foot. "Blake's on her way up in a minute and you *do not* want her to find you."

Finally understanding the situation, Faith sat bolt upright. The movement dislodged her sleeping partner, and Noah tumbled sideways off the sofa, landing on the floor with a thump.

"What the–?"

"We fell asleep!" Faith hissed, climbing to her feet. She massaged the arm which had been trapped between them, willing the pins and needles to ease off. "We have to *go*."

Alert now, Noah jumped up, shooting an embarrassed glance at Diane. "Sorry! We must've fallen..."

"I don't care." Diane jerked a hand towards the door. "Get yourself out of here and back downstairs. *Separately.*"

"Does anyone know–" Faith began, but her friend cut her off.

"Not yet." Diane was already turning to go. "Blake was still in the hub when I left. I'll try and distract her, let you get out of here." At the door she paused. "Be quick, though. Ella's leaving today. If you want to see her, it needs to be soon."

"Ella's what?" Faith began, but her friend had already gone.

"They found a potential place for her last night." Noah ran a hand over his hair in a vain attempt to tidy it. "I was going to tell you, but..."

Faith hurried to the table in the centre of the room and gathered up the record books. Hastening to the shelves, she began to replace them. "Wait. She's leaving *today*?"

"I guess so." He came to stand beside her. "There was some urgency about her filling the space. They've had some sickness and needed people to fill in immediately. It's a place called Matriarch House."

"Really?" Faith pictured the building. It was right in the centre of the city. The academy girls had been given a tour of it a couple of years previously. She shuddered to think of Ella being in a place where Danforth regularly spent time.

"Madeleine was keen to get her in there, to see if she could gather vital information about the chancellor."

"I'll bet." Faith's heart was racing. If Ella was leaving so quickly, would Noah follow soon? Turning to him, she reached for his hand. "Thank you."

He looked puzzled. "For what?"

She shrugged. "For being here. For coming to find me last night. For... understanding." She moved a step closer. "I'm glad we know where we stand." She motioned towards the door. "Now we'd better go, before–"

"Not yet."

He closed the gap between them, easing Faith back against the bookcase. Taking her head in his hands, he leaned in and kissed her with a sweetness that made her ache. This kiss felt important, and she knew Noah was thinking it might be the last they shared for a while. When he pulled away, she felt tears pricking her eyes.

"Do we need to go down separately?"

Blinking them away, she nodded. "Probably makes sense. You go first. Make sure you check that the hallway's clear at the bottom of the stairs."

"Okay." He moved away reluctantly. "I'll go to the hub, act like I'm heading there from the storage room." Reaching for her hand, he squeezed it. "But before I go, let me say this. My spine feels like I slept on the tunnel floor. But, honestly? I enjoyed last night's sleeping arrangements more than I can say."

He winked. Before Faith could respond, the door closed behind him.

Chapter Thirty-Two: Noah

His palms were sweating, but Noah focused on breathing in and out as he and Evelyn walked along the street. After permitting him to complete some more practical training in and around the library, Robyn had finally given the go-ahead for him to appear as a drudge in a more public place. The last few days had gone well, as far as he could tell, but he knew the leaders still doubted him. He was looking forward to proving them wrong.

Evelyn had dressed in finer clothes than usual. Having ascertained that the mission would take her nowhere near BellaLab Corp, she had been happy to act the part of a Bellator citizen wealthy enough to have her own drudge. Noah was accompanying her through the city on a shopping trip. She had visited various shops already, and Noah had assisted her: carrying purchases, ferrying things to and from the comcar she had hired for the morning, and bringing her snacks and drinks when she required them. It meant mixing with other shoppers, sales assistants, the comcar driver and, on one terrifying occasion, a pair of Bellator guards.

They'd been at it for more than an hour, and the tension in his body was beginning to make him ache. Evelyn seemed to be enjoying herself, not speaking to him unless she was barking an order, making sure she stopped frequently to browse, demanding things of him which kept him on his toes. Noah knew that was the point of the outing. And despite his discomfort, he was doing well.

Right now, they were standing in line at a fancy delicatessen. His mouth was watering at the array of fine cheeses and meats which were laid out under the glass of the counter in front of him. Such delicacies were unknown in Eremus, yet many of the women here enjoyed them on a regular basis. The shop was busy, and he was carrying a number of parcels from the clothing store they had just visited. The burden was awkward, and his arms were beginning to ache, but he was determined not to draw attention to himself by shifting the load into a more comfortable position.

Ever the mistress-of-disguise, Evelyn was conversing with the assistant behind the counter as though she was a long-lost friend. Again, Noah knew they were spending as long as possible in each shop, so he could be thoroughly tested. Neither Madeleine nor Robyn would send him to a placement in the community without being confident he could successfully pull off the drudge subterfuge.

He found himself thinking of Ella, who had left to begin her own placement three days ago. Apparently, she was doing fine so far: her cover story had been accepted and she had managed to integrate herself into the canteen at Matriarch House with no major problems. Noah hoped she was alright. He was eager to follow in her footsteps and feel like he was doing something useful. But the leaders wanted more proof of his capabilities before they signed off on a placement for him.

He wondered if the mistrust was linked to him being male. There was a kind of entrenched prejudice in every Bellator woman, he had discovered. They couldn't help it. Even the most forward-thinking members of the Resistance shot him curious looks sometimes, and he knew that the negative image of men they'd had drilled into them from an early age was difficult to escape. Even Faith struggled with it sometimes.

He sighed. Only time and exposure to males who broke the stereotype would fix the problem.

A sharp elbow in his side brought him back to the here-and-now. As the assistant moved away to wrap her purchases, Evelyn glared at him. Instantly, Noah understood. Though it hadn't attracted any major attention, his loud exhalation had not gone unnoticed by the Resistance member he was supposed to impress. Dipping his head further, he resolved to become invisible in the eyes of all Bellator females. When Evelyn turned back to the counter, she looked a little less furious.

The assistant was holding out Evelyn's purchases. "Will that be all?"

As Evelyn nodded, Noah stepped forward to collect the shopping. Thankfully, there were only two small packages this time. He balanced them on the top of the existing pile, praying they would return to the comcar before going anywhere else. Dropping the pile of boxes in the middle of the street would undermine all his successes.

"Be sure to visit us on Liberation Day, won't you?" the assistant trilled. "We're launching a new range of artisan produce that day, to celebrate Bellator's achievements." She glanced down in an attempt at modesty. "The chancellor has chosen us to cater the banquet, you know."

Noah wondered what banquet she meant. And, as his stomach rumbled, how nice the food might be. And then, it occurred to him that perhaps, as a member of the government's catering staff, Ella might be involved in some way.

"What an honour," Evelyn trilled.

"It *really* is." Noah sensed the woman's delight at the accolade. Leaning forward, she dropped her voice. "And the ceremony is so important this year, what with the recent trouble and all. I mean, Chancellor Danforth has had so much to cope with... with all the lies this terrible rebel group has been spreading."

"You're so right." Noah found himself in awe of Evelyn's acting ability.

"And as for this Faith Hanlon girl..." Noah stiffened as the woman tutted in disgust.

"Hmmm." Evelyn was making a great show of studying the range of cheeses under the glass of the counter. "What do you make of her?"

The woman leaned closer. "Well the poor girl has obviously been through a lot. When I read that leaflet, I couldn't believe some of the claims she was making. They've obviously got a real hold on her."

"They?" Evelyn mused.

Noah had to admire her. She was an excellent spy, blending in, saying just enough to get the woman talking. He could see why she was such a valuable asset to Madeleine.

"Eremus." The woman almost whispered the word. "Surely it has to be... *men* behind all this?" Noticing the queue of customers had grown, she stood back, as though knowing she needed to conclude the conversation. "Anyway, I'm certain the Liberation Day ceremony will prove a wonderful opportunity for the chancellor to reassure everyone. There are so many rumours..." she blew out a breath. "One doesn't know what to believe. But her speech will be broadcast to the entire city. I'm sure she'll offer a powerful message. Put everyone's minds at rest for good."

"I'm sure you're right."

Evelyn bristled as the woman behind her shuffled a little closer. *Time to go*, Noah thought. Evelyn clearly agreed. Leaning forward, she brought the conversation to a close.

"The banquet's at Matriarch House as usual, yes? And Danforth's speech will be broadcast from the square?"

"It will indeed." The woman beamed with pride. "You shop here that day, you'll be dining on the same food as the dignitaries." She leaned across, brandishing something in her hand. "This flyer has all the details. We're open all day, but I'd advise popping in early. You know how busy the square can get, and we're expecting great demand as people leave. Wouldn't want you to miss out."

"I'll be sure to pop in." Evelyn accepted the flyer graciously.

Turning to Noah, she slipped the flyer between two of the packages. The delicate balance disrupted, the parcels at the top began to slide sideways. Refusing to panic, Noah bent his knees, jamming his foot against the counter. The tower of items teetered for a moment, but his rapid shift of weight worked to counterbalance the load. Forcing himself to take slow, deep breaths, he managed to realign the pile without issue.

Once the packages were under control, Noah followed Evelyn, who had already stalked out of the shop. He resisted the urge to scream at her for abandoning him. As they made their way to the side street, they passed several other women. Evelyn smiled politely at them all, but, to Noah's relief, did not stop.

When they reached the comcar, the driver was waiting.

"Everything in order?" the driver asked as she opened the back of the car so Noah could unload the packages.

"Yes, thank you."

When he had safely unloaded the parcels, Noah slipped the leaflet the woman in the deli had given to Evelyn into his pocket. He turned back to Evelyn, bracing himself for her next challenge.

"Where to now?" the comcar driver asked.

"I think I'll take a walk," Evelyn waved a hand. "Want to pick me up from the Liberty Park Café in an hour?"

"Of course." The driver glanced down at her wristclip. "See you at the south exit at two p.m.?"

"Thank you."

Within seconds, the comcar was gliding away. When it had turned the corner, Evelyn glanced up and down the empty alleyway before turning to Noah.

"You're not as good as you think."

Knowing it would prove her statement correct, Noah refused to react. He'd felt like he'd done quite well, up until the unconscious sigh and the near-accident in the final store. But *completely* fading into the background seemed the only way to convince the women of the Resistance that he was up to the job.

"Hmmm." Evelyn tapped a foot on the ground. "You're determined, I'll give you that. I just don't know if you're ready to be out here alone."

This time, Noah had to fight to keep his head levelled at the ground. He retained the drudge pose, refusing to react. No way would he give Evelyn the satisfaction of reporting him to Madeleine.

He was surprised when she chuckled. "Not bad. I'm *trying* to provoke you, you know. You mostly do a decent job of resisting the temptation to react." She looked out at the street ahead. "Final task, then. Follow me to the cafe, but keep a beat behind as always, alright?"

Noah inclined his head to show he understood.

"When I get there, you'll wait outside. There's a designated area for drudges, though there aren't usually more than one or two there at once. It shouldn't be too much of a struggle for you if there are others. It's not like drudges even speak to each other in public."

Noah had found himself wondering how much drudges spoke to one another in *private*. Aside from Arden, who was hardly a *normal* example, he hadn't spoken to any drudges at all. That would come if and when he took up a placement. He swallowed the nerves which coursed through him at the thought.

Without waiting for a response, Evelyn set off, retracing their route out of the alleyway and heading back along the main street. Noah felt a little easier, knowing that his tasks were almost complete. Another hour, where he'd only have to walk and stand still whilst maintaining the drudge posture, didn't seem too tricky. And then he'd be back at the library.

Perhaps he could steal a couple of hours with Faith once he returned, before he had to serve dinner.

Pushing the hopeful thought from his head, he focused on keeping up with Evelyn. She was a lithe woman who moved with the speed of a gazelle. It required all his focus to retain his posture whilst keeping the appropriate distance behind her as they travelled so quickly.

The busy streets of the shopping district disappeared behind them, giving way to the wider streets of the residential area which was home to Liberty Park. Noah had never been there, but Evelyn had described it as she had briefed him about the day's events. A large green space, it had existed before the Women's Liberation Movement and had once been named after a famous man. Nowadays, its name reflected the Bellator women's freedom from men.

The cafe to which they were now heading was in the very centre. As they passed beneath the curved archway which marked the entrance to the park, Noah felt some of the tension drain away. Being outdoors always made him feel more at home. And while the manicured lawns, well-trimmed trees, and boating lake were a far cry from the wilderness of Eremus, they gave enough of a flavour of home to put him at ease.

Reminding himself not to get too relaxed, Noah focused on keeping his movements as smooth as possible. On the way to the café, they passed multiple Bellator citizens: two red-faced women sprinting along together; a teacher of some kind, accompanied by several children who she was attempting to teach about plant names; and a pair of intellectual-looking women, who sat on a bench pouring over some papers. Noah felt a surge of satisfaction as not one of them gave him a second glance as he passed by.

At the café, Evelyn indicated the area where drudges should wait before slipping inside. The space was empty, and Noah took up residence at the rear, where he could see the lake, though he could not gaze out across it as he wanted to. Keeping his eyes low, he watched the water rolling back and forth across the coloured pebbles with a rhythm he found soothing.

Drudges relied on their hearing far more than ordinary people, he had learned. Their permanently lowered gaze meant their vision was limited, but it was amazing how much you could learn from listening. Noah enjoyed the sound of the water flowing across the stones, but he could also hear birdcalls, the rustling of smaller creatures in the undergrowth, and the footsteps of anyone passing by.

He identified another jogger, her feet pounding the pavement hard. After that, a woman he was certain was older shuffled past with a dog, their passage sounding very different than the runner's had. When the near-silence made him confident he was alone, he moved under the cover of a clump of trees which fringed the waterline.

Placing his hand on one of the trunks, he closed his eyes. Raising his head, he stretched his neck for the first time in hours. The relief was intense. Breathing in deeply, he transported himself to Swallow Lake, where he, Flynn, and Paulo had spent many a pleasant hour fishing and swimming. An unexpected pang of homesickness swept over him.

His reverie was interrupted by a new set of footsteps. It was more difficult to work out this woman's purpose, though. She was not accompanied by friends, or a dog, nor was she jogging. The pace of her step did not even imply a definitive direction. But this wasn't unusual, Noah reminded himself. Unlike the Eremus citizens, the Bellator women had leisure time. They came to places like parks simply to meander, the speed of their passage irregular as they stopped to glance out at the lake or bent down to smell a flower.

But something about the woman's approach set him on edge. Inching closer to the edge of the thicket, he peered out, confident that no one could see him. From here, he could see the path stretching in both directions. To his left, it was empty. But when he glanced right, he could see a figure approaching.

As he'd expected, the woman was not in any kind of hurry. She ambled along, stopping several times to look out over the lake and smell the blossom on a tree branch which arched down from over her head. Eventually, she took a seat on one of the benches which flanked the path, her back to the trees where Noah was hidden.

Once settled though, she didn't seem to relax. As Noah observed her, praying that Evelyn wouldn't choose this particular moment to exit the café and come looking for him, she frequently glanced one way up the path and then the other, took a breath, then repeated the process.

Not like she was simply enjoying the view. There was something odd, Noah thought, about the way she *kept* looking back and forth. If she were merely seeking refuge from a busy day, she'd be still, relaxed. But her posture, the way her gaze flickered back and forth, suggested otherwise. She was watching, observing people. And not in an idle, absent-minded way.

He had to get closer. Checking that the area was clear of other people, Noah prowled through the trees until he stood directly behind the bench where she sat. Making sure he was still hidden from view, he leaned against the trunk and planted his feet in a firm position so he couldn't stumble and give himself away. Then he focused on the woman again.

She was dressed in plain, dark clothing which, on closer inspection, was faded and looked as though it had been mended several times. Her boots were well-made though, and an unusual shade of blue. She turned her head to the side again, and Noah caught a glimpse of her face. He clamped a hand over his mouth to silence his gasp. From the distance, she had looked like any other woman. But up close, he knew her well.

It was Sarah Porter.

Chapter Thirty-Three:
Faith

Sophia was sitting up in bed, alone. She looked miserable. A tray of food sat in front of her, but the contents were untouched. Still hooked up to machines on both sides, she was clearly unable to leave the room. Her only companion was the medic who popped in every couple of hours to take her temperature and blood pressure. She never stayed long, and she didn't seem to say much to her patient.

Faith traced a finger across her friend's face on the screen, willing her to stay positive. "I haven't forgotten you, Soph. I promise."

Could her friend really be pregnant? If so, did she know? How must she be feeling? Did she think Faith had given up on her?

With all that had happened lately, Sophia did not seem high on Madeleine's list of priorities. In fact, since Danforth's press release denouncing the validity of the leaflets, the Resistance leader had been pretty much locked in her office, barking at anyone who tried to gain access. Rumour had it, she had been so crushed by the failure of the leaflet mission, she was on the point of giving up.

Robyn was keeping things going. Ella had left for her new position a few days ago. Diane was being given ever more responsibility and had been buried in some tech project with Blake, often working until the small hours of the morning. Even Noah had been permitted to resume his drudge training, and was out for the day with Evelyn.

Only Faith, it seemed, had no purpose. And with little to do other than sit and stare at Sophia, she felt like she was going to go mad.

She pushed her chair back from the table. Enough was enough. She would *demand* to speak to Madeleine. Ask if she had thought any more about rescuing Sophia. At least it would give her something else to do.

When she reached the hub, it was deserted. She headed for the office without hesitation. Knocking sharply, she walked in without waiting for a response.

Inside, the Resistance leader was hunched over a datadev. Expecting criticism for her intrusion, Faith was surprised when Madeleine simply waved her into a chair. She gestured to a spare pair of headphones which lay on the desk.

Faith slid into the seat as requested. Slipping the headphones on, she listened.

"Will you be calling on Hammond again, do you think?" Anderson asked.

Faith waited, wondering whether they would need to decipher the other side of the conversation from Anderson's replies. As she heard a second voice, she sat bolt upright.

"I don't think so." It was Danforth. Another meeting in Anderson's office. Clearly, they had much to talk about. *"You saw the beating Kemp received. I don't think she knows anything."*

Madeleine and Faith exchanged knowing glances. It was a relief to hear that they believed Kemp now, though she would certainly have to watch her step.

"You'll have to keep a close eye on her, though." Danforth sounded stern. *"Make sure she isn't slipping off anywhere she shouldn't be... that sort of thing."*

"Of course."

"On to other matters, then." Danforth cleared her throat. *"Laura Meadows, for example."*

"Have Hammond's methods proved more fruitful with our little rebel?"

Faith recoiled from Anderson's words, and the sound which followed them. It was suspiciously like a snort of laughter.

"They have. To an extent at least. The Meadows woman has given us a couple of addresses linked to the rebel group she belongs to. One on Hyde Street. Madeleine Leigh's old residence, in fact."

Faith found herself admiring Laura. Whilst she hadn't remained silent, she had given up a location which was no longer of use to the Resistance. It was a solid strategy. But as Danforth went on, she knew they wouldn't have been satisfied with a single location.

"She confirmed Leigh's involvement with the rebel group. And that she's dead." Faith couldn't help sneaking a look at Madeleine, who looked heartened by the false claim. *"She also gave us an address on the east of the city, in the Garner district. My guards are on their way to check it out as we speak."*

Faith glanced at Madeleine in alarm.

"A safe house?" she mouthed.

"Not one we use often," Madeleine whispered "I'll have Blake check it out."

She began tapping commands into her datadev as Danforth continued. Faith relaxed slightly, knowing Blake would be on the case within minutes. She hoped it would be soon enough.

"There may be more to come. She definitely hasn't told us everything. I'll have Hammond try again later today." Danforth sniffed. *"Moving on, have there been any more conclusive results on the femgazipane trial?"*

"I'm afraid not." Anderson sounded reluctant to give the response. Faith wondered if she was scared. *"We're still not seeing the hormone levels Sanders wants."*

Faith felt a hot sweat sweep across her body at the doctor's name.

"I'm sorry it's not better news," Anderson hesitated. *"The others just don't seem to be adapting to it as quickly as Sophia did, no matter what we do."*

There was a sharp bang, as though Danforth had hit the desk with something. Faith and Madeleine jumped.

*"I want to know **why**."* Danforth spat out. *"We know it's possible, now that Sophia's pregnant. We've got to..."*

Faith tuned her out for a moment. It was true, then. Sophia was actually going to have a baby. She found it difficult to imagine. Hearing a gasp of horror from Madeleine, she refocused.

"...start increasing our numbers. It's imperative that we get some more of these girls on the metraxilone pills."

Faith looked at Madeleine. Metraxilone. The mysterious second drug. And now Danforth was suggesting they give it to the academy students en masse.

In the academy office, Anderson sounded doubtful. *"But Sanders doesn't want them to have it yet. Not until their hormone levels are optimised. She said–"*

"I don't care what she said." Danforth's tone was harsh. *"I want results. Those damn leaflets have done some serious damage. There are actually some citizens who still believe the information, **despite** my announcement."*

Faith glanced at Madeleine again. While the leader's face remained serious, there was a more positive lift to her chin, and a determination in her eyes which hadn't been there a moment earlier.

"We need something big." Danforth sounded like she was pacing. *"Something to convince the women of this city to get behind me once and for all. But one pregnant girl isn't enough. I need several. We have to be certain that it works. Or we'll have to consider... alternative strategies."*

The chancellor's words were ominous. But Faith didn't have long to ponder what she meant as Anderson went on.

"Of course, it works. You've done exactly what you set out to do!" Anderson was fawning now. It made Faith shudder. *"Reproducing without male seed. It's going to change everything! I mean..."*

Faith slumped back in her chair. *Finally*, it made sense. Danforth wanted to eradicate men altogether. If she had found a way to get women pregnant without male input, it would solve all her problems.

In the background, Anderson was still fussing. *"But Sanders says there's no guarantee the metraxilone will work if the hormone levels aren't right."* The sound of footsteps stopped, as though Anderson's words had stopped Danforth in her tracks. *"You know the two drugs work in tandem. It might be dangerous for the girls if they're given the second drug before the first has—"*

"I don't care whether they're ready or not." Danforth's voice was low and urgent. *"We need more successful pregnancies."*

"Of course we do, that's why we're—"

There was another loud bang, silencing Anderson's interruption.

"Enough!" Danforth sounded menacing now. *"Choose the six girls with the most promising hormone levels. Start them on the metraxilone. Today."*

"But what if–"

"What if nothing." Danforth dismissed Anderson's protest. *"We have to make this work."*

They heard the sound of footsteps again, followed by the creak of a door opening. Then a pause. Faith imagined Danforth turning to Anderson before she swept out of the office.

"If we make this work, all talk of rebellion will disappear. For good. The women of Bellator will believe us. There will be no doubt. They'll thank us, adore us." Danforth's final words sent a chill down Faith's spine. *"And if that's the case, why worry about a few dead school girls?"*

CHAPTER THIRTY-FOUR: NOAH

He was seething.

The last time Noah had seen Sarah, she'd been conspiring with Jacob to outwit the other members of the council. Then, like him, she'd disappeared. It was Sarah who had stood by Jacob's side even when his actions endangered the Eremus citizens. Sarah who had done the bulk of Jacob's dirty work. Sarah who had kidnapped Avery.

There was no sign of Avery right now. But Sarah was here, in the city. Presumably up to no good. Noah's heart raced as he pondered what she might be doing. Reconnaissance for Jacob, no doubt. As one of the few females in his party, she could easily infiltrate the city. Presumably, she would report back whatever she discovered to the ex-leader, wherever he was holed up.

Behind him, Noah heard the café door open and close. Praying it wasn't Evelyn, he swung around to look. A couple of older women emerged from the café, laughing together. Their relaxed good humour was jarring, considering the situation.

Noah glanced back at Sarah. Clearly rattled by the appearance of the women, she had stood up. Shooting them a nervous glance, she pulled up her collar and glanced back in the direction she'd come from.

She was leaving! His heart pounding, Noah considered his next move.

If he followed her, he'd be putting himself into a huge amount of danger. Evelyn would be furious, and as a drudge, he didn't even have the luxury of keeping his eyes fixed on his quarry. With his head lowered, how could he track Sarah? Parts of the city were still unfamiliar, and he could hardly stop a Bellator woman and ask for directions.

But if he let her go, who knew what damage she might do?

Curling his hands into fists, he watched her set off. He *had* to risk following her. Jacob's unpredictability made him dangerous. He was as much a threat to the Resistance plans as he was to Eremus. Madeleine needed to know what he was up to. And no one would have a better chance than he would, right now.

Resuming the drudge posture, he stepped out from his hiding place. He trailed her, keeping his eyes lowered and his pace slow. She made her way out of the park and took one of the quieter streets which led away from the busier thoroughfare.

Good, Noah thought. Less chance of either of them being noticed.

He wondered if she was heading back to meet with Jacob. Learning the location of their hideout would certainly prove useful. To both Eremus and the Resistance. He tried to keep track of the streets they moved along, picturing the maps he had studied with Ella. But after making several turns, he lost his bearings.

His mind went to Evelyn. What would she do, when she emerged from the café to find him gone? Had he ruined his chance of helping the Resistance forever?

It was too late now. All he could do was hope Sarah led him to a key location. Returning from the mission with some useful information was the only way he could guarantee Robyn and Madeleine would listen to him.

The blue boots were moving more slowly now. Perhaps Sarah was close to her destination. He wondered where she had gotten the unique footwear. Stolen them, he presumed. But he was grateful for her choice, as they made her far easier to track.

When she turned a corner and came to a sudden stop, he was taken by surprise. With only a second to make a decision, he attempted to bypass her as though he were simply going in the same direction. But she was too quick for him. Shooting out a hand, she grasped his arm.

"Are you following me?"

Her fingers felt like a vice. Noah froze. Fighting the instinct to respond, he tried to act like the Bellator drudge he was pretending to be. Head down, angled away from her. Remaining silent.

She stepped closer. "What do you want?"

Again, he kept his mouth closed. How much did Sarah know about drudges? Whilst staying silent would be the right thing to do in front of an ordinary citizen, with Sarah, it might have the opposite effect.

"Can't you speak?" Her breath hissed in his face. Noah remained still, feeling her frustration at his lack of response. "I mean, you're *definitely* following me. Why else would you turn down what's so clearly a dead-end?"

Noah's heart sank. Jacob's second-in-command was wilier than he'd given her credit for. Suspecting that he was following her, she had headed down an alley which had no exit. Trapping him. Making it blatantly obvious that he was shadowing her.

Sighing, he turned towards her, keeping his eyes lowered. "I was following you."

Sarah pushed him a little further down the alley. "Why?"

Praying they were out of sight of the street, Noah raised his gaze to meet hers. "Because, *Sarah,* I wanted to know where you were going."

Her eyes flew wide as she recognised him. "Noah Madden? What are... why are you?" She gestured to his clothing. "What's this?"

Noah wondered how much he could tell her. "I'm posing as a drudge. Supporting the Resistance." That much she knew already. Jacob had been working towards the alliance before he had left Eremus.

"So you... this costume... it allows a man to be..." she glanced behind them at the street beyond, "out in public... in the city?"

"Kind of." Noah didn't elaborate. Keeping his voice low, he voiced his own question. "What are *you* doing here?"

She spun back to face him. "It's none of your business."

"You're with Jacob, right?" Glancing out of the alleyway, he noticed some ordinary citizens emerging from a shop and moving off down the street. Taking another step into the shadows, he pressed her. "What is he planning?"

"As if I'd tell *you.*" She stared at him, her eyes zeroing in on his mask. "They're servants, right? The drudges?"

He nodded. Perhaps if he let her talk, she might give something away.

She narrowed her eyes. "Where are you based?"

Not wanting to admit that he didn't hold a specific role as yet, he shrugged. Anger flashed in Sarah's eyes. "Does Madeleine have you spying for her?"

"That sort of thing, yes. You'd be amazed the things I've discovered." Noah hoped the lie was convincing.

Sarah's eyes lit with interest. "What sort of things?"

"None of your business."

He felt a flash of satisfaction as he echoed her earlier words. But it didn't last. Sarah wasn't going to tell him anything or lead him anywhere. He'd blown it. The best he could do now was make his way back to Resistance headquarters without attracting attention to himself.

"On that note, I'd better go." He began edging closer to the street. "I'll *certainly* have some interesting information to report back this morning."

Sarah's eyes flashed with fear at his words. She did not want him reporting back to Madeleine about *her*. Before he could step out in the street, her hand was on his arm again.

"Not so fast," she muttered in his ear. "I'm *certain* that the Bellator servants rank a whole lot lower than the women of the city. If I were to cry out... right now, accuse you of attacking me," she gestured across the street, where a group of Bellator citizens were standing outside a shop. "How do you think they'd react?"

"You wouldn't." Noah jerked his arm free.

"Try me." Sarah stepped out in full view. "Help!" She cried out. "Help me!"

Noah didn't wait for the women's reaction. Jamming his head as low as it would go, he hurried off up the street, praying he would be out of sight before the women had a chance to react.

Chapter Thirty-Five: Faith

"Have you seen Noah?"

Faith looked up, startled. Ever since the news about the academy girls had come in, she had been sitting in the hub racking her brain for ways they might help them. But when rescuing Sophia had been deemed difficult, rescuing *multiple* girls was an impossibility.

Evelyn stood in the doorway, her face creased into a frown.

"No. Isn't he supposed to be with you?"

"*Supposed* to be." Evelyn scowled. "He disappeared while we were out."

Faith sat forward, her heart thundering. "What do you mean, he disappeared?"

"Exactly that. I was in the café in Liberty Park. He was supposed to wait outside for me. When I came to fetch him, he was gone."

"You think something happened to him?"

"Who knows?" Evelyn stomped past her, heading for the office. "And he'd actually been doing well up to that point."

Faith followed the older woman into the office. Robyn and Madeleine looked up as they entered.

"Evelyn, you're back." Madeleine greeted her briskly. "Good. We need you."

"I lost–" Evelyn opened her mouth to speak, but Madeleine cut her off.

"No time." She jabbed a finger at the screen. "The academy girls are in grave danger. We're working on a plan to help them."

Evelyn took a seat, all thoughts of Noah forgotten. "I'm listening."

"Anderson is about to start the girls at the academy on a radical second drug." Madeleine leaned forward. "An action she's been advised against by the medics."

"We can't rescue them all right now." Robyn looked stricken. "We don't have the manpower. But we can't just do nothing."

"We think we've come up with a way to help them," Madeleine continued. "A temporary solution, at least."

"Alright." Evelyn didn't hesitate. "What do you need me to do?"

"We need placebos." Madeleine blurted out. "Pills with which we can replace the real drug."

"And then we have to get them into the academy." Robyn frowned. "Somehow."

"We can't use Kemp." Madeleine butted in. "They're watching her too closely."

"What about Arden?" Faith spoke for the first time. "Could he help?"

Madeleine scratched her head. "Possibly. It would be bigger than anything he's done in the past. But I think he'd be up for it, if the girls' lives are at risk."

"You can contact him?" Faith asked.

"Should be able to, yes." Robyn turned to Evelyn. "Can you manage the placebos if I can work out a way to get them inside the school?"

"Definitely. Lily has a contact in one of the med centres." Evelyn stood up. "When do you need them?"

"As soon as possible."

"I'm on it." Evelyn moved towards the door. As she reached it, she turned. "By the way, you should know that Noah did very well today, until he–"

Running footsteps in the hub made her pause. Faith's eyes went wide as Noah appeared behind her. He was pale and breathless, but alive.

"Hi." His gaze went to Evelyn. "Sorry about…"

"It's fine." She narrowed her eyes. "Everything alright?"

He opened his mouth, but Faith caught his eye. She gave a tiny shake of her head. Taking the hint, he glanced back at Evelyn.

"Yes thanks. Never better."

She regarded him for a moment before turning away. "Very good. I must get on."

She swept out of the office, with Robyn not far behind.

When Faith looked back at Madeleine, she had returned to her screen. Jerking her head towards the hub, Faith raised an eyebrow. Noah nodded.

Once out of earshot, Faith pulled him to a table in the corner. "You alright?" She looked him up and down. "Evelyn said she'd lost you! I was so–"

Noah ran a hand across his forehead as he slumped down on to the bench. "I'm okay. I had to run, that's all."

"From what?"

He leaned closer, dropping his voice. "From Sarah Porter, of all people."

Faith recoiled at the name. "You saw her? Was she with–?"

"No sign of Jacob." He held her gaze. "I followed her. It's why I left Evelyn. But I figured, if I could find out where their group was hiding out, it would be useful information for Madeleine." He hung his head. "But she spotted me. Even threatened to expose me."

"What do you mean?"

"She screamed for help. I think she was going to have me arrested for harassing her." He flushed at the memory. "I didn't wait around to find out. Ran as fast as I could, loitered in the backstreets, eventually made my way back here."

Faith's heart thundered as she imagined him on the run. "So you don't know–"

"I don't know anything, other than Sarah was in the city today."

Faith glanced at the door to the office. "You should probably tell Madeleine."

"And give her another reason to send me back to Eremus?" He rolled his eyes. "She already doubts me."

"Evelyn said you'd done well, until you disappeared." Faith laid a hand on his arm. "And she didn't give you away."

"Not yet, anyway." Noah groaned. "You think she might keep it to herself?"

"Probably. For the time being, at least." Faith hoped she was right. "They have too much going on right now." She wondered how much she would be permitted to confide in him. "Sophia's definitely pregnant. And Danforth's desperate to push ahead with using the drugs on the academy students. She wants more pregnancies, so she can make some big announcement to the citizens. Convince them she's their saviour, once and for all."

"At the Liberation Day Ceremony?"

"What?" Faith frowned.

"I overheard the woman at the deli discussing it with Evelyn. There's some big celebration next week, isn't there? Danforth gives a speech."

"You're right." Faith's mind was racing. Liberation Day was always a big deal in the city. Everyone turned out to listen to the chancellor speak or watch her on the news. "*That's* why she's so desperate for results. Liberation Day will be the perfect time to announce her news."

Footsteps from the other side of the hub announced a newcomer. They looked up to see Diane approaching. "Robyn came in to speak to Blake." She flopped down onto the bench next to Faith. "And we were right in the middle of testing–"

"It's pretty urgent." Faith beckoned her friend across, dropping her voice. "Sophia's definitely pregnant. We think Danforth wants to announce her *big success* to the Bellator citizens at the Liberation Day Ceremony. But she'd rather have more than one pregnancy to crow about."

Diane's eyes flew wide. "The academy girls?"

"Yes. But they're not ready for the second drug, according to the doctor in charge of the study."

"So she's putting their lives at risk?" Diane sat bolt upright. "What are we doing about it? These are girls we know! We can't let them–"

Faith held out a hand to stop the flood of words. "We're not. Robyn's speaking to Blake about contacting Arden. They're going to replace the drugs with a placebo. Keep them safe." She turned to Noah. "Danforth told Anderson there were some women in the city who believed the information from the leaflets, you know. She's worried."

"Really?" Noah sat forward. "That's great."

"I wonder..." Faith turned to Diane. "You know how Blake managed to keep Stella's broadcast going for longer than usual last week?"

Diane nodded. "Could she hack into the feed for *Danforth's* speech, do you think?"

"She's pretty good." Diane cocked her head on one side. "It's possible, I guess."

"What are you thinking?" Noah asked.

Faith's mind raced over the possibilities. "What if... what if we could switch the feed during Danforth's talk and *I* could talk to the citizens? They'd all be listening on Liberation Day. Perhaps a live audience with me might have more impact than the leaflets alone. Might change their minds – stop them believing every word that comes out of Danforth's mouth."

"You could tell them what she's doing to the girls at the academy before she gets the chance to announce her triumph." Diane looked excited. "Preempt her."

"You think that might work?"

"It's certainly worth a try." Diane gestured to the office door. "Shall we?"

Moments later the three of them waited for Madeleine's response. Her face was unreadable as she considered Faith's proposal.

"I'd have to check with Blake. Make sure she thought this was possible."

"Of course." Diane stepped forward. "But I'm fairly sure she would. We've been working on the tech she used during Stella's broadcast last time. We've made some alterations, improved it. Hacking into Danforth's speech and switching the feed is definitely something she could do."

"What if Danforth's team could track it? Trace it back here?" The leader hung her head. "It's bad enough she's torturing Laura for information about the Resistance. So many people live here in the library. I don't know how many more lives I can put at risk."

"I'm sure Blake would do everything she could to scramble the signal." Diane's eyes flashed with determination. "Keep Faith on as long as she could, without compromising headquarters."

Madeleine turned to Faith, her face earnest. "*If* we do this, you'll have to make sure your speech is very carefully written. Get across the key points fast. We'll have no idea how long you'll have."

"I can do that." Faith felt more positive than she had in a long time.

Madeleine sat upright in her chair. A calm settled over her, and she looked almost regal.

"Alright. I'll consider it." She gave a sharp nod. "We finally know what Danforth's up to. She wants to present her citizens with a solution to the reproductive issues the city has. To show them they can exist without any form of male input." The leader shook her head in disbelief. "If we can replace the metraxilone with the placebos, the girls at the academy will be safe. It's the best we can do for them, for now.

"But it's not enough. Danforth still has one successful candidate. If she presents Sophia to the citizens, it will be extremely convincing. We cannot allow that to happen. If this works..." Madeleine jabbed a finger at Faith. "Your speech could act as a distraction."

Faith held her breath. "A distraction for what?"

"For a rescue. If all eyes are on the Liberation Day celebrations, security elsewhere will be more lax. We know Danforth is struggling for guards right now. If all the attention is focused on you, we can take advantage." Her eyes gleamed. "We can get Sophia out."

Faith's heart felt like it was going to burst. "You mean it?"

Madeleine nodded. "It makes sense. If we remove all of Danforth's advantages, she'll have nothing to impress her citizens with. It will require some careful planning, but I think it's–"

The door to the office burst open, cutting her off. The three of them turned to see Ella, her face stricken.

"I'm sorry…" she was panting, "I know I'm not supposed to come here without permission, but I had to come… to let you know…"

Noah was at her side in a second. Taking her arm, he brought her forward and eased her into a chair.

"What is it?" He soothed. "Take your time."

"I just came from Matriarch House. Got sent home early."

Faith sucked in a breath. "They know you're from Eremus?"

"No. Not that." Ella heaved in an unsteady breath. "I was bringing in a food delivery. From a van outside, to the kitchens." She blanched, and her eyes filled with tears. "I heard a commotion… running feet… shouting… and then… and then…"

She broke off. Alarmed, Faith took a step closer. "What happened? Are you in trouble?"

Another vehement shake of the head. "Not me." She paused, bringing her eyes up to meet Madeleine's. "I'd just stepped into the building when a figure came running towards me. Smashed straight into me. We both went flying. But before we could get up, guards came flying at us from nowhere." She paused, dropping her gaze. "At first I thought I'd been discovered. That it was me they were after."

There was a silence, as though Ella didn't want to go on.

"But they were after the other person?" Madeleine prompted. Ella refused to look up. "What happened to them?"

"The guards grabbed hold of her, but she struggled." Ella's eyes went wide. "So hard. She managed to pull free of them… she tried to run, but…" She gasped a breath, forcing herself to go on. "She didn't even make it to the door."

"Did the guards…?" Diane's voice was full of dread.

"They shot her." Ella's voice was full of disbelief. "Right there in front of me. Before she could reach the street."

The group fell silent. It was clear from Ella's face that the shot had been fatal. Faith felt sick as Madeleine asked the next question.

"Ella, did you recognise the person who was shot? Do you know who it was?"

Ella turned to Madeleine again. "Not at first. But she collapsed to the ground close to the door, underneath a light." She paused. "That's when I knew. I think she'd been trying to escape. Stop the torture."

Madeleine's hands were trembling. "Was it-?"

Ella nodded. "It was Laura."

CHAPTER THIRTY-SIX: NOAH

Spotting Evelyn sitting alone at a table in the hub, Noah made his way over. Since their return from the mission he'd abandoned, he had barely seen her. For the past few days, she had been busy sourcing the placebo pills from a local medcentre, and working out how they could be delivered to Arden at the academy without attracting attention.

It was proving tricky, and her exhausted expression was evidence of how hard she'd been working to manage the crisis.

"Evelyn?" He approached with caution, knowing he was interrupting a meal. "How are you?"

She glanced up at him, her face unreadable. "I'm tired."

"May I?" He gestured at the bench across from her. When she didn't object, he sat down. "I wanted to apologise. And to thank you." He took a breath. "I did have a good reason for leaving the other day."

"Really?" Evelyn eyed him as she broke off a piece of bread and popped it into her mouth. "What could possibly have been important enough for you to totally abandon your mission?"

"I saw someone... from my old life." Noah ploughed on. "A woman from Eremus. She was one of the people who went with Jacob when he left."

Evelyn's expression altered, the ridicule disappearing. "In the city?"

"Yeah. I... I followed her because I wanted to see if she'd lead me back to Jacob."

"And did she?"

"No." Noah hung his head. "She caught me following her and threatened to alert the guards." He held up a hand at her stricken expression. "Don't worry – I ran. Managed to get back here without being seen."

"Thank heavens for small mercies." Abandoning her meal, Evelyn stood up. "Come on then. We need to tell Madeleine you saw Sarah. Eremus deserves that information too."

She made her way towards the office, clearly expecting him to follow. As Noah trailed behind her, he hoped the information didn't go against him.

Inside, Madeleine and Robyn were pouring over some maps. They glanced up at Evelyn's entrance.

"We're not quite ready for you yet–" Madeleine began.

"This can't wait." Gesturing to Noah, she took a seat. "It seems Noah spotted one of Jacob's associates in the city the other day."

Madeleine tensed. "He must be planning something. And with everything we have going on, we could do without any unknowns." She turned to Robyn. "We should speak to Flynn and Anna. They might know something more." She glanced at Noah, a begrudging respect in her eyes. "Thanks for letting us know. There are a lot of plans in the offing at the moment. Since Kemp's torture and the news about the academy student testing, Danforth's gone mad. Laura's death was the last straw."

"It really was." Evelyn let out a heavy sigh. "We *have* to take more definitive action now."

"Laura risked *everything* for the Resistance." Robyn muttered. "She gave her life rather than betray us. She deserved better."

"She did. And we won't let her death be for nothing." Madeleine's face had taken on a steely determination. "That's what this new mission is about. We can't allow Danforth to carry on like this. But we don't need Jacob throwing a spanner in the works."

Robyn turned to Evelyn. "Did we manage to contact Arden?"

"Not yet." Evelyn scowled. "The usual methods just aren't working. I have someone watching the academy, waiting for him to come outside so we can get a message to him, but so far... no luck."

"The placebos are ready to go, though?"

"They are. But until we can get them into the building, make the switch, we can only assume that some of the students are already on the metraxilone."

"Keep trying." Robyn gave a nod. "But go and get some rest, first. You look exhausted."

Nodding her thanks, Evelyn left the room. Once she'd gone, the leaders turned back to Noah.

"Okay. As well as protecting the academy students and looking at hacking into Danforth's feed for the speech so that Faith can talk to the citizens, we also want to get Sophia out. Danforth wants to present her fertility miracle to the city at the Liberation Day ceremony. We can't allow her to do so."

"You think they'll try to bring Sophia to the square where the speech is taking place?" Noah was horrified.

"She's too sick for that. It won't look good." Madeleine swiped a hand across her datadev. "Blake witnessed them taking some photographs and video of Sophia earlier today." She spun the device to face them, showing screenshots of Sophia propped up on multiple pillows. "They made her face up so she had some colour and had her smiling and posing. We think she plans to show that footage to the crowd."

"So we're planning to use the distraction of Faith's speech to get Sophia out. But we need your help." Robyn smiled. "I know you had a shaky start with the drudge stuff, but Evelyn told us you did very well the other day. And now we find ourselves with an ideal solo mission for you."

"Great." His heart beat a little faster. *This was what he had come here for.* "What does it involve?"

Madeleine took over with a brisk nod. "Our plan for Sophia relies very much on us having someone on the inside." She raised an eyebrow.

"In the hospital?" Noah was surprised. "We don't already have someone there?"

Madeleine shut off the datadev. "We used to. Danforth's paranoia has led to her increasing security checks significantly in recent weeks. We had to remove our original contact for fear of her being discovered. And we can't see a way of getting anyone new in quickly, unless..."

Again, her eyes moved to Noah.

"We feel..." She rephrased, "We think Danforth will be keeping a close eye on things at the hospital. She knows the Resistance exists. She knows we're trying to take her down. She'll be very careful about allowing new female technicians or medics in the wards."

"But she doesn't *know* we have an alliance with Eremus." Robyn's voice was low and serious. "She won't suspect that we have a *male* spy."

"We don't think she'll check the drudges." Madeleine's eyes were fixed on Noah's, hawk-like. "We intend to replace one of them with you."

"You're going to kidnap a drudge?"

"Yes. One who's a similar height and hair colour as you." Madeleine's tone was calm as always. "Once he's here, he'll be treated with the utmost care and respect. We will expect him to confide in us. Tell us details about his job, his role and duties, so he can be replaced quickly."

"By me?" Noah felt a shiver run down his spine.

"We'll get you in place as soon as possible." She tapped a finger on the desk as she spoke. "Definitely, by Liberation Day. When Faith gives her speech, you'll be in situ to let the Resistance members into the hospital."

"Does Faith know?"

Robyn shook her head. "She's been busy with her speech. We figured it was one less thing for her to worry about."

"But–"

Robyn held up her hand. "I know, you'll want to tell her. But first, we want her to finish the speech. Could you hold off telling her til she's done?"

"I don't–" He spotted the look on Madeleine's face. "I suppose."

"In the meantime," Robyn added, "I'll head to one of our safehouses. Make contact with Eremus. I wanted to fill them in on our plans anyway, but with the news about Sarah, we definitely need to speak." She glanced at Noah. "Come with me, if you like."

Once Noah had changed into his drudge uniform, he hurried back down along the hallway, surprised when he ran into Faith in the doorway of the hub.

"Hey," she smiled. "How are you?"

"Fine." He attempted to return her smile. "You?"

"I'm good, actually. I'm so happy they've finally agreed to rescue Sophia." A sadness crossed her face. "I mean I'm sad about Laura, obviously, but..."

As she trailed off, he pulled her back out into the hallway, letting the door to the hub close behind her. "No one thinks you didn't care about Laura. It's alright for you to be pleased that they're going to save Sophia. You care about her."

"But I..."

"She's the reason you came back here." Noah smiled, gently. "And I know you. You're the kind of person who's totally devoted to the people they love. You'd do anything for them."

"I would." She gazed up at him, her eyes misty. "And that includes you. I don't know what I'd do if you were in danger too."

Guilt sliced through him at her words. He would tell her later, he promised himself. He had promised he'd keep the news to himself for now. Instead, he tried to return the weight of feeling.

"*I* would too." His voice was a whisper. "I'd do anything for the people I care about. And that includes *you*."

The goodbye kiss she gave him stayed in his mind all the way to the safe house. He barely noticed the people they passed, finding it easier than ever to remain in the drudge posture as long as his focus was on Faith. When they arrived at their destination, Noah was surprised at how quickly the hour-long journey had passed.

Glancing both ways, Robyn slipped down a side street and into an alleyway behind the houses. At the third house along, she unlatched the gate and led him into a small yard. She pulled a key out of her pocket and unlocked the door.

She was smiling as she closed the door behind them. "Well, I haven't seen you in action in public until now, but if the last hour is anything to go by, you'll convince even the most suspicious of Bellator citizens."

By the time Noah had time to react to the compliment, Robyn was unloading things from her pack. "Hopefully, we won't be here for long. I could do with getting back to HQ by the time the team brings the drudge back. But sometimes," she fiddled with the walkie talkie, "it takes a while to get a response from Eremus." She rolled her eyes in annoyance.

Noah had to bite his lip. "It's not like we have time to sit around *waiting* for the Resistance to get in touch. We're pretty busy trying to keep the community safe, warm, and fed."

Robyn flushed. "Sorry. I forget that things in Eremus are so difficult sometimes."

Noah took a seat at one of the chairs which surrounded the table. "It's fine."

Twisting the knob at the top of the walkie talkie, Robyn sat down opposite him. "Let's hope someone's around today with a good signal."

She brought the walkie talkie to her lips. "Eremus, this is Resistance One. Do you read me? Come in, Eremus."

"Reading you Resistance One. This is Eremus. Over."

"Paulo!" Noah sat bolt upright.

Robyn's lips curved upwards in amusement. "You know who it is?"

"My brother."

Leaning in, she clicked the button again. "Hey, Eremus. How are things?"

There was a short pause before the walkie talkie crackled again. "Good thanks. The recent raid has made a real difference."

Noah had never thought he'd miss his bossy older brother, but the familiar voice sent a surge of warmth through his body.

"No problem." Robyn replied. "Wanted to let you know that Sarah Porter was recently sighted in the city. Presume there's been no sign of Jacob on your end?"

"No." Paulo sounded alarmed. "And if Sarah's in the city..."

"Jacob is too." Robyn bit her lip at the confirmation. "How are the Danforth students doing?"

"They're fine. How are Noah and Ella?"

"Also, fine." Robyn's tone was reassuring. "Ella started a placement in the city a couple of days ago. And Noah is also preparing for his own assignment." She paused. "I brought him here to speak to you."

For a second, there was silence. And then, Paulo's voice came again. "You there, little brother?"

Robyn passed the walkie talkie across the table.

"Noah?" A loud crackle made him jump.

He raised the device to his lips and took a breath. "How's it going?"

"Good. It's... good to hear your voice." There was a pause so long that Noah thought they'd lost contact. Tactfully, Robyn moved to the kitchen, rattling mugs and filling the kettle with water. Eventually, the walkie talkie crackled again. "Sorry. I was just sending someone to get Anna."

Noah tried not to get his hopes up at the mention of his ma. If she was a long distance away, she wouldn't make it to Paulo before he and Robyn had to leave. "Thanks," he managed.

"Where's this placement then?"

Noah glanced at Robyn, but she nodded encouragement. "At the hospital."

Paulo took a while to reply. "Really? Be careful there."

"I will." Noah breathed, relieved to have escaped a lecture. "I've been practising hard... ever since I got here."

This time when Paulo spoke, it sounded like he was chuckling. "I'm sure you have."

Not knowing how to respond to his brother's compliment, Noah pushed on. "It's Liberation Day next week. The Resistance has a lot planned. I'm part of a much bigger mission."

Robyn appeared beside him, taking the walkie talkie from his hand. "Danforth always makes a big speech. We're planning to disrupt it."

"How?"

Robyn held the button down and gestured to Noah. Understanding that she wanted him to take the lead, he leaned forward.

"We're planning to replace Danforth's words with Faith's." Noah felt a sense of pride well within him. "She's going to expose all of Danforth's lies, talk about the experiments, the school, and her time in Eremus."

"Interesting." There was a brief dip in the sound before Paulo continued. "...had an idea which we wanted to discuss with you. We want to prove that the people of Eremus aren't monsters."

"How do you intend to do that?" Robyn interjected.

"Send back one of the hostages. Show that they've been treated well." Paulo paused, as though he expected them to reply. When they didn't, he went on. "We were going to speak to you about when might be an appropriate time to do it, but it sounds like this ceremony might be the perfect opportunity. We could make a show of bringing the student back to Bellator, *while* Faith is speaking. Demonstrate that the people of Eremus aren't monsters. That we can be trusted. Undermine everything Danforth has preached about our community."

Robyn frowned. "We couldn't guarantee the safety of the person returning the hostage."

"We know that... we're willing to take the risk." There was another pause. "We're worried... if we wait much longer, Jacob will take action. *Especially* after what you just told me. If Sarah's in Bellator, Jacob's planning something. Something that could be devastating to both our communities."

Leaning over, Noah pulled the walkie talkie from Robyn's grasp. "But you're not *with* Jacob. Eremus doesn't have anything to do with him anymore."

"The women of the city don't know that. They'll believe what they see. If the first male they are exposed to is Jacob, he could ruin it for everyone. But if it's Flynn... doing something decent, honourable, then..."

At the mention of the man who was like a father to him marching into Bellator in broad daylight, Noah froze. Recognising his discomfort, Robyn leaned forward, easing the walkie talkie out of his hand. "I'll take your suggestion back to Madeleine. Let you know what she says. Personally, I think it would go a long way towards showing the Bellator women what Eremus is really like."

"...please say you'll consider it." Paulo's reply was clipped.

"We will."

There was another lengthy pause. Robyn leaned closer to Noah. "It'll be dangerous for whoever does it, but it might turn the tide of opinion. Lord knows we need as much help as we can get."

Noah nodded, sensing the conversation was almost over. It was staring him in the face now: Robyn had brought him here to give him a chance to say goodbye to his home, his family. In case he didn't come back from his mission.

Robyn shot him a questioning glance. "Are you al–"

But the walkie talkie crackled again before she could finish asking the question.

"Noah?" This time the voice was female. "Noah? Are you there?"

At the sound of the familiar voice, Noah felt tears in his eyes. Robyn passed the device back to him and rose, taking her coffee with her into the next room. Appreciating her sensitivity, Noah settled back in his chair. Taking a deep breath, he pressed the button.

"Hey, Ma. How are you?"

Chapter Thirty-Seven:
Faith

She rubbed her aching neck, glancing at the time on her wristclip. Ten p.m.

As Noah had headed out with Robyn, Faith had come to the library to write her speech. Feeling like she finally had a purpose, she had set to work as though her life depended on it. If delivering this speech was her way of contributing to the Resistance, then she was determined to do it well.

But putting the words together to convey everything that had happened to her over the past few months was proving more difficult than she had anticipated. Her thoughts kept drifting to the explosion in the forest, Kemp's beating, Sophia's forced pregnancy, Laura's death. So many terrible events.

How could she possibly convey them all in a short time? Describe the heinous crimes that Danforth had committed, was still committing, and would continue to commit, unless someone stopped her?

It was the reason the speech was so important. But also why it was so damn difficult to write.

Faith slumped back in her chair. She had around a page of decent material now, but she'd written and discarded so many sentences she'd lost count.

Deciding to take a break, she wandered out of the library and went downstairs. Most of the Resistance members would be in bed now, but there was a fair chance that Diane would still be up. After failing to find her in the bunk room, Faith headed for Blake's office.

Inside, Blake was huddled over a datadev. The techie had been working flat out ever since she'd agreed to help the Resistance hack into Danforth's speech on Liberation Day. She barely looked up as Faith entered, but Diane waved a hand from her position at another desk.

"How's the speech coming?"

Faith took a seat on the stool in front of Sophia's monitor. "Don't ask."

She stared at the screen. Sophia was sleeping now and looked fairly peaceful. In her waking hours she was anything but.

Hold on, Faith willed her. *We're coming for you.*

"That bad?"

Faith turned to see Diane's eyes on her. She shrugged. "Not *that* bad. I just needed a break." She looked over at her friend. "What are you doing?"

"What are we *not* doing, is more the question." But Diane's eyes glowed with pride. She loved working alongside Blake. At Faith's inquisitive gaze, she sat back. "See this?" She brandished a flat, rectangular piece of plastic. "It's a keycard, like the ones they use at the hospital."

Faith's mind went back to the night she had broken into the Bellator Hospital. She'd had to steal a keycard from a medic to access the datadevs in the restricted area.

"We've been trying to clone them." Diane tapped the card against the desk. "So anyone going into the hospital could use them, rather than having to steal one, like you did."

"It would certainly reduce the danger involved in breaking and entering." Faith gave a wry grin. "If you had a key."

Blake grunted. "It would if we could get it right."

Faith frowned. "It doesn't work?"

Diane glanced at her unofficial mentor. "We're almost there with it."

"Hmph. Not close enough." Blake's eyes remained fixed on the screen. She looked exhausted. "Not for Noah to use, anyway."

Faith froze. "What do you mean, *for Noah to use*? Why would Noah..." She glanced at Diane. "Where is Noah going?"

Diane frowned. "He didn't tell you?"

"No." A surge of anger rolled through Faith. She turned away, glancing at the screen again. Sophia slept on. "He didn't tell me."

Abandoning the keycards, Diane moved towards Faith. "Maybe Madeleine swore him to secrecy. He's heading to the hospital in a couple of days—undercover—as a drudge. He's part of Sophia's rescue."

"A very important part," Blake added.

"He's the one who'll be gaining access to the Fertility Ward. Opening the door for the Resistance to get in." Diane looked impressed.

"*If* he can pull it off."

Faith felt her heart constrict. She'd known Noah would leave at some point, and with all there was to organise for Liberation Day, it made sense for him to be put to work. But knowing that he would be in such a dangerous position was not comforting news.

Diane's face darkened at Blake's comment. She leaned closer. "He'll do fine."

"I hope so."

"He will! Evelyn told me he did a great job the other day. She really put him through his paces." Diane turned to Blake. "Speaking of Evelyn, has she had any luck yet?"

"Don't think so. Let's see." Blake tapped a few buttons on her keyboard. "She's still in place. No movement as yet."

"And there's been no sign of him?"

"No sign of who?" Faith asked.

"Arden. Evelyn's hiding at a location close to the academy." Blake ran a tired hand across her forehead. "We've had someone there for the past two days now, trying to get the placebos to him, but..." she shrugged, her face taut with worry, "no success as yet."

"And you're worried..."

"Every minute we don't make the switch is a minute that students are being given metraxilone." Blake sighed. "There's nothing we can do but wait, though." She glanced at Diane. "And there's plenty more that needs to be done in the meantime."

Faith shot Diane a questioning look.

"We're under pressure to get the keycards to work, plus Blake is trying to work out the logistics of hacking into the Liberation Day feed. If we don't manage to do that, your speech will never be heard."

Faith turned to Blake. "You can't just do what you did with Stella's last broadcast?"

Blake whirled on her. "I can't *just* do anything. It's a complex procedure, which changes almost daily. I manage to hack in, Danforth's tech wizards block me. I have to investigate as many avenues as possible. That way, if one method fails, there's a backup. I have to give us the best chance of this working."

As she bent her head over the datadev again, Diane explained. "We're pretty sure that Danforth's tech people have put additional security measures in place. We're looking at ways to get round them, but it might not be possible to do it remotely."

"Which means...?"

"Which means we may need someone to go in and *manually* disconnect their system." Blake shot them a dark look. "Something I was trying to avoid."

"That sounds pretty dangerous." Faith shuddered.

"It's extremely dangerous." Blake massaged her temples. "And we can't really spare the manpower. We're stretched to breaking point already with this mission."

She was right. Their final operation involved multiple teams in multiple places, all at the same time: Robyn's team, who were going to retrieve Sophia from the hospital; Evelyn, who had been charged with guiding Flynn and Helen safely into the city; a small group including Olivia and Diane who were keeping an eye on things in the square; Faith, Blake and Madeleine, who were running things back at the library...

The list went on and on.

"No." Blake sat up straighter in the chair. "I'm not out of options yet. If people would just keep quiet and leave me to work..."

Faith let out a breath. "Sorry."

"It's fine." For once, Blake looked apologetic. "I'm just feeling the pressure, that's all. But we all have to play our part." She wagged a finger at Faith. "Just be certain to make every one of those words you're writing count. Okay? And... since I've no idea how long we'll be able to breach Danforth's feed for, you'd better pack a lot into the beginning of your speech."

As Blake turned back to her screen, Faith tried not to feel buried under the weight of the very pressure Blake had mentioned. "I guess I'll get back to it, then," she began, "and make sure I–"

A beeping sound from Blake's datadev interrupted her. The tech whiz leaned forward, flicking a switch on the dashboard in front of her.

"Evelyn!" She barked into her headset. "Tell me you've you got some good news."

She listened, her head cocked to one side. For several minutes, the room was silent. Faith felt like she should be holding her breath as they waited for Evelyn's report. Blake's face was unreadable.

Eventually, she gave a terse nod. "Will do. Thanks for the update."

She cut the call and slumped against the back of her chair. Diane and Faith exchanged glances, knowing not to rush her. When Blake finally turned to them, her eyes were sombre.

"Evelyn spoke with Arden. He has the placebos and will make the switch as soon as possible."

"That's great!" Faith burst out. "Now we don't have to–"

"You don't understand." Blake paused, a hitch in her voice. "It's too late."

Diane moved forward, placing a hand on her shoulder. "What do you mean?"

Blake's expression was bleak. "Because they've been administering the metraxilone to six of the senior girls for the past forty-eight hours."

Faith and Diane's eyes met, anticipating Blake's words before she spoke them.

"When they went to wake the girls this morning, two of them were dead."

CHAPTER THIRTY-EIGHT:
NOAH

When Noah got back to the library, he looked for Faith. Guilt had gnawed at him the whole way back from the safe house. She deserved to know that he was leaving. He owed her the truth.

The last words his ma had spoken to him played over and over in his head.

"I'm glad we had this chance to talk, before... you know." She had paused, as though gathering herself. "I'm glad you felt you could be honest with me. It means a lot." Noah had bent his head, hiding his expression from Robyn. "And, despite what you might sometimes think... I'm very proud of you."

There had been a crackle, as though the walkie-talkie had been on the point of giving up. Noah lunged forward, clutching the device like some kind of lifeline. But her final words had come through loud and clear.

"I love you, Noah. Just try to keep a cool head, okay? For me?"

It took him more than an hour to find Faith. He began in the library, knowing it was her sanctuary. But the space was empty, aside from the books on its shelves, which stared down at him in pity.

He tried the bedroom she shared with some other Resistance members, to no avail. Madeleine's office, the hub, even opening the door to the exit tunnel. Faith was nowhere to be found. He racked his brain for somewhere else she might be. Had she left the building? But Madeleine hadn't allowed her to go anywhere recently. Surely, with the mission ahead, she wouldn't risk discovery?

He gave up, trailing back to the storage room, though he doubted he would be able to sleep without speaking to her. Tugging the door open, he almost had a heart attack when he spotted a figure lying on the mat on the floor. Faith. He ducked inside, closing the door behind him. Creeping closer, he knelt down beside her. *Had she been crying?*

"Where have you been?"

He cradled her face in his hand. Her eyes fluttered open, widening as she recognised him.

"What happened?" He stroked a thumb over her cheek. "Are you okay?"

She shook her head, the tears returning. Slowly, she shuffled backwards, making space for him beside her. Gesturing to the empty space, she looked up.

After a moment's pause, he lowered his body until it lay next to hers. "What is it?"

Her eyes widened. "You didn't hear?"

"I only just got back. Came straight to find you."

"The team didn't get the placebos into the academy in time." She paused, breathing hard. "Two of the girls... girls I've known since I was ten years old... they're..."

She didn't need to finish the sentence.

He shifted closer, until their bodies pressed against one another from shoulder to hip. "I'm so sorry."

At his whispered condolence, something in her seemed to break. Thrusting her arms around him, she buried her face in his neck and sobbed. Noah wrapped his arms around her as tightly as he could manage, trying to contain her grief. Her entire body shuddered, racked with sobs. Not knowing what to say, he simply held her. Stroking a hand down her back, he waited until the fit of tears began to subside. When her breath evened out a little, he tried to pull back, searching for something to say.

"I can't imagine–" he began, but she didn't let him finish.

Her eyes desperate, she lunged forward, pressing her lips to his. The kiss wasn't gentle. As their mouths collided, he felt the contact as bruising, almost violent. He knew he should back away. She wasn't in the right state of mind for this. It was a bad idea. They had decided to wait.

But his body responded to her passion in an almost primal way. He returned the kiss, feeling the strength of her emotions in the way she pressed her body up against him. But when her hands pressed against his chest and her lips moved lower, he knew he had to stop her.

Something was driving her. He instinctively knew she wouldn't be the one to end this. Grief was overwhelming her and she was trying to bury it with desire. He didn't want their first time to be like this. And, if she was in her right mind, neither would she.

His body aching, he pushed away, resisting her. Her hands had moved lower, pulling up the hem of his shirt, her fingers exploring the bare skin beneath. Shivering, he took hold of her hands and removed them. Holding them, he hauled in a deep breath.

"Stop."

Her eyes flew open. "W-what?"

He attempted a smile. "We should stop. This isn't going to help."

She blinked, the heat in her eyes fading. Already he could see the despair return.

"It might feel good now, to block out the hurt..." he inched backwards, "but you'll hate yourself when it's over and the sadness comes back."

"I'm sorry." She flushed. "I didn't–"

He pulled her close, sensing the danger was over. "It's okay. Understandable. And... in case you weren't clear on this... I was enjoying it. It's just..."

"I know." Her voice was barely a whisper. "We said we wouldn't. And to do it now, when I'm..." She reached up, brushing a stray hair from his face. "Thank you. For stopping me."

"No problem." He groaned. "Honestly, it was one of the hardest things I've had to do."

She shifted closer, laying her head on his chest. "I can't believe they're gone. We thought we had it under control, but..."

He brushed a lock of hair off her forehead. "We did all we could."

"It wasn't enough."

"One day it will be." He cradled her head against his chest. "At least the placebos are there now. The rest of the girls will be safe."

"For now." She sighed. "We just have to hope that the rest of the mission goes to plan. That we can get them out for good. Did you get through to Eremus?"

He nodded. "They want to play their part too." He hesitated. "There's something I need to tell you."

"They're sending you undercover to the hospital." She shifted. "I already know."

He braced himself for her anger. "I'm sorry I didn't–"

"It's fine." She leaned her head back to look at him. "I knew you had to go at some point. I can hardly judge you for helping with the very thing I've wanted since I returned to Bellator. You have an important part to play in Sophia's rescue."

"So do you." He felt her shrug beneath him. "You *do*!"

"I suppose." She leaned back against his chest. "I just feel like I'm doing so little when you're going to put yourself directly in the firing line to save my best friend."

"I think," he gathered his thoughts, "I think it's natural that you're scared for us. For me." He took her chin in his hand and pulled her gaze to meet his. "I love that you care so much... for me. But this is what we both came here for. To improve things. So we have to be brave. Do what's asked of us. And hope we come out the other side unscathed."

"But I feel like I won't be doing *anyth–*"

"You're wrong. You'll be doing something very important. We can't all do battle with guns and knives and fists. Some people are meant for that." He thought of Paulo and Flynn. "But others, people like you and me, we have to find different ways to fight. My way is to act a part. Adopt a disguise. Go undercover and try to help free your friend. Yours–" Faith opened her mouth to speak, but he held up his hand. "*Yours* is to speak out about what you know."

"But what good are words?"

"What do you mean?" He faked shock. "*Wars* have been won with speeches, in the past. Did you know that? Instead of violence, people protested. Brought the truth to the eyes of people who'd been lied to. It's a vital stage of this fight. Once the women of Bellator see the truth, they'll support the Resistance in bringing Danforth down." She tried to lower her gaze, but he hung on to her chin. "*You're* the person delivering those all-important words. Don't tell me that's not important."

"I'm so afraid it won't be enough." Her voice was barely a whisper.

Leaning forward, he pressed his lips to hers. When he pulled away, the pain in her eyes had dimmed.

"It will be enough. You just have to find the right words. You can do it. But promise me you'll stop thinking what you're doing isn't important?"

"I promise."

She leaned in, returning the kiss. Her lips were soft and warm. Noah wondered if he'd ever get used to kissing her. For a moment, he relaxed into it, but when her arms crept around his neck and she shifted closer, he pulled away.

"Do you think maybe you should go and get some sleep?" Her face fell. "Not that I want you to go. Obviously."

"Could I maybe… stay?" She blushed. "I mean… if you're being sent away soon, we might not have too many more moments to be alone."

"Stay?" He glanced around at the limited space. "Really? It won't be too comfortable. Ella wanted to stay in here with me the day we arrived." He held out a hand at Faith's expression. "She was nervous, that's all. She wanted to be with a familiar face."

Faith lowered her eyes. "I'm willing to bet that Ella wasn't willing to lie this close to you."

A thrill ran through him. "Alright. If you're *sure*. But if you wake up in a couple of hours with a stiff neck, feel free to go back to your usual bed."

"I will." She shifted her body until she was lying the length of the sleeping mat again. When he didn't follow, she frowned. "Come on, then. We both have to lie the same way for this to work, surely?"

Tentatively, he eased his body in place alongside her. The mat was so small that he had to loop an arm around her waist just to ensure she didn't slide off. Nose to nose, they exchanged nervous smiles.

"I don't think this is very practical." He kissed her again.

"How about if we…" she blushed, "if we lie with my back to your front. Like spoons."

He felt a rush of heat at the suggestion but tried to keep his voice even. "I guess that might work."

Faith wriggled around until she was facing the opposite direction. Then, sighing, she nestled into him.

"That okay?"

It was better than okay, but for a moment Noah couldn't find the words. After a brief pause, he managed a strangled, "Fine," but wasn't sure if he'd manage to get any sleep at all with Faith pressed up against him.

When she stilled, however, Noah found a sense of calm settle over him. As her breathing steadied, becoming deeper and more rhythmic, he relaxed his arms around her and dropped a soft kiss on the back of her head, breathing in the scent of her hair.

"Noah?" The words were sleepy.

"Uh-huh?"

"Be careful out there, won't you?"

He squeezed her tighter. "I will. I promise."

When he woke, the room felt different. It took him a few minutes to work out that he wasn't alone. Beside him, Faith stirred, rolling to face the ceiling. She opened her eyes and smiled.

"Hey," she murmured.

"Hey, yourself. This is… new." He held her gaze, feeling the tension at the unfamiliar intimacy. "You okay?"

"A little better than I was last night." She shrugged. "Because of you."

Something surged inside him at her words. "I'm glad."

"I've actually been awake a while." She shifted slightly. "I was just... lying still... trying to stay in the moment. Enjoy a little peace before the storm begins."

"You think we're ready?"

She paused before answering, considering her words. "As ready as we can be."

"You thought about what I said?" Noah nudged her gently. "About your speech? How much it matters?"

"I did."

"And?"

"I know you're right." She reached for his hand. "You make me feel strong. Safe. When I'm with you–"

"You too?" He tried to clarify. "I mean... it's the same for me. When I'm with you, I feel like I could do anything."

She smiled, sadly. "You were exactly what I needed last night." She glanced away. "I'm pretty sure I'd like to wake up next to you *every* morning."

He was silent for a moment, taking in the enormity of her statement. "That's... that's quite a declaration."

"It's how I feel."

"Me too." He pulled her to him.

"That's good to know."

She leaned forward, until their lips met. Noah closed his eyes, savouring the moment. *Who knew how many more times they would be together before he left?*

After a moment, she broke the contact. "I have to get out of here. Before there are too many people around."

"You're ashamed of me?" He cocked his head to one side.

"No. I just..." She blushed. "I like things... us the way we are. I don't want people weighing in with their opinions."

"I get it." He stretched his arms over his head. "Better get moving, then. Don't want anyone to catch us. I'll wait a few minutes before I follow."

With a final kiss, she manoeuvred her way to the door, turning back to gaze at him before she opened it. When she was gone, he lay back, straightening his spine in a way he hadn't been able to all night. It was a relief, but at the same time he missed her presence.

Eventually, he decided he had given her enough time to escape without alerting suspicion. Rubbing a tired hand across his face, he left the store room and wandered into the hub. It was quiet, being so early. He was just helping himself to a coffee and a roll smothered in jam when the door to Madeleine's office opened.

He turned with a smile, ready to greet whichever leader was emerging. Instead, he found himself faced with an unfamiliar drudge. Behind him stood Robyn.

"Noah!" she greeted him brusquely. "Just the person."

She moved into the hub, beckoning to the newcomer to follow her. The new drudge's eyes darted around the room, seeming uncomfortable with his surroundings. When they reached Noah, Robyn stopped.

"I was just coming to find you." She paused, waiting for the drudge to catch up to her. "We had a team at the hospital last night. They managed to find a drudge that looked enough like you." She gestured to the man standing behind her. "Meet Rowan. You'll be replacing him at the Bellator Hospital first thing tomorrow."

Chapter Thirty-Nine: Faith

"This is where you'll be sleeping."

Faith gestured to the mat on the floor of the store room. Her heart lurched as she stared at it, remembering the previous night. Turning back to her companion, she managed to smile.

"I know it doesn't look like much, but–"

The drudge stepped into the tiny room behind her. "It's no worse than I'm used to."

"Really?" Faith cast him a concerned glance.

He gave a small smile. "You think the hospital gives us comfortable beds?"

"Of course, they don't." She glanced away, embarrassed. "It's just– I mean I've never seen the drudge quarters, anywhere."

"This is fine. Warm, dry, private." He stepped inside, stooped to push a hand down on the mat. "This is thicker than those in the drudge quarters, too." Faith noticed he didn't use the word *home*.

She stared at the newcomer. The Resistance had really lucked out with the drudge they had taken from the hospital. Robyn and Blake had grabbed him at the rear of the hospital as he headed away from the night shift. Blindfolded, he'd been bundled into the back of a comcar and brought back to the library. But after the initial shock of the kidnapping had worn off, he had listened as Madeleine explained the reason for his kidnapping.

Surprised to discover that rumours of the Resistance were true, he had been quite amenable to their questions once he'd been assured they would treat him well. He'd even helped Noah to prepare for his mission, demonstrating how to blend in as his replacement. Despite his lack of sleep, he'd worked with Noah all day, explaining the hospital systems, sketching a map of the key areas, and going over the different duties Noah would be required to complete.

It was imperative that Noah absorb the relevant information fast. He had to be in place to start Rowan's next shift.

This evening.

Having spent the day tucked away in the library finishing her speech, Faith had not found out about Noah's imminent departure until an hour earlier. Since then, she'd been unable to focus on anything. Once Rowan had finished working with Noah, Robyn had asked Faith to show him around. Faith suspected the job was aimed at keeping her away from the office, where Noah was receiving his final instructions. But she had been grateful for the distraction anyway.

During the tour, she had really warmed to the man. As with Arden, Madeleine had named him. Faith could see the pride Rowan took in being introduced to others. The name meant he, a lowly drudge, mattered. Faith's determination to deliver a powerful speech had solidified as she'd accompanied him around the building. The appalling treatment of the drudges was something else Danforth had normalised. Yet another reason the chancellor's reign had to end.

But showing him to the store room was another reminder that Noah was leaving in a matter of hours.

"You okay?"

Looking up, she found Rowan's eyes resting on her. She was relieved to discover that his were a light blue, rather than Noah's vivid green. She had to admit, Robyn and Blake had chosen well. Hiding in the alleyway at the rear of the hospital, they spent a long time observing the drudges to make sure they chose the one most like Noah. And aside from the eyes, the two men were very much alike.

The similarity in their shape was uncanny. Dressed alike as drudges, and viewed from behind, they could have been twins. But up close, Faith could see many differences. Rowan's hair was a similar colour to Noah's, but his chin was narrower and his lips thin, where Noah's were full. His nose was a touch larger than Noah's too, but all of this would be covered by the mask.

Faith found it comforting that the pair looked so similar. This, in addition to the scant attention paid to the drudges by the Bellator women, would keep Noah safe. At least, Faith hoped so.

"Faith?"

She was jolted from her reverie. "What? Oh, I'm sorry," she stammered. "Yes, I'm fine. Thank you."

Rowan looked as though he wanted to press her for more, but his reticent nature took over and he lowered his eyes respectfully. Faith marvelled at how intuitive he was. He'd read her mood accurately, understanding, despite her smile, that something was wrong.

She hurried to cover the silence. "Won't you have been missed today? I mean," she searched for the word he had used, "in the drudge quarters. The others, they won't have... reported you gone?"

He shook his head. "Unlikely. Drudges disappear, from time to time. We don't question it."

Faith frowned. "You don't?"

"Who would listen?" Rowan shrugged. "Sometimes drudges die. The consequences of disobedience are severe. If a drudge is beaten by one of the Bellator citizens, no one questions it. We don't have rights."

"But..." Faith struggled to understand.

"And sometimes drudges run away." Rowan raised an eyebrow. "Mostly, they're discovered and brought back. But our lives are–" he paused. "If a drudge is brave enough to risk it, we let them go."

"Do any of them escape? For good, I mean."

Rowan shrugged. "I don't know. I've never had the courage to try it myself. We hear of those who get caught, because they're–" He stopped, biting down on his lip.

"Danforth gets rid of them?"

"They're classed as malfunctioning. Because they disobeyed orders. Danforth has them executed. Quietly, though."

"She's clever."

"*Too* clever." Rowan growled. "So to answer your original question, no. The drudges might notice I'm not in my bed. But they won't report it. When Noah arrives tomorrow to replace me, they'll notice him. But they probably won't question it. As long as he's convincing as a drudge, they'll just assume I've been replaced."

Sucking in a breath, Faith sagged against the doorframe.

"You're worried about him."

"A little." She blushed at the lie.

Rowan held her gaze. "From what I've seen today, he'll be okay. He acts the drudge well. And I've done everything I can to keep him safe."

Faith managed a smile. "I'm sure he'll be alright." She backed away. "You get some rest. You deserve it."

She watched until the door had closed behind him. Then she hurried to the door of the library and headed up the stairs.

Her sanctuary was quiet, but the high ceilings and old books didn't distract her the way they usually did. Collecting a datadev from the front desk, she moved into the side room which housed the research documents and curled up on the sofa under the window. She tapped the button on the front of the device and waited while it whirred to life.

Her speech was almost there now. Noah had restored her belief in a shared future with him and a better world for them all. His words of encouragement had proved a catalyst for renewed inspiration, and her thoughts had been flowing freely ever since. Her words could make a difference. She knew it now.

But there was one group of people she needed to add.

When the screen loaded, she opened the document and began typing. Her fingers flew over the keys, describing Rowan, Arden, and the rest of the drudges who the women of the city never saw. Their individual personalities. She was ashamed that she too had regarded them as less than herself until very recently. Until someone pointed out how unjust their treatment was, reminded the citizens of the city that these men were human too, nothing would change. The drudges deserved a better life as much as anyone.

When she had finished, she sagged back against the sofa. The speech was ready. She could do no more.

She still quivered whenever she thought about delivering it. She would be telling the truth, uncovering lies, casting light on things which had been hidden from the citizens of Bellator for years.

But the chancellor would deny every word she said. She *had* to be convincing.

Learning of Eremus' action had given Faith confidence. She had been surprised by the Eremus plan to bring a hostage back to the city, but knew that Flynn's arrival at the ceremony would send a powerful message. Who could deny Eremus' compassion if they permitted another Danforth student to return safely to the city? The action would offer concrete proof to support her words. Surely, then, the women of Bellator would believe them.

She ran her finger down the datadev screen, scanning the sentences she'd spent so long constructing. The words she had played with, writing and reordering, replacing and rephrasing, so she could deliver a speech worthy of the danger the Resistance members were putting themselves in. Everyone else would be directly in the line of fire, whether it was Flynn approaching the stage at the ceremony, Kemp and Arden doing their best to protect the academy students, or Noah at the hospital. All of them risking their lives. To make their efforts worthwhile, the speech had to have the desired impact.

There were so many things the Bellator citizens needed to know. Faith could only hope she got the chance to tell them everything. And that they listened. And, she closed her eyes and said a silent prayer, that Sophia's rescue would go smoothly.

The two events were bound together: Liberation Day would act as a distraction, allowing the rescue to go ahead. Because many of the hospital staff would be otherwise occupied listening to Danforth's speech, they would be less attentive to their surroundings. With Noah on the inside and many of the staff looking the other way, the Resistance was hoping they could get Sophia out without anyone noticing.

Faith turned back to the words on the datadev screen. *Were they enough?*

Closing her eyes, she recited the words aloud, imagining the crowds in the Main Square transfixed by her voice, believing her words, rising up and rebelling against Danforth until everything was perfect. Sophia wasn't pregnant, the academy students were safe, the drudges were free, and the Eremus folk were able to roam in and out of Bellator without fear.

A noise startled her, and she turned to see Noah standing at the entrance to the Records Room. He was smiling, but the expression on his face was somehow also sad.

"Make sure you deliver it just like that."

Her face heated at his words. "Like what?"

"With passion." He walked towards her, offering her a hand. She took it and he pulled her upwards, forwards, framing her face in his hands. "With that tone in your voice."

Breathless, she eyed him. "What tone?"

"The one which is totally convincing." He held a finger to her lips as she tried to protest. "Which demonstrates how much you believe in your words. Because that means others will too."

She blushed. "You think so?"

"I know so." He circled his arms around her, pulling her close and whispering in her ear. "You'll blow them away." He leaned back a little, so she could see his face. "And while you're delivering the speech of a lifetime, I'll be letting the Resistance into the hospital so they can bring Sophia home to you."

She closed the gap between them, holding him tightly. For a moment, they simply stood with their arms around one another. In the silence, Faith could feel his heart beating against hers. She laid her head on his shoulder, feeling like it belonged there.

Eventually, she felt his shoulder rise as he inhaled deeply. "Faith, I–"

"You came to say you were leaving, right?" She held her breath until she felt him nod. "Okay."

He leaned back a little, cradling her chin in his hands. "You want to come down and–"

She shook her head, cutting him off. "If you don't mind, I'll say goodbye here. I know most of the people downstairs suspect there's something between us, but I'd rather not slam it in their faces with a tearful farewell."

He raised an eyebrow. "It would be tearful?"

Stepping away, she punched his arm lightly. "Don't mock."

His face turned serious. "I'm not. I'm trying to accept the fact that I got to spend the last few days with you without anyone judging or disapproving. And now I have to leave," he paused, closing his eyes, "and I don't know when I'll see you again."

Her breath caught in her throat, but she attempted to lighten the mood. "You're saying *you're* the one who'll be tearful?"

He grinned, seeming to appreciate her attempt to relieve the tension. "Very possibly."

"Then we should definitely say our goodbyes here. Safer." She winked. "You know, for your reputation."

He chuckled. "Thanks. Wouldn't want people to think I was afraid."

She studied him closely. "Aren't you though?"

"I'm terrified." He held her gaze. "Does that make you think less of me?"

"I'd think less of you if you weren't."

Leaning forward, she pressed her lips to his. Softly at first, then with more determination, as though she was trying to sear the memory into her mind.

After a moment, she broke away. "Better go then. Don't keep them waiting."

He held her gaze, his eyes blazing. "Promise me you'll give that speech everything you have?"

"I promise." She cocked her head to one side. "Promise me you'll do *everything* you can to go unnoticed and convince everyone you're just an ordinary drudge?"

"I promise."

Leaning in, he kissed her softly one last time. She closed her eyes as he eased away from her. He released her hand last, and she shivered at the loss. His footsteps faded as he walked away.

When she opened her eyes, he was gone.

Chapter Forty: Noah

He stood in the narrow hallway, glancing left and right. After two days in the Bellator Hospital, he still found it difficult to get his bearings. The building was enormous, and the one night he'd had to go over things with Rowan had not been enough.

Right now, he was transporting a huge bundle of soiled blankets to the laundry. If he could remember where the laundry was. Without raising his head to study the signs, he had to go by memory.

Stay under the radar. Rowan's warning echoed in his ears. *Make sure the women don't notice you.*

It was easier said than done, when you didn't know where you were going.

The first of his two shifts at the hospital had taken place at night. The hallways had been quiet, and there were far fewer people. Today, he was working in broad daylight. There were medics and patients everywhere, and the constant flow of traffic through the building was adding to his confusion.

The drudge tasks weren't difficult. And the women he had come across usually bypassed him without a word. The other drudges, however, were less accepting. None of them had spoken to him yet, but he'd felt them studying him as he moved around the hospital. They knew he was not Rowan.

But they also knew he was not an ordinary drudge.

Hearing footsteps approaching, Noah made a decision. Turning left, he headed up the hallway, hoping he had chosen the correct route.

When he heard a babble of sound up ahead, he knew he had not. Phones ringing. The noisy *bing-bong* of the hospital intercom. The whirr of an air-conditioning unit. Numerous voices demanding attention.

He was headed for the hospital's main reception area.

But he couldn't alter his route now. The footsteps echoed down the hallway behind him, coming closer every second. An abrupt about-turn would raise suspicion. He had to keep going.

Drudges use the lesser travelled routes in the building. Rowan's voice came back to him. *They complete their jobs with the minimum of fuss.*

A trickle of sweat began to make its way down his spine. *Keep walking,* he admonished himself. *Keep your head down. Act as though you're supposed to be here.*

But he knew he wasn't.

"What on earth..." He felt the angry glare of the receptionist even though he wasn't looking at her. "What is *he* doing here?"

Resisting the urge to glance upwards and get his bearings, Noah ploughed on. The faster he was out of sight, the better chance he had of melting into the background again. Circumnavigating several pairs of feet, he ignored their owners, who tutted at him. With a sudden rush of relief, the laundry's location came back to him. Angling himself towards the correct exit, he picked up the pace.

Drudges never hurry. For a moment, he hated the sensible voice in his head.

If he'd already been spotted, surely it didn't matter?

"*Good* morning." Behind him, he heard the receptionist speak again. This time, she was addressing an incoming patient. "Yes, I know. I'm so sorry. I can't *imagine* what he's doing. Rest assured, I'll be reporting him to–"

Reaching the exit, Noah left the reception, blood pounding in his ears. He braced himself for footsteps behind him. The hospital had guards. If the receptionist was as good as her word, they would be after him within minutes.

But the bustling sounds died away. Three hallways later, he found himself in the quiet thoroughfare the drudges used to access the main equipment and storage rooms. The laundry was right behind it.

If he could make it there and deliver the sheets as expected, he might be okay. The drudges were all the same to the women. If the receptionist had no way of identifying him, perhaps he could lose himself in the next task, and get away with it.

He pushed open the door of the laundry, heading for the baskets which held the incoming sheets. Finding an empty one, he unburdened himself. As he hurried to the exit, he wiped his sweaty palms on his uniform. It had been a close call. But he was fairly confident he'd escaped identification.

He moved into the storage room, hoping to collect a mop and bucket. Perhaps he could head towards the Fertility Ward. He *had* to be certain of the layout of that part of the hospital before tomorrow. One false step on Liberation Day could blow the whole mission. He would not let Faith or Sophia down.

As he approached the cleaning supplies, he felt a hand on his shoulder. His body went rigid. Since entering the hospital, no one had touched him. The women didn't go near the drudges, and he had yet to see one drudge make physical contact with another.

He drew in a slow breath, trying not to panic as fingers dug into his skin. Before he could react, he found himself being pushed behind a section of shelving.

Fighting every instinct he had, he remained silent. There was no point giving himself away until he had assessed the situation. He allowed his assailant to spin him round, maintaining the drudge posture as he was thrust back against the shelving.

Noah found himself staring at a pair of regulation drudge shoes. He found himself noticing a dark stain on the toe of the left foot. It was shaped like a teardrop. Hearing the sound of ragged breathing, he jerked back into the moment and noted the tension in the uniformed body of the drudge.

"Not speaking, huh?" The voice was low and hoarse. "*Still* trying to convince people that you're a drudge?" Noah swallowed hard, but kept his eyes on the ground. "You ready to start talking?"

Noah's mind was racing. He'd expected trouble from the Bellator women, if they discovered his lie. But an attack from a drudge was something he hadn't anticipated. He waited for the man to go on.

"What did you think you were *doing*, charging through reception with a ton of dirty laundry just now?" The hold on Noah's shoulder tightened. "Way to attract the *wrong* kind of attention."

Drudges appeared powerless. Their slim frames and the way they carried themselves gave the impression of weakness. But the work they did was arduous. They were wiry, more powerful than they looked. Noah found he didn't want to test the strength of the grip on his shoulder.

Even if he could break free, where would he go? If the drudges themselves suspected him, didn't trust him, he had no chance of staying undercover. And if he left the hospital, his mission was a failure. His only chance was to try and talk the drudge down.

"Who are you?" His attacker was becoming impatient. "I know you're not a drudge." Hot breath assaulted his face as the drudge leaned closer. "The women might not be wise yet, but I knew it from the moment you walked in. We all did."

Sighing, Noah raised his gaze. The eyes staring at him seethed, reflecting first anger, then curiosity, then a primal fear.

"There are no cameras here." The drudge jerked his gaze upwards. "Do you think I'd risk this if there were? Now talk."

Noah breathed in slowly. "I'm not a drudge. You're right." Ignoring the sharp intake of breath, he ploughed on. "But I'm not here to hurt you."

"You hurt us *all* when you make mistakes like the one you just made. I was behind you when you strolled into the reception area." Noah remembered the footsteps he'd heard behind him. "I would've stopped you, if I'd been able to." The man dropped his gaze, seeming uncertain for the first time. "Don't you know the kind of trouble you could cause for the drudges here?"

Suddenly, Noah understood. Drudges didn't matter. The city's women bypassed them without a thought for their well-being. As long as they did their jobs, they were ghosts. But if they stepped out of line, a world of pain awaited them. The group of men was invisible, totally dispensable to the women of Bellator. It was criminal.

"I'm sorry about just now." Noah wriggled his shoulder. The drudge released his hold, but didn't step away. "I just... got lost."

"It's not the first mistake you've made though, is it?" The drudge's eyes bored into Noah's. "It didn't make too much of a difference when you were working at night. But in the daytime..." His face creased with worry. "We'll all be punished if it keeps happening."

Noah stared at the man in front of him. He seemed more worried than angry now. He was frightened that Noah's presence was a threat to the drudges' safety. And after a couple of days in the role, Noah knew he was right.

"As I said, I'm sorry. I didn't mean to cause a problem for you all."

The drudge narrowed his eyes. "Who are you? I mean… you're not a drudge. But you're male. So… what are you doing here?"

"Would you believe me if I said I was part of a group who wants to fight against Danforth's rule?" Noah held the man's gaze. "A kind of Resistance?"

The drudge frowned. "We hear whispers about a Resistance. You're saying it exists?"

"I am." Noah leaned forward. "We want to fight against the injustice of the Bellator system. Fight for people who can't fight for themselves."

"I'll bet you don't want to fight for the drudges."

"Why would you say that?

"Because," the drudge's eyes flashed with anger, "the Bellator women don't care about us. We can disappear," his voice cracked, and he dropped his gaze, "and no one even notices."

"Disappear?"

"Yes." Suddenly the drudge's hands were on Noah's arms, shaking him. "Only a few days ago, I woke up to find a friend of mine was gone. Literally vanished, overnight. I mean…" the man faltered. "He didn't do anything wrong, not as far as I could tell. But he was here one day, gone the next."

Something clicked inside Noah's head. "You mean Rowan?"

The drudge frowned. "Who?"

Realising that the name would mean nothing, Noah searched for a way to describe the missing drudge. "Your friend… does he look a lot like me? Did he go missing on Tuesday night? After he'd finished his shift?"

"You know something about it?" The drudge pushed Noah into the shelving again. "Did you do something to him?"

"No!" Noah hurried to explain. "The Resistance took him so that I could replace him. They needed someone undercover in the hospital. But they had to get me in without raising suspicion. So I had to replace an existing hospital worker."

"You're saying he was kidnapped by the Resistance?"

"Yes." Spotting the fury in the drudge's eyes, Noah hurried on. "But he's safe. They're looking after him."

Noah couldn't decide which was worse. The terror he had felt all his life as a member of the hidden community or the sense of total anonymity that went along with being a drudge. In Eremus, he'd always known that he could be discovered and executed at any given moment. Here, a single drudge mattered so little that they could disappear without anyone saying a word.

Relief flooded the drudge's eyes. "So he's not dead? They won't hurt him?"

Noah shook his head. "He's fine. When this is over, they'll make the switch back. He'll be just–"

The drudge's expression changed again. "Why should I trust you? I'm assuming you'd say anything to get me off your back right now."

"I can see that you'd think that." Noah shrugged. "But I assure you, it's true. Can you trust me? Believe that I'm telling the truth?"

"Believe that there are women who care enough to protect a lowly drudge? I doubt it." The drudge released Noah abruptly. "Unless you can prove it."

Noah's heart clenched at the challenge. "I don't think I can–"

"I. Don't. Care." The drudge leaned close to Noah's face one last time. "I'll leave you alone, for now. But come up with proof that my friend is alive and well soon, or I'll make your life a living hell."

"Alright! Alright." Noah's mind was racing. "Meet me outside the drudge quarters at the end of shift today."

"You have proof?" The drudge sounded suspicious.

"I do." Noah held his breath, hoping that the drudge would agree to his terms. "But I can't provide it right now.

The drudge gave him an appraising look. "I'll be there. But this had better not be a trick of some kind."

"It's not. I promise you–"

But the drudge was already stalking away, leaving Noah alone.

Chapter Forty-One: Faith

"Again."

Faith took a deep breath. Blake had been drilling her for the past three hours. The Liberation Day celebrations were tomorrow, and she was determined they would both be ready. Faith had recited her speech more times than she could count. Her throat was sore, she could feel a headache building, and her back ached from sitting upright in the uncomfortable chair. It would be worth it, she told herself, when the Bellator women heard her words.

But the pressure was immense.

She glanced at the camera. When she had asked why Blake had set it up to face a blank wall, she'd been informed it was to keep their location anonymous. A thought which terrified Faith. She imagined Bellator guards discovering them, storming in through the doors with guns blazing. The piercing red light on the camera made her think of the laser point of a gunsight.

Several dense cables trailed from the powerful spotlights Blake had trained on her. They made the space feel claustrophobic, the heat they threw out making Faith's body pour with sweat. She kept leaning too close to the microphone, feeling foolish as it squealed in protest.

But with every run through, she was getting better. Blake's obsessive preparation was paying off. Faith would keep going as long as the tech genius wanted her to.

A grudging admiration for the woman had grown every second she worked alongside her. Blake never stopped. When she wasn't adjusting lights, listening to Faith talk or shifting the microphone's position by a miniscule degree, her eyes were glued to the screens in front of her. She had laser focus: flipping switches and turning dials, her fingers flying back and forth over her keyboard with alarming speed.

Every so often, she was interrupted by a message from another Resistance member out in the field. Breaking off briefly, she dealt with each request with ruthless efficiency before turning her attention back to Faith.

There was no doubt about it. Blake was a huge asset to the Resistance, despite her lack of social graces. Faith only hoped one day she might prove half as useful.

At a nod from the woman in question, Faith opened her mouth. But before she could launch into her opening line, there was a shrill, repetitive bleeping sound.

Faith glanced at Blake. Usually so composed, the tech genius had gone white.

"No. No, no, no, no!" Her hands flew to her mouth. "Dammit!"

"What is it?"

Blake jerked her head towards the datadev. An alert message had flashed up on the screen, accompanying the alarm. "I was afraid something like this would happen."

Faith leaned forward, trying to read the message, but Blake swiped her hand across the screen and the message disappeared.

"Additional security measures." She started typing with a new intensity. "Danforth knows we're planning something. Every day, she's had her tech team try something new to shut me out. But this..." she ran a despairing hand through her hair, "this is..."

"You can't fix it?"

"Not from here." Blake glared at the screen. "Remember I told you I'd need someone on the inside."

"You said you didn't have anyone to spare."

"We didn't." Blake paused in her typing, squinting at the myriad lines of code which crawled across her screen. "But I need someone there now. Someone who can *physically* disconnect a cable. Then reconnect it elsewhere." She began to type again. "I'll need to show them how to do it today, so they can replicate the move tomorrow, just before the broadcast begins."

"But why–"

Blake glared at Faith's question. "If we do it today, Danforth's team will know. They'll reconnect the cables and guard the control room more heavily. It'll be ten times harder to get to it after that." She shook her head. "No. It has to be done right before the ceremony, so there's no time for them to realise something's wrong." She raised her wristclip to her mouth. "Open contacts."

"Wait." Faith realised what she was doing. "I thought you said you didn't have anyone down there."

"Strictly speaking, I don't. Not an experienced member of the Resistance, at least." A hologram of names and numbers appeared in the air in front of Blake. She swept a finger down the list. "Knowing this was a possibility, I made sure we had someone down there, in case the worst happened. It's just a case of hoping she responds quickly."

"But who–"

At a warning glance, Faith closed her mouth. But when Ella's contact details appeared, she gasped. Before she could question the choice, Blake had sent the message.

"*Ella's* your c-contact?" Faith stuttered. "But she's not technical at all."

"She's our best option. She knows Matriarch House well and she's already inside." Catching Faith's expression, Blake raised an eyebrow. "She doesn't *need* any technical expertise. All she has to do is locate a cable, unplug it, and reconnect it somewhere else. I can take care of the rest from here."

She returned her attention to the datadev as a new message flashed up on the screen.

"Excellent." She smiled grimly. "She'll call us in a few minutes." Blake tutted at Faith's expression. "Relax. I'm just going to talk her through the process. Then all she has to do is repeat it tomorrow."

"All?" Faith began, but there was no time to dwell on it as Madeleine appeared at the door.

"We just heard from Kemp." She wiped a hand across her forehead absentmindedly. "She got the placebos from Arden. Made the switch sometime during the night."

"How did she manage that with them watching her?" Faith asked.

"One of her roles is directing the drudges." Madeleine laughed, the sound hollow. "It's considered a lowly position, but it puts her in close contact with Arden, so it suits her just fine. Lily included some sedatives in the package with the placebos. Once Kemp had the drugs, she slipped a sleeping pill into Professor Lannion's coffee."

Faith pictured the over-enthusiastic sports teacher. "She was the one watching Kemp?"

"Last night she was." Madeleine shrugged. "Anyway, it worked. Lannion passed out in the professors' lounge. Kemp stole her keycard, accessed the drug stores, and made the switch."

Faith's heart leapt at the good news. "That's great."

"It is." Madeleine looked relieved. "The girls are safe."

"For now."

Madeleine winced at Blake's trademark bluntness. "Yes. For now."

"*For now* is good enough." Faith tried to put a more positive spin on the situation. "Once the mission succeeds, we can rescue them for good."

"We can." But Madeleine sagged against the doorframe. "Thank goodness."

Faith wondered if the leader was remembering her decision to leave the academy girls where they were. When Robyn had suggested they consider a rescue, Madeleine had overruled her. It was too risky, she argued, and Danforth wouldn't administer unknown drugs until she had evidence of how well they worked.

Madeleine knew she'd been wrong. The guilt was etched permanently on her face.

Shaking herself, Madeleine turned to Faith. "You all ready for tomorrow?"

Jolted from her thoughts, Faith sat straighter in her chair. "I think so."

"Almost." Blake flashed a rare smile. It was gone so quickly, Faith wondered if she'd imagined it. "I've really been putting her through it, but she's taken it like a pro. We're nearly there."

As Madeleine left the office with a smile, Faith wondered if Blake had omitted telling her about the technical issue to avoid a lecture or to ease the leader's burden. She didn't have time to dwell on it. A pinging sound from Blake's wristclip indicated an incoming video call.

Immediately alert, Blake swished a finger across the screen. Ella's face appeared, close up, the hologram floating eerily in midair.

"Blake? Can you hear me okay?" She peered at the screen, giving them a generous view up her nostrils. "I still don't fully have the hang of this thing."

"All good. We can see *and* hear you." Blake's tone was more reassuring than usual. "Perhaps hear you a little too clearly, if you know what I mean." Ella's face paled at the warning. "You have your earcoms in, right?"

"I do." Ella dropped her voice to whisper-level. "No one but me can hear you. I'll keep the talking to a minimum. Only speak when there's no one within earshot. There's no one around right now?"

"No. It's pretty quiet at the back of the building." Ella rotated her gaze left and right. "Most people are busy elsewhere, prepping for the big day."

"That's what I was hoping." Blake tabbed to another screen. "Alright. I'm going to direct you to the control room. Can you switch to forward mode on your wristclip?"

"I think..." Ella squinted at the screen, her eyes looming even larger. "Here we go."

The view from her feed changed. Now they could see the hallway ahead of her.

Blake flicked a switch on the dash, silencing the feed. She turned to Faith. "While I'm directing her through the building, I want you to keep an eye on this."

She jabbed a finger at a diagram on the second screen.

"What is it? Some kind of schematic of the building?"

"Yep. Every time Ella passes a camera, mark it on the map. Might as well note them down while we have this insight, for future reference.

Matriarch House is Danforth's main base. Who knows when the intel might prove useful?" She stared at Faith. "Got it?"

"Got it."

Blake flicked the switch again. "You with us, Ella?"

"Yep."

"Keep your wristclip pointing forward but high. We're trying to mark the camera positions."

"Got it." The image wavered as Ella started walking. The direction changed as she levered her arm upwards. "That okay?"

"Perfect." Blake pointed as the first camera came into view. "See it?" She gestured to a specific point on the map. "Ella's right here."

Faith marked a star on the map. Confident she knew what she was doing, Blake returned her attention to Ella.

"Okay. So there'll be someone on duty in the Control Centre. Hopefully only one person. You're going to have to distract them. Did you bring the cleaning equipment?"

"Uh-huh."

"That's your reason for being there." Blake paused, drawing in a breath before continuing. "See the blue door on the right? That's where you're headed. I'll stay quiet now, give you a chance to concentrate. Remember to keep your explanations short and simple."

Faith could hear Ella's shaky breathing as she walked down the remainder of the hallway. When she reached the control room, she paused a second before knocking.

It was several seconds before the door was jerked open. The woman on the other side looked harassed.

"Yes?"

"I need to get in here to clean." Ella brandished a cloth in the air.

The woman frowned. "Right now?"

Ella hesitated. "Hammond's orders. She wants to make sure the equipment is in tiptop condition for the big day."

"Tiptop condition?" The woman didn't move. "We service it regularly. It's not like–"

Ella leaned forward. "Thought you might want a little break too. They just whipped up several batches of cookies in the canteen. To keep up morale, you know?" She kept up a steady chatter so the techie couldn't interrupt. "Why don't you pop down and grab a few? They'll be gone before you know it."

The woman looked interested. "Well," she cast a glance over her shoulder, "I guess I could..."

"It wouldn't take you long." Ella stepped back, and Faith imagined her gesturing in the direction of the canteen. "I'll be finished by the time you get back, and out of your way."

"I guess you're right." The woman shot Ella a grateful grin. "I could use a break."

"See you soon then," Ella trilled.

She waited until the woman had passed her before darting into the control room. Once the door was closed, she spoke again. "All clear for now. But I'd like to escape before she gets back to complain about the distinct *lack* of cookies. What do you need me to do?"

"Go to the rear of the room." Blake didn't waste time. "You're looking for a machine called a server. It will have..."

Ella was there before she had finished the sentence. She rotated her wristclip in a semicircle. "You see it?"

"There!" Blake exclaimed. "The big grey box."

Ella approached it with caution. "What next?"

"Look at the back." Blake waited while Ella obeyed. "Let me see it... wait a minute... There! See the blue cable?"

"This one?"

"No!" Beside Faith, Blake jumped out of her chair. "The *light* blue one."

"H-here?" Ella's fingers were shaking as they closed around it.

"That's it." Still tense, Blake leaned closer to the screen. "Follow it. You should find it's connected to a smaller black device. It's called a firewall."

Ella trailed the cable through her fingers, stopping when she hit the firewall. "Now what?"

"Unplug it." Blake waited, but Ella didn't move. "What are you *waiting* for?"

"You're s-sure this is right?"

"I am." Blake's breathing quickened as she watched Ella grab hold of the cable and begin tugging. "NO!" It was practically a scream.

The image distorted as Ella jumped. "What?"

"There's an attachment on the end of the cable where it meets the firewall. You need to depress the little lever to release it. Otherwise you'll break the cable. It'll be useless." Blake slammed her hand on the table. "Worse, they'll know someone was messing with it."

The image stabilized as Ella moved back toward the box and released the cable. Blake continued to offer instruction, her voice calmer now. "Now move it out of the way."

The camera feed swung wildly as Ella followed Blake's instructions. For several moments, they couldn't see what was going on in the Control Room. There was a shifting sound, followed by a dull thud.

"Is t-that right?" Ella aimed the camera at the equipment. Faith could tell she was finding it difficult to keep her wrist steady.

"Yep. Now, see the thin grey cable?" Blake's voice was terse, tense. "You need to unplug it. Then replace it with the original – the light blue one. And *quickly*."

Ella did as Blake had asked. The task took her a while, her hands slipping off the cables several times. She was clearly sweating. When she was finished, she sat back. "Is that right?"

"Yes." Blake leaned in closer, her voice urgent. "Now reverse the process." As Ella complied, Blake continued to bark instructions. "Repeat this tomorrow, just before the ceremony. *Exactly* this. Got it?"

"G-got it."

"And you're certain you've memorised the steps?" Blake didn't wait for a response. "Because if you don't manage to get this done, I can't bypass the firewall, which means..."

"No one will hear Faith's speech. *I get it.*" Ella stood up. "When does this need to happen?"

"No more than an hour before the ceremony begins." Blake lectured. "It has to be done *before* Danforth starts speaking, or–"

Recognising the terror on Ella's face, Faith laid a hand on Blake's arm. *Enough,* she mouthed. Blake gave a curt nod.

"I'll make sure it's done," Ella whispered, "and–" There was a sound behind her. She spun round, the video feed revealing the woman she had sent to the canteen in the doorway.

"There were no cookies." She took a step into the room.

"That's odd." Ella kept her cool. "I'm sure I heard someone say they'd just laid out a fresh batch."

"Not that I could see."

"Perhaps they ran out." Ella walked past the woman, making her way to the door. She turned. "I'm heading down there now. I'll see if they're making a fresh batch."

She pulled the door open.

"Wait a minute." The woman's tone was suspicious. "Did you finish cleaning?"

"I did thanks." Pulling a cloth out of nowhere, Ella waved it in the air. "All done. I'll see you later. Bring you cookies, when they're ready. Least I can do, since I sent you on such a goose chase."

Once she was outside the door, Ella switched the feed back to her face. "That was close. And now I guess I have to conjure up some cookies from somewhere and keep up the pretence."

"You can manage that?" Faith asked.

"Sure. I have full access to the canteen. And I'd better make good on my promise." There was a rustling sound, like Ella was on the move again. "But we'd better start thinking up a different excuse for tomorrow. Because that one's not going to work twice."

Chapter Forty-Two: Noah

He stood on the porch outside the drudge quarters. The rain was pouring down, and the sky grew darker by the second. All day he'd been considering the best way to prove his words to the drudge, and he'd finally admitted that the only way to make the man stand down was to show him Rowan was alive.

The day shift was over, and that meant a lot of movement in and out of the hospital building. The drudge dorms were cramped and crowded. This was the only place he could guarantee an audience with the man alone.

He hopped from one foot to the other, willing the drudge to arrive. Every second that he didn't return could be a second he was standing in the guard's office reporting Noah. The drudges on the night shift had already left, and most of those who had finished work had already returned. Noah had endured several mistrustful glances from the men as they filed past him. But no one had exited the hospital for the past two or three minutes.

Where was he?

A creaking sound alerted him to the hospital exit door opening. Noah tensed, as a single set of footsteps moved across the courtyard. The steps were slow, dragging almost. Noah was curious, but knew he couldn't look up to greet the new arrival. He had to rely on the man realising that the person in the doorway was him.

A pair of feet stopped beside him. Recognising the teardrop stain, Noah opened his mouth to speak.

"Not here. We'll be seen." The drudge's tone was rough and urgent. "Follow me."

The man surprised him by circumnavigating the drudge quarters. The rain was cold on Noah's head as he trailed behind him. He wondered if he was being a fool, trusting the drudge. Who knew what the man might be leading him into?

They rounded a corner. The drudge slid into an alcove in the wall, beckoning Noah to follow. Once they were both squeezed into the gap, the drudge looked up.

"Relax. No cameras here." He gestured upwards. "There are only a few places in the building without them. We should be safe from prying eyes for a few minutes."

Noah raised his eyes slowly. He was about to launch into an explanation when he noticed the drudge's face. "What..." he gasped. "What happened to you?"

There was a cut along the side of the drudge's eye, running down his face and under his mask. Noah knew the wound had not been there earlier in the day. The blood had been stemmed, but glistened, as though the injury had happened very recently. The area around the eye was swollen and red, and Noah suspected the drudge would have significant bruising by the following morning.

"It's nothing." The drudge glanced away.

"Doesn't look like nothing." Noah waited. "Honestly, how did it happen?

The man shrugged. "I was late finishing my last job. The medic wasn't happy."

"So she... what? Hit you?"

The drudge met his gaze with defiance. "Why do you think I'm so late out?"

"To be honest, I thought you might be reporting me."

The man gave a humourless chuckle. "Not yet." He gestured to his eye. "But you can see why we're all so concerned about you getting us into trouble because you have no idea what you're doing."

Noah shifted uncomfortably under the man's gaze.

"Where's this proof then?" Taking the hint that the subject was closed, Noah considered his next action. Blake's warning was ringing in his ears. He was about to go directly against his instructions.

But one look in the man's eyes told him he had to do something convincing.

"It's here." His fingers moved to the sleeve of his drudge tunic and the man stiffened. Noah held his hand out flat in front of him. "I'm just..." he gestured to his clothing. "I need to get something out of my sleeve. To show you I'm telling the truth."

The man followed his gaze, as though he was assessing whether what Noah had concealed could be dangerous. "Do it slowly, then."

Nodding, Noah repeated his earlier motion. Rolling up his right sleeve, he slid a finger into the seam, locating the tiny hole which Robyn had made for him. He removed the device from inside and held it up.

"I'm not supposed to show you this." He shrugged. "It's for emergencies only. But if you're determined to report me unless I can prove Row– I mean, your friend's, alive..."

"What is that?"

"It's a very small version of a wristclip. You know... like the women wear?" Noah watched the drudge nod before he continued. "It allows me to contact the Resistance. That's where your friend is."

"Okay." The drudge agreed. "Just keep your hands where I can see them."

Noah fumbled with the identical pocket in his opposite sleeve, until he had freed the tiny earcoms. Sliding them into his ears, he pressed the power button to turn the clip on. A tiny green light glowed on the device. As he activated the call button, he said a prayer that Madeleine would forgive his disobedience.

After a few seconds of silence, a tiny bleeping sound emitted from the clip. He waited, his heart pounding. It didn't take long for some-one to pick up the call.

"Noah?" It was Blake. "What's wrong?"

"Nothing," he reassured her.

"Then why are you calling?" Her tone became hostile. "You're risking–"

"I know. Believe me, this is important." Noah took a deep breath. "Do you know where Rowan is?"

"What?" Blake's voice was clipped. "*Why?*"

"Because there's a drudge who's threatening to expose me unless I prove his friend is still alive."

There was a silence.

"Blake?" he hissed. "Are you there?"

"Sorry." She didn't sound sorry. "I see your predicament. I've sent Faith to fetch Rowan. She shouldn't be long."

At the mention of Faith's name, Noah's heart lurched.

"Your position, is it secure?" Blake asked. "The last thing we want is for you to–"

"It is." Noah glanced up at the drudge. "For now. But hurry."

"Hang on." Blake paused. "Is he with you right now?"

"He is."

"Give him one of the coms."

Noah slipped one of the tiny buds out of his ears and proffered it to the drudge. The man looked at it like it might explode.

"Put it in." Noah gestured to his ear. "They've gone to get him. You should be able to speak to him in a moment."

"Really?" The man's eyes widened. "You're not... This isn't some kind of trick?"

"There's no trick." Noah pointed to his ear again. "Go ahead."

With shaky hands, the drudge put the earcom in. "What do we do now?"

"We wait."

Noah almost smiled. The antagonist who had threatened him in the store room was gone. This was a man concerned for the life of a friend.

"It shouldn't be too long." Remembering the warning not to reveal details about headquarters, Noah kept his reassurance vague. "He can't be far away. In fact–"

"Noah?" Blake's voice cut across his. "He's here."

Relief flooded through him. "Great."

"You both listening?"

"We are."

"The next person you hear speaking will be a man we have named Rowan." Blake's voice took on a businesslike tone. "He's a drudge we took from outside the hospital three nights ago. I've asked him to keep this brief. He will say enough to reassure you that he is alive and well. You are *not* permitted to ask him any specific questions about our location. Are you in agreement?"

"I am." The drudge's response was eager.

"Alright. Here we go."

There was a slight shuffling, and the sound of a throat being cleared. "Hello?" As Noah watched, the man in front of him drained of colour. "Hello? Is anyone there?"

"Thought you were dead." The drudge's voice was heavy with emotion.

There was a pause, as though Rowan was just as startled.

"You're okay, then?"

"I am. Yes. Fine, in fact." Rowan sounded breathless. "Are you?"

"I am n-now." The drudge coughed, covering up the catch in his voice. "You'll be coming back?"

"So they say. After..." Rowan paused. "They haven't told me everything, but... the man who replaced me... he's there for a reason. A good one."

"So he says."

"*Trust me.*" Rowan urged his friend to understand. "I think... once he's done what he came for... we'll see each other again. And... things might even be... better."

"You really believe that?" The drudge glanced at Noah, his eyes a tornado of mistrust and desperate hope. "You believe *them*?"

"I do." There was a short pause. "Don't do anything stupid, will you?"

"Me?" The drudge attempted humour. "Stupid?"

"Yes. You." Noah could picture Rowan rolling his eyes. "Just hang tight. I'll be back before you know it. And don't give this guy a hard time. Okay?"

The drudge eyed Noah, his expression softening. "Okay."

"Noah?" Blake's sharp voice cut across the air. "We good now?"

Noah met the other man's gaze. "Okay?" he mouthed the same question Rowan had asked.

The man nodded.

Noah sagged against the wall. "We're good. Thanks."

"Alright." Blake was straight back-to-business. "Hide the devices again. *Carefully.* See you on the other side."

The line went dead. Noah turned off the clip. Slipping the com from his ear, he held his hand out for the other. Once he had it, he began to fumble with his sleeve again.

"Let me."

The drudge leaned close, taking the clip from Noah's fingers. Deftly, he slid the device back into its hiding place, smoothing the surface so the hole was invisible and rolling the sleeve back down again. After repeating the process with the earcoms on the opposite side, he stepped back.

"You won't be causing me any more trouble from now on, then?" Noah raised an eyebrow. "Tomorrow's an important day for me. For all of us. I don't need any unexpected interruptions."

"You won't get any from me." The drudge's face had transformed since the conversation with Rowan. He looked almost kind. "And don't worry about the others." He gestured towards the drudge quarters. "I'll pass the message round that you're okay."

"Thank you." Noah smiled his appreciation before realising that the man couldn't see it behind his mask. "I'd appreciate that." He gestured to the painful-looking cut. "Can you get someone to look at that? I mean... do drudges get medical treatment?"

The man shrugged. "Someone inside will have a needle and thread if it needs stitching. I doused it with some antiseptic before I left the hospital. I'll be fine."

"If you're sure." Noah made move to leave, longing for his bed now that the situation had been resolved. But a hand on his arm stopped him. He turned back to the drudge.

"I'll go one better than warning the others to keep away." The drudge leaned closer, his eyes earnest. "I get that you might not be allowed to tell me what you're doing. But if you're able to let me in on any of your plans, please do. I'll do what I can to help you with them."

"Really?" Noah felt a surge of hope at the man's offer. Having some internal support would make things so much easier. "Thank you."

The man shrugged. "You called him Rowan, huh?"

"Well I didn't, but..."

"Must be nice to have a name." The drudge's gaze was wistful.

"Shall we think of one for you?" Noah considered. He remembered the main character from the last book he'd read. "How about Liam? It means strong."

"Liam." Noah suspected the drudge was smiling behind his mask. "I like it."

The next morning, Noah headed for the fertility wards. Following his new drudge friend's advice, he was carrying a mop and bucket. They would give him a plausible task to complete, Liam had said, should he run into any of the hospital staff while he was down there.

Madeleine had been right about the Liberation Day celebrations distracting people. The hallways he walked down were decorated with banners in the colours of the Women's Independence Party. Large screens had been set up in the wards, waiting rooms, and other common areas. There was a sense of expectation in the air.

At eleven a.m., every woman in the city would be listening to Danforth's speech. It meant, if all went to plan, Faith's words would reach a huge audience. Noah felt a surge of hope. Maybe, just maybe, they could do this.

Sophia was being kept a long way from the rest of the hospital, for obvious reasons. Danforth didn't want strangers stumbling on her dangerous experiment. As Noah reached the hallway leading to the fertility wards, he resisted the automatic urge to glance both ways. Stealth was almost impossible, when he had such limited vision.

He had one more task to complete before the rescue could take place. And the only place he was going to complete it was here. Taking in a deep breath, he followed the hallway until he reached its end.

Placing the wet floor sign, he doused the mop in the soapy water before squeezing it out. As he began to clean the floor, keeping his movements slow and even, he listened. Aside from the rhythmic swishing of the mop on the floor, the hallway was silent. From what Liam had told him, the area outside the door to the fertility wards was covered by a single camera.

Silently thanking Arden for his advice, Noah faked a sneeze, risking a glance upwards as he did. The hair on the back of his neck prickled as he spotted the camera, perched high in the corner. Now all he had to do was avoid its silent gaze.

Noah worked his way across the floor gradually. He could feel a ribbon of sweat trail down his spine as he crept closer and closer to the camera. He forced himself to maintain the same speed, making achingly slow progress towards the space underneath it. From there, he knew, he would be invisible.

When he reached his goal, he kept the mop moving but lifted his gaze slightly, noting the position of the chairs lined up at the edge of the space, the window in the wall to his right, and the position of the fire exit door on the other side of the hallway. The one he was supposed to open for the Resistance group when the time came. He swallowed hard.

Finally, he turned his eyes to the door which led off the waiting area and into the wards. His heart beat faster. His next task was a tricky one. He had to get his hands on a keycard which would allow the team access to the restricted ward. The replacement card Blake had given him was burning a hole in his pocket. But until a medic emerged from the ward, he couldn't hope to make the switch. All he could do was wait.

Taking advantage of the empty space and the camera's blind spot, he looked up for the first time in hours. He had to suppress a groan as a jolt of pain shot through him. Sighing, he massaged his neck with one hand, attempting to ease the discomfort. He would never get used to the unnatural posture.

Trying to get his bearings, Noah peered out the window. A few streets away, he could see the carved stone tigers mounted on the roof of Matriarch House. Another outward display of Danforth's power. Another fragment of the façade.

Was Ella in the building right now? Noah found himself hoping she was, digging up more dirt to use against the chancellor when the time came. For the second time in as many minutes, he felt guilty. Yes, he wanted Ella's work to help bring Danforth down, but he hoped she wasn't putting herself at risk.

Ella had always been the cautious sibling, but Jacob's treatment had changed her. In the old days, Ruth had been the sibling far more likely to rush in without thought. These days, he wasn't so sure. The thought of his best friend brought a pang of homesickness. He'd never gone this long without seeing her before. And while speaking to his ma and Paulo had been amazing, it had made him yearn to spend an hour lying in the den with Ruth teasing him.

A shrill bleep indicated a keycard was being used to open a door. Snapping his head down, Noah resumed his mopping. As a medic emerged from the ward, he prayed that she wouldn't notice the section he was working on was already wet.

Spotting the wet floor, the medic slowed her pace. She wore sensible black loafers, but you couldn't be too careful. The mismatched laces caught his eye. One was black, the other brown, as though she had lost the original. As she passed him, Noah watched her slip a keycard into the side pocket of her scrubs. Before she could get much further, the ward door was flung open and an authoritative voice boomed down the hallway.

"Susie, wait!"

"Yes, Doctor Sanders?"

Noah continued to mop, creeping a little further along the hallway as he listened. Neither woman seemed to register his presence. He marvelled again at the amount of information drudges were privy to simply because the women of Bellator didn't notice them.

"While you're fetching the scans, can you collect Sophia's blood results?" The woman was definitely more senior. "Don't let them fob you off. Wait until they're ready. I don't care how long it takes. We need them as soon as possible."

"They're pretty backed up." The medic sounded hesitant. "The wait was more than an hour first thing this morning. It'll be worse now. They're on a skeleton staff because of the celebrations."

"Just get down there and wait." The doctor tapped an impatient foot. "Don't come back without them."

"Will do."

"I'm a little concerned about her hormone levels. Make sure you check them again later, okay?" The doctor didn't wait for a response. "I'll be leaving in about ten minutes. Danforth has me down as a guest speaker in the Liberation Day presentation. She wants me to provide a voiceover for the citizens when they show the footage of Sophia. Explain the progress we've made with her, and what it means for the future of Bellator."

"Of course." Susie sounded more animated at the prospect. "How do you think they'll react?"

"A pregnancy created without male seed?" The doctor sniffed dismissively. "They'll be impressed, of course. Shame we don't have any other pregnancies to show off yet. We just can't seem to get it right with those academy girls."

Noah thought of the students who had died as a result of the experimentation. Realising he was clutching the handle of the mop too tightly, he forced himself to relax. This was good information. He just had to keep his cool.

"The footage we took of Sophia yesterday is great, though. She's starting to show already." The doctor clapped her hands gleefully. "There'll be plenty for our citizens to marvel at."

"There certainly will."

"Alright. I'll be back around four."

"What about–"

"Sophia will be alright without us for the next hour or so." The doctor tutted. "It's not as if she can get out without a keycard. Now hurry along. The faster you're in the queue, the faster you'll get back."

The door to the ward swung closed behind the doctor and Susie turned and walked away. Waiting a few seconds, Noah collected the bucket and followed in her wake.

CHAPTER FORTY-THREE: FAITH

The Liberation Day celebrations had begun. Danforth's speech was due to start in forty-five minutes.

Everyone was in place. Robyn's team had just left the library in a comcar headed for the hospital. Concerned about Sophia's condition, Madeleine had insisted on Lily being with them. Sophia had been through so much. If she needed medical help, Lily was most qualified to give it. Noah was already in place, laying the groundwork for Robyn's arrival.

Diane was with the team in the square, which was there to monitor citizen reactions to the speeches. Ella was making her way to the control room at Matriarch House to disconnect the firewall. Evelyn waited in a safehouse on the outskirts of the city with Flynn and Helen.

Frustrated at not being able to actively participate in the mission, Madeleine was holed up in her office watching the square from various angles through the security cameras Blake had hacked into. The tech genius herself was in charge of comms, in addition to making sure the speech went live.

Faith was terrified.

If the mission went to plan, they were one huge step closer to breaking down the barriers between Eremus and Bellator. To stopping the experimentation on the academy girls. To freeing the drudges. Each team member's role was crucial, but she knew her speech was a vital part of the operation. It *had* to go well.

Trying to calm her nerves, she drew in a breath and then blew it out slowly.

"Could you be quiet?" Blake tutted. "I'm trying to concentrate."

"Sorry." Faith lapsed into silence again.

A moment later, Blake spun to face her, eyes blazing. "Would you, p-*lease*, get it together."

Faith blinked, realising the obsessive drumming of her fingers on the desktop was not conducive to calm.

"I'm *sorry*... it's just... I..." She fell silent. "Never mind."

Blake sighed. "Would you like to see the schedule again?"

Clicking a couple of buttons on her keyboard, she gestured to the screen in front of her. A second later, Faith was staring at a list of the Liberation Day proceedings. She checked her wristclip. Ten thirty. The Bellator orchestra would be playing.

Faith remembered the academy students being marched into the hall every year so they could watch the broadcast. She was ashamed to say she had never paid much attention to the speeches. On one occasion, she had persuaded Sophia to sneak away with her to avoid the dull event. They had hidden in one of the student bathrooms, stuffing their faces with pastries saved from the celebratory breakfast.

Faith sighed. Such frivolous rebellion seemed a world away.

When Faith had been forced to watch, the only part she'd enjoyed was the orchestra. It was the highlight of the ceremony, in her opinion. Sophia would slide a hand into hers and they would close their eyes, allowing the beautiful melody to wash over them.

"Could we–" She stopped.

Blake's eyes snapped back to hers. "What?"

"Nothing. Sorry. I'm distracting you."

"Spit it out." Blake cocked her head to one side. "Whatever it is, if it relaxes you even a *little* it will be worth it. For me, at least." She flashed a rare smile at Faith's confused expression. "You're like a bomb waiting to go off. And when you explode, I'll be collateral damage."

Faith laughed, surprised at the humour, bleak though it was. "I was wondering if we could tap into the ceremony broadcast. Listen to the orchestra. I mean, only if it's possible... convenient..."

Blake had already turned back to the screen. Disappointed, Faith chided herself for hoping that the tech genius might share her love of music. But after a rapid tapping on the keyboard, she heard it: quietly at first, but increasing in volume as Blake adjusted one of the sliders on the control panel in front of her. A hundred instruments swelling together in glorious harmony.

They would have opened the ceremony with The Women's Anthem, Faith knew. It was not a tune she was particularly fond of. Right now, they were playing a piece that was unfamiliar. Its melody was beautiful, rising and falling with a haunting sadness that brought tears to her eyes. Blinking rapidly, she sucked in a breath as quietly as she could, hoping the woman beside her wouldn't notice.

"They're incredible, aren't they?" Blake's voice had taken on a tone Faith had never heard before, one filled with awe. "The way all those instruments can weave such a wonderful sound."

"You like music?" Faith tried to keep the surprise from her voice.

Blake turned to her, more slowly this time. "That shocks you?"

"Um, maybe. I–"

"Oh, would you stop being such a mouse! It drives me mad." Blake lifted the mug which was ever-present at her elbow, draining it of the coffee which was her life blood. "What are you afraid of?"

"I'm not–" Faith stopped. "Well, maybe a little."

"I'm hard on *everyone*." Blake sniffed. "You should have learned that by now."

"I guess so."

"And I was especially hard on you when you first got here, because..." Blake hesitated. "I suppose I doubted your allegiance, with you coming from the academy, then having been in Eremus." She drew back, studying Faith closely. "You have to admit, you're hardly built for combat."

"I know I'm not strong." Faith cleared her throat. "Not physically, but–"

"Oh hush." Blake had turned back to the screens again. "That's not what Madeleine wants from you. I know that now."

Faith stayed quiet, revelling in the frank conversation. It was refreshing to see Blake so unguarded. She wasn't sure she would witness it again.

"You've shown loyalty since you arrived," Blake continued. "It's just... Madeleine's plans aren't always so obvious to begin with. But your speech today...," her tone became reverent, "it's going to make a massive difference."

"Um, yeah." Faith searched for intelligent words and came up empty-handed. "I hope so."

"If it works, that is."

There was the Blake who Faith knew. "Yeah. If it works."

The tech whiz glanced at her. "Better not mess it up then, had you?"

Faith laughed shakily. "I'll do my best not to. I mean–"

The familiar intermittent pinging announced an incoming call. Blake jerked to attention, all traces of humour vanishing.

"You there already, Robyn?"

For a moment, there was nothing but silence. Faith leaned forward, straining to listen.

"Robyn?" Blake's voice notched up a tone. "Is there a problem?"

There was the sound of rapid breathing, followed by rustling sounds. They waited.

"You could say that." Robyn sounded tense. "We've hit some traffic. There are a ton of diversions taking vehicles away from the celebrations in the centre. They're snarling up the roads everywhere. We're stuck on Elliott Street heading north right now. Got any bright ideas about alternative routes?"

Blake started typing. "Give me a minute."

"Thanks." There was a brief pause. "We've seen some additional security measures, too."

"What do you mean, *additional security*?"

"Guards. Posted in various key locations. Stopping vehicles, asking questions." Robyn broke off, groaning. "Shoot! There's one up ahead. *Lily, can you*–?" They waited, while she gave directions to the other members of her team. "*Damn*. We can't avoid it." The rustling sound was back, as though Robyn was shifting in her seat. "I have to go. Keep working on a different route for us, would you Blake? I'll try and talk our way past the guards."

The call cut off abruptly. Blake pulled her earcoms out. "Dammit!"

Faith's heart contracted as the techie banged her fist against the desk. For a moment, she sat still. Faith had never seen her at a loss before.

"Can I–?" she began, but Blake brushed her words aside.

"No."

Bending over her datadev again, she tapped away at the screen until a city map appeared. Large sections of the streets were coloured with red, a bold representation of the traffic Robyn's team found themselves stuck in. Bending forward, Blake placed a finger on Elliott Street, her eyes searching for routes which might be less congested.

Faith sank back in her chair. "I'm sure there's an alternative route. There *has* to be."

"There *will* be." Blake frowned. "It just depends how long it takes Robyn to deal with the guards. And how quickly we can reroute them. Because," she paused, her voice quivering, "if we can't get them there soon, our window of opportunity to grab Sophia will be gone."

Chapter Forty-Four: Noah

Noah hovered outside the lab, trying not to look out of place.

He hadn't wanted to risk following Susie all through the hospital, so when she had stopped to talk to a colleague, he'd moved on past. He'd ditched the mop and bucket and collected a cleaning trolley from the equipment store, hoping it would help with his cover. Extremely thankful he'd overheard the earlier conversation, he'd headed for the lab where he knew medics delivered samples and collected results.

Now all he had to do was wait.

All he could do was hope that she would come along soon. Or that she was already inside the lab. It was unfamiliar territory for him. With no good reason to enter, he had been forced to try and look busy outside, all the while watching for a pair of black loafers with mismatched laces to appear.

So far, he'd had no luck. And time was running out. With less than half an hour until Danforth's speech began, he still didn't have the means to access the ward.

He pictured Robyn's team arriving at the fire door with no way in. Sophia languishing in the Fertility Ward. The expression on Faith's face when she realised he had failed.

He swallowed hard. There was another possibility. One which he did not want to face. It was quite plausible that Susie wasn't inside the lab at all. What if she had already come and gone by the time he had arrived? Or been directed elsewhere by her superior on a more pressing matter?

His palms were sweating. Even when he located her, he had no idea *how* he was going to make the switch. While he knew where her keycard *was*, he couldn't approach her directly. Even bumping into her accidentally seemed like it was asking for trouble.

He needed to find a spot where he could pass her when she was distracted. Slip his hand into her pocket without being noticed.

It was easier said than done.

The door to the lab opened. He took an involuntary step back, knowing he looked suspicious. A burst of music blared from inside, followed by the blare of an announcer. *In twenty minutes, Chancellor Danforth will make her address, until then...* The noise faded as the door closed.

Noah found himself staring at a pair of cream-coloured heels. The woman didn't notice him. But as she clattered down the hallway, his heart sank. Definitely not the person he was looking for.

Only twenty-five minutes left. He had to do *something*. And he had to do it soon.

The rattle of a trolley from further down the hall made him turn. Remembering at the last minute not to look up, he flattened himself against the wall so that the drudge pushing it could pass. But the trolley came to stop beside him. Hands began sorting through the items on the top shelf.

"Need a hand?" The voice was muttered, low. But, unmistakably, Liam.

Noah marvelled at how the drudge managed to speak without attracting attention. The mask covered his mouth, disguising its movement, but he also made sure that neither his body nor his face altered. The words were barely a whisper, but Noah had heard them.

He didn't dare risk a reply. But Liam seemed to have a plan. He gestured to the trolley. To Noah's surprise, it did not contain the usual collection of cleaning products. Instead, it had been converted to a kind of merchandise stall. Brightly-coloured ribbons and sashes, commemorative pin badges and pens with the Bellator motto were laid out on the top shelf, all in glorious Liberation Day colours.

Noah remembered seeing similar trolleys about the hospital earlier in the day. Some of the drudges had been assigned to supervise them, so the busy staff could help themselves to the celebratory merchandise in between their shifts.

His heart began to beat faster as he understood Liam's plan. If Susie came out soon and stopped to browse what was on the trolley, switching the keycards would be far easier.

He felt a surge of gratitude. Liam didn't know him. But, with the knowledge that his friend was safe, and that Noah was part of a movement which intended to make things better for drudges, he was willing to help.

All they needed now was Susie.

The door opened again. Inside, the announcer continued to speak.

As you can see, the stage is set for Chancellor Danforth's arrival, which should be any minute now. Viewers have been speculating about her outfit. Last year, you will remember, she wore..."

As a medic exited the lab, both drudges tensed. But the shoes which emerged were simple black pumps with no laces. Before Noah could lose hope, the woman stopped dead.

"Hey, Suse!" She caught the door with her foot. "Did you get yourself kitted out for the celebrations? You know the boss likes us to be matriotic."

There was a movement from inside the lab. When the *right* pair of shoes stepped into view, Noah thought his heart might explode.

"Not yet, no." Susie stepped out into the hallway. "I'm going to be stuck here for at least an hour. Might as well have a look while I'm waiting."

She came closer, her fingers rummaging through the items on the trolley. "Let's see... the badges are cute, but... oh! Look at this scarf!"

"It's pretty!" her friend cooed. "Try it on! I'll bet it..."

Noah tuned the voices out, inching closer to the medics. Susie draped the scarf around her neck and posed. As the other woman began admiring it, Liam nudged him.

The women were distracted. Noah listened closely, checking that the hallway was clear. Then he took his chance. Slipping his hand into his pocket, he retrieved the dummy keycard. He leaned closer to Susie. As she arranged and rearranged the scarf, he repeated the move.

One card out. The other card in.

"I think we should have one each." The sensibly-shoed medic giggled. "Twins!"

Edging backwards, Noah stationed himself at the side of the trolley again. Neither woman appeared to have noticed anything amiss. He waited while they selected a number of items each, exclaiming over each one in turn. Eventually, the first woman turned to go.

"I'd better be off. Promised I'd get back so we could all watch the speech together on the ward."

"I think I'll be watching it right here." Susie's tone was gloomy.

Inside, Noah was celebrating. The ward would be empty. Maybe things were finally going his way.

"I'll see you later." Susie opened the lab door as the other medic walked away. "Have a good one."

Inside, the announcer's voice had reached feverpitch.

As Chancellor Abigail Danforth takes the stage, the crowd in the square bursts into applause. She looks as self-assured as always. Rumour has it, she has a big announcement to make, this year. We can only wait and see what...

The door swished shut, muting the voice. Beside Noah, Liam let out a long breath. Checking there was no one near, Noah gave a tiny nod of thanks. He hoped Liam understood the intention.

Danforth was about to begin. Which meant Faith's own speech would follow. He had to get back to Sophia before that happened.

As he set off along the hallway, his hand closed around the keycard in his pocket.

Chapter Forty-Five: Faith

"*C*itizens of Bellator, I stand before you today a proud woman.*"*

Danforth's words rang out hollowly across Blake's office. As Blake had requested, Faith started the timer on the datadev in front of her. The schedule had allowed forty-five minutes for Danforth's address. It was vital they time their interruption. Other parts of the plan depended on it.

She tried not to concern herself with the fact that they weren't quite ready.

"*I'd like to thank the Bellator Orchestra who, as always, showed us how the beauty of music can lift us from our daily grind.*"

Faith watched as Danforth's crocodile smile beamed out at the crowd. How many of the women in the square, she wondered, still believed what the chancellor told them?

"*Welcome to our Liberation Day Ceremony! Today, we have much to celebrate, and I'm very proud to…*"

Faith turned to Blake, tuning out the vicious words. "Are we good to go?"

Blake tapped on her coms. "Still trying to contact Robyn."

Though everyone else was in place, they had yet to hear back from the Resistance leader. Blake's posture radiated tension. Hunched over the datadev, she was tauter than the strings on one of the Bellator Orchestra's violins.

Faith glanced around. They were as prepared as they'd ever be for her speech. She had her notes neatly laid out in front of her. Blake had checked and tested the equipment several times. Microphone, lights, camera: they were all in the perfect position.

Controlling the outside factors was proving more difficult.

"Can I help?"

As Blake glanced at her, she braced herself for the usual rejection. *No, Faith. I have it in hand.*

Faith saw the response rise to Blake's lips automatically, but at the last moment, something changed. Rolling her neck, she gestured to the second set of earcoms.

"I want to double-check that Ella's been able to disconnect the firewall." Blake chewed on her lip, and Faith could see her struggling with asking for help. "Could you contact her, while I try to reach Robyn?"

Grateful for something to do, Faith didn't waste time. Selecting her friend's name from the contacts list on the datadev, she made the call.

It took several moments to connect. The repetitive pinging sound set Faith's nerves on edge as she waited. She adjusted and readjusted her earcoms. *What if Ella hadn't made it to the control room? What if she'd been caught sneaking inside? What if–*

"Blake?"

At the sound of Ella's voice, Faith pumped a silent fist in the air. Beside her, Blake jumped.

"It's Faith. Everything go to plan?"

"Hold on. I've bypassed the firewall. I'm just connecting the cable now." There was a brief pause. "There was a tiny delay getting in."

Faith's heart pounded as she waited for an explanation.

"Okay, I'm done. The firewall's down."

"Great." Faith gave a thumbs up to Blake, who relaxed her spine a fraction. "Did something go wrong?"

"No. It was easier than I expected, actually." There was a rustling noise. "But when I got to the control room, the techies were on their way out."

"They were *leaving*?" Faith frowned. "Right before Danforth's speech started?"

"Yeah. There was a guard standing at the door when I arrived. She was asking if everything was in place. One of the tech ladies confirmed they were ready." Ella sounded a little breathless. "I had to keep on walking, so I didn't arouse suspicion. That's what caused the delay. But as I walked away, I heard the guard say Danforth needed them in the square."

"That's why they left?"

"Guess so. I wandered around for a couple of minutes, then went back. They were all gone by the time I got there."

"Maybe..." Faith considered, "Maybe Danforth needs them to be... I don't know... more hands on. You think?"

"Maybe. Anyway, it made things a lot easier for me. I didn't have to use a ruse to get inside. It was deserted." There was a clicking sound Faith assumed was the door opening. "Everyone's watching the speech in the canteen. I'm heading back there now, so no one notices I'm missing."

"Sounds like a plan." Faith drew a breath, knowing it was time to play her own part now. "Anyway, thanks for your help."

"No problem." There was a brief pause. "Try not to worry, Faith. You're going to be great."

The line went dead before Faith found the words to respond. It was so like Ella to understand exactly how she was feeling. Swallowing hard, she turned back to Blake. "Any luck?"

"It's just ringing out. She'd have answered by now, if she was able to." Blake rubbed a hand across her mouth. "The guards must still be detaining her."

"If she doesn't get there..." Faith's heart lurched.

"Don't you think I know?" As Blake cut the call, Faith noticed her fingers were shaking.

"What can we do?" Faith sat up straighter. "There must be something."

Blake frowned. "What we need is something big to distract the guards. Something that would cause them to move to a different part of the city. The square, perhaps." She scrolled through her contacts. "I wonder if Diane... No, that wouldn't work."

A thought struck Faith. "What about Flynn?"

Blake cocked her head to one side. "What *about* Flynn?"

The Resistance had been in contact with Eremus several times since Paulo had told Noah about their plan. They'd agreed that Flynn's idea of coming to Bellator with one of the Danforth students was a powerful one. One which would support their cause. He'd been given approximate timings for the event and the Resistance had arranged for him and Helen to sneak into the city through the tunnels the night before.

Evelyn had been assigned to greet the pair. She had checked in with Blake several times to confirm their arrival. She had met them on the outskirts of the city the previous night and brought them in darkness to a small safehouse close to the centre. It was a risky move, but they'd managed it. Now they were close enough to the square to get there in minutes. The plan was for them to stay there until Faith's speech began. Once they were certain Blake had managed to successfully hack into the feed, they would move towards the square, aiming to arrive as Faith finished speaking.

Although the added security presence around the square amplified the risk of using the more central safehouse, it was essential that Flynn be able to time his arrival as precisely as possible.

Flynn would be carrying a weapon, held to the head of his hostage. Helen was in on the plan, and well aware that the weapon was only for show. It was a necessary move, aimed at preventing Danforth's guards from attacking. It would, they hoped, protect him as he walked through the city streets, allowing him to reach the square without coming to any harm.

As long as he had a Bellator citizen by his side, under his control, the guards would not shoot. But they would, Faith was certain, shadow him at a distance. There was no way a male could wander the streets without attracting attention.

Right now, it might be just the distraction they needed.

"Flynn and Helen are supposed to wait until I start speaking to appear, right?"

"They are." Blake frowned. "*And*?"

"What if we brought them out early? Like... *now*?"

Blake looked as though she was considering the idea. "You mean..."

"An Eremus man on the streets will be quite the distraction."

"The timing's wrong, though. If he comes out too soon, he'll be putting himself in more danger than we intended."

"Maybe." Faith knew she was right. "But he's already taking a huge risk coming here in the first place."

"I suppose..." Blake raised her eyebrows. "I mean, you're right... the disturbance will have guards from all over the city racing over there." She chewed on her lip. "But..."

"Do you have any better ideas?"

"No."

"Why don't we ask him, at least?" Faith reasoned. "Give *him* the choice?"

Still, Blake hesitated.

Faith's eyes moved to the screen. Danforth was still speaking, as she had been for the past five minutes, according to the timer. Faith's speech was supposed to cut in at ten minutes.

"Blake," she kept her voice soft. "We don't have long."

"We'd better get on with it then, hadn't we?" Blake started scrolling her contacts. Seconds later, the call connected.

"Evelyn," her voice was urgent, "change of plan..."

CHAPTER FORTY-SIX: NOAH

Danforth's voice rang out across the entire hospital. In the lobby, the staff rooms, the wards, the waiting areas, every screen was broadcasting her speech. As Noah headed towards the Fertility Wards, he caught snatches of the chancellor's words, her disembodied voice emanating from multiple directions.

"...a day for celebrating our independence from the other half of our species, those detestable males who seek to..."

He picked up the pace, trying to escape her vicious words. His hatred of Danforth was deep-seated. He'd been brought up by people who cursed her name, but his close encounters with her recently had only served to support their low opinion of the chancellor. The poison which spewed from her mouth under the guise of her being protective of her citizens made his blood boil.

The hallway leading to the fertility unit was as quiet as it had been the day before. On the way, Noah had picked up a trolley with various items of cleaning equipment. Taking a leaf from Liam's book, he planned to improvise, washing down the walls of the corridor as he waited for Robyn.

At least he knew Sophia was alone, for the time being. It was one thing that had gone in his favour.

But time was ticking on. As he approached the end of the hallway, he ran through the plan in his head. Cover the security camera. Check that the keycard worked. Wait for Faith's speech to begin. Let Robyn and her team in through the fire door. Keep watch while the team got to work. Then, finally, secure the fire door behind the escaping team.

First things first. Positioning the trolley underneath the security camera, Noah grasped one of the towels from the top. He stretched the material between his hands, preparing himself. Then, his body taut, he launched it in an arc over his head. When he flattened his back against the wall and looked upwards, he had to fight the impulse to thrust a hand of triumph in the air. The towel had landed right over the camera, blinding anyone who might attempt to see what was going on in the hallway from a distant security room.

Straightening his spine, he glanced up at the screen on the wall. The image showed a crowded square, the women of Bellator keenly focused on their leader. Danforth's face was glowing, her arms outstretched like some kind of prophet.

"*Today,*" she boomed, "*I have something miraculous to show you. Something which, I'm sure you'll agree, will change our lives forever.*"

Noah's heart clenched. That Sophia was being used as a guinea pig was bad enough. That Danforth would put her on display this way, as nothing more than a pawn, made him feel sick.

"*But first,*" Danforth gave a little laugh, "*We will hear from the esteemed Doctor Sanders, who will give you a little background before the... big reveal.*"

The screen split, showing an image of the doctor Noah had heard giving Susie instructions earlier. She wasn't in the square itself, it appeared, but the background suggested she was in a conference room of some sort, probably within the hospital. She wasn't far away, then. But at least Noah knew she was otherwise occupied, for now.

Tuning the woman's voice out, he crossed the hallway, approaching the ward door. Slipping the keycard from his pocket, he held it against the keypad.

Nothing happened.

Fighting panic, he tried again. He moved the card away from the keypad, forcing himself to wait a few seconds before holding it against the keypad once more.

There was no green light welcoming him into the restricted area. No telltale beep indicating the door was unlocked. The silence taunted him.

He took a step back. Robyn's arrival would mean nothing if he hadn't managed to get the door open. His palms sweating, he studied the keypad. It looked a little different than the ones he had seen previously. They were usually simple black boxes, sensors which registered the keycard as soon as it was within proximity. It made it easier for medics who were carrying equipment or pushing trolleys to get inside. But this one was thicker.

This ward was restricted. Access might be more difficult. Noah leaned closer to the keypad, noticing a long, slender opening which ran down one side. An idea occurred to him. Praying he was right, he slipped the keycard into the gap, swiping it down until it slid out at the base.

There was no happy beep. But a red light on the top of the device flashed. *Did that mean the key wasn't working?* Repositioning the card, he repeated the motion, more slowly this time, making sure that the edge of the card was pressed flush against the back of the opening.

He almost passed out as the light flashed green and a cheerful beeping sound emanated from the device. It was followed by the sharp click of the lock releasing.

Glancing both ways, Noah eased the door open. *Did he dare to go inside?* It wasn't, strictly speaking, part of the plan. But he knew for a fact that no one was inside but Sophia. Surely, she would appreciate being forewarned of the rescue?

His hands shaking, he pocketed the keycard and walked in. Faced with two doors, he took the one labelled FEX02. Inside, he found himself in a small vestibule. Four doors opened off it. One was open, revealing a small office. Two were labelled, *Bathroom* and *Store Room.* The ward had to be the last one.

He hurried to the door. Not wanting to startle its only patient, he eased it open. There were four beds, but only one was occupied. Its inhabitant was propped up against pillows, her face pale and her eyes closed. Noah moved towards her. *Was she sleeping?*

As he approached, her eyes flickered open. A defensive expression flashed through them. It was quickly replaced by shock.

"Noah?" She sat bolt upright. "What are you–?"

"Hey," he murmured.

As quickly as it had appeared, the surge of energy vanished. Sinking back against the pillows, Sophia raised a weary hand to her forehead.

"I'm sorry." Her voice was timid. "I'm just so tired. I can barely stand up to walk to the bathroom." She took a couple of deep breaths. "You're not a hallucination, are you?"

"I'm not." Noah was at her side within seconds. He reached for her hand. "See?" He glanced at the door. "We don't have much time though. Can you just listen for a moment?"

"Sure." Her eyes flickered with interest. "Go ahead."

"I'm here as part of a rescue mission." He tried to focus on the vital information. "It's too complex to explain now, but a team from the Resistance is on their way. My job is to let them in when they get here." He mimed unlocking a door. "Once they arrive, they'll get you out of here. Take you somewhere safe. Okay?"

Sophia's eyes filled with tears. "It's *more* than okay. But..."

"What?"

She gestured to the various tubes attached to her body. "What about these?"

Noah's eyes followed the tubes to the various machines which surrounded her. "I'm sure it can be dealt with. There's a woman with the team – Lily – who has some medical knowledge. She'll know what to do."

"I guess..." She took a deep breath. "I've seen them put these in so many times, I could almost do it myself. What I mean is... if I need to, I can tell someone what to do... to take them out." Sophia covered her eyes with her hands, her shoulders shaking. "I'm sorry. It's just... it feels like I've been here a long time."

"I understand. And you have." Noah squeezed her hand. He hesitated before continuing. "I'm sorry, but..."

"You need to go?" She gave a watery smile.

"Yeah." He frowned. "But I don't want to leave–"

"It's okay." She cut him off. "I can tolerate anything, if I get to leave this hellhole at the end of it."

"I'll come back for you, I promise." Noah held her gaze. "I won't leave you here any longer than I have to."

"Thanks." Her smile faded as he turned to go. "One last thing, though. Is Faith... I mean, is she–?"

He turned back, smiling now. "She's fine. At Resistance Headquarters right now, playing her own part in the mission. And waiting for you, of course."

"I knew she wouldn't abandon me."

"Abandon you? You're the reason she came back to the city."

As Noah turned to leave, Sophia relaxed back against the pillows. Though still pale, she looked much happier. He only hoped everything went to plan now.

Checking that the hallway outside was still empty, Noah replaced the keycard in his pocket. He armed himself with a wet cloth and disinfectant spray, then knelt down underneath the window which gave him a good view of the side street. Squirting the wall, he began to scrub.

Sanders was wrapping up her part of the broadcast. A glance at the screen told him Danforth was preparing to address the crowd again.

Faith's speech would begin soon.

Until then, there was nothing to do but wait.

Chapter Forty-Seven: Faith

"We have to start." Faith closed her eyes. "*Now.*"

"Not until we know that they're out of trouble."

When Faith opened them again, Blake was dialling Robyn's number. *Again.* The sound of the unanswered call ringing out was beginning to feel like some kind of torture. Flynn had quickly agreed to leave the safehouse early, acting as a distraction. But though he had gone out into the streets several minutes ago, the Resistance leader had yet to respond to their call.

They could only assume she was still being detained.

On the other screen, Danforth had taken over from Doctor Sanders. It brought them one step closer to the chancellor's big reveal of Sophia's pregnancy. When photographs of Faith's best friend would be shown as evidence of the chancellor's triumph. When the gentle Sophia would be used as *proof* that males could be eradicated forever.

It made Faith sick to her stomach. They *had* to interrupt before she had the chance to show the images.

"Shouldn't we..." she tried again, but Blake waved an impatient hand in her direction.

Tired of being ignored, Faith sat up as tall as she could. "*Listen* to me! We can't just–"

The ringing sound stopped.

Please let it be Robyn. Faith held her breath. *Please let them be back on their way, ready and able to rescue Sophia.*

But no one spoke.

Instead, they could hear the sound of traffic. Comcar engines whirring. The beeping of several horns. A distant radio playing what could have been Danforth's speech.

"*Hello?*"

For a moment, Faith's heart soared. "*Robyn!* It's so good to hear your–"

"*Excuse me?*" The reply made no sense.

"Robyn? Can you hear–"

But Blake was frowning. "She's not talking to you. She wants us to *listen*. Find out what's happening." Blake leaned closer, straining to hear.

"*Do you think you could let us go now, Officer?*"

"They're still with the guard." Faith's shoulders slumped. "The plan didn't–"

Blake held up a hand, silencing Faith as Robyn spoke again.

"*We've been answering your questions for more than fifteen minutes now. The traffic is clearing and we'd like to be on our way. As I've said, several times, we're simply making our way to the other side of the city to celebrate Liberation Day with friends. I don't appreciate you–*"

A sharp crackling interrupted Robyn's speech. The next thing they heard was a disembodied voice.

Emergency Alert! Back up requested. All guards not on duty in the immediate area surrounding the square must proceed to the west of the city. Incident of concern on Hanover Street. Further instructions to follow.

Blake elbowed Faith. "Not working, huh?"

Faith ignored her. Straining forward, she tried to work out what was happening with Robyn. There were several unidentified sounds. A shuffling or rustling of some kind, followed by a throat being cleared.

"Thank you for your cooperation. You may proceed with your journey now."

Blake and Faith exchanged glances. Were the guards really leaving?

A second later, Robyn's voice came on the line. "Thank you." Her voice was flooded with relief. "Whatever you did, it worked. We're on our way now. Should reach the hospital within fifteen minutes."

The call went dead, but there was no time for celebration.

On the screen, Danforth was smiling broadly. *"What I'm about to show you is something very special. A triumph of..."*

Blake's fingers flew over the keypad, preparing to hack into the feed which was broadcasting Danforth to the rest of the city. Her attention shifted to Faith. "You ready for this?"

Faith leaned towards the microphone.

With a flourish which was most unlike her, Blake clicked a button. Holding three fingers in the air, she started a silent countdown.

Three.

Two.

One.

On the screen, Danforth's expression faltered.

"I'm very proud to..." she glanced to the side of the stage. "I'm very... p-p–" Her face filled with fury. "W-what's g-go–"

Blake pointed a finger at Faith.

"You're on," she mouthed, with a smile.

Faith took a deep breath. "Citizens of Bellator. My name is Faith Hanlon."

Chapter Forty-Eight: Noah

"*I may not have long to deliver my message, so I urge you to listen closely.*" As Faith's voice boomed from the speakers, Noah held his breath. "*You are all being lied to by the woman who stands before you today.*"

Faith sounded determined and confident. Exactly the way she had when he'd stumbled on her rehearsing in the library. Noah stopped scrubbing and turned. Only moments ago, Danforth had been grinning down at them. Now, Faith's serious face filled the screen mounted at the back of the stage.

The wounds on her face were almost healed now, but the fading scars gave the impression that she had seen battle and survived. She looked tough. And determined.

"*Terrible things are happening within the Bellator boundaries, while you are kept in the dark. Lie number one: there are dangerous experiments going on within the grounds of the Danforth Academy. Experi-*

ments which put the lives of its students at risk. I know this, because I am one of them."

Noah felt a surge of hope. Faith had waited so long to play her part in the Resistance's work. Every word was heartfelt. The citizens in the square stirred, shock and confusion dancing across their faces as Faith continued.

"Lie number two: Eremus still exists." A whisper ran through the crowd at the revelation. *"And, far from being a den of vicious brutes, it is a thriving community filled with both men and women who choose to be there. Again, you can trust my word on this, because I have been there."*

Danforth was still standing by the microphone at the front of the stage. Her eyes were fixed on the screen, and her face was twisted with fury. Faith's words were already having an impact. The fact that the Resistance had used the speech to disguise Sophia's rescue mission was the icing on the cake. Noah glanced at the street. Any minute now, Robyn would be there.

"But let me tell you more. As I said, the Danforth Academy students are being cruelly used. Their presence at the establishment is not, as you have been led to believe, a privilege. It's a curse."

Faith paused, and Noah could feel the crowd leaning closer to listen. For a moment, he searched the faces, wondering if he might spot Diane. Her team would be there, listening, talking to the citizens, measuring their reactions. But the square was packed, and it was impossible to make out individuals.

He turned his attention back to the screen, where Faith continued to speak. Despite the pressure, Faith's words were measured, weighty, and ringing with importance. The crowd was transfixed.

"Even as I speak, these young, vulnerable women are being forced to undergo horrendous experiments in the name of progress. I have wit-

nessed this and even," she winced, as though the memory was painful, *"been subject to the testing myself."*

Faith took a breath, keeping her eyes fixed on the camera. Noah felt like she was staring right at him. If even half the audience felt the same way, her speech would have a powerful effect.

"Not only that, the revolutionary discovery your chancellor is about to reveal is a direct result of this testing. It's an advancement in modern medicine she feels sure you will be thrilled by." Faith paused, leaning closer to the microphone. *"I wonder if you'll feel quite so thrilled when you learn that the experimentation has already caused the deaths of three young Danforth students?"*

This time, there was an audible gasp.

Faith pressed on, refusing to allow her audience time to recover.

"I presume you're wondering how I know about lie number two: the Eremus community. A few weeks ago, I was kidnapped by them and taken to live in the forest." A ripple of shock ran through the crowd at her words. *"Like you, I believed their community to be long gone. Like you, I thought the rebel males in the forest were..."*

Noah glanced out of the window again. There was still no sign of the team. He wondered how much longer Susie would be in the lab. If she returned to the ward before they had rescued Sophia, things would get far more complicated. Saying a prayer that Robyn made it before it was too late, he turned his attention back to Faith.

"...what I found there shocked me. Not because the people in Eremus are all male or all monsters. But because what I found was a large, mixed community forced to live in very difficult circumstances because of our chancellor's treatment. The kidnapping was a desperate attempt to draw attention to their plight. Their suffering. The chancellor has her guards hunt them down, because..."

The noise of an engine in the side street caught Noah's attention. He tensed, ready to move to the door. But the vehicle sped by without stopping. Noah glanced back at the screen, wondering how much longer Faith had before Danforth's people cut her off.

His eyes sought out the chancellor. He found her at the side of the platform. She was waving her arms uselessly at an unseen offstage presence. Noah revelled in her fury for a moment, but as Faith began to speak again, his eyes were drawn back to hers.

"...majority of the people were kind to me. Some even became my friends." She smiled slightly, and Noah wondered if she was thinking of him. *"When I came back to the city it wasn't to flee from Eremus. It was to try and save a friend. A fellow student who the chancellor was... **is** hurting."*

Noah's hands were shaking. Not with fear, or even anticipation of the dangerous mission to come, but with admiration for the young woman who was giving her all to the speech that could change things, for the better, for everyone.

"There are many other things I would like to tell you." Faith gave a slight shake of her head. *"I may not have time. But understand my message. Until you begin to question the leader before you, the atrocities I have described will continue."*

Danforth had disappeared from the stage. Noah pictured her roaring at her technical team backstage as they struggled to restore the broadcast feed before any more damage was done. He turned back to the screen, praying Faith would be allowed to continue.

"You may recognise my face from the leaflets that were distributed throughout Bellator a couple of weeks ago. Leaflets which were dismissed by our chancellor as the work of extremists. Of a group of rebels who want nothing more than to disrupt our city's peace."

There was still no sign of life on the street outside. Noah leaned closer to the window, casting his gaze this way and that, hoping to see a comcar pulling up. But the street remained stubbornly empty.

If Robyn's team didn't get here, the mission would fail. He recalled his earlier promise to Sophia. Considered the look on Faith's face if the team returned empty-handed. He couldn't just sit here and do nothing.

Making a decision, he crossed the hall again. He could speed things up, at least. If he went inside, he could remove the tubes from Sophia's arms, get her into a wheelchair and bring her out here. She would be ready and waiting when Robyn arrived.

And he had to believe that she would arrive. Soon.

Behind him, Faith continued, her voice growing more animated by the second. *"I can assure you that these so-called rebels do not aim to lie to you, nor to harm you. All they want is to expose the chancellor for the liar she is! To open your eyes to what's going on around you. You should know that Laura Meadows, the Resistance member arrested for her part in delivering the leaflets, was executed by the chancellor. Not, as she claimed,"* Faith's voice took on a cynical tone, *"given the care she needed to be rehabilitated. And there are many others who suffer at Danforth's hands."*

Noah made his decision. Swiping the keycard through the gap in the rear of the reader, he pushed open the door.

"Another group who you should spare a thought for is the drudges..."

Faith's voice faded as he strode inside. Without hesitation this time, he entered Sophia's room. Her eyes met his immediately, and he got the impression they had been fixed on the door since he'd left the room.

"Are they here?" Her voice trembled. "The team?"

"Any minute now." He didn't want to lie. "But I figured... if I got you ready, it would save time."

The hope in her eyes faded, but she forced herself to sit up. He hated how weak she looked.

"Alright." She glanced around. "*Anything* we can do to increase the chances of success. Can you disconnect the cannulas? I know it's not the sort of kit you have in the caves, but your ma must have told you about them." She searched for reassurance. "Right?"

"Of course." Noah looked at the tubes. "I should probably find something to cover the wounds with. In case they..." he hesitated.

"*There's* the boy whose ma trained him to assist her." Sophia managed a weak smile at his practical suggestion. "I think there's some cotton wool over there. Self-adhesive bandages, that kind of thing." She pointed to a trolley at the side of the room. "Hurry though."

Noah washed his hands in the sink before searching the trolley. Finding what he needed, he donned a pair of gloves and began to remove the cannulas one at a time. Sophia looked away, wincing as each needle left her skin.

Noah found himself hating Danforth even more.

When he was finished, Sophia had three, neatly-covered injection sites.

"A job well done." She grimaced as she complimented him.

"Do you have anything warmer?" Noah gestured to the thin tunic.

"Susie wears a cardigan sometimes. It might be in the office, if we have time to grab it."

Noah hurried to the office and located it. As he wrapped the thick woolly material around Sophia, he could feel her trembling. She had been slight when he met her, but now her body felt skeletal. Helping her to the edge of the bed, he tried not to gawp at her swelling stomach.

It was the only part of her which was full and rounded, as though the baby was sucking all the goodness in her body for itself.

Dragging his eyes away, Noah grabbed the wheelchair from the corner of the room. He thought Sophia might argue that she could walk, but the effort of removing the tubing seemed to have sapped all her energy. She was floppy as a ragdoll, as he helped her transfer from the bed to the chair.

When she was settled, he wrapped a blanket around her and brought her to the door of the ward. Easing it open a crack, he peered through. The hallway was still, thankfully, empty.

He turned to Sophia. "I'll go and check if the team are there before I wheel you out."

Propping the door open so he could keep an eye on her, Noah slipped across to the window. The street outside remained empty. His heart sank. If the team didn't arrive soon, they would lose their chance.

His heart racing, he contemplated alternatives. He could take Sophia out of the hospital himself. But a drudge with a vulnerable patient would not go unnoticed for long. He glanced back at the frail body in the chair. Sophia needed care. He couldn't push her all over the city in a wheelchair.

Perhaps he could hide her somewhere inside the hospital. But where? The moment Sanders discovered her missing, she would tear the place apart. There was no way she wanted to lose her one and only success.

On the screen, Faith launched into the final section of her speech.

"So many of your fellow citizens are suffering." Noah glanced up and down the hallway in desperation. The speech had done its job, but he was out of options. He gazed up at Faith. Despite his own dire situation, he was confident that her words would make a difference.

"This suffering is purposefully hidden from you. The Resistance aims

to show you the harm which is being done, in your name, to other, more vulnerable people, both inside and outside the boundaries of your city."

"I-is that Faith's voice?" Sophia was leaning forwards. Her eyes lit up as they found the screen. "It is!"

"You need to listen to them, to us, to our message." Faith was winding up, her face earnest. *"To know that things in Bellator are not as rosy as the chancellor would have you believe."*

A screech of wheels in the street outside made Noah jump. Glancing outside, his heart soared as a comcar drew up outside. He yanked the door open as Robyn and Lily leapt out of the vehicle.

"Sorry for the delay. Unavoidable, I'm afraid." Robyn stepped into the hallway her eyes zeroing in on the young woman in the chair. "Oh! You have her ready and waiting."

"Hadn't you better get going?" Noah gestured to the screen. "It's almost over."

Lily's eyes slid to the screen. "Isn't Faith *amazing?*"

"Hurry, Lil. There's no *time.*" Robyn crossed the hallway, heading for the open ward door. "Hi Sophia. I'm Robyn and this is Lily. We're here to take you somewhere safe. Okay?"

Sophia nodded her understanding. As Robyn pushed the chair out of the ward and towards the exit, Lily checked the injection sites on her arms.

"Nice job!" she grinned at Noah.

He marvelled at her lack of panic. Between them, Robyn and Lily had Sophia in the comcar in seconds. As the door slammed behind her, Robyn turned to Noah.

"Quick thinking, getting her ready. Really saved us some time." She opened the passenger door of the comcar. "Make sure you cover your tracks, won't you? For your own safety."

The door slammed behind her, the comcar pulling away before she had time to wave. Noah moved back inside, relocking the fire exit. The sound of Faith's voice drew him back to the screen.

"It is time for us to make changes. To question the system. To hold accountable those who make the rules which put some of us at risk at the expense of others. And, if necessary, to stop them." She paused, drawing in a deep breath. *"Our movement does not intend to disrupt or destroy this city, but to work together to change it for the better. N-not i-in–"*

The image on the screen began to break up. There was a loud crackle, and Faith's face disappeared.

Cover your tracks. Robyn's parting words came back to Noah as the spell cast by Faith's speech was broken.

Using a broom handle from the trolley, he retrieved the towel from the camera. Packing away his cleaning equipment, he prepared to leave. From underneath the camera's watchful gaze, he raised his eyes to the screen once more.

Danforth had resumed her place centre-stage. She looked shaken but was preparing to speak. No doubt she was ready to denounce Faith's claims and attempt to return her citizens to their usual state of ignorance.

Noah grinned. The damage was done.

But before she could say anything, there was a disturbance towards the rear of the crowd. The Bellator women parted like sheaves of corn on a windy day, drawing back in horror and fascination as two figures made their way towards the stage.

The taller of the two was hooded and held a gun to the temple of the smaller figure, a female, whose face was exposed. Squinting his eyes, Noah recognised a pale and wary-looking Helen. On the stage, dozens of Bellator guards had sprung into action around Danforth. By the time the strange pair reached the stage, there were more than twenty guns trained on them.

Noah had known it was going to happen, but he still wasn't ready for it. He'd have recognised the mystery figure anywhere, despite the hood. The man's gait was as familiar to Noah as his own.

Guiding Helen before him, Flynn headed for the steps which led up to the stage. Danforth's guards bristled as he came to a halt at the bottom.

Flynn lowered his hood, and Noah felt his knees buckle. The only father he'd ever known looked calm and rational in the face of immense danger. He kept Helen close, the gun pointed at her head.

Noah knew how the situation looked to the majority of the audience. They would assume Flynn was the standard violent male, a terrifying threat to Helen, using his masculine power to gain some kind of sway over the crowd.

But what choice had Danforth left them?

Noah could only hope that the false threat would protect Flynn, giving him the opportunity to speak. Danforth wouldn't want to risk the life of a Bellator citizen. Not with so many onlookers.

Once Flynn opened his mouth, all they could do was hope that his words, in addition to Faith's, would be enough to turn the tide. To reverse the years of hatred.

A strange expression crossed Danforth's face as Flynn called to her. The microphone didn't pick up his words, but after a moment the chancellor nodded. Slowly, Flynn directed Helen up the steps, keeping the gun pressed to her temple. As he neared the centre of the stage, Danforth backed away, taking the guards with her.

As Flynn stepped up to the microphone, Noah's eyes followed the chancellor. Flanked by her guards, she stood to one side, her arms folded. Noah had expected her to look angry. Frightened. Wary even. But the expression on her face was one of extreme confidence, as though she had expected, or even planned, the Eremus man's appearance.

As Flynn opened his mouth to speak, Noah's heart began to pound.

CHAPTER FORTY-NINE: FAITH

The microphone squealed as a nervous Flynn cleared his throat. The sound reverberated throughout the crowded square. Faith's heart went out to him. Microphones were tricky things, and the Eremus man had no experience with them at all. Wincing at the shrill sound, he pulled back. But when he leaned forward again, he stood tall.

"I know the sight of a man is a frightening one for you all." He stared out at the women in front of him, his gaze unflinching. *"And I must apologise for my threatening appearance here today."* He gestured to Helen. *"Unfortunately, these actions were necessary for me to gain access to your city."*

Faith's body ached with tension. The speech had gone better than they could have hoped, but they were still waiting for confirmation of Sophia's rescue. Having completed her own part of the mission, Evelyn had joined Diane's group in the square. Once Flynn and Helen had taken the stage, the Bellator citizens had surged forward, seeming intrigued, curious, fascinated.

Faith had to confess she felt the same.

"I am here today to support Faith Hanlon. To corroborate her story about Eremus." Flynn's earnestness brought tears to Faith's eyes. *"And to provide evidence of our good intentions."*

A noise at the back of Blake's office made them both jump. Turning, Faith saw Madeleine in the doorway.

"They're back." She was out of breath. "Robyn's team... they came through the tunnel just now."

As Blake pumped a fist in the air, Faith felt her entire body sag with relief. *Finally,* Sophia was safe.

"Where are they?" She stood up. "I should–"

"Leave it a few minutes." Madeleine stood in her way. "The journey here really took it out of her. Lily asked that we give her time to get Sophia settled in. Check her over."

Faith started to argue, but changed her mind at the look on Madeleine's face. She had waited this long to be reunited with her friend. A few more minutes wouldn't make a difference. The important thing was that Sophia was here. They'd rescued her.

As she returned to her chair, she said a silent thank you to Noah. Without him, Sophia would never have escaped Danforth's clutches.

"Something's not right." Blake had turned back to the datadev. "It shouldn't have been this easy for Flynn to get up there."

Madeleine joined them, leaning over the back of Faith's chair. "You're right. But what are we missing?"

"Nothing!" Faith turned to her. "He's holding a Bellator citizen hostage! *That's* why Danforth's allowing it."

"You think?" Madeleine tapped a finger against the screen, zooming in on the stage. "She doesn't even look perturbed."

Faith peered at the chancellor. She had to admit that Madeleine was right. Danforth stood a few feet back from Flynn. She almost looked like she was smiling.

"I thought she'd at least put up a bit of a fight." Blake frowned. "Helen is a single citizen. One Danforth cares nothing about."

"Maybe so," Faith stared at her, "but it would be fairly tricky to explain away her actions if she let Flynn shoot a vulnerable teenage girl in front of a crowd of hundreds."

Madeleine's eyes stayed glued to the screen. "Well, I'm not convinced."

"Me neither." Blake shook her head. "Danforth's too calm."

"Look at the crowd." Faith pointed. "They're *listening* to him. It might actually be working."

Blake grunted, her expression unchanged as Flynn continued to speak.

"We do not wish to be at war with this city. In fact, we would like to coexist peacefully with the women of Bellator."

"Danforth could have instructed her tech team to cut the feed by now. Limit the damage to the square alone. There must be *someone* left in Matriarch House." As Madeleine leaned closer to the screen, Faith thought of Ella, hoping that she had made sure she was well away from the Control Room. "I mean, this is going out to *every* household in Bellator. Why would–"

She stopped. Faith went cold as she saw the reason why. Flynn had taken a deliberate step away from Helen. First, he raised his hands aloft in an unmistakable gesture of peace. Then, very deliberately, he lowered the gun to the ground.

"What's he *doing*?" Madeleine's face was stricken.

With the weapon on the stage beside him, Flynn turned back to the crowd. *"I hope this serves as a symbol of our desire to end the feud. We have to start to build trust. So I'm starting by showing that I trust you. That you won't simply execute an unarmed man. The people of Eremus..."*

"This wasn't part of the plan... w-was it?" Faith stammered.

One glance at Madeleine's face told her it wasn't. Flynn was supposed to keep the gun trained on Helen at all times, to protect himself.

A wave of fear washed over her. "Won't Danforth just..."

"Shoot him?" Blake was never one to mince words. "You'd think so."

But Danforth had made no move toward Flynn, nor had she given her guards any further instructions.

Flynn paused to glance at the chancellor, as though he too had expected some kind of reaction. When she did nothing, he continued. Faith spotted the first vestiges of hope in his posture. Standing tall, he motioned to the young woman beside him with a now-empty hand.

"I hope that Helen's presence here serves as further evidence of our peaceful intentions."

For the first time, Flynn glanced at the screen behind him. Catching sight of his face, magnified to alarming proportions, he faltered. Faith understood his anxiety from her own experience. For her, at least, the technology in use on the stage was familiar. To Flynn, it was totally alien.

Once again, she was struck by the bravery of the man, prepared to stand vulnerable in front of hundreds of women who hated him. Noah might not be his biological child, but she could see Flynn's influence on him. Forthright, honest, and resolute, he was a product of the man who stood on the stage today. The man who had volunteered to take him on and bring him up as his own.

Faith blinked away tears as Flynn recovered. He pushed on, driving his point home.

"What Faith said is true. Eremus has been holding a number of the Danforth students hostage." He hung his head. *"In hindsight, the kidnapping is an action we very much regret. All I can say is,"* he stared

up at the crowd, his expression fierce, *"that the Eremus people did not see any other option at the time."*

The camera zoomed in on Flynn's face, showcasing his every emotion to the entirety of Bellator.

Blake leapt to her feet. *"Why* would she allow a close up?" She stared at Madeleine, open-mouthed. "I mean–"

On the stage, Flynn continued to press his message home. *"I know it's a lot to ask that you take me at my word, but I assure you that these girls have been treated..."*

"Look at Danforth!" Blake jabbed a finger at the chancellor. "This is a woman who *hates* men. Who has done everything she can to rid the city of them completely. It doesn't make sense that she would permit one to speak to her people like this. Not for this length of time. He doesn't even have the gun anymore!"

Faith stared at the chancellor. She wore her usual mask of calm, her expression revealing nothing. Considering there was an Eremus male sharing the stage with her, she seemed utterly unperturbed.

Flynn's expression, in contrast, was passionate, honourable, open.

"I urge you to listen to one of your own. Trust in a fellow Bellator citizen." He gestured to Helen. *"This young woman asked if she could speak to you all. She wishes to share her own experience with you. I hope that her words will further convince you that Eremus wishes you no harm."*

He turned to Helen, who took a tentative step forward. Faith could see how nervous she was. Before she reached the microphone, she stumbled.

Flynn reached out a hand to steady her, and a gasp ran through the crowd. The unplanned gesture could not fail to demonstrate the gentleness of the man on the stage. The way Helen took his hand without hesitation, as though it was the kind of behaviour she expected from him, was even more powerful.

Faith felt hope flare inside her.

How could the crowd fail to see Helen's lack of fear? Here was a Bellator female *willingly* accepting the help of an Eremus male. A man who, since he'd stood in front of the crowd, had shown nothing but courage and decency.

Once Helen spoke, adding her words to those of Faith and Flynn, the citizens of Bellator would *have* to believe. Have to admit the things they had been told did not add up. Have to question their leader's behaviour.

And, with Sophia's rescue, Danforth no longer had the shiny miracle she intended to distract her citizens with.

She had nothing.

Beside Faith, Madeleine's fists were clenched, and Blake was shaking her head in disbelief. Ignoring them, Faith strained to listen to Helen's words.

"Fellow citizens," she began, her voice shaking slightly.

But before she could say any more, a thunderous roar split the air. The crowd erupted into panic, their screams of terror shrill and haunting.

Faith tensed. She pressed closer to the screen, where a dense column of smoke billowed into the sky above the city. Citizens hurried in every direction, panic etched on their faces. Madeleine, Blake, and Faith exchanged glances, searching for an explanation.

But before they could make sense of the chaos, the screen went black.

A NOTE FROM CLARE

Thank you for reading Defiance! Reviews make a huge difference to authors and readers. If you enjoyed the book, please consider writing a short, honest review on Amazon. I cannot tell you how much I'd appreciate it! (While you're there, click on my author page and follow me for more information about upcoming releases!)

I love building relationships with my readers. If you enjoyed Defiance and would like to receive updates when I have a new book out, sign up for my readers' club:

https://clarelittlemore.com/newsletter?signup=defiance

You'll receive a regular newsletter with giveaways, book recommendations, special offers, the occasional free short story, and (of course) details of all my new releases. I promise there will be no spam. I hate spam.

Want more?

Want to continue Faith and Noah's story?

Alliance is the fourth and final book in The Bellator Chronicles!

Get it now!

A brutal loss. A shocking discovery. A harrowing sacrifice.

The rebellion lies in ruins after an explosion rocks the city. But when Faith discovers the Chancellor's end game, she knows she has to act. Even if it means putting herself in harm's way.

Reeling from his traumatic mission, Noah returns to headquarters to discover Faith missing. He's desperate to mount a rescue. But her position behind enemy lines makes her useful, and the Resistance want her to stay where she is.

As tensions mount, Noah despairs of ever seeing Faith again. A risky assignment offers him one last chance to find her and help the Resistance bring the Chancellor down. If it fails, the revolution is over. For good.

Even if they succeed, there are no guarantees that everyone will come out of it alive.

OTHER BOOKS BY CLARE LITTLEMORE

The Flow Series

Binge-read the entire series now!

Flow

Break

Drift

Quell

A drowned planet. A terrible secret. A girl desperate for answers.

In a world where sea levels have risen to unimaginable levels, an isolated society exists. Life in The Beck is tough. Floodwaters constantly threaten existence, and rules must be followed to ensure the survival of the entire society.

Sixteen-year-old Quin knows the Governor is hiding something. When she receives a sudden promotion to the Patrol Sector, she hopes the extra freedom will help her expose his lies.

Life in Patrol is not what she expected, though. The new recruits train hard, and failure is not tolerated. When she attracts the attention of the handsome, mysterious Cam, he warns her that asking questions could get her killed.

But Quin can't resist. She digs deeper and discovers that there's more to Cam than meets the eye. With her heart and her life on the line, Quin has to decide how far she is willing to go to protect the people she loves.

If you love The Hunger Games, Divergent and The Giver, this gripping dystopian series by Clare Littlemore will keep you up all night.

ACKNOWLEDGEMENTS

Writing a book can be a long and lonely process. Defiance was not an easy book to write, and it would not be what it is without the support of a number of very important people.

As always, I need to say a huge thank you to my editor Beth Dorward. Defiance started off as an extremely lengthy story, and has ended up as two entirely separate books! It has had to undergo massive changes throughout the editing process (and there's still more to come with the second half of the original manuscript). Beth is always patient, practical and thorough, and I really appreciate her being there to steer me in the right direction with my writing. Thanks also to my cover designer, Jessica Bell, for continuing to create eye-catching covers which maintain the theme of The Bellator Chronicles whilst bringing something fresh to the mix. (In addition to creating a fourth cover at the eleventh hour for a book I never expected to exist!)

I also need to mention the wonderful Lyn Blair for her unwavering support with so many aspects of this series. She has read the book in many forms, from its most raw to the final version. Her advice is always welcome, and she has helped me work through numerous plot twists which would otherwise have given me sleepless nights. Last but not least, to my mum, who always reads my books prior to publishing, proofreading for any last-minute grammar errors. With Defiance, she did this numerous times (sometimes almost overnight), for which I am eternally grateful.

After that, there are too many people to name. So to those of you who you listened while I tried to work through a complex subplot, beta-read an early edition of Compliance or bolstered me when I was concerned I'd never see the book published, thank you. To those of you who brought me endless cups of tea while I tapped away at the keyboard (you know who you are), commented on early ideas for cover designs, or helped me to edit my blurb, thank you. If you considered my suggestions for possible titles, spotted an errant proofreading error, or waited until I'd finished the chapter I was working on before I helped you locate your football boots, thank you. If you bought copies of the earlier books in The Bellator Chronicles and waited for this one without complaint, thank you.

Finally, to my readers. Thank you for your patience in waiting for this book. I know it's been a long time coming (far longer than I anticipated). I hope it was worth the wait.

9 781999 838171